WISE HER STILL 3 fold

The Book of Reflections

TIFFANY BUCKNER

WISE HER STILL 3fold

The Book of Reflections

Anointed Fire Christian Publishing

United States Copyright Office

© 2017, Wise Her Still Three-Fold

The Book of Reflections

Author: Tiffany Buckner

info@anointedfire.com

Published by Anointed Fire™ House

Website: www.anointedfirehouse.com

ISBN-13: 978-0-9993380-1-8

ISBN-10: 0-9993380-1-3

Most of the stories in this book are fictional. Names, characters, businesses, places, events and incidents are either the products of the author's imagination or used in a fictitious manner. Any resemblance to actual persons, living or dead, or actual events is purely coincidental.

I have tried to recreate events, locales and conversations from my memories of them. In order to maintain their anonymity in some instances I have changed the names of individuals and places, I may have changed some identifying characteristics and details such as physical properties, occupations and places of residence.

Although the author and publisher have made every effort to ensure that the information in this book was correct at press time, the author and publisher do not assume and hereby disclaim any liability to any party for any loss, damage, or disruption caused by errors or omissions, whether such errors or omissions result from negligence, accident, or any other cause.

Dedication

As with all things, I dedicate this book to the one and only true living God, YAHWEH. I pray that your name is glorified in every single story, paragraph and detail of this book. I love and adore you with every inch of who I am.

Contents

Acknowledgments

Thank you to the many women and men who purchased Wise Her Still and Wise Her Still Too, either for yourself or your loved ones. Your dedication, reviews and feedback have truly encouraged me to keep the series going. I sincerely thank God for you.

Special thanks to Apostle Bryan Meadows and his beautiful wife, Patrice Meadows, for launching the Mentorship Modules. The program put pressure on me to finally finish this book ... a project that was three years behind. Your sacrifices have not gone unnoticed and I, like many others, truly appreciate you more than words can express.

Introduction

Wise Her Still Three-Fold is a compilation of fictional stories written to inspire, correct and instruct women from all walks of life. Each story is carefully penned to help the readers to not only relate to the main characters, but to better understand how each characters' choices rendered the results he or she received. It is not uncommon these days to hear women referring to their harvests as attacks, not realizing the concept of sowing and reaping. Wise Her Still Three-Fold will help you to look at your own life and discover the reason you have the results you have today, be they good or bad. This will help you to change your life by simply changing your perspective.

Just like the previous Wise Her Still books, Wise Her Still Three-Fold is thought-provoking, funny and bursting at the seams with wisdom, knowledge and revelation. Each fictional story is broken down and every wisdom nugget has been unearthed so that you can get the lesson without having to go through the valley of experience.

Chapter 1

Religious Parakeets

A religious parakeet is a person who preaches a word that he or she does not sincerely believe. Such souls memorize scriptures and preach what they've heard others preaching, but when the Word in them is tested, they are found to be unbelievers.

We often ask God for things that we don't have the faith or know-how to believe Him for. The same is true with many religious leaders. Many preach a message that, when tested, is found to be nothing more (to them) than a good sermon.

But what happens when a prayer manifests itself right in the eyes of the doubtful? The answer is simple: they question it.

_____

It was a Sunday morning and Pastor Aaron was twenty minutes into his sermon. He was preaching about the power of God and testifying about how God had changed him from being a promiscuous, adulterous, drinking and partying man into the man of God that he is today. Many in the congregation shouted as the man of God spoke of how God can change anyone who wants to be changed.

Evening Glory Church was filled with a lot of prestigious believers, including politicians, lawyers, doctors and entrepreneurs. The growing church was the home of more than three hundred believers, with more than two hundred of those members being regular attendees. The church was well put together. It boasted of several large television monitors, a state of the art surround system, an ATM in the hall and a large event room. Additionally, one side of the church was blocked off because the church was undergoing a massive expansion. The updated building would be able to seat one thousand members.

As Pastor Aaron made his way off the stage, the doors of the church suddenly opened. In walked a frail young woman by the name of Brenda. The scar on Brenda's right chin told a story of hardship — one that most of the members did not understand.

Brenda was known around the city of Detroit because she'd once been a drug-addicted prostitute with an extensive criminal history. Nevertheless, it was no secret that Brenda had been drug-free for more than three years and she'd left the streets after a brief stint in rehab. When she was in rehab, she met a Pastor by the name of Diane. After Brenda left rehab, she'd taken Diane's advice and recommitted herself back into the rehab, where she underwent treatment for her addiction.

Diane had been a volunteer at the rehab. A former prostitute herself, Diane's testimony helped many women to leave their ungodly lifestyles behind to pursue God. After Brenda met Diane, she decided to return to rehab and take Diane up on her offer to be mentored by her. Brenda beat her drug addiction and started mentoring young women as well, but her mentor, Diane, moved to California a year after meeting her. She had been offered a great opportunity at a mega church in Los Angeles. She would be helping to get prostitutes off the streets of California and helping the church reintroduce victims of sex trafficking back into the modern world. Brenda was hurt to see her go, but the two vowed to stay in touch and Brenda committed to helping others the way Diane had once helped her.

In search of a new church home, Brenda walked into Evening Glory for the tenth time. She was late because she didn't have a car; she relied on a cab to get her to church. No one at the church had volunteered to let her ride with them because the majority of the members were afraid to be affiliated with Brenda in any way. They were worried that their names would be tainted or that Brenda would return to her old lifestyle. Despite their obvious prejudices against her and their reservations about her, Brenda continued visiting Evening Glory.

When Brenda walked into the church, most of the members glanced at her before returning their attention to the Pastor. A few of them even leaned over to gossip about her because of her casual attire and her rugged look. Brenda wore a pair of white-washed blue jeans, a gray T-shirt with the American flag on the front and a short leather jacket. She didn't have a lot of clothes, so she wore what she had. Her shoulder-length blonde hair was long and hard to manage, nevertheless, Brenda did her best to make her hair look presentable.

Pastor Aaron smiled at Brenda before continuing on with his message. He also had his reservations about her, but he couldn't allow his feelings to be made obvious.

After service ended, many of the church's members stopped and chatted with each other; this was the Sunday norm. Brenda walked around the building, stopping to greet a few members before heading back out. She wasn't offended by the behavior of the people because Diane had forewarned her about what she called "church folks." "To them, you will always be a drug-addicted prostitute,"

Diane once told Brenda. "The only difference is ... to church folks, you are now a saved prostitute who's battling a drug addiction."

Brenda also noticed that many of the women in the church did not like their husbands or their sons speaking with her. One of the members had once publicly scorned her nineteen year old grandson after she noticed him talking with Brenda. Brenda was congratulating the young man on his acceptance to a nearby university when Mrs. Rodgers, the boy's grandmother, rushed over and began to criticize him. "Jeremy Lazarius Rodgers!" screamed the noticeably upset mother. "Go and sit in the car right now! Don't you make me act up in church!" The embarrassed young man apologized to Brenda as he slowly walked away. Mrs. Rodgers then stood in place, giving Brenda a scolding look, but instead of confronting her about her attitude, Brenda simply smiled and said, "God bless you." After that, she walked away.

After service, Brenda walked up to the Pastor's wife, Jacqueline. Jacqueline was a sweet-spirited woman, but it was obvious that she was no fan of Brenda's. Nevertheless, she was as kind, or better yet, tolerant, as she could be with her.

Jacqueline: Hey, sweetie. You're looking good as usual.

How's life treating you?

Brenda: Great! You know, I just got hired as a waitress over at The Pilgrim Hut, plus, I just got my acceptance letter from school. I will officially be a college student in June. Can you believe it? A 40-year-old college student?

Jacqueline: That's great! I'm so very proud of you. You know, you're never too old to grow.

Brenda: You're right. It's all just happening so fast, but I thank God for it. But that's not what I came over here to talk to you about.

Jacqueline: What's on your mind, sweetie?

Brenda: A dear friend of mine will be in town in two weeks and when I told him what church I was going to, he said he would stop in and visit.

Jacqueline: Okay.

Brenda: Yeah. Well, he happens to be a pastor and I was thinking that maybe I could connect you all with him and maybe he could be your special guest or something. I don't really know how that kinda stuff works *(chuckles)*.

Jacqueline: Why didn't you talk with Pastor Aaron?

Brenda: Well, when dealing with married couples, I prefer to speak with the wife first. It just keeps any confusion down.

Jacqueline: I understand, but Aaron is who you need to talk to. As a matter of fact, he's heading this way right now. *With that, Jacqueline gestured for her husband to walk over.*

Hey, babe. Brenda wants to run something by you.

Brenda: Well, it's not really a big deal. I was just saying to the Mrs. that a good friend of mine will be in town in two weeks. He just so happens to be a pastor. I told him about this church and he said that he was going to stop in and visit. I thought it would be a good idea to connect you and maybe he can visit as a guest pastor or something...

Pastor Aaron: That's really nice, but anytime we have guest speakers, we book them months in advance, plus, I have to know them by the spirit. Tell your friend he's more than welcome to visit, but I definitely can't put him on the program.

Brenda: Oh, yeah ... sure. No problem.

Pastor Aaron: But hey ...Tell him to leave his business card with us and we'll definitely check him out.

Brenda: Will do. Thanks and just know that I love the both of you very much.

Jacqueline: And we love you too.

After Aaron and Jacqueline left the church to head home, the frustrated first lady could hardly contain herself.

Jacqueline: I'm telling you ... that Brenda character is trouble with a capital T! She wants some strange man to be a guest speaker at our church? A guest speaker? In whose house?! She wants us to turn over the mic and the stage to some crooked pastor who was probably one of her customers!

Pastor Aaron: Yeah, she caught me off guard with that one. But we have to remember where she came from. I think she said she's been clean for over two or three years, but all she knows is the street life. I guess we shouldn't be surprised when she makes odd requests like that.

Jacqueline: I guess you're right. I know it's bad for me to say this, but I wish she'd find another church to call home. I am just not comfortable with her at all.

Pastor Aaron: I didn't expect her to stay this long, but she is a soul, so we have to do what the Lord wants us to do. We need to keep leading her and we have to be careful with her. She's fragile. One bad move and we could be the reason that she ends back up on the streets.

Jacqueline: I'm trying, baby. I'm really trying.

The following Sunday, Brenda was at church on time. This time, she brought three women with her. The women looked as rugged as Brenda. It was obvious that they were either on drugs or had done drugs for a large portion of their lives. Once service started, Brenda noticed that the seats immediately around them were empty. Most of the church's members had deliberately sat as far away from the troublesome-looking quartet as possible. Nevertheless, Brenda had already forewarned the women and they were able to enjoy Pastor Aaron's sermon without being distracted by the many eyes that kept glancing over at them.

After service, Brenda took her friends to meet the pastor and his wife. Pastor Aaron greeted the women and Jacqueline hugged them as they introduced themselves. Jacqueline's heart was racing. Is this what their church was about to become? Was their church about to be filled with pimps, prostitutes and addicts? She cringed at the idea as she forced a smile on her face. Sensing his wife's discomfort, Pastor Aaron gently placed one of his arms around her. He then gave her a gentle nudge as he bid the women farewell. With that, Brenda and her friends left and Jacqueline looked at her husband. Her eyes were filled with frustration and fear. "It'll be alright," said Pastor Aaron as he kissed his wife and then walked away to greet a few more members.

That week, the local buzz was that Apostle Brody Jefferson was going to be in town and he'd be speaking at Glory Chapel. Apostle Jefferson was an internationally known celebrity pastor from California. He was so highly requested that anyone who wanted to book him for a speaking engagement would have to do so a year in advance. Nevertheless, he'd left that weekend open and one of Glory Chapel's members had successfully convinced him to visit their church.

Glory Chapel was a small church headed up by a local Pastor named Marcus Rancifer. Glory Chapel had just undergone an expansion and it could now seat over three thousand members. Paying for such a huge expansion was a leap of faith and many criticized Pastor Rancifer for taking that leap, especially since his church was the home of only one hundred members. Nevertheless, the budding Pastor obeyed God and he went for a three-thousand seater. This decision not only brought him much criticism, but it cost him a few members who thought he was wasting the church's funds.

Pastor Rancifer had a testimony himself. He was once a former heroin addict and thug. He'd spent more than twelve years in the state penitentiary and he'd also watched his first wife die from a heroin overdose. She died in his arms and it was at that point that he decided to turn his life around. This conversion happened more than twenty years ago and the good pastor had dedicated his life to serving God and serving his community. He was particularly compassionate towards drug addicts, prostitutes and anyone who'd come off the streets in search of God. For this reason, Pastor Rancifer's church was filled with people from all walks of life, including former addicts, prostitutes, pimps and politicians.

It was Saturday evening and Brenda was at the local

supermarket with her good friend, Apostle Brody Jefferson. Thankfully, the supermarket wasn't that busy, so Brenda and Brody were able to shop without much interference. Apostle Jefferson's seventeen-year-old daughter, Kimberly, had wandered off in search of the candy aisle, while the Apostle and Brenda headed towards the bread aisle. Just as they turned onto the bread aisle, Brenda heard a familiar set of voices. It was Pastor Aaron and First Lady Jacqueline.

Brenda: Hey, you two!

Aaron and Jacqueline looked up and were surprised to see the great Apostle Brody Jefferson standing next to Brenda.

Pastor Aaron: Hi. Oh my! What an honor it is to be in the presence of the demon slayer himself, Apostle Jefferson! It is an honor and a pleasure, man of God.

Brenda: Oh, where are my manners? Apostle Jefferson, these are the people who pastor the church I've been attending. This is Pastor Aaron and First Lady Jacqueline Holmes.

Apostle Jefferson: Oh wow. The pleasure is all mine.

Jacqueline: I can't believe you're standing right here in front of us. Wow. I'm at a loss for words. I've been a fan of yours since I was a child. I watch your show every Wednesday. I can't get enough of it.

Apostle Jefferson: Thank you. I've heard a lot about your church. It's always an honor to meet fellow servants of the Lord.

Pastor Aaron: Likewise. God is so good. How do you two know each other?

Brenda: Oh. This is the friend I was telling you about who was coming to town. He's the one I wanted to connect you with.

Pastor Aaron: Seriously?

Jacqueline: Wait. This is who you were talking about? Why didn't you tell us that it was Apostle Jefferson? Brenda, you know we would have loved to have him.

Brenda: I tried, but ...

Apostle Jefferson: Hold on, Brenda. It doesn't matter who I am, right? We are all servants of Christ Jesus, so your availability should not depend on whether I'm some small town preacher no one has ever heard of or a mega mogul. And to your question, Pastor Aaron, I met Brenda through a mutual friend of mine named Diane Sedgewick. Diane was instrumental in getting Brenda and so many other women off the streets. She moved to California to head up my church's program against sex trafficking. She'd introduced me to Brenda a year ago and told me about the great things that Brenda was doing here in Michigan.

Pastor Aaron: What exactly are you doing, Brenda?

Brenda: Haven't you noticed some of the people I've been bringing to church with me? Sure, they're a little rough around the edges, but they are prostitutes and former prostitutes that I'm either helping or have helped get off the streets. They're trying to turn their lives around.

Pastor Aaron: Oh wow. I think we owe you a huge apology. We thought ...

Brenda: You thought I was still in the streets, right? No. I'm never going back out there. I love God too much and I finally love me. You don't owe me an apology, plus, I warned every woman that has ever come to church with me about the looks they'd get. They weren't offended. They enjoyed your services.

Apostle Jefferson: This is just a part of the faith walk. We've got to go. It was definitely nice meeting the two of you, but Brenda is supposed to be cooking for me and my wife this afternoon and if you've never had her curry chicken, you haven't lived yet.

Jacqueline: Okay. Where is Mrs. Jefferson? I'd love to meet her.

Apostle Jefferson: Back at the hotel catching up on her rest. She was going to ride with us, but she was too tired, so she asked me to ride with Brenda. I'm in good hands, though.

Jacqueline: Oh wow. I can't think of many women who'd be comfortable doing that.

Apostle Jefferson: Doing what? Letting their husbands go shopping with another believer who happens to be a woman? Let me say this before I go. You don't test the past of the saint; you test the spirit of the saint to see if there are any spirits in the saint. That's what the Bible tells us to do; right? So, if I tested Brenda's spirit and found demonic spirits hiding out in her, my job isn't to judge the house; it's to clean it up because she is the temple of the Holy Spirit. You don't walk into a church building and talk about how dirty it is. You grab a broom and get to work. If I found unclean spirits lurking, I'd speak with Brenda and let her know that they were there, and then, I'd ask her if she wanted to be free. I wouldn't avoid her because if I did, I'd be silently allying myself with the Devil. In a sense, I'd have an agreement with him that if he kept her away from me, I'd leave him alone. By doing so, I'd leave God's true temple filthy and God would judge me for it. We really do have to go though, but I hope you can at least tune in to Sunday's service. We're expecting a great move of God and a lot of people are gonna get set free.

Pastor Aaron: It was good meeting you, but we're already free. Thanks for the tidbit of info. We've got to go as well.

With that, Pastor Aaron grabbed his wife's hand and the two walked out of the store, abandoning their shopping cart. Frustrated and embarrassed, Jacqueline told a few people about them seeing Apostle Jefferson out shopping with a prostitute. Nevertheless, she was not prepared for the public rebuke she'd receive on Sunday.

It was Sunday morning and Glory Chapel's seats were filled. More than three thousand people came out to the church. People were standing in the aisles and the ushers were running around frantically looking for more chairs to accommodate the overflow.

Back at Evening Glory Church, only 25 of the members were present. Twelve of those members were on the ministry team. Every other member was at Glory Chapel and Pastor Aaron knew it. Nevertheless, he decided to continue services as usual. Jacqueline, on the other hand, wasn't feeling well so she'd decided to stay at home. She had a mild case of the stomach flu and a major case of humiliation.

At Glory Chapel, Brenda stepped onto the stage to introduce Apostle Jefferson. She testified about her struggle with drugs and how she'd become a prostitute. According to Brenda, she had been raped by her stepfather at 12 and she'd told her mother. Instead of putting her stepfather out or having him arrested, Brenda's mother assaulted her with a knife. This was how she'd gotten the long scar on the side of her face. After Brenda was released from the hospital, she ran away. One day, a man posing as a good Samaritan offered Brenda a meal and a place to stay and she'd agreed to it. Little did she know that the man was a sex trafficker. He was responsible for Brenda's drug addiction and her lifestyle. After testifying about her salvation and deliverance, Brenda welcomed Apostle Jefferson and his wife, Prophetess Kimea Jefferson to the stage. The couple hugged Brenda, and Prophetess Jefferson reached for the microphone. Brenda smiled as she handed the mic to the woman of God and they hugged again. After that, Brenda went and stood alongside Apostle Jefferson as the Prophetess prepared to address the crowd.

Prophetess Jefferson said, "Before I hand the mic to the man of God, let me go ahead and put the devil in his place. I don't ordinarily address rumors, but I want to address this one because it not only is an attack against my husband's integrity, but it is an attack against the character of this awesome woman of God. I think Apostle and I could have gone without addressing the rumors because we're used to the devil attacking our names, but I could not stand by and watch him attack sister Brenda like this. After all, this woman has brought hundreds of women off the street in one year! One year, y'all! And she's doing phenomenal work for the Kingdom of God. You know, it's amazing that God will use a former prostitute to draw souls to Himself, but the Devil is using church folks to throw darts at her integrity. Apostle Jefferson and I just arrived early yesterday morning and we had plans to go to Brenda's house. She was supposed to be cooking her delicious curry chicken for us and we had agreed to go to the store with her. Y'all, I was tired! I hadn't slept the night before because I spent the night packing and preparing for this trip. Ladies, you know how we are. Anyhow, Brenda was supposed to pick us up from our hotel at five and when she arrived, I was too tired to go. I asked Apostle Jefferson to ride with her to the store. The plan was that they'd go to the store and stop back by to get me once they were finished shopping. I did this because I trust the God in my husband and I trust the God in Brenda. You see, we don't judge a book by its cover; we ask God to help us to see what's on the pages. Sometimes, the most anointed gifts don't look anointed. That's because God doesn't want you trying to discern folks with your eyes; He wants you to test the spirits! Anyhow, our daughter, Kimberly, rode with them because, of course, we have to exercise wisdom and make sure that the enemy doesn't have any grounds to falsely accuse us. While at the store, Apostle and Brenda ran into a local pastor and his wife. The couple knows Brenda's history and when the conversation didn't go the way they wanted it to go, they left the store offended. Now, there is a rumor circulating that Apostle Jefferson was at the store with a prostitute. Little did they know my daughter was on the other aisle and she heard everything. People of God, this is why we have to be careful because the enemy would much rather attack our names than our health, our finances or our marriages. If the devil can ruin your name, he doesn't have to worry about you being a threat because your name goes before you. For example, when you all heard that Apostle Jefferson was going to be in town, you made plans to come to Glory Chapel because of the weight the man of God's name carries. God has given him a good name and people know that Apostle Jefferson is a true vessel of God. He is a man truly after God's own heart. When God blessed Abram, He told him that he would make his name great. Not long after that, He renamed him Abraham and called him the father of many nations. In second Samuel, chapter seven, He told David that He has made his name great. Of course, we know He changed Saul's name to Paul, and in Proverbs 22, verse one, He said, "A good name is to be chosen rather than great riches, and favor is better than silver or gold." He also talks about causing the names of sinners to be forgotten or blotted out. Lastly, the names of God's children are written in the Book of Life. What does this mean to us? It tells us that names are very important to God. We cast out devils in the name of Jesus. The sick are healed in the name of Jesus. Acts 19 tells a funny story about seven unbelievers who tried to cast a demon out of a demon-possessed man. Okay, think about it. There are seven men against one demon. They were known as the sons of Sceva. They went into the man's house thinking their names were about to be great. I can imagine them now ... they probably told all of their family members, church members and friends that they were about to go and perform an exorcism. I can imagine that there was a crowd outside waiting to see or hear about the man's deliverance. Honestly, those folks probably had a bet going on to see who would come running out that front door. The sons of Sceva didn't believe that Jesus Christ was the Son of God. That's why they addressed that demon saying, "We command you using the name of Jesus, whom Paul preaches about." Those clowns tried to attack the devil when they, themselves were not saved! They tried to attack that demon without wearing the shield of faith, the breastplate of righteousness, the belt of truth or having their feet covered with the gospel of peace. In other words, they walked up to that demon spiritually naked. How did that devil respond? It said, "I know Jesus. I even know Paul, but who in the world are you?" It then proceeded to kick their religious behinds, ripped off their religious garments and it sent them out of the house naked. Can you imagine the crowd when that front door sprung open and out ran seven naked, bruised and ashamed exorcists? That devil stripped them of their clothes and their dignity because they were spiritually naked. This tells us that a good name is even known in the spirit realm! Because of this, the enemy targets the names of believers, especially believers who are doing the work of the Lord. We knew the enemy was going to try to attack us for coming into this region and we were fully prepared for every dart that he threw out. With that being said, guard your heart and your name! Do not let your good be evil spoken of, people of God. And whatever you do, don't give life to rumors, especially ones that come from blind church folk. If someone stops and tells you that they heard Apostle was out with a prostitute, tell them that Jesus hung out with Mary Magdalene after He cast seven demons out of her. Tell them that Brenda is like Mary Magdalene; she has been set free by the Lord, Himself. After that, ask them if they want her to cast those gossiping spirits out of their tongues. I have personally witnessed her casting demons out of several people and I could have only wished that she would have cast them out those gossiping leaders before the devil could use them."

With that, the crowd laughed, shouted and praised the Lord. Jacqueline, of course, was at home, watching the service live. Humiliated, she decided to cut the television off. How could they recover? Sure, Prophetess Jefferson hadn't said their names, but everyone who'd heard the rumor had heard it directly from the first lady herself. Additionally, she couldn't sue the Jeffersons for slander because Prophetess Jefferson had not mentioned any names; she'd simply addressed the rumor. Angry and scared, Jacqueline went into her closet to pray. Her prayers were right-sounding prayers laced with witchcraft, but they would not and did not work.

Apostle Jefferson's message that night was about the power of God. He spoke of how God changed him; how He'd changed Pastor Rancifer and how He'd changed sister Brenda. After his powerful sermon, more than two hundred people gave their lives to Christ that evening.

Pastor Rancifer's church went from being a small church with a little over a hundred members to a large and growing church with more than 2,500 members in less than two months! In less than a year, the church was undergoing another expansion. Additionally, most of Pastor Aaron's members resigned from Evening Glory and became members of Glory Chapel. Five months later, Glory Chapel closed its doors and the church was closed for seven years before it was reopened by Pastor Aaron and his new wife, Sabrina. You see, Pastor Aaron's problem was he'd stopped acting like the head of his home and he allowed his wife to slowly become religious, judgmental and hateful. Even though he'd witnessed many of her dark behaviors toward the members, he did not address them in the manner in which they should have been addressed. Not long after his church fell apart, Jacqueline left him for another man. It was only then that he began to acknowledge that Jacqueline was truly backslidden. Humbled and reconciled to God, he spent the next few years rededicating his life to the Lord and God re-entrusted him to lead His people.

Brenda continued to do the work of the Lord. She brought in thousands of women off the streets and she led them to Pastor Rancifer's church where she knew they would not be judged. Instead, they'd receive the love they needed to begin the healing process. In less than five years, Pastor Rancifer's church was housing more than ten thousand members and Brenda was well on her way to starting her own church alongside her new husband, Craig.

What happened in this story? The answer is obvious. The pastor preached a message that he, himself did not believe. This is not uncommon in many of today's churches. People are oftentimes victims of their own limited perceptions and because of this, many churches are filled with people who proclaim God with their mouths, but their hearts are filled with unbelief. People tend to measure God's abilities based on what they see. For example, people who saw the frail young Brenda walking in the church's doors saw a troubled soul they believed would blemish the church's prestigious reputation. They couldn't see Brenda for who she had become, nor could they see the potential for change in any of Brenda's friends. For this reason, God often uses former prostitutes to reach out and recover victims of the sex trade. You see, a former prostitute is not afraid to reach out to or receive a woman who's currently in prostitution. She knows how to reach her and she knows how to address her. She even knows when the woman is trying to manipulate her. Nevertheless, many people who are in the church have allowed the church's walls to become the walls of their prisons. Their love does not extend outside of the four walls of their local churches. As a matter of fact, their love doesn't even cover everyone within the four walls of their churches. Why is this? Because people oftentimes fear what they do not understand. Humans are creatures of comfort who barricade themselves in whatever lifestyles or mindsets they've been subjected to for any lengthy period of time. This includes dysfunctional lifestyles and thinking patterns. When introduced to religion, people often barricade themselves in religious reasoning by taking what they've experienced and what they believe and pairing it up with what they've learned in church. This means that every man's understanding, when not in subjection to the Holy Spirit, is a byproduct of his limited reasoning and his lack of knowledge. Howbeit, when a person is introduced to Christ and that person allows the Lord to give him a new heart and a new mind, he doesn't weigh the Word against his own personal opinions and past experiences. If anything, he will use his past experiences to confirm the Word, but he will not use the Word to justify his experience. For this reason, traditional church-goers who don't venture out and get to know God for themselves will, in a sense, edit the Word until it agrees with their lifestyles and/or mindsets. They will then attempt to determine who's holy and who is hell-bound. This line of reasoning helps the bound believer to stay in his comfort zone, or better yet, his religious prison.

Brenda was Kingdom fruit. She was the manifested evidence of God's Word in action. When she stepped into her destiny, every unbeliever masquerading as a believer had no choice but to reveal the condition of his or her heart.

I will never forget what the Lord said to me back in 2015. He said, "Your ministry will only go as far as your love." Those few words were powerful enough to help me better understand why some churches get stuck and stop growing. Many leaders want sheep they can relate to and they are afraid to pastor anyone who they can't lead with their understandings. What they do not realize is that God calls us to lead His people by His Spirit, meaning, we don't have to understand them. We just need to stay submitted to God and remain prayerful; that way, we can hear from God regarding them. In other words, God will send a leader sheep who will cause that leader to go outside his or her understanding. This will cause the leader to seek God all the more. Remember, when Solomon was crowned king, he asked God for wisdom to lead His people.

1 Kings 3:5-9: At Gibeon the Lord appeared to Solomon in a dream by night, and God said, "Ask what I shall give you." And Solomon said, "You have shown great and steadfast love to your servant David my father, because he walked before you in faithfulness, in righteousness, and in uprightness of heart toward you. And you have kept for him this great and steadfast love and have given him a son to sit on his throne this day. And now, O Lord my God, you have made your servant king in place of David my father, although I am but a little child. I do not know how to go out or come in. And your servant is in the midst of your people whom you have chosen, a great people, too many to be numbered or counted for multitude. Give your servant therefore an understanding mind to govern your people, that I may discern between good and evil, for who is able to govern this your great people?"

This tells us that Solomon understood that he, as a man, could not lead the people without the direction of God. This also tells us that anyone who shepherds God's people should remain prayerful when leading God's people. Any leader who attempts to lean on his or her own understanding is a leader who will have much blood on their hands.

Some ministries don't grow because the leaders have limited love; they cannot properly cover anyone who does not look like, sound like or reason like them. For this reason, they reach out to people who are relatable, people who won't stretch them. When someone comes to their churches who they cannot relate to, they will not promote them. Instead, they will judge them and place them in what can best be described as perceptive bondage. In this, they will cause them to become slaves of their personal perceptions of them, meaning, they will impose their opinions upon those souls. If anyone should come outside their views of them, they will rebuke them. For example, let's say that a man named Darren was perceived by his leaders to be an incurable womanizer. Darren sincerely turns his life over to God and practices sexual purity for three years. One day, he introduces a woman to his leaders. He explains to them that she is an evangelist at a nearby church and he's been seeing her for three months. Later on, he tells his leaders that he is serious about Angela (his friend) and he believes that God has spoken to him and revealed that she is his wife. Nevertheless, the leaders can't seem to get past who Darren was three years ago. They think that Angela is too good for Darren and that he'll eventually hurt her. Because of this, they assure Darren that he has not heard from God and they tell him that if he doesn't release Angela that God will judge him. Darren is confused. He trusts his leaders, but he is confident that he's heard from God. He is now in a difficult position, being forced to choose between staying under the influence of his leaders' perceptions of him or accepting the wife that God has blessed him to find. This is how perceptive bondage works.

Think of a set of security cameras at a mall. When security sees the monitors, they see what's currently happening throughout the mall. Let's say a crafty thief was to gain access to some of the videos they'd taken in the past, videos of past security footage. The thief successfully distracts security and it is that time when the officers are out of the office that the thief makes his way into it. He places the memory card in the video player and presses play. After that, he leaves the office. When the officers re-enter the office, they don't notice anything unusual, so they sit down and begin to view the video monitors. Little do they know they are viewing old footage! The thief utilizes that time to steal many valuable things from the mall. This is how the thief, Satan, works. He causes saints to run off memory! Perception is a dangerous thing when it's not challenged by prayer.

Pastor Aaron's church could not grow any further because the pastor had reached his love's limits. When he started leaning to his own understanding, he set himself up to fall and fail! When leading God's people, one cannot make room for the spirit of error! Having a prejudiced attitude towards broken souls could easily drive them back into the arms of Satan. It is hard to save or recover a babe in Christ who has experienced church hurt. This means that a leader can inadvertently cause the natural or spiritual death of the person he or she is leading if that leader doesn't have enough love to cover that person.

Over the years, God has placed me in the midst of many, many people from different backgrounds and cultures. He started doing this when I was in the world and now I understand why. We all come from different backgrounds. We've had different experiences and we have different beliefs. Some of us have been driven into darkness because of our experiences, but God brought us out. Nevertheless, He didn't bring us out of darkness so that we can exalt ourselves against those who are still blinded by sin. He gave us the light of His Word so that we could lead the unsaved and the backslidden back to Him. Many believers fail the love walk while trying to master their faith walk. Little do they know that faith without love is the very pulse of religiousness. Love isn't just a word; it's an experience. It is the very heart, essence and depth of who God is. Without it, we are godless.

1 John 4:20 (ESV): If anyone says, "I love God," and hates his brother, he is a liar; for he who does not love his brother whom he has seen cannot love God whom he has not seen.

Know this: Hell is full of people who gave out more hugs than they did love. They spoke scriptures, attended church services often and danced around in the sanctuary, but they failed the test of love. It is the very test that testifies for you or against you.

Hebrews 13:2 (NIV): Do not forget to show hospitality to strangers, for by so doing some people have shown hospitality to angels without knowing it.

Chapter 2

Evaluate the Seed, Not the Need

I grew up around a lot of men who were womanizers and even though it warped my view of men back then, once I came to Christ, the knowledge I received from watching them was nothing short of invaluable. Think of it this way. If you were a teenager in a room full of poker players, you'd learn each man's poker face. If you were able to see each player's hand and watch them bluff their way through a game, by the time you were old enough to play against them, you'd be able to defeat them easily. The reason for this is because you were allowed to sit on the sidelines and learn while investing nothing but your time and attention. This means you had nothing to lose, but everything to gain. During your time as a passive student, you didn't just learn to master playing poker, you learned to master the poker players as well. That's how it was for me.

I didn't have to invest anything in those men; after all, they were either related to me or they were older friends of the family. I watched them manipulate

women, take advantage of them, and then, toss them away like recycled trash. At the same time, I didn't just see the error in the men, I was able to see the common denominators in the women. I learned to look for patterns and this helped me to better understand how Satan plays the game.

———————————

"Whatever! You just make sure that check clears at the end of the week. That's all you need to be worried about!" shouted Desiree before hanging up the phone. She was having another intense argument with her ex-boyfriend and the father of her two children, Lenny.

Desiree was a 27-year-old mother of three. Her last two children, Jasmine and Hayden, were the products of her five-year relationship with Lenny. Her oldest child was a seven-year-old by the name of Anna. She and Lenny had been broken up for over a year, but Desiree wasn't completely over the breakup or the betrayal. You see, Lenny left Desiree to be with a woman named April, a woman he'd met over the internet. He'd had an affair with April for five months before finally abandoning Desiree altogether and moving in with April. Nevertheless, Lenny's relationship with April had been short-lived. Three months into their relationship, he'd discovered that she was sending lewd photos of herself to her ex-husband, so he left. Nowadays, Lenny was living as a single man and he was angry with Desiree because she did not reconcile with him after he'd given her what can best be described as an over-the-top emotional plea for forgiveness. Sure, he'd entertained a few women since his breakup with April, but no woman he came in contact with compared to Desiree. He wanted Desiree back, but the feeling was not mutual.

Desiree hadn't forgiven Lenny for his betrayal and it showed. Try as she may, she could not seem to be kind to Lenny. She wanted him to suffer the same way he'd made her suffer. To make matters worse, Lenny had been a great father when he and Desiree were a couple, but after they broke up, he didn't show much interest in his children. His primary focus was reconciling with Desiree while Desiree's primary focus was getting even with Lenny.

It was late Monday evening and Desiree had just left the braid shop. The braid shop was in a small shopping center just a few feet from a grocery store. Desiree's mother was keeping her children and Desiree wanted to do a little grocery shopping before picking them up. Because the braid shop was only a few feet from the store, Desiree walked over to the store.

Life for Desiree and her children had gotten difficult since Lenny's departure. Lenny had been the primary breadwinner in that relationship and the family depended on his income for food and housing. During her relationship with Lenny, Desiree worked part time as a parking lot attendant at the local mall. Now that Lenny was gone, Desiree was working two jobs. She was still working as a parking lot attendant and she also worked as a cashier at a Chinese restaurant. She was receiving child support from Lenny, but it wasn't much because Lenny was the father of four children. He'd had two children with a girl named Latoya before he met Desiree and the state was already taking child support out of his wages for Latoya's children.

Desiree's shopping cart was halfway full and she was almost ready to go to the checkout counter, but she wanted to stop and get some fruit before checking out. Feeling tired, she leaned over the front of her shopping cart as she held her cell phone to her ear. She was reassuring her mother that she would be picking up her children within the next thirty minutes to an hour. "Ouch!" The voice was loud and angry. Desiree had hit a man's ankle with her shopping cart. The friction from the impact caused the cart to bounce back and hit her in the chest area. With that, Desiree's phone fell to the floor and broke.

Desiree was leaning forward because of the pain, but she kept apologizing to the handsome stranger. A little boy who appeared to be around seven or eight years old ran to her phone's rescue, picking up the phone, its batteries and the back cover. His big blue eyes danced with excitement as he handed the broken phone back to Desiree. "I think it's broken," he said. "My dad can fix it though. He can fix anything." Desiree smiled at the miniature Samaritan. "Thank you, cutie," she said. "It was an old phone. I think this is just a sign that I need to get a new phone. Aren't you the sweetest thing? Thank you." Still holding the change from the braid shop, Desiree handed the child a five dollar bill, but his mother intervened. "Oh, thank you, but I don't want him to think that he's supposed to get paid for every good deed that he does." With that, the mother took the five dollar bill out of her son's hand and handed it back to Desiree. She then thanked Desiree and asked her if she was okay. Desiree nodded. "Yeah, that hit just knocked the wind out of me. I'll be alright. Thank you." After that, Desiree thanked the young boy again. The boy's mother started pushing her cart onto the next aisle, but the young boy slowly walked behind her. Desiree managed to get the young man's attention. Still somewhat bent over, she jogged over to the child and put the five dollar bill in his pocket. With that, she placed one finger over her mouth, indicating for the child to keep quiet about what she'd just done. The little boy's eyes lit up as he nodded with excitement. He then rushed off to catch up with his mother.

"I saw that." The voice was strong, but hushed. Desiree turned around to see the man she'd just hit with her shopping cart. Standing straight up, Desiree joked, "You didn't see anything and you don't know anything. I'm sorry. Are you okay? I guess I wasn't paying attention." The handsome stranger seemed to ignore Desiree's question as he made his way toward her shopping cart. He reached into the cart and picked up the roll of cabbage that she had. "My name is Ed. I like long walks at the park and I love a woman who can cook." Desiree didn't smile or laugh, but inwardly, she was flattered.

Desiree: I'm okay too. The shopping cart knocked the wind out of me, as you probably saw, but I'm okay. Thanks for asking.

Ed: I didn't ask you if you were okay because I can see that you are fine and I do mean that. You, my lady, are fine!

Desiree: I am not your lady, but thank you.

Ed: I think my ankle is starting to swell.

Desiree: What do you want me to do? I'm not a doctor or a nurse.

Ed: Apologies don't heal wounds, but I am confident that if you give me your phone number, I'll feel much better.

Desiree: And how would me giving you my number help your ankle?

Ed: Oh, I'm not worried about my ankle. It's starting to swell, but it'll be okay. It's my pride that I'm worried about. You see, if a beautiful woman hits me with her shopping cart and then, proceeds to sneak a five dollar bill into a child's pocket while his mother wanders off aimlessly, she is obligated to give me her number.

Desiree: And what if I don't?

Ed: Then the pain from my ankle could cause me to become delirious. Who knows? I just might go and find that sweet, naïve mother and tell her all about her son's deception.

Desiree: *(Laughing)* You wouldn't do that to an innocent little boy who went out of the way to help a damsel in distress, now would you?

Ed: In my right mind, I wouldn't. But you hit my ankle pretty hard and I felt something in my brain move. It felt like that piece of the brain that's responsible for sound reasoning. Who knows what I'll do at this point? Jokes aside, I think you're a beautiful woman and I'd like to get to know you better.

Desiree: Okay. That's better. My name is Desiree, I have three children and I work two jobs. Is that enough?

Ed: But are you single though?

Desiree: Yes, I am, but that doesn't mean I'm available.

Ed: Listen to me you beautiful, single and unavailable woman. I need to stop by the checkout counter and pick up some ice for my ankle. The more we stand here and talk, the more light-headed I'm beginning to feel.

Desiree: Are you serious? Are you okay?

Ed: No. My ankle is still throbbing and my pride has a dent in it. I may need medical attention or, at minimum, your attention.

Desiree: You're not going to give up, are you?

Ed: Not until you're scribbling my name next to your name and placing little bitty hearts around it.

Desiree: You're nice and all, but ...

Ed: Isn't that the little boy coming with his mother? I'll be right back.

Desire: *(Laughs)* No. Let me see your phone so I can put my number in it.

Ed: Wise move, my lady. Wise move.

Ed handed his phone to Desiree. She laughed as she added her name and number to his contacts.

Desire: Here. It's done. Don't call me after nine.

Ed: You didn't give me the wrong number, did you? Because there's no way I can check since you seem to have dismembered your phone.

Desiree: I gave you the right number.

Ed: Who's your phone carrier?

Desiree: Why? Are you going to pay my bill?

Ed: I might. But no, seriously, who's your carrier?

Desiree: We Cell-You Wireless.

Ed: You're kidding, right?

Desiree: No, I'm not.

Ed: Okay, so even though destiny can be cruel at times, it was meant for you to bump into me. I just wish you hadn't done it with your shopping cart.

Desiree: What do you mean?

Ed: My cell provider is We Cell-You Wireless and I literally just left there getting a new phone. My old phone is less than a year old, but the camera went out on it and I need my camera.

Desiree: Is that right? So, you like to take pictures of yourself?

Ed: No. I need it for work.

Desiree: What do you do?

Ed: Ah, see ... you're interested in me after all, but I think we need to take things slowly. I can't tell you where I work already. You could turn out to be a crazy lady.

Desiree: You may be right. Are you sure you still want to call me?

Ed: I'll take my chances, but anyhow, if you want, you can have my old phone. I have it out in my car, and like I said, it's still relatively new. The camera just doesn't work on it.

Desiree: That's awfully nice of you, but I don't know you and ...

Ed: Lady, stop it. You need a phone and I have one. Don't read too much into it. Just take the phone so I can call you later.

Desiree: How will it work, though?

Ed: You'll just have to take the memory chip out of what's left of your old phone and put it in the new one.

Desiree: I guess. Okay.

Ed: Just watch my shopping cart while I run out to my car. I'll be right back.

Desiree agreed and Ed jogged towards the store's exit doors. A few minutes later, Desiree could see the little boy who'd picked up her phone walking out of the store with his mother. His mother was still walking ahead of him and obviously distracted. She appeared to be talking on a bluetooth headset and laughed hysterically as she talked about something her husband had done. At that moment, Desiree saw Ed coming back into the store. He greeted the distracted mother as she passed him by. After he saw that the mother was too distracted to notice him, he bent over and handed something to the apparently excited little boy. The little boy then placed whatever Ed had given him into his pocket. Ed then signaled for him to be quiet. He excitedly nodded his head as he jogged to catch up with his mother. Desiree giggled as Ed made his way back to her.

Desiree: What did you give him?

Ed: Him who?

Desiree: That little boy. What did you give him?

Ed: You didn't see nothing and you don't know nothing.

Desiree: Whatever.

Ed: I gave him, not one, but two five dollar bills. Did I mention that I tend to be a little on the competitive side?

Desiree: They have medication for that, you know ... Anyhow, thank you for the phone, but duty calls. I have to go and pick up my children before my mother calls the cops and reports me missing.

Ed: Do you know how to take the memory card out of the old phone and put it in the other one?

Desiree: I'll figure it out.

Ed: Give me the phone. I'll do it right quick and then you can go.

Desiree handed Ed her phone and he switched the memory card out for her. After that, they said their goodbyes before Desiree made her way to the checkout. She then called her mother back to tell her what had happened.

Ed called Desiree that evening and she learned some really interesting things about him. He was unlike any man she'd ever dated. Ed was thirty years old; he had no children and he worked as an insurance adjuster. He was also a deacon at a local church, plus, he owned his own home. Additionally, his singing voice was nothing short of amazing. Desiree felt intimidated by Ed. In her heart, she questioned why a man like Ed would be interested in a woman like herself. Nevertheless, she didn't want to ruin any opportunity that she had with him, so she never posed her question out loud to Ed.

On their first date, Ed took Desiree to a really nice (and expensive) restaurant. He was definitely a successful, debonair man, but at the same time, he appeared to be a humble man who knew what he wanted. Compared to the other women in the restaurant, Desiree felt somewhat under-dressed, but Ed reassured her that she looked beautiful.

A few Sundays later, Ed invited Desiree to visit the church he served at. When she saw Ed wearing a suit and serving around the church, she instantly fell in love with him. He was the perfect man in her eyes. At the same time, he was definitely an upgrade from Lenny. Desiree smiled as she thought to herself how Lenny would react when he saw the successful, Mercedes-Benz driving Ed picking up his children from school.

As the months passed, Desiree found herself falling more and more for Ed. He was the perfect gentlemen and his sense of humor had no ends. She'd already introduced her children to him and they all seemed to love him. At first, her son, Hayden, was a little bothered by the idea of his mother being with any other man besides his dad. Nevertheless, Ed surprised Hayden with one of his favorite video games, and after that, Hayden loved him.

Everyone around Desiree knew about Ed, including Lenny. Of course, Lenny was very jealous of Desiree and Ed's blooming relationship. He'd once even told Desiree that Ed wasn't truly interested in her. According to Lenny, Ed was only there for the sex. Because of Lenny's opposition of her relationship, Desiree had gone as far as to stop him from seeing his children. Howbeit, Ed encouraged Desiree to let Lenny see his children and she obliged.

Four months into their relationship, Desiree was starting to feel like Ed wasn't spending as much time with her or her children as he once had. At the same time, she was beginning to suspect that she was pregnant; after all, her menstruation was three weeks late. To make matters worse, Desiree suddenly realized that she hadn't met any of Ed's family or friends. He appeared to be a private man.

For the last couple of months, Ed had paid Desiree's car note and given her some money to help out around the house. He was giving her more money than Lenny gave her in a six-month span. Even though Desiree wanted to question Ed about his strange behavior, she didn't want to scare him off. Desiree's mother seemed to like Ed as well because he was a good provider. She'd even reasoned with Desiree by saying, "You need to hurry up and lock that man down. Put a hole in the condom or something! Don't let that man slip through your fingers. If I were you, I'd lock him in with a baby." Desiree had taken her mom's advice, but since Ed didn't like wearing condoms when they had sex, Desiree had simply stopped taking her birth control pills.

It was a little after nine o'clock on a Friday evening and Desiree was laying on her bed. Ed hadn't called her all day, nor had he returned her calls. Ordinarily, Ed would take her out every Friday and they'd go out of town to one of Ed's favorite hangouts: a beach in Miami. After that, they would retreat to a hotel and stay the night. Of course, Desiree's mother volunteered to keep the children while Desiree worked on securing her relationship with Ed.

Home alone, Desiree found herself recanting her life. She'd miscarried her first child after finding out the father of that child was married. Not long after that, she'd met James, the father of her daughter, Anna. One year into their relationship, she'd found out that she was pregnant and James didn't like the news. He asked her to abort the baby and when she refused, he'd stormed out of her house and left. Later that day, he called and invited her on a weekend getaway. He claimed to have had a change of heart and he wanted to celebrate the news of Desiree's pregnancy. Young and naïve, Desiree believed him and agreed to the getaway.

One day before she was supposed to leave with James, Desiree received a phone call from James's best friend, Falcon. Falcon told Desiree that he'd just finished hanging out with James. He'd sensed that James was upset and about to do something stupid, so he'd asked him about his plans for the getaway. At first, James claimed that he was just trying to get used to the idea of being a father, but after a few beers, the truth came to light.

James was planning to take Desiree to one of his parents' properties where he planned to put something in her food or drink to cause her to have a miscarriage. Nevertheless, he had trouble getting access to any abortion pills or anything he felt would effectively cause the death of his unborn child. Because of this, he reasoned within his heart to take Desiree to the property and start a fight with her. He would then kick her in her stomach to cause a miscarriage.

It goes without saying that Desiree did not believe Falcon at first, but after talking more with him, she realized that James had gone from being frantically upset about the news of her pregnancy to being a gleaming father-to-be. His change of heart had been too dramatic. After she hung up with Falcon, Desiree called James to test him. "I won't be able to go with you this weekend," she said. "My mother just found out that I'm pregnant and she wants me to go and live with my aunt Betty until the baby is born." Drunk and still reeling from the news, James couldn't hold back his anger.

He talked about them running away together and when that didn't work, he then started telling Desiree that he wasn't ready to be a father. For a few minutes, James thought Desiree was in agreement with him, so he told her that one of his friends was supposed to be getting in touch with a woman who worked at a local abortion clinic. According to James, his friend had purchased abortion pills from the woman before and he'd already given the guy the money to give to the woman for the pills. He was just waiting to hear back from him.

It was then that Desiree could not deny Falcon's claim anymore. After she refused to have the abortion or go anywhere near James, James skipped town and for more than a year, Desiree didn't know where he was. He finally resurfaced after his mother fell sick, but he still wanted nothing to do with his daughter, Anna.

Not long after Anna was born, Desiree met Lenny. Lenny seemed to be the perfect man for her, even though she wasn't fully attracted to Lenny physically. Determined to have Desiree, Lenny had taken flowers to Desiree's mother at her workplace and told her that he was interested in her daughter. He pleaded with her to talk with Desiree for him, and after learning that Lenny was a fireman, Mrs. Banks agreed to talk with her daughter. Five years and two children later, Lenny walked out of Desiree's life to pursue another woman.

Now, here it was happening all over again. Desiree was possibly pregnant, but of course, Ed didn't know this. Nevertheless, he was clearly trying to avoid her and Desiree knew what that meant. Ed was likely seeing someone else or he'd had his fill of her.

Music filled the atmosphere as Desiree lay on her bed with tears in her eyes. Why didn't Ed want her as much as she wanted him? What had she done wrong? Was she really pregnant? If so, how would Ed react? He was very different from James and Lenny; he appeared to be far more mature. After all, he was a deacon at his church and he was really good with Desiree's children. With that, Desiree decided to do the one thing she'd been putting off doing. She decided to take the pregnancy test she'd purchased a week prior.

Ten minutes later, Desiree found herself pacing the hallway of her apartment. How could this have happened? She dialed Ed's number again, but he still would not answer. Suddenly, Desiree had a revelation. What if Ed had taken another woman down to the same hotel he took her to every Friday night? Desiree looked at the clock. It was a little after nine. A creature of habit, Ed had a pattern. Normally, he would take Desiree to the beach around nine and they'd be back at the hotel around 10:30. Desiree rushed to her computer to get the number of the hotel. She knew that if Ed was there, he wouldn't be in his room just yet, but he would be checked in.

"Yes, do you have a guest by the name of Edward Crenshaw?" Desiree's voice sounded desperate. The clerk seemed almost sympathetic. "Hold on, sweetie," said the clerk. "Edward Crenshaw.... Edward Crenshaw.... Yep, here he is right here. Would you like me to transfer you to his room?"

Desiree's heart filled with terror, agony and fear at the same time. "Um, yeah, but first, what room is he in?" The clerk paused for a few seconds. "He's in room 442. I'll transfer you now." With that, Desiree suddenly heard a click, followed by the sound of ringing. She knew that Ed would not be in his room just yet and she knew that he wouldn't answer the line if he was in the room. With her heart racing, Desiree grabbed her car keys and purse and rushed out of the door. A few seconds later, she rushed back in the house, grabbed her pregnancy test, wrapped it up in a napkin and dropped it into her purse. After that, she rushed out of the house and started speeding to Miami.

Desiree arrived in Miami at 10:42 pm. She felt like she was having an out of body experience as she drove around the parking lot looking for room 442. Suddenly, she spotted Ed's car. Desiree parked her car next to Ed's car and made her way towards room 442. Her heart raced as she approached the door.

Desiree found herself standing in front of Ed's room feeling overwhelmed. Her emotions had gotten the best of her; she was ready to confront her cheating beau and tell him the news. She knocked on the door, trying not to knock too loudly. "Who is it?" The voice was definitely Ed's voice. "Room service," said Desiree as she lowered her voice. "We didn't order room service," responded Ed. Desiree could hear the sound of a woman's voice coming from the other side of the door as well. "Baby, I called earlier and asked them to change the pillowcases," said the woman. "Maybe they didn't do it while we were gone."

Ed felt a wave of fear come over him as he approached the door. Room service doesn't normally come that late in the evening, but he knew that he had no choice but to open the door. When he did, his worst fears were confirmed. Standing in the doorway was a teary-eyed Desiree. "Who is that?" asked the woman sitting on the bed. Ed panicked, but before he could close the door, Desiree stepped in and started shoving him. "So, this is why you're not answering my calls, Ed? I'm sitting at home, crying my eyes out while you're out here with someone else?! What about us, huh?! What about what we had?!"

Ed was frightened. "Desiree, I never said that you and I were in a relationship. Please don't make a scene. You and I were just two consenting adults who ... " Desiree couldn't believe what she was hearing. She interrupted, "Consent to this!" With that, Desiree reached into her purse. Thinking she had a gun, Ed punched her and snatched her purse. Desiree fell to the floor and began to cry aloud.

By this time, Kirsten, Ed's new lover, was on the bed screaming. Ed dumped Desiree's purse on the bed as she rushed out of the room to call the police. Nevertheless, there was no gun. The only thing that was out of the ordinary was an object wrapped in paper towels. Thinking it was a small knife, Ed unwrapped the object and was horrified at what he saw. It was a positive pregnancy test.

When the cops arrived, Ed was sitting on the bed still holding the pregnancy test. He looked scared and almost child-like himself. After everyone gave their side of the story to the officers, the policemen decided to not arrest

Ed because, as they said, he'd responded to what he believed to be a credible threat. The officers asked Desiree if she needed any medical attention, but she said that she didn't. They then asked her to leave, threatening to arrest her if she came back to the room. Desiree agreed. She loaded her belongings back into her purse and left Ed still sitting on the bed holding the pregnancy test.

Ed's friend, Kirsten, was visibly shaken. She asked the police to stay with her until her brother arrived. She'd called him a few minutes after Desiree called the police and he was on his way. When Kirsten's brother finally arrived, Ed touched her arm. "I'm sorry for all this," he said. Kirsten didn't respond. She walked out the door and Ed could hear her reasoning with her brother in the parking lot. "The cops are still in the room," she said. "I don't want you to go to jail. Let's just go ... please!" Minutes later, the sound of screeching tires could be heard leaving the parking lot.

Ed waited a week to contact Desiree and when he did contact her, it was via text message. It read: *I know you probably don't ever want to see me again, and I don't blame you. The truth is, I'm not ready for anything serious just yet. I thought you understood that. I apologize if I didn't make it clearer. I hope all is well with you and I hope you can forgive me for what transpired last Friday. I also hope you* can forgive me for what may appear to be a heartless request. *Dez, I'm not ready to be a father. I know it's a little too late for us to have this talk, but I'm just not ready. At the same time, you're already struggling to raise three children. Having another child at this point is not a good idea. Please hear my heart when I say this. Will you consider an abortion? I'll pay for it and I'll even pay for your time off work. Please don't be mad at me for this. I'm sorry. Please let me know what you're going to do.*

Desiree was numb as she read the text, but she wasn't surprised. She handed the phone to her mother who was sitting a few feet away. Her mother decided to respond to Ed and her text read: *This is Desiree's mother. She is going to have that baby and you're going to pay for it. If you don't want children, don't do what it takes to have them! Do not contact my daughter anymore unless you're contacting her to tell her what you're going to be doing for your child! If you text or call her again and upset her, I will send my nephews to your place of employment and I promise you they will adjust your attitude one punch, kick or bullet at a time! Call my bluff, Ed. Please try me!*

After that, Ed never contacted Desiree again. Seven months later, Desiree gave birth to a healthy baby boy who she named Edward — after his father. It goes without saying that Ed requested a paternity test once he'd received court documents indicating that Desiree was taking him to court for child support. The paternity test came back showing that Ed was indeed the father of Desiree's youngest son. He was then forced to pay Desiree $1,100 a month in child support. Additionally, he was not an active part of his son's life.

The End.

If you're a woman, you likely sympathized with Desiree. If you're a man, you likely sympathized with Ed. Nevertheless, both of them were wrong. You see, Desiree is trading sex for love and financial security. Let's call this what it is — it is prostitution legalized by ignorance. Honestly, I think that if we start calling things what they are, many people will wake up and realize that they are a part of the problem and stop playing the victim. I'm a woman, so in society's mind, I'm supposed to side with the woman, but I cannot side with sin regardless of the gender of the person who plays with it. The fact is that Desiree tried to use Ed! At the same time, Ed successfully used Desiree! He is equally wrong and the person who will suffer because of Ed and Desiree's choices is their son.

Ed and Desiree's mindsets are pretty common. Let's first expose the personality operating in and through Ed. I've seen this personality in a lot of low-income areas. Men like Ed garner a little success for themselves and they almost always chose to marry a woman who is of equal caliber. This means that they tend to marry women who are just as successful as they are or women who come from successful families. Now, don't get me wrong; this doesn't mean that the women in low-income areas are not good enough for successful men, but this is to say that a lot of successful men like to prey on women in low-income areas. They use their jobs and titles to manipulate women into sleeping with them. Of course, we could put the bulk of the blame on the women. After all, they are consenting adults who can make their own decisions. While this is true, you have to understand that it is the nature of a human and an animal to try to survive, especially when children are involved. The truth is ... a lot of children who are walking around today are not the products of loving relationships. They are the products of two manipulative souls trying to fulfill a void, a need or a desire. Women tend to sleep with men because they think they love them, they're attracted to them, and they want to have a future with them. Now, when a woman becomes a mother (in most cases), she starts making choices based on her need and the needs of her children. Sure, she continues to desire a man that she's attracted to, but her love for her children may compel her to settle for men that she's not too interested in. Again, this isn't always the case;

everyone is different, but this is common.

Men tend to sleep with women for several reasons. Most women think that sex, for the promiscuous man, is all about him satisfying his sexual appetite, but it goes much deeper than that. Sex, for an uncommitted man, is centered around his belief system, his voids and his instinctual need to conquer. He may believe that sex establishes his identity as a man; it makes him feel needed, wanted, and most of all, it makes him feel empowered. The sexual experience and the orgasm are huge bonuses, but if you analyze how each man chooses his sexual partners, you will learn a lot about the man himself. For example, three men or personalities I came in contact with in my youth come to mind. Two were relatives and one was a friend of my dad. We'll call them Will, Jason and Greg.

Will was a relative of mine who would never pursue beautiful, confident women, even though many of them were interested in him. He didn't think too highly of himself, so he chose women he felt were inferior to him in the looks arena. In other words, he got with women who saw him as being out of their leagues. He used these women to build his self-worth. With them, he was confident (arrogant even) and sure. When a beautiful, confident woman approached him, he would get nervous and would not return her calls. Nevertheless, if a woman who, by society's stands, was considered unattractive were to approach him, he'd morph into a very confident man. He needed his women to build him up and because no woman or person has the ability to build us up spiritually, he found himself getting bored with the women he'd chosen for himself. Because of this, he wouldn't be faithful and he'd always abandon one relationship to enter another one. This was all centered around his low self-esteem. Sex was just a bonus.

Jason was another relative who was a womanizer. Nevertheless, Jason's promiscuity was centered around his desire to be successful at something and his need to finally reach his mother. You see, Jason wasted his life selling drugs and doing a lot of foolish things trying to make easy money. His father was not at all happy with his choices and his mother wasn't the most nurturing mother to him, especially after he started making bad choices. Jason found himself in and out of prison and he found himself wearing the one label no man wants to wear: failure. Howbeit, Jason was successful at one thing and that was nabbing women. He would often come to our house, and even though I was a young girl, I noticed that every woman Jason introduced to us was motherly. She was nurturing and overly committed to Jason. It goes without saying that Jason had "mommy issues." At the same time, he liked the attention and the accolades that he received from the men in our family and from his friends. So, just like a man shows off his prized car collection, Jason would often show off his prized collection of women. Jason was finally successful at something. Sex, to him, was all about having bragging rights and making the women want him all the more. He loved watching women argue over him and he loved being able to choose between women because he was finally able to find success at something and that was, as he used to call it, being a player. Jason also used women for money. He would often date working women who he knew he could charm into supporting him. Sex, for Jason, was just a bonus.

Finally, there was Greg. Greg was a close friend of my dad and he was similar to Ed from the aforementioned story. Women, for Greg, were like stimulants; they were, in a sense, caffeine for his self-esteem. They made him feel alive, wanted, and most of all, they made him feel powerful. Just like the effects of coffee wear off, the effects of every one of Greg's women would eventually wear off.

Greg had a fairly decent job and he always seemed to be making more money than he knew what to do with. Nevertheless, having a good job and a house to call home wasn't enough for Greg. He loved to play the hero with women. Greg would date women who were struggling financially. He preferred women who were used to dating men like Jason, men who took from them but never gave. Greg would get with these women and spend a lot of money on them. He'd lease cars for them, pay their car notes, pay their rent and take them on long, expensive vacations. He'd send roses to their jobs and even show up at their workplaces to perform grand acts of affection in front of their co-workers. He would lead his women to a place where they would have to depend on him. He wouldn't let them move into his house, but he would spend a few nights at their houses. He would even encourage them to move into more expensive houses, and again, he'd pay their rent for them, in addition to paying the down payments on their cars. He would then pay a few of their car notes; that was, until the effects of the relationship began to wear off. He loved the high he felt in new relationships and he loved playing the hero. He loved being praised by women and he loved having power over women. That's why he put them in positions where they could not afford the houses and the cars he'd gotten for them or persuaded them to get for themselves. After he had them in financial bondage and dependent on him, he'd pay a few more bills for them before leaving to start that same pattern with another woman.

Greg eventually made a move on me when I was 12 years old. He fondled me until I was 14 and I finally got the courage to tell my parents. Before I told my parents, he'd asked me to run away, saying that he had a house that my parents didn't know about. He promised to take care of me and even teach me to drive. I was petrified at the idea, after all, I didn't like his inappropriate behaviors toward me in the first place. After he'd asked me to run away with him, I finally got the nerve up to tell my parents what he had been doing for two years. Thankfully, he'd never gotten the chance to have sex with me because my siblings were always home and I was always trying to avoid being alone with him, but the few times that he'd caught me alone were nightmarish for me.

Unfortunately, my parents didn't do much about Greg's behavior and he was allowed to return to our home. His need for power was still very much alive, but he was afraid to bother me anymore. Because of this, he would pull a few dollars out of his pocket and give it to my siblings. He would pretend that he didn't see me. That was his way of regaining his power and punishing me for telling on him.

Greg's need for power led him into pedophilia. He was over 40 years old and he could never seem to settle down with one woman because the effects of each relationship were short-lived. Sex, to Greg, was about power and control.

The point is ... every man uses sex differently. The orgasm and the experience itself are just bonuses. A man can sleep with a woman that he's not attracted to just to fulfill a deep-rooted need for acceptance, a sense of love (if but for a moment) and to feel in control, especially if he's lost control of his own life. After that, he will decide whether the sexual encounter was good based on how it made him feel. Please understand that good sex, to a man, isn't based on how well a woman performs in the bedroom. It is based on whether he experienced what he came to experience or not. For example, to a man who is angry with his mother and women as a whole, sex may be his way of retaliating against the female gender; it may be his way to legally abuse women. At the same time, he gets to gratify the desires burning from within his flesh. For this reason, he may be forceful, insensitive and selfish in the bedroom. On the other hand, for a sensitive man who did receive a lot of love and hugs from his mother, but he did not receive, for example, discipline, sex may be his way of (and I hate to say this) giving back. He will often pursue dominant women who make him work for their affection. He will likely be a passionate soul who uses sex to experience the intimacy he felt with his mother. He will also provoke his women so that he can receive the discipline he feels he needed from his mother. This personality is what we refer to as the Ahab spirit. He will oftentimes be found in a marriage being starved of sex by his Jezebel-infested wife. He has to earn his right to have sex with her, and for that reason, he will oftentimes go months, even years, without having sex. Sex, for him, is all about the reconciliation experience.

Desiree used sex to get what she wanted from men. She wanted to be married; she wanted to have a family and she wanted to be taken care of financially. At the same time, she was clearly under the authority of her mother and it is obvious that her mother has the Jezebel spirit. Desiree's mother taught her to use her body to ensnare men. When Desiree met Ed, her mother encouraged her to intentionally get pregnant by him. For her, Ed was nothing but an opportunity for her daughter to escape poverty.

It is clear that Desiree's father wasn't in the picture as well. Women who have been abandoned by their fathers oftentimes look for love and acceptance from other men.

Below are a few truths you can extract from this story:
1. In her current state, Desiree could never petition Heaven for a husband because she had not forgiven her ex, Lenny. Ed represented an opportunity to get back at Lenny and to make Lenny jealous.
2. Ed appeared to be a good man because he was the deacon at a local church. It is not uncommon for womanizers to hide behind religious garments;

they wear them as costumes. Ed wasn't a deacon with snakish ways; he was a snake impersonating a deacon!

3. Desiree was a smart girl who did dumb things. She should have invested the time she spent trying to secure a relationship with men into building her relationship with God and getting a college degree. The same is true for any woman. Many women spend their time chasing behind men, trying to find someone who'll stick around and love them. Years later, these same women wake up next to their newest investment opportunities, only to realize that they are about to lose again.

4. Desiree considered her need; she needed her bills paid and she wanted a father for her children. She also wanted to please her mother, so she considered the need and not the seeds that God had placed on the inside of her. For this reason, she sowed pieces of her broken soul into relationships, hoping to finally get what she longed for. This never happened.

5. A man can invest in a relationship and pursue a woman vigorously, only to later realize that he doesn't love her. This is similar to what women do to their personal friends. Many single women will become best buddies with other single women, only to dump those women once they've gotten married

or gotten into relationships that they think will end in marriage. When they were single, they proudly boasted that they would be close friends forever and nothing would come between their friendships. They even made plans for their future spouses to hang out, but once one of the women got into a serious relationship, she had a change of heart. Sure, when she told her friend that they'd be friends forever, she meant it at that time, but when her status changed, her mind had to change with it. Broken men do the same in relationships because they too are not yet settled. They'll plan to spend their lives with the women they've chosen for themselves and when they say that they will never leave them, they mean it (in that hour). They are speaking from their need, but once their needs change, their minds change.

Of course, there is a lot that can be taken from this story, but the moral of the story is: broken people attract other broken people. Ladies, it is never wise to enter into relationships based on your need because your need belongs to God. This means that you should take your requests before the Lord and let Him fill them. Additionally, God has to be your everything. As you build upon your relationship with the Lord, He will supply all your needs according to His riches in glory by Christ Jesus (see Philippians 4:19). He will also remove all of your voids and give you a new heart and a new mind. In other words, He will change the way you think! Nevertheless, if you take that need and hand it to a man, he will, in turn, hand you an impossible list of needs that he has. You will find yourself working overtime trying to please a man who simply cannot be pleased — he needs to be delivered! If you receive him as your "head" or God-assigned authority over you, it is because you need to be delivered as well.

Don't be driven into relationships by your needs. Work on your relationship with God and work on having all of your needs met; that way, you won't be so intimidated or wowed by every man who approaches you in a BMW or, for some of you, a Kia.

Chapter 3

Captivated

In today's day and age, it is not uncommon to see believers who seem to be too busy for God. They won't take the time out to read their Bibles or pray to God consistently. For this reason, we are in the midst of a starving generation, and one thing about starving people is ... they'll eat anything, especially if it tastes good to them.

The Bible warns us about having itching ears, and at the same time, the Bible also warns us about false prophets. One of the most common questions that people ask is, "How do I tell the difference between a false prophet and a true one?" The answer is simple. Prophets of God are the mouthpieces of God, meaning, they are like human loudspeakers. God holds them up and speaks through them. This means that God's Prophets are in His hands; they are submitted to Him. A false prophet, on the other hand, is not submitted to God. Sure, false prophets disguise themselves as God's Prophets and many are faithful members of small and

large churches; they prophesy and perform miracles. Nevertheless, they are not faithful to God. Their integrity does not match the words that they preach, plus, false prophets hold themselves up in an attempt to draw people to themselves, but not to God. Nevertheless, when you come in contact with a false prophet, that person will always pretend to be drawing souls to Christ, when in truth, they are drawing souls to themselves. Because of this, having an intimate relationship with God is imperative to differentiating a false prophet from a true one.

It was Anastasia's birthday and she was ecstatic. Her dad was coming by her house to take her out to eat and later that evening, she was supposed to be visiting her best friend's new church. There, she hoped to finally meet the man who her former pastor had prophesied that she'd meet. She'd been single and abstinent for three years and Anastasia was beginning to become impatient. Nevertheless, after visiting her former church two weeks prior, she'd received a prophetic word that she was going to meet her God-appointed husband at a big event. Anastasia assumed it was the event at her best friend's new church because it was the only event she was planning to go to.

Anastasia leaned forward and applied another coat of lipstick. She wanted to look her best for her outing with her father because the church event was going to start in less than two hours. This meant that she would not have enough time to return to her house to freshen up for the event since the restaurant that she was eating at was in the same town as the church she would be visiting. Both places were a little over a half hour away.

Anastasia turned sideways to make sure that her stomach didn't look bloated. Her fitted blue dress matched her big blue eyes, and her dark brown hair flowed down the center of her back. She was beautiful to behold and she knew it. Howbeit, as beautiful as she was, Anastasia was a woman of faith. Her dad was a pastor who'd dedicated his life to serving the Lord. Her mother, on the other hand, was not saved. Anastasia's dad met her mother when he was a young, backslidden son of a preacher. He'd gone to Miami, Florida for a weekend with his friends and it was there that he met Anastasia's mother.

Anastasia's mother was an Armenian exotic dancer by the name of Nairi. Nairi migrated to the United States at the tender age of fourteen. Her parents sent her to live with her mother's brother, hoping that she could further her education, but instead, Nairi had been sexually molested by her uncle. When she turned eighteen, Nairi ran away from her uncle's house and started living with a woman she'd met while working at a local restaurant. The woman (Syn) saw how beautiful Nairi was and quickly befriended her. After several months of friendship, Syn finally told Nairi what she did for a living. She was an exotic dancer. At first, Nairi was apprehensive about living with Syn, but her relationship with her uncle seemed to get more and more volatile as she approached her eighteenth birthday.

Finally, on her eighteenth birthday, Nairi's uncle had come home drunk again. He then demanded that she sign a contract he'd drawn up, stating that she was betrothed to him. When Nairi refused to sign the contract, her uncle attacked her and vowed to kill her. Fed up with his abusive ways, Nairi took a pair of scissors off an end table nearby and stabbed her uncle before he could sexually assault her. After that, she fled his house and never looked back. She never knew what became of her uncle, but she didn't care. She ran to Syn's house and moved in with her. Syn then introduced Nairi to her lifestyle.

Anastasia had only met her mother twice in her life. She'd met her once when she was three years old and a second time when she was eight years old. After that, Anastasia's mother seemed to have completely disappeared.

Anastasia's father was of Swedish descent. His family

moved to the United States when he was only four years of age. Royce, Anastasia's father, grew up in church. His father was raised in the Roman Catholic church; that was, until he'd been introduced by a close friend of his to an American Baptist pastor by the name of Henry Bartholomew. Fascinated with Mr. Bartholomew's faith, Royce's father (Mr. Erickson) renounced Catholicism and became Baptist. A few years after his conversion, he'd begun studying a new trending faith now referred to as non-denominational Christianity. After a series of dreams where he claimed to have met the Lord, Mr. Erickson finally made one last conversion; he became a non-denominational believer. A few years after his conversion, he became a pastor himself. He then met Royce's mother and they had two children: Royce and his sister, Annabelle. They decided to move to the States when Royce was four because Mr. Erickson said he'd dreamed that he was preaching in an American church.

Royce was nineteen years old when he met Nairi. He'd visited a beach near his hotel room in Miami, Florida, and there, he saw Nairi walking by herself. Her beautiful tanned skin was accented by her long dark hair. Her earth-toned swimsuit made her skin look like melted gold. Royce had once described her as one of the most beautiful women he'd ever met.

When Royce saw Nairi for the first time, she was walking along the shoreline and she was visibly upset. Royce was also alone because he'd spent the majority of the day surfing with his friends. His friends retreated to their hotel rooms to take a nap, but Royce stayed behind to do a little more surfing. Smitten with the exotic beauty, he rushed over to see if he could console her.

Royce was the nicest man Nairi had ever met. He was handsome, well-spoken and respectful. Additionally, his sense of humor was refreshing. He appeared to be loving, sensitive and somewhat innocent. He wasn't like the monsters who would throw money at her whenever she danced. His big blue eyes looked child-like and his dark brown hair never seemed to be combed properly. Nairi really liked Royce; he was definitely one of a kind. Nevertheless, when Royce told her that his father was a pastor, she knew that his father would never approve of her.

Royce traveled to Florida to see Nairi every weekend that he could. He did this for a period of five months; that was, until he discovered Nairi's secret. Not only did he feel like he'd been lied to, he believed that Nairi was doing far more than dancing. He believed that she was prostituting herself, so Royce stopped calling Nairi and he stopped returning her calls. Seven months after he broke up with

Nairi, Royce's father received a call from Syn, Nairi's boss and roommate. Nairi had just given birth to a healthy baby girl who she named Anastasia. She was planning to return to her home country of Armenia, but she did not want her parents to know that she was a mother. She feared that they would be ashamed of her, or even worse, try to pressure her into giving her daughter to a family member. Syn had been raised in a foster home and she did not want Anastasia to suffer through the abuse, rape and the sense of rejection she'd suffered through. She'd finally convinced Nairi to to let her call Royce's home and tell him about his daughter. Royce's father answered the phone and Syn told him about Anastasia. Of course, Mr. Erickson was not happy about the news; after all, he'd told his son about the dangers of premarital sex. Now, here it was that his son had not only engaged in fornication, but he'd repeatedly done it with a stripper. Nevertheless, Mr. Erickson and his wife drove down to Florida with an embarrassed Royce in tow. Royce was ashamed of Nairi's lifestyle. He was also embarrassed at the idea of being bossed around by his parents in front of Nairi; after all, every time he'd visited Florida, he'd pretended to be strong, independent and sure of himself.

When Royce and his parents entered the hospital room, Nairi had her back turned to them. She did not want them to see her face. She hoped that they would just take baby

Anastasia and leave. At the same time, she didn't want to see her daughter being taken away from her, even though she knew that she was doing what was best for Anastasia. Royce would not hurt her and she knew it. She didn't want her family to be anywhere near Anastasia and after hearing about the American foster system, she didn't want Anastasia to get caught up in it either. Nevertheless, she knew that they would question Anastasia's paternity so when Royce and his parents entered her hospital room, Nairi blurted out, "They perform blood tests at this hospital. Just ask the nurse to give you the forms."

Royce was not happy that Nairi had her back turned. He was ashamed, but at the same time, he wanted to see her big beautiful eyes one more time. Royce's mother made her way around Nairi's bed. She wanted to see her face. When she saw the pain in her face, she gestured for Royce and his father to leave the room. Thirty minutes later, she came out of the room with her eyes fixed on Royce. She approached him with tears in her eyes, and without warning, she slapped him. After that, she grabbed Mr. Erickson's hand and the couple returned to the room without Royce. An hour later, the couple emerged from the room holding Anastasia. A social worker approached the couple just as they were exiting the room and they followed her into another room. That's when Royce decided to give in to temptation; he decided to go into

Nairi's room.

Nairi didn't expect Royce or his family to return, so she was sitting up on her bed, staring at the door. She was grieving her daughter. When Royce entered the room and saw her crying, his heart broke. When he'd met her at the beach, she had been crying and he'd consoled her, but now, she was crying because of him. "I'm sorry," said Royce, staring at the woman he'd never truly gotten over. Nevertheless, Nairi was angry with Royce. She picked up her pillow and threw it at him with force. "Get out of my room!" she screamed repeatedly until Royce finally complied.

Royce's parents helped him raise Anastasia. They'd both passed away in 2003; Mrs. Erickson died one day before Royce's birthday and Mr. Erickson passed away a day after Anastasia's eighteenth birthday.

Royce had never gotten over Nairi, and for that reason, he remained a single father his entire life. He'd tried dating, but he was always too afraid to invest himself into a serious relationship. He was afraid that he'd hurt another woman, so he dedicated his life to full-time ministry.

Anastasia stood in the mirror and examined herself one more time. The sound of the doorbell startled her. She knew it was her father coming to pick her up, so she grabbed her purse and headed out the door. "You look beautiful," said Royce. "The older you get, the more you look like your mother." Anastasia smiled. She hated discussing her mother with her father because he seemed to only want to talk about her beauty, but he would not answer the many questions that Anastasia had about her. For that reason, almost every time they'd attempted to discuss Nairi, they'd gotten into an argument. "You look good too, Dad," said Anastasia. "I just might get you hitched after all." The duo laughed as they entered Royce's car.

The church event wasn't as populated as Anastasia thought it would be. It was nothing like Wendy, Anastasia's best friend, had described it would be. There were maybe fifteen people in the church, including Anastasia and her father. Anastasia searched the crowd, hoping to see a man that she was interested in, but every man there was either married, unattractive or elderly. Disappointed, Anastasia sunk in her seat. She was almost twenty-five years old and she had no good prospects for a husband. Sensing his daughter's mood change, Royce placed his hand on her hand. "You don't have to look for your husband," he said. "In the right time, he will find you." How did he know? Anastasia hadn't told her father about the prophecy, but he'd somehow managed to figure out, yet again, why she was so solemn. "This isn't about a man," said Anastasia. "I'm just tired." Royce smiled at his daughter as he squeezed her hand. He knew better. Anastasia wanted to be a wife and mother more than anything and he believed it was because she wanted to prove to herself that she would be nothing like her mother.

After the event, Anastasia was somewhat gloom. As they traveled towards Anastasia's house, her father tried to cheer her up, but nothing seemed to work. Anastasia closed her eyes and anytime Royce asked her if she was okay, she tried to excuse her behavior by saying that she was sleepy. The truth was Anastasia was beginning to doubt God and she was definitely beginning to doubt the prophetic.

Anastasia: Dad? I have a question.
Royce: Well, hopefully, I have an answer. What is it, sweetie?
Anastasia: You believe that prophets still exist, right?
Royce: Of course.
Anastasia: Okay, before I ask you, I want you to promise me that you won't try to pastor me. I just want to have a question answered. I need you to be my dad right now.
Royce: Anastasia, I can't promise you anything. The Bible tells us not to vow anything, but what I can tell you is I'll do my best to answer you and I'll try to not act like a

pastor.

Anastasia: I met a man the other day who said he was a pastor. Ron; that's what I think his name was. Yeah, it was Ron. Anyway, he said that he is a pastor at a church called New Age Assemblies.

Royce: Okay. Where is this going?

Anastasia: Well, first I ran into Pastor Bingham the other day at the library and ...

Royce: Your former pastor?

Anastasia: Yes, him.

Royce: What's he doing now?

Anastasia: I think he said he's about to open a new church down in Phoenix.

Royce: I hope you're not planning to go there.

Anastasia: I considered it. I know that him cheating on his wife was wrong, but he's human.

Royce: Of course, he's human, but to lead God's people, we must first set an example, and then, when we make a mistake, we must confess that mistake and repent of it. He did neither.

Anastasia: You're doing it again.

Royce: Doing what?

Anastasia: Trying to pastor me. Dad, I just want to ask a question; please just let me ask a question.

Royce: Okay, I'm sorry. What's your question?

Anastasia: Anyhow, Mr. Bingham seems to have changed a lot. He looked a little different to me.

Royce: Yeah, sin will do that to you.

Anastasia: Dad!

Royce: I'm sorry. Keep going.

Anastasia: Okay, so I asked him how his new wife was and he said that they were expecting their first child. We talked for maybe fifteen minutes, and just when I was about to leave, he started prophesying to me.

Royce: What did he say?

Anastasia: He told me that I was going to meet my husband really soon and I'd meet him at a church event.

Royce: Oh, so that's why ...

Anastasia: No, that's not why ... Just listen, okay? Anyhow, I believed him, so I guess; yeah, I was sorta going to this event hoping I'd meet the guy. I can't lie; I was a little disappointed that I didn't meet him, but that's not what I want to discuss with you.

Royce: There's more?

Anastasia: Yes, Dad; there's more. The conversation between me and Mr. Bingham carried on all the way to the checkouts and there was a man standing behind us in line. After Mr. Bingham checked out, he looked at his watch and told me that he needed to go. After he left, the guy behind me started talking to me. First, he offered to pay for my items, but I told him no. He paid the cashier anyway. After that, he kept making small talk with me. He's the guy I was telling you about. His name is Ron and he pastors a church called New Age Assemblies. Anyway, I could tell that he was trying to get me to wait on him to finish checking out, so I stood still and waited. He looked to be around 35 years old, but I wasn't interested in him romantically. Anyhow, once he finished checking out, we walked out to the parking lot together and he asked me why I believed that prophets still existed. I told him about you and I told him that it was in the Bible. He told me to show him proof, but I couldn't. He then invited me to visit his church for Bible study that Wednesday and I went.

Royce: Anastasia ... no!

Anastasia: Listen, Dad! Pastor Ron was on to something! You're a good preacher; don't get me wrong, but he had me sitting at the edge of my seat. At first, I didn't want to believe what he was saying, but after tonight, I think I can safely say I'm questioning the prophetic.

Royce: That means you're questioning God.

Anastasia: How does me questioning the prophetic sum up to me questioning God? Tell me, Pastor Royce.

Royce: First, watch your tone with me. Secondly, the fact that you said that I'm a good preacher tells me that everything I've taught from the pulpit was nothing but a sermon to you; it had no true depth or meaning. I'm not offended about that because I'm your father, so I can imagine that it's hard to receive from me, but to question God means that your faith was never truly grounded.

Anastasia: There you go again! Can we just have one conversation without you trying to tell me what I should or shouldn't do? Why can't you just listen?!

Royce: Anastasia, we are going to end this conversation now because even though I'm your father, I am also a vessel of the living God. With that being said, you can't put a muzzle on me and tell me to listen to lies without giving me the opportunity to address those lies! What you're trying to do is make your case and that's fine. Everyone's path to God is different. If you need to follow this man and join his church for a season, that just may be the path you have to go. It's false doctrine, but life is a far better teacher than I am. The only thing I can do is pray for you.

Anastasia: Okay, it's settled then. I'm going to be joining his church.

Royce: Okay. That's your choice.

A few minutes later, Royce pulled up in front of Anastasia's house. Still angry with her father, Anastasia got out of the car without saying a word. She slammed Royce's car door and stormed towards her house. Royce was heartbroken, but he knew that Anastasia had to find her own way. She needed to finally understand that God wasn't supposed to be serving her; she was supposed to be serving Him. "Lord, just protect my baby," said Royce as the teardrops formed in his eyes. "I put her in your hands, Lord. Have your way." After Anastasia made it safely into her house, Mr. Royce pulled away.

Royce knew how impatient his daughter was and he'd often warned her that her lack of patience had the potential to lead her into some dark places. He'd witnessed his daughter going on prayer lines and visiting a lot of churches. She had particularly become fond of prophets. Nevertheless, as he pulled away from Anastasia's house, he knew that his prayers were being answered. He knew that Anastasia was about to get a wake up call.

For more than three months, Anastasia did not call her father, and to her surprise, he didn't call her. She'd become an active member of New Age Assemblies and everything seemed to be going well. She'd even met a guy by the name of Joshua and their relationship seemed to be blossoming quickly. Anastasia was happy; she finally felt free, but there were a few things about the church that troubled her. At New Age Assemblies, the women were not allowed to speak inside the church, nor could they hold any positions of power. It was clear that they were not even allowed to question their husbands. It was hard to tell, but all of the married women looked unhappy and controlled; they looked like they were under a spell, plus, they weren't allowed to wear makeup. Nevertheless, Anastasia had what she wanted: a blossoming relationship that seemed to be heading towards marriage.

It was a Tuesday afternoon when Anastasia ran into Joshua at the mall. She was about to leave the mall when a hand came from behind her and opened the door for her. It was Joshua and he didn't look too happy. Wearing sunglasses as always, he asked, "What do you have in the bag?" Anastasia was surprised. "I bought some lip gloss and a new pair of shoes. Why?" Joshua sighed and began to walk away. Anastasia was confused. "Did I do something wrong?!" she yelled out. Nevertheless, Joshua did not answer her question. Instead, he walked across the parking lot and got into his vehicle. Stunned, Anastasia watched as Joshua pulled his car close to the mall's entrance. He then exited the car and opened the passenger's side door. "Let's take a ride," he said taking off his sunglasses. His eyes seemed somewhat different. They appeared to be darker than usual, nevertheless, Anastasia was determined to make things work between her and Joshua; after all, she was sure that he was going to propose to her soon.

"Where are we going?" Anastasia's inquisitive voice broke the silence as Joshua turned onto the busy freeway. They'd been driving for just a little over fifteen minutes and Joshua hadn't said a word to Anastasia. He didn't appear to be angry, but it was clear that he had something on his mind. "Josh, if I've done something wrong, I'd rather you tell me. I hate the silent treatment." Suddenly, the car slowed down and turned. Anastasia turned her head and to her surprise, they were pulling up in front of a fairly large home. The house looked great, but it definitely needed a new coat of paint, plus, the yard was a mess. Strewn about the yard were children's toys and uncollected newspapers. "Whose house is this?" asked Anastasia. Nevertheless, Joshua did not answer her. Instead, he put the car in park, got out and walked over to the passenger's side. He then opened the door for Anastasia. "Follow me," he said.

The house's nearest neighbor was half a mile away. Even though the house was pleasant to look at, it had a creepy feel to it. Anastasia wasn't sure who the house belonged to until Joshua pulled out his key and unlocked the door. He then led her upstairs into a beautifully decorated bedroom. The room's walls were painted white, but they were framed with a gold, ornamental border. Joshua's bed was a fancy, gold-plated canopy bed with white and gold drapes that fell from a beautifully hung post on the ceiling. The bed's comforter was pure white, but the throw pillows were tan and crimson with gold specks in each pillow. Each wall was lined with narrow, vertical paintings wrapped in gold frames. The floor was covered with a plush white carpet and the air had clearly been fragranced with some sort of perfumed oil. "Take off your shoes," said Joshua as he removed his shoes and walked into the bedroom. Anastasia didn't know how to respond to all of the emotions she was feeling. On one hand, she was was uneasy, terrified and confused, but on the other hand, she was taken aback by what she felt was the most beautiful house she'd ever seen. Now, she was entering the beautiful utopia that Joshua slept in every night.

The curtains on the bed were already pulled back and held to the bed's posts with a beautiful gold ribbon. "Sit down," Joshua said, pointing to his bed.

Anastasia: Josh, I don't think this is a good idea.
Joshua: I never said it was okay to call me Josh. Call me Joshua.
Anastasia: Okay, Joshua; I don't think this is a good idea.
Joshua: What?
Anastasia: Me being in your bedroom. I don't believe in sex before marriage. I told you that before.
Joshua: Have a seat.

Anastasia reluctantly sat on Joshua's bed as he reached for the bag she was carrying. Not wanting to upset him, Anastasia handed him the bag.

Joshua: Pastor Ron always said you will know when it's time.
Anastasia: Time for what?

Joshua held up the lip gloss that Anastasia had purchased. He then opened his bedroom window and threw it out the window.

Anastasia: Wait! What was that for?! That lip gloss cost me fifteen bucks!

Joshua: If you wait too long to marry your bride, the devil will get in her and she will start dressing and behaving like a harlot.

Anastasia: Josh ... I mean Joshua, you are talking crazy. I am not a whore and lip gloss is not makeup. We use it to moisturize our lips.

Joshua: I'm sorry I waited so long to make you mine, Anastasia. I knew I was going to marry you the first time I saw you. I'm sorry I took so long.

Anastasia didn't know how to feel. She was flattered by Joshua's words, but still disturbed by his behavior. Joshua made his way to the bed and sat next to Anastasia. He then leaned towards Anastasia and closed his eyes. It was clear that he was ready to share their first kiss. Anastasia stared at Joshua as he continued to lean forward. Not wanting to ruin the moment, she leaned in and began to kiss him. At first, all seemed normal, but about thirty seconds later, Joshua seemed to be getting more and more forceful. He kept forcing his tongue into Anastasia's mouth and the more Anastasia tried to pull away from him, the more forceful he became. Suddenly, he began to unbutton his shirt and that's when Anastasia successfully managed to pull away from him. She pulled her body onto the bed in an attempt to get away from Joshua. "Joshua, what are you doing? I told you that I don't want ..." Before she could finish speaking, Joshua struck her with his fist. "You're not supposed to question me. Didn't you read the by-laws?" he asked calmly. The force from the blow was so hard that it put Anastasia in a state of semi-consciousness. Dazed and confused, she watched as Joshua disrobed himself and climbed into the bed. Everything else seemed to be nothing but a blur.

The next day, Anastasia woke up in Joshua's bedroom, but he was not there. Her entire body was sore. Confused, she struggled to remember what had happened the day prior, but at first, the only memory she had was sitting on Joshua's bed. Anastasia climbed out of the bed and that's when she noticed that she was wearing a white gown that clearly did not belong to her. It was a beautiful, elegant gown that draped all the way down to her feet. She made her way to the on-suite bathroom and from there, she let out a piercing scream. Her right eye was swollen and she had hickey marks all over her neck and chest. Some of the hickey marks were clearly bite marks. Suddenly, she remembered Joshua striking her. Fear struck Anastasia as she rushed back into the bedroom, hoping to find her clothes. That's when the bedroom's door opened and in came an older blonde woman who introduced herself as Misty.

Anastasia: Call the police! I've been raped! He raped me! Wait! Is he here?!

Misty: Is who here?

Anastasia: Joshua?

Misty: No. He went to get your wedding present.

Anastasia: Wedding present? I'm not married to that scumbag! Call the police! Please! Look at what he did to my face.

Misty: I almost forgot that you're new here. He didn't rape you, dear. He honored you. The devil got in you, so he cast him out of you; that's all. You're one of us, now.

Anastasia: Is everyone around here crazy? Who's us? What are you talking about? Now, I remember you. I saw you at the church. You're that woman with all the kids.

Misty: Yeah, well, those children are our children now.

Anastasia: Our children?! What are you talking about? Where am I?! Can you just call the police for me?!

Misty: Joshua is on his way back, so I'll let him explain everything to you. I was the same way at first. I panicked when he married me, but now, I'm honored to be called his wife.

With that, Misty left the room and closed the door.

Anastasia was even more confused and terrified than she'd been before. Suddenly, she remembered that her cell phone was in her purse. She rushed around the bed and grabbed her purse off the nightstand. After fumbling through it, she became impatient and dumped its contents onto the bed. Her phone was gone. It was clear that Joshua had taken it. Pacing back and forth, Anastasia contemplated jumping out of the window, but the bedroom was on the second floor. "Think. Think." Anastasia spoke softly to herself. She tried to remain calm, but her heart was racing. That's when she remembered a cell phone that Pastor Ron had given her after she'd joined the church. All of the members had been given a cell phone that could only dial Pastor Ron's number. Maybe she could reach the pastor and have him call the police. To her surprise, that phone was still in one of her purse's side pockets.

Anastasia paced back and forth in front of the window as Pastor Ron's phone rang. She could see Joshua's car pulling into the yard. "Please answer," she whispered in a soft, panicked tone. "Please answer."

Pastor Ron: Hello?
Anastasia: Hello, Pastor Ron. I'm at Joshua's house. Please, please call the police for me. I need help.
Pastor Ron: What's wrong, dear?

Anastasia: He raped me yesterday and he hit me. Now, he's holding me hostage.

Pastor Ron: I know how confusing this must be to you. I told that boy to let me talk with you before he ...

Anastasia: Before what? You knew he was going to rape me?

Pastor Ron: It's not rape, dear. You're one with him now. Congratulations. You are now married. Now, it may take you some time to adjust, but ...

With that, Anastasia hung up the phone. She rushed back to the window, but it was clear that Joshua was now in the house. She could hear him coming up the stairs towards the bedroom. Anastasia rushed around the room looking for a weapon, but she could not find anything. Suddenly, she remembered a few things her dad taught her. She reasoned within herself to remain calm.

Anastasia could hear Joshua talking outside the bedroom door. He was on the phone talking with Pastor Ron. He peeped in and looked at Anastasia who, by this time, was sitting on the bed. He then pulled the door up in an attempt to keep Anastasia from hearing his conversation, but she could hear him well. "No, she's here," he said. "I apologize. I didn't plan to do the ceremony yesterday. I saw her at the mall buying makeup, so I knew that I needed to step up to the plate. Like you said, I will always know when it's time. Sure. Why, thank you. I will. Yes, sir. You're right. No, she'll be okay. Remember Misty and Jeannette were like that at first too. *(Laughs)* Yeah, Jeannette still holds the record for the worst fight ever. No, it was my left arm. The doctor said it was broken in three places. She laughs about that now, too. Yeah. Okay. Don't worry. I took it and threw it away. No, she can't. You know me, Pastor; I do think ahead, even when I'm under pressure. Nope. Just a few scratches, that's all. I'll be okay. See you Sunday. Yeah. Thanks. We don't need anything. Pastor Ron, she'll be fine; stop worrying. Okay. Tell everyone I said hello. Okay. Thanks. Bye."

With that, Joshua entered the room. "Put this on," he said as he tossed a bag onto the bed. Anastasia didn't answer him. She reached for the bag and saw a dress similar to the ones worn by the women at the church. "You're not going to understand this immediately," said Joshua. "But someday, you will come to realize that I did the noble thing; I rescued you. And now, we are one. You are now my wife and I am your husband. I will send Misty into the room in an hour or two to help you understand the honor that I have bestowed upon you. There's so much I want to tell you, but as of right now, you don't know when to be quiet and I don't want to be forced to silence you time and time again. Misty will help you understand, so you'll know when to speak and when to be silent. In case you're wondering who Misty is to me, she is also my wife. You have another sister as well. Her name is Jeanette, but she's being quarantined right now because some evil force has entered her. Anyhow, Misty will come and talk to you after you've showered and put your clothes on. But before I leave, I must say a prayer to cover you." After he finished speaking, Joshua bowed his head and began to pray silently. Anastasia sat on the bed, refusing to lift her head. She was terrified, but at the same time, she was trying to follow one of the survival lessons her father taught her.

After Joshua left the room, Anastasia went into the bathroom to shower. The pain in her body was almost unbearable; the swelling around her eye was starting to go down, but it was being replaced by what appeared to be a dark purple-like color.

Anastasia dropped her gown and stepped into the shower. She began to cry as the water from the shower ran down her bruised body. For the first time, she found herself sorely missing her father. Was this it for her? Would she be stuck with Joshua for the rest of her life, never to hear from her father again? Her priorities took a sudden shift and suddenly, she wasn't so desperate to get married.

Anastasia turned to find the soap. What she found was a poorly shaped substance that was clearly homemade.

Anastasia reached for the soap and began to wash her body with it. The soap didn't lather well, but somehow, it had been infused with the smell of roses. As a matter of fact, the smell of the soap was almost overpowering.

After her shower, Anastasia dried off and put on the dress that Joshua had given her. "Okay, let's do this," she whispered as she lifted her head, revealing the face of an angry woman with a plan.

Just as Joshua had said, Misty came into Anastasia's holding place. When Misty walked into the room, she was carrying a breakfast tray. On the tray was a ham and cheese sandwich and a small glass of orange juice. "I know you think you're not hungry," said Misty. "They all say that at first. Pastor Ron had me to mentor six of his wives and every last one of them claimed to not be hungry the day after their weddings. But I'll tell you this. It is better to eat and obey the man of God than it is to dishonor him by refusing the food he's bought. Make things easier for yourself, sweetie." Anastasia couldn't seem to take her eyes off Misty. She was an older woman with blonde hair, gray eyes and a rotten tooth that made her breath almost unbearable. Age and circumstance had taken its toll on her and robbed her of her beauty. Nevertheless, it wasn't hard to see that she had once been a very beautiful woman.

Anastasia slowly reached for the sandwich. She knew that she needed to get along with Misty if she ever wanted any hope of escaping. She also knew that she needed to show interest in the food that Misty had prepared for her if she wanted to make a good impression on her. Anastasia lowered her head, bit into the sandwich and began to slowly chew. It was obvious that she didn't like the food because of the length of time it took her to chew it. "What's wrong?" asked Misty. Anastasia closed her eyes and forced herself to swallow the chunk of meat. "I'm a vegetarian," responded Anastasia. "Oh, you should've said so. That's not a problem," said Misty. With that, she reached for Anastasia's sandwich. Lifting up the top layer of bread, she pulled out the meat and handed the sandwich back to Anastasia. "Thank you," said Anastasia as Misty returned the sandwich to her. Misty stared at Anastasia as she slowly ate the sandwich. "I can see why he chose you," she said. "You're really pretty and you're really nice." Anastasia was uncomfortable, but she didn't want to offend Misty. "Thank you," she responded. "How long have you been with him?" Misty's countenance lit up. She was obviously proud to be Joshua's first wife. "Twelve years," she said. "Obviously, I'm a little bit older than him, but I was given to him as a gift." Misty's response surprised Anastasia. "A gift? Who gave you away?" she asked. "My Paw-Paw," said Misty proudly. "His name is Dale and he's a reverend at New Age. Anastasia knew exactly who Misty was talking about. She'd had a few uncomfortable encounters with Reverend Dale when she'd first started going to the church, but she'd written him off as a strange, possibly perverted old man. Now, things were starting to make sense. Reverend Dale had been instrumental in connecting Anastasia with Joshua. He would sit close to Anastasia anytime the church had a meeting and he'd start asking her a bunch of uncomfortable questions. Miraculously, Joshua would come to the rescue and sit between the Reverend and Anastasia. The uncomfortable reverend would then make his way to the ministers' section at the front of the church. It was in that moment that Anastasia realized that the two men had been playing a game similar to the game "good cop/bad cop." Reverend Dale played the bad cop, of course, robbing Anastasia of her peace and making her uncomfortable, but Joshua would show up as the heroic good cop. He would chase the bad guy away and restore order.

"I think my menstruation just came on," said Anastasia. "What am I supposed to do?" Misty smiled. "It's okay. We're women, so it happens. I have some pads in my room. I'll go get some for you." Misty stood to her feet and picked up the food tray. She walked to the door and turned back to look at Anastasia. "He's going to quarantine you, so don't be alarmed. I'll tell you more when I come back."

What did she mean by quarantine? Anastasia's overactive imagination seemed to take over. She imagined some lonely, dark room with a musty odor, an infestation of mice, and a mattress lying on the floor. Nevertheless, nothing could be worse than being in a beautiful room with an ugly spirit, so the thought didn't terrify her too much.

Anastasia stood to her feet and walked over to the window. She could see six children outside playing. The oldest of them all was a little girl who appeared to be around ten or eleven years old. She stood out like a sore thumb because she wasn't playing with the others. Instead, she sat on a lawn chair with her arms crossed. It was obvious that she was upset with someone. The youngest of them all was a toddler who appeared to be around two years old. He was a handsome young man with the blondest hair that Anastasia had ever seen. "If you're thinking about escaping, don't do it. He has this place booby trapped and all of the windows have alarms on them. I know it's scary right now, but you'll get used to it." Misty's voice broke through the silence. Anastasia turned around to see Misty holding a shopping bag. "Your supplies are in here," said Misty as she placed the bag on Anastasia's bed. "Whose children are these?" asked Anastasia. "They're mine, they're Jeannette's, and now, they're yours too. We have eight in total. I have three and

Jeannette has five, but the children aren't considered mine or hers. They are ours." Anastasia was disgusted. She'd seen a few shows about cults and it was clear to her that she was now involved in one. "What did you mean that he's going to quarantine me?" asked Anastasia. "What am I being quarantined for?" Misty seemed to be surprised at Anastasia's question. "Why darling, because you're unclean! You're menstruating. He's probably gonna quarantine me for even being near you, but hopefully not. But you'll be okay. You'll be in the room with Jeannette. I think you're going to love her. She was feisty like you at first, but look at her now. She has given our husband five children and she wants to give him more. That's why she's in quarantine." With that, Misty touched Anastasia's shoulder. "I have to go now, but you'll be okay. The quarantine room sounds bad, but it's actually pretty nice, compared to Pastor Ron's quarantine room. His looks like a rat-infested dungeon."

An hour later, Joshua finally returned home. Anastasia could see him out the window. He was carrying a few shopping bags. What amazed Anastasia the most was that none of the children seemed interested in him and vice versa. He made his way into the house and Misty met him at the front door.

A few minutes later, Joshua entered Anastasia's room.

Horror gripped Anastasia as Joshua walked closer to her. "I heard that you've had an unfortunate turn of events. You're unclean, so you have to be placed in quarantine, but no worries; you will be in good company. You will meet your other sister there and she'll help to better prepare you for your new journey. I bought you some undergarments and a few gowns. You won't be needing any civilian garments for a while because you'll be in the house, adjusting to your new role. Follow me." Anastasia knew to remain silent. She grabbed the bag of pads off her bed and followed Joshua to the quarantine room. "Make sure you don't touch anything outside this room," he said.

When the door of the room opened, Anastasia was surprised at how elegant the room was. It had its own kitchen, a small living area and three twin sized beds. Sitting on one of the beds was a beautiful brunette woman. She was wearing a white gown and holding an infant. The baby appeared to be around three months old and the mother appeared to be somewhat deranged. She glared at Joshua as he stood in the doorway. "I want another baby!" she screamed. "You're my husband!" With that, Joshua gently shoved Anastasia into the room, closed the door and locked it from the outside. Anastasia was terrified. She stood in the doorway holding her bags, trying to figure out what to do. "You can take the bed in the middle," said Jeannette as she walked towards the baby's crib. "The one closest to the window is mine and the one closest to the door is Misty's." Anastasia made her way to her new bed. "Did you choose him or did he choose you?" asked Jeannette as she placed her sleeping baby in his crib. "What?" asked Anastasia. "What do you mean ... choose?" Jeannette sat on her bed and adjusted her gown. "Were you kidnapped or did you come on your own accord? Or were you a gift?" Anastasia was afraid to answer. She didn't want to use the wrong words and get in trouble with Joshua, but at the same time, she didn't want to lie. "Kidnapped," answered Anastasia as she dropped her head. "I was dating Joshua, but I didn't know about all this." Jeannette pulled her hair into a ponytail. "Let me guess," she said. "He followed you to the mall or a store and got upset about something you purchased. He then asked you to get in his car, and now, he claims to have rescued you from a life of harlotry." Anastasia felt a wave of relief hit her. She turned around to face Jeannette. "Exactly," she said. "How did you know?"

Jeannette: I was sixteen when he took me; I'm almost twenty-two now.
Anastasia: Wait. Can't he hear us? I'm sure this room is bugged.
Jeannette: No. Every time he has ever bugged this room, I found his devices and destroyed them. I have a little gadget that helps me find his devices, but of course, he

doesn't know that. I blame it on the kids every time. He thinks I'm in love with him. He thinks I want to have more children with him, so he finally stopped bugging the place.

Anastasia: Well, don't you?

Jeannette: No, I say that so he can keep me in quarantine. Misty let me in on a little secret of his. He hates children and he despises pregnant women. Of course, she's in love with him. She told me that bit of information, hoping that I would stop getting pregnant by him. By that time, I was pregnant with my second child. What she didn't know was I hated every minute of Joshua's presence, so she gave me the ammunition I needed to keep him out of my room.

Anastasia: What do you mean, "your turn?"

Jeannette: Well, sicko Joshua tries to be fair. He alternates whose bed he's going to sleep in so, for example, if he sleeps with Misty on Monday, he'll make his way into my room on Tuesday. Now, that he has you, we'll both get an extra day off. I'm sure Misty hates that.

Anastasia: She actually likes sleeping with him?

Jeannette: Oh yeah! She's just as sick as he is. She hates when my turn comes around, so she pretended to like me so she could find out when I was menstruating and what I was thinking. I made her think that I was obsessed with him. I told her that I wanted to have as many babies as my womb could carry. Of course, she went back and told Joshua, so he placed me in quarantine a few times trying to break me. So, I started using my head. I would claim that I was menstruating when I wasn't menstruating, and then, when I was menstruating, he'd find out the hard way ... if you know what I mean. It was hilarious. One time, he actually vomited. And then, there were the other times when I lied and told him that my menstruation had just gone off. I told him that I'd just finished my three day purification. The truth was that I was ovulating. I knew that if I got pregnant, he wouldn't touch me for at least eleven months. He despises pregnant women.

Anastasia: I thought the church encouraged men to be fruitful.

Jeannette: They do. That's the problem. Joshua doesn't exactly agree with the church when it comes to children, but he wants to move up the ranks, so he's not going to publicly disagree with them. The church is against every form of birth control, so Joshua tries to be careful. He quarantined me this time because he said I keep having babies.

Anastasia: So, you get pregnant on purpose?

Jeannette: Yeah. I hate him sleeping with me and he hates children. I've learned to give Misty the gift of having her crazed husband as many nights as possible.

Anastasia: Have you ever tried to escape this place?

Jeannette: Not really. He may hate the children, but I don't. I love my children and it would be hard to escape with them, plus, he has promised us that if one of us were to ever escape, he'd kill everyone who was left behind, including the children.

Anastasia: I can't imagine spending my life here. Truthfully, I can't imagine spending a week here.

Jeannette: I understand. Take it one day at a time, and if you ever think about escaping, remember, you are putting our lives and our children's lives in danger.

Anastasia: I wouldn't do that. I have an idea, but I need at least a week or two before I'll know if it's plausible. How often does the mailman run here?

Jeannette: Every day around three o'clock. He brings the mail up to the door, but of course, Misty is there to collect it. I've gotten his attention a few times and I've tried just about everything I could think of, but I think that he thinks I'm just some teenage girl who keeps flirting with him. Anytime I get his attention, he'll wave at me, get in his truck and leave.

Anastasia: Yeah, a guy wouldn't be too helpful. We need a woman. Are there any female mail carriers that come here?

Jeannette: Yes. I think the guy is off on Tuesdays, so she fills in for him then. I tried to get her attention once, but she intentionally ignored me.

Anastasia: On Tuesdays at three, right?

Jeannette: Yeah. What are you thinking?

Anastasia: I've bought myself about two weeks in quarantine. Joshua asked me how long my periods last and I told him fourteen days.

Jeannette: And he believed you?

Anastasia: At first, no. I told him that my normal menstruation is seven days, plus, I have two huge fibroids. I told him that my ob/gyn wanted to do surgery on me to remove the fibroids, but obviously, I didn't make it to my appointment. So, he placed me in quarantine for two weeks.

Jeannette: You have fibroids?

Anastasia: No, of course not. I told him that to turn him off. I remembered a sermon that Pastor Ron did a few weeks ago, saying that fibroids were demon babies forming in the womb.

Jeannette: You're pretty smart. I think we're going to get along just fine.

Anastasia: Thanks. Are we allowed to open the windows?

Jeannette: Yeah, why?

Anastasia: I think we need to keep the windows open everyday so we don't set off any alarms. We'll open it around two o'clock. If they ask about it, tell them I kept wheezing for air.

Tuesday finally came around and Anastasia did everything she could think of to get the female mail carrier's attention. She waited until Misty collected the mail and went back in the house. After that, she hissed, waved and made strange sounds, but nothing seemed to work. "She heard me," Anastasia said to Jeannette. "She's ignoring me because she thinks I'm taunting her."

Tuesday came around again and this time, Anastasia kept making sounds in her attempt to get the woman's attention. "You're a loser," Anastasia said as the mail lady made her way to her truck. Anastasia then took one of the kids' toy dolls and threw it at the woman. "Loser, loser, loser!" Again, the woman intentionally ignored her, only stopping to look at the doll that was now lying next to her feet. "Excuse me!" shouted Anastasia as the mail carrier entered her jeep. With that, Misty came outside and looked up at Anastasia. She had her hands on her hips. She apologized to the carrier and then stormed back into the house. A few minutes later, the bedroom door flung open.

Misty: What the heck are you thinking? Do you want to get us all killed?! What in God's green earth is wrong with you?!

Jeannette: I was asleep. I didn't see anything. What happened?

Anastasia: I wasn't talking to the mail lady. I was talking to my daughter. She kept asking me to throw her a doll so she could play with it.

Jeannette sat up on her bed and looked at Anastasia. "What daughter?" asked Misty. "Never mind," responded Anastasia. "You wouldn't understand. I don't want you to think I'm crazy." Jeannette knew that Anastasia was working on something, but she didn't know what. Jeannette then looked at Misty and said, "You can't tell Joshua about this. He'll kill us all if you do. She has a few days left in quarantine and I'll make sure this never happens again." Misty agreed. "Don't ever do that again!" shouted Misty to Anastasia.

Misty left the room and Jeannette turned to Anastasia.

Jeannette: Why did you call the woman a loser and throw a doll at her? Are you trying to ruin our only chance of getting free?

Anastasia: Please, just trust me. A mail carrier visits several homes a day. For them, it's just routine, but I need her to snap out of that routine thinking anytime she pulls up in this yard. I need her to be on high alert; it's the only way I'll ever get her attention. That way, she'll always glance at this window, even when she tells herself not to. Trust me. I know what I'm doing.

Jeannette sighed. "I sure hope so," she said. "I sure hope so."

Misty was sure to mention to Joshua that Anastasia was now claiming to have a daughter. She didn't tell him about Anastasia trying to get the mail lady's attention; she simply told him that she'd spoken with Anastasia and she claimed to have a daughter. Joshua couldn't wait to get her out of quarantine to question her further about this alleged daughter.

Friday came and Anastasia was feeling somewhat hopeless. She watched as Jeannette ran into the bathroom and scrubbed her face to make herself appear to be somewhat deranged. She used a dry washcloth to scrub under her eyes until her skin became red. She then grabbed the soap from the shower, ran some water over it and began to lather her hands with it. When her hands lathered, she began to wipe her eyes. "Ouch, ouch, ouch!" she screamed. "I hate this part." Jeannette wanted her eyes to be red. "What are you doing?" asked Anastasia. Jeannette held her head down and began to dishevel her hair. "Getting ready to buy myself some more time," she responded. "Joshua is a crazy man, but he's also a punctual one. He'll be in here in three minutes." With that, Anastasia rushed around the room and collected her belongings. She put them in a shopping bag and rushed over to her bed. She sat down and waited for the door to open. Just like Jeannette said, Joshua was a punctual man. The door opened and he gestured for Anastasia to get up and follow him. Like a mad woman, Jeannette dashed across one bed after the other. "I'm ovulating!" she screamed. "Let's not waste this moment. I put the baby to sleep and now, I'm ready! Did you hear me, Joshua?! I'm ovulating!" Anastasia made her way out of the room, laughing inwardly at Jeannette's Oscar-worthy performance. It was now her turn to perform and she hoped she could be as believable as Jeannette. Joshua closed the door behind Anastasia. He then locked the door. Jeannette leaned against the locked door. "Go get him, girl," she whispered. "Go get him. I'm counting on you."

Anastasia calmly followed Joshua back to her room. Joshua was surprised at how positive and relaxed she appeared to be. "You're going to need to take a shower because I want to see you tonight," said Joshua. Anastasia walked around the bedroom, touching everything in her reach. "Okay," she said. "I want to see you tonight as well." Joshua became uncomfortable.

Joshua: Why the sudden change? What happened to you? Why are you suddenly happy to see me?

Anastasia: Misty and Jeannette helped me to see the error of my ways. I didn't realize that you'd saved me from myself. I was headed down a dark path. Of course, lip gloss would have led to lipstick, and before long, I would've been buried under layers and layers of makeup. The devil obviously had my mind, but you saved me from him. So now, I want to voluntarily repay you.

Joshua: Is that right?

Anastasia: Yes, it is. When I saw how honored Jeannette

was to have your children, I realized that to reject you meant rejecting the one thing I'd been praying for.

Joshua: And what's that?

Anastasia: To have babies. I want lots and lots of babies and I'm going to name them all after you. Of course, there's Joshua Jr., Josiah, Josslyn, Joshka; I thought that was cute, and ...

Joshua: Hold on a minute. Let's not rush things. You're not ovulating because your cycle just went off.

Anastasia: No. My menstruation went off a week ago, but my fibroids were just bleeding, so I'm definitely ready. Plus, I've been seeing our daughter.

Joshua: Yeah, Misty mentioned something about you having a daughter. What's that about?

Anastasia: No, not me ... us. A little girl has been following me around for the last week or so. She always catches me in the bathroom.

Joshua: Was it Mandy?

Anastasia: No. This little girl hasn't received her earthly body yet and that's why she's kinda transparent when I see her. She told me that she is our future daughter. She said that we are going to have triplets on our first try and she was the oldest of them all! One of them, she said, was a little slow, but that's okay. We're going to love them all. Joshua, you can't understand how excited I am.

Joshua: So, you're hallucinating?

Anastasia: No, it's not a hallucination, baby. Don't you get it? I saw our daughter; well, at least, one of them! And she looked just like you. Baby, she looked just like you. As a matter of fact, Jeannette showed me a picture of your mother (God rest her soul) and our daughter looked just like her. She told me that she wanted to be named after her grandmother. So, I'm going to name her Madelyn. The others will be named after you, of course. Honestly, I think it may be your mother trying to reincarnate herself, but we'll see.

Joshua looked sick. He couldn't look at Anastasia, so he kept staring past her. He hated his mother. "I'll be back," he said in an eerily calm tone. "Don't unpack just yet." A few minutes later, Misty came back into the room. "Well, darling, the hubby wants to quarantine you for another week. He said that you're getting visitations from the devil, plus, you're still unclean." Anastasia smiled. "Not the devil; I've met our daughter. Can you ask him if he'll take me out of quarantine tomorrow? I want to show him how much I appreciate him, plus, little Madelyn has been telling me things to tell him. We've got a lot to talk about."

The door to the quarantine room flung open and in walked Anastasia. When Jeannette saw Anastasia walking into the room, she almost choked on the coffee she was drinking. She fought hard to hold back the laughter, but she couldn't hold back the tears. She knew Anastasia had done something crazy, but what could she have done to land herself back in quarantine in a matter of minutes? Misty greeted Jeannette and told her she'd bring her dinner up in a few minutes. Jeannette nodded, still fighting to hold back the laughter. Once the door closed and the women were sure that Misty couldn't hear them, they erupted in laughter.

Jeannette: What on earth did you say to him?

Anastasia: I told him that our invisible, futuristic daughter has been following me around, talking to me. I told him that she'd said that we were gonna have triplets on our first go around and one of them would be slow. I also told him that I was ready for him.

Jeannette: What did he say?

Anastasia: He looked like he'd seen a ghost. I literally saw all the blood drain from his face.

Jeannette: He's probably on the phone with Pastor Ron now. Just be advised that they're gonna try to perform an exorcism on you; they'll likely do it Sunday, so be ready.

Anastasia: Oh, I know. I remember seeing them perform one on Deacon Rubert's wife. That's okay. I'm ready for them. I'm not worried about the exorcism. I'm determined to get that mail lady's attention this Tuesday. She will hear and see me Tuesday.

Jeannette: I do have some news for you. Misty was in my room a few minutes ago, and according to her, Joshua has pegged another woman. He plans to kidnap some woman he's been dating, but she doesn't know what day he wants to do it on. She said that she thinks he's planning to take the woman on Monday because he wants her to prepare a feast Monday evening.

Anastasia: Well, we've got to stop him.

Jeannette: Stop him? How?

Anastasia: Play along with me. I told Misty that my futuristic daughter has given me some messages for Joshua. I did this so that I could get a handle on him. I need you to call Misty back to the room. Take her to the side and pretend that you think that I'm loony. Tell her that I keep talking about my daughter with Joshua. No, wait! Tell her that I keep talking to an invisible person. Act like you like me, but you're a little worried. I want her to think that you're not too fond of me because if she thinks we're close, she'll get suspicious and warn Joshua.

Jeannette: Okay, but why?

Anastasia: Just trust me on this. By the way, I saw Joshua when he pulled his car in today. His driver's side rear tire is low and needs more air. Don't tell him I said that. We'll just pretend that Madelyn, our future daughter, told me. Call her. Just follow my lead and trust me on this.

Jeannette picked up her phone and called Misty. "Can you come up for a minute?" she asked. Her voice sounded concerned and Misty was sure she knew what Jeannette wanted.

When Misty came into the room, Jeannette asked her if they could step outside the room together. Misty hesitated and then, checked the hall to make sure that Joshua wasn't upstairs. "Sure," she said. When the women went outside the room, Jeannette put on her performance. "I don't know about this one," said Jeannette. "I think she's a fruitcake. She keeps talking to an invisible person, saying that its her daughter." Misty looked around again. She then leaned in and spoke in a whispered tone. "I agree. I told Joshua that she's gonna need more than a quarantine. He's calling Pastor now to see if they can arrange an exorcism." Misty's breath was atrocious. Jeannette subtly held her breath while Misty continued to talk. "After I tell him what you said, I'm sure they'll try to arrange it for tomorrow. I think Joshua is scared. He keeps flinching every time he hears a sound." Without warning, Anastasia pulled the door open. "Can the two of you come in here?" she asked. Her eyes were big; she looked scared. Both ladies entered the room and Jeannette made her way to Anastasia's bed. She kept mentally coaching herself to not laugh at whatever came out of Anastasia's mouth. "Madelyn; that's my daughter. Madelyn gave me three warnings for our precious Joshua and I need to tell him." Jeannette stood to her feet and walked to the window. She had to turn around because Anastasia's performance was almost believable, yet funny.

Anastasia: Madelyn told me that Hell has an assignment against her dad. She said she overheard three spirits talking and one said it was going to let the air out of one of Joshua's tires. The other said that Joshua was going to be in a multi-car accident. He will be preparing to take another bride for himself, but the bride he has chosen has many many demon spirits in her. The demons will make her grab the car's steering wheel and she's going to pull his car out into oncoming traffic. Madelyn couldn't understand the other one because it was speaking in a strange language, but she said that she was going to try to interpret what it said. Please, please warn our husband!

Misty: I can't take that story to Joshua. He'd have you committed.

Anastasia: Just tell him to check his car's tires. Tell him the story and tell him to check the tires.

Misty agreed and left the room to tell Joshua about Anastasia's descent into madness. Five minutes later, Jeannette and Anastasia watched as Joshua walked out to his car. Both women hid so that should he look up, he wouldn't see them. Joshua walked around his car, starting at the passenger's side. When he walked over to the driver's side and saw his near-flat tire, he covered his mouth with his hand. He then rushed into the house. Thirty minutes later, Pastor Ron's car pulled into the driveway. "Wish me luck," said Anastasia as she practiced crossing her eyes.

Within minutes, the bedroom door opened. "Follow us," said Joshua to Anastasia. Before he could close the door, Jeannette rushed across the bed. "Hello Pastor! I'm ovulating! Please tell Joshua to visit me tonight!" The door shut and off went Anastasia to the living room with the two men. In the living room, there were two other men who were members of the church.

Pastor Ron: I know you may not understand this, dear. This is probably all overwhelmingly new for you, but I want you to know that we all love you and we're here to help you.

Anastasia: What's going on, Pastor?

Pastor Ron: We are about to perform an exorcism on you, but I need you to remain calm. We want to talk to Madelyn.

Anastasia: You can't talk to Madelyn. She's not here right now.

Pastor Ron held up a battered wooden cross. "Shut up, devil! I want to talk to Madelyn! Madelyn, come forth and speak to me!" Anastasia's eyes crossed and she collapsed to the floor. "Madelyn, come forth!" yelled Pastor Ron repeatedly. "I need to talk with you." The men were all holding crosses and throwing water on Anastasia as she rolled around on the floor groaning and covering her ears.

Without warning, Anastasia stopped rolling on the floor. The room was silent for a couple of minutes; that was, until a child-like laughter started coming out of Anastasia. The laughter went from child-like to evil. Pastor Ron began to back up as Anastasia stood to her feet. She blinked her eyes as if she'd just woken up from a deep sleep. She kept wiping her eyes in a child-like fashion and every time she turned and looked at one of the men, she acted as if she'd never seen him before.

Anastasia: Where am I? Who are you people? Where's my mommy?

Pastor Ron: Who are you?

Anastasia: My name is Madelyn.

Pastor Ron: What is your business here, Madelyn? Why are you bothering Joshua?

Anastasia turned to look at Joshua. "Because he's our daddy," she responded.

Joshua was immediately filled with fear. Anastasia's facial expression was one he'd never seen before. Her eyes appeared squinty and her voice was childlike, but monstrous. "Daddy, we're coming for you," said Anastasia to Joshua. Joshua backed up. "What does she mean?" he asked Pastor Ron with terror in his voice.

Pastor Ron: Madelyn, you told a friend of ours that you

overheard three demons talking about what they were going to do to your daddy. What did you hear them say?

Anastasia: I can't tell you.

Pastor Ron: Why not?

Anastasia: Because they're here. Two of them went in him and the other went inside him.

Anastasia pointed at the two men Pastor Ron had brought with him.

Suddenly, Pastor Ron didn't trust the two men anymore. "Take a seat," he said to the terrified men when he noticed them feeling around on their bodies. Anastasia then turned to look at Joshua again. "Mommy's ovulating. It's time to give me an earthly body." Joshua shook his head in denial. "How amazing this is!" shouted Anastasia. "In my former life, I was your mother, but now, you're about to be my dad. We've got a lot of catching up to do."

Pastor Ron: How did you know that Joshua's tire was on flat?

Anastasia: Because they did it.

Pastor Ron: Who is they?

Anastasia turned to look at the two ministers again.

Anastasia: I can't tell you.

She then leaned in and whispered to the pastor.

Anastasia: I can't tell you because they're watching me.

Pastor Ron held up the makeshift cross again. "I command you to tell me!" Anastasia covered her eyes and started walking away. In a child-like voice, she repeatedly said, "No," as she walked around the room. "Tell me now!" screamed the frustrated pastor. "Okay, okay!" said Anastasia. "But first you gotta make them leave!" She then pointed at the two men again, and Pastor Ron gestured for them to go outside.

When the men were gone, Anastasia set her eyes on Joshua. "I was playing outside when I heard them talking. I was playing close to your car. When I heard them start talking about you, I hid. One spirit said that it was going to kill you by letting the air out of one of your car's tires. The other one said it would get you when you tried to take your next bride. I think it said that she belonged to the devil; he was angry at you for taking her, so he made you have an accident. I couldn't understand the other spirit because it spoke in a strange language, but I remembered what it said. I am now in the process of translating it."

Joshua was terrified. He had planned to take his next bride that following Monday, but of course, his plans were now foiled. "Demon, come out of her!" screamed Pastor Ron. "She is not yours! Come out now!" He then held up the cross and pressed it to Anastasia's forehead. Anastasia let her eyes roll back into her head, groaned a few times, and then, violently began to shake her head. A few minutes into the exorcism attempt, Anastasia fell to the floor. When her eyes opened again, she appeared to be confused. "Where am I?" she said. "Why am I on the floor? Can someone get me some water?" Joshua yelled out to Misty. "Misty, bring water!" He then helped Anastasia get up off the floor. The two men then prayed for Anastasia and Joshua had Misty return Anastasia to the quarantine room. Pastor Ron said that she needed to stay there for at least another week so that any demonic residue that was in her would be completely gone. Joshua wholeheartedly agreed. He was now afraid of Anastasia.

Misty was quiet as she led Anastasia back to the quarantine room. She was afraid that the devil hadn't been cast all the way out of Anastasia; after all, she still appeared to be unusually calm. "Can I get you anything else?" she asked as she held the door open to the quarantine room. "No," said Anastasia. "Thank you for being so nice to me. I'm going to give you a big, big surprise on Thursday." Misty's heart froze with terror. What did she mean? Why did her voice still sound child-like? Was Anastasia planning to harm her, or worse, was the voice coming out of Anastasia's mouth coming from a demon? Misty closed the room's door, locked it and rushed back to her room to pray.

Meanwhile, Jeannette sat on her bed staring at Anastasia. She was eager to hear what had transpired.

Jeannette: Anastasia?
Anastasia: Well, that exorcism went well. I think they cast the gas out of me. I do feel a lot better.

Jeannette laughed hysterically.

Jeannette: So, you just faked an entire exorcism? You are something else! If I ever get out of here, I am writing a book about you. We've definitely got to stay in touch.
Anastasia: Oh no, I didn't fake it. Misty's roast beef is the devil and I think they cast it out of me.
Jeannette: So, what's the plan? Why did you tell Misty that you were going to give her a gift on Thursday?
Anastasia: I want her to think that I've settled into the idea of being here; that way, she can stop monitoring me so closely. Plus, I need her to be afraid of me.
Jeannette: Why?
Anastasia: So she'll go out of her way to avoid me.
Jeannette: Aren't you afraid that Joshua's fear of you may put you in danger? I mean, what if he decides to hurt you

or worse?

Anastasia: That's why we have to get out of here. What I did was risky and it won't be long before he thinks that way. But he thinks I need a week in quarantine, so I'm safe this week; which means, this week is our only chance to get out of here. Do you have a life-like baby doll around here somewhere? One that looks like an infant ...

Jeannette: In the closet. Why?

Anastasia: I'll tell you later. I really need you to trust me on this one.

Jeannette: I'm scared, but look at me. I have nothing left to lose.

Tuesday finally arrived and Jeannette was having second thoughts. She hadn't slept the night before, plus, her baby sensed her frustration, so he wouldn't stop crying. Anastasia smiled. The day was starting off the way she'd planned it.

Jeannette: Are you going to tell me the plan or what? I couldn't sleep at all last night.

Anastasia: I know. I'll explain it later when we're at the police station.

Jeannette was surprised at how confident Anastasia was in her plan. Her confidence helped to settle Jeannette's fears somewhat, but there was still the issue of the crying baby.

Anastasia: We're going to have to do something that may scare you, but you're going to have to trust me. It is our only hope.
Jeannette: What is it Anastasia?
Anastasia: We're going to have to use the baby. Don't worry, he won't get hurt, but it will be a terrifying experience for you. Trust me, I saw this on TV once. It'll work; I promise.

With that, Anastasia explained her plan to a terrified Jeannette. Jeannette hesitated, took a deep breath, and then, reluctantly agreed. The women then started preparing for what would be their best performances ever.

Like clockwork, Misty came into the room at eight that morning to bring the women their breakfast. She looked tired and she didn't say much. Concerned that she may be suspicious about their plans to escape, Jeannette asked Misty to sit down. "What's wrong?" she asked. "Why are you so glum today?" At first, Misty didn't respond. She looked over at Anastasia's bed. Anastasia was under the covers (as usual) pretending to be asleep. "Come outside with me," said Misty as she made her way towards the door.

Once outside the room, Misty told Jeannette that Joshua had been depressed and somewhat jumpy for the last few days.

Misty: Ever since that girl came here, things have been different. He seems distant and he won't shut up about this other girl he was supposed to marry on Monday. I can tell he really likes her, but now, Pastor Ron says that it's not a good idea for him to marry her. I mean I'm glad he didn't marry the girl because I'm not sure if we have enough room for her, plus, Anastasia hasn't settled in, but I feel like he's taking it out on me.

Jeannette: How so?

Misty: He doesn't say much, and of course, he hasn't touched me since her exorcism. He won't even eat that much. When she was going through the exorcism, they asked her ... oh wait, they asked the demon how it got into her. Do you want to know what it said?

Jeannette: What?

Misty: Through my meatloaf! That devil said that it entered her through my meatloaf! Now, he won't even eat anything I cook! How does a demon get into meatloaf in the first place, Jeannette? I told him that I didn't think she got fully delivered and now, I wish I hadn't said that. Now, he's jumpy and cranky, plus, he's thinking about putting me in quarantine.

Jeannette: Why? What have you done?

Misty: Nothing at all. He's frustrated because normally, I give him good advice whenever he has a problem, but I can't help him with this problem. How am I supposed to know what to do about her? I think he wants to get rid of her, but he doesn't know how. Plus, he thinks I'm doing something to the both of y'all because he said ... well, that you've been acting like you've got demons. And he's blaming it all on me and my meatloaf! He keeps asking me what I put in it!

Jeannette fought hard to keep from laughing, but she couldn't keep from smiling, so she dropped her head to ensure that Misty wouldn't see her. She pretended to be upset, but in truth, she was fighting off laughter. After she was able to collect herself, she lifted her head.

Jeannette: Listen. Just keep encouraging him. I'll be out of quarantine in a few days and I'll talk with him then. Until then, just keep his mind off things. I want to get rid of her as much as you do. She needs more help than the church can offer her.

Misty: I feel a little better. I thought y'all were becoming friends.

Jeannette: Me? Friends with her? Ridiculous! I just pretend to be her friend because I have to sleep in the same room as that fruitcake, but you can rest assured that as soon as I get out of here, me, you and Joshua are going to have to sit down and figure out what we're going to do about her. So keep your head up. All will be well. And by the way, I love your meatloaf.

With that, Misty hugged Jeannette and Jeannette reentered the quarantine room. After Misty locked the door, Anastasia sat up on her bed. "What time is it?" she asked. Jeannette then pointed to a clock near the television. It was 2:35 that afternoon and it wouldn't be long before the mail carrier arrived. Jeannette watched nervously as Anastasia wrapped her infant son in his blanket. "Be careful with him," she said. "Please, be careful. I'm begging you." Anastasia assured her that she would.

At 3:15, the mail carrier arrived. She was later than normal, and the wait had been agonizing for both Anastasia and Jeannette. Anastasia walked over to the window with the infant in her hands. As the mail carrier turned into the yard, Anastasia held the baby out the window. Just as she'd predicted, the woman pulled into the yard with her eyes fixed on the window. The women had intentionally kept the infant awake so that he would be cranky. As planned, the infant began to cry as he was awakened from his sleep.

Anastasia then began to hold the baby outside the window as if she was thinking about dropping him. The mail carrier got out of her jeep, but before she could rush towards the window, Anastasia pulled the baby back into the house. She then sat on the floor quickly and handed the baby to Jeannette, who then, handed her the baby doll. Anastasia wrapped the doll in the blanket and then stood back up, holding the doll over her head. She shook the doll violently for a few seconds, and then, she began to hold and cradle the doll as if she was feeling regretful. The mail carrier didn't know what to do. She ran towards the door of the house, and then, turned back around and ran to her jeep. She then called the police to report the incident. Anastasia stayed near the window, pacing and holding the doll like a loving mother.

Four minutes later, three police cars pulled into Joshua's yard and the officers bolted from their vehicles with their weapons drawn. Hearing the commotion outside, Misty opened the door of the house where she found herself staring down the barrel of a gun. The mail carrier pointed to the room where Anastasia was and a few of the officers rushed up to the room, but the door was locked. A hostage negotiator stood beneath the bedroom window trying to get Anastasia's attention. Afraid, Jeannette took her infant and hid in the closet.

The officers were afraid to kick the door down because they worried that Anastasia would throw the baby out the window if they were to do so. So, the hostage negotiator used his loud speaker to get Anastasia's attention. "Don't hurt the baby," he said. Open the door for the men outside your room. They just want to help you. Anastasia looked into the officer's eyes.

Anastasia: I don't have a key. We are locked in this room. Misty has the key.

Officer Santiago: Who's Misty?

Anastasia: The woman who opened the door for you. Tell them if she doesn't give them the key, they can kick the door down. I won't hurt the baby.

The officer then lifted his Walkman. He radioed to the other officers that the perpetrator was cooperating and had agreed to not harm the baby. He told them that Misty allegedly had the key, but of course, Misty claimed to not know where the key was. "Please get me out of here," Anastasia said to the negotiator. It was at that moment that the officer realized that Anastasia was behaving more like a victim than she was like a crazed mother. That, coupled with the fact that her room was key entry only told the officer what he needed to know. "Place Misty in handcuffs until we can sort this all out," he said speaking into his Walkman. He then looked up at Anastasia. "Are you sure you're not going to hurt the baby?" he asked. Anastasia opened the blanket, revealing that the infant she was carrying was actually a toy. "I just needed to be rescued," she said. "The real baby is in the closet with the mother. "We're being held against our will." Officer Santiago wasted no time telling the men to break the door down. "She's possibly a victim," he said over the Walkman. "Treat her as a victim, but place her in cuffs." Anastasia covered her ears and sat on the floor. The door suddenly split as the officers began to kick it in. Within seconds, the officers were in the room and Anastasia was in handcuffs. "Be careful," Anastasia yelled to one of the officers. "My friend is in the closet with her baby. We were both kidnapped." The officer opened the closet door to see Jeannette cradling her baby and trying to keep him calm. "It's okay, ma'am" said the officer. "Your nightmare is over."

Once outside of the house, Anastasia and Jeannette conveyed their stories to the officers. Jeannette had been reported missing almost six years prior and was presumed to be dead. Anastasia had just been reported missing a few days prior. Her car was found in the mall's parking lot, but when the officers ran her tag, they'd gotten her name and phone number. When they were unable to reach Anastasia, they conducted a small investigation and found that she was employed as an administrative assistant to a local attorney. They called the attorney's office and discovered that Anastasia had not been to work for a few weeks and this was not normal behavior; ordinarily, she had been a very punctual employee who'd never called in sick to work. They were able to get Royce's name and number from the law firm because Anastasia had him listed as her emergency contact. Royce spent the last few days agonizing over his daughter and searching frantically for her. He told the officers about Pastor Ron, but he didn't remember the name of Ron's church. Stricken with grief and worry, Royce had been calling and going by the police department every day to see if there was any progress in the case.

While Anastasia was talking to the officers, she noticed a familiar vehicle pulling into the yard. The car looked just like her dad's car. When the door of the car opened, Anastasia couldn't believe her eyes. She covered her mouth and tears fell from her eyes as Royce got out of his car. "Daddy, Daddy, Daddy!" screamed Anastasia. Royce cried and tried to make his way towards his daughter, but a few officers held him back. "That's my baby!" he exclaimed as he tried to push through the officers who were now holding him. "Let him go," said Officer Santiago. "I remember him from the precinct." With that, the officers moved and Royce rushed over to his daughter. The two held each other and cried hysterically. "I'm so sorry," cried Royce. "I should have protected you. I'm so sorry."

Misty's angry voice could be heard over the commotion.

"Get your hands off me!" she yelled at one of the officers. "Joshua is my husband! I am not being held against my will and neither are they! He rescued them from a life of harlotry and this is how they repay him! My children will be home from school any minute now! So, all of you workers of iniquity need to get off my property before they come home!" Misty lifted her head just in time to see Royce wrapping his arms around his daughter. His love for Anastasia was undeniable. When Misty saw the love that Royce had for his daughter, her heart began to ache. She longed for genuine love, a love she didn't have to work for. She'd settled for Joshua, hoping that someday, he'd learn to love her. She wanted to believe that Joshua loved her, and for a while, she'd been able to convince herself that he did, but after seeing Royce strongly embracing his daughter, Misty realized what she'd been longing for: undeniable, unmistakable love without conditions. Her eyes began to fill with tears as she watched the love between Royce and Anastasia. Her husband had never been satisfied with her alone; her children hated her, and she didn't know who she was outside of Joshua. At that moment, something in Misty surrendered. She didn't care about life anymore; every ounce of hope that she once had died. She stopped resisting arrest and headed towards the patrol car with the officers who were ushering her.

Anastasia looked around to find Jeannette, but at first, she didn't see her. A few seconds later, she locked eyes with Jeannette who, by now, was sitting in the back of an unmarked patrol car with her children. Anastasia could see Jeannette's mouth moving and her words were obvious. "Thank you," said Jeannette as the patrol car pulled away.

A few hours later, Joshua returned home and pulled into the driveway. As usual, he was wearing his favorite pair of sunglasses. The officers didn't want to alarm him, so they parked their cars around the corner and hid around his house. Joshua looked noticeably frustrated as he opened the backdoor of his car and began to pull out a large item. It was a shovel and to the officers, it was clear that he was planning on burying someone. "Freeze!" shouted one of the officers as Joshua closed the car's door. "Put your hands in the air and do not move!" Joshua was in shock. He didn't know what to do, so he dropped the shovel and took off running. Nevertheless, one of the officers easily chased him down and tackled him to the ground. "You have the right to remain silent. Anything you say can and will be used against you in a court of law. You have the right to an attorney. If you cannot afford an attorney, one will be provided for you before any questioning if you wish. Any questions?" Joshua didn't answer the officer's question. Instead, he began to berate the officer for touching him. "Why are you touching me?" he asked. "You are a heathen; you are an unclean man. You're not supposed to touch me. Do you know who I am?" The officers ignored Joshua as they escorted him to his car. Joshua didn't resist arrest physically, but verbally, he continued to lash out at the officers until a familiar face walked up to the primary officer who was escorting him. She was accompanied by a female who, even though not wearing a uniform, was obviously an officer. "That's him," said Misty. "I've been his hostage for twelve years now. My Paw, Reverend Dale over at New Age Assemblies took me against my will and gave me to him." Misty looked Joshua straightway in the eyes. "It's over," she said. "I tried time and time again to convince myself that you loved me, but the truth is — deep down inside, I knew that you didn't. I even tried to convince myself that my Paw loved me and that's why he gave me to you, but I saw Anastasia with her father and something in me woke up. I don't know much about love, but I realized in that moment that my Paw didn't love me either and you know what? That's okay because I'm about to learn to love my self!" Joshua was speechless. He stared at Misty as the officers escorted him towards the police cruiser that was waiting for him. As the officer shoved Joshua's head into the cruiser, he looked back and Misty and said, "When I get out of here, you are going to quarantine."

Joshua was eventually sentenced to 345 years in prison.

The New Age Assemblies cult was dismantled and Pastor Ron was charged with two hundred counts of kidnapping and attempted kidnapping, sex trafficking, child endangerment, possession of child pornography, torture and two counts of murder. While in custody, Pastor Ron proudly admitted to having killed two women he'd taken as wives. Both women had attempted to escape several times. Frustrated, he'd buried both women alive in his backyard. As it turns out, when Joshua turned to him about Anastasia, he'd advised Joshua to do the same thing which, of course, was the reason Joshua was unloading a shovel when the officers pulled up. Pastor Ron was sentenced to death, but after a year in prison, he was murdered by one of the inmates who, ironically enough, happened to be the nephew of one of the women he'd killed.

Anastasia learned a very valuable lesson and that is — wait on God. His timing is perfect. Because of impatience, she'd joined a cult and nearly lost her life. She did not honor her father because she took his love for granted. Her anxiousness and dishonor gave way to rebellion which, in turn, opened her up for false prophets and false prophecies.

The story about New Age Assemblies' evils was shared on national and international news channels. Anastasia had moved back home with her father because she was still traumatized from the events that had taken place. Two weeks after the story ended, there was a knock on Royce's door. "I'll get it," said Royce as he pulled his famous meatloaf out of the oven. He then joked with Anastasia, "My meatloaf will help to undo all the evils that Misty's meatloaf did." Anastasia laughed as she watched her father make his way towards the living room door. She then spun around in her chair and started running her fingers against the kitchen counter.

"Hello," a familiar voice echoed through the living room door. Royce couldn't believe his eyes. The beautiful woman standing in his doorway was none other than Nairi, Royce's ex-lover and Anastasia's mother. Teary-eyed, Nairi, couldn't take her eyes off Royce. "I've dreamed about this moment all of my life," she said. "I know I don't deserve ..." Before she could finished speaking, Royce wrapped his arms around her and began to cry. That's when Anastasia walked into the living room. Nairi's face was resting on Royce's shoulder when she suddenly opened her eyes and saw what she later described to be the most beautiful woman she'd ever seen.

Nairi's heart raced with fear and excitement. Realizing that Anastasia was behind him, Royce released his grip on Nairi and moved to the side so the two women could see one another clearly. Anastasia slowly made her way towards her mother. She then reached up and started touching Nairi's face. A few seconds later, Anastasia fainted, but she fell into the arms of her father who then carried her over to the couch.

Anastasia's eyes opened and she saw what she later described to be an angelic like face hoovering over her. Nairi didn't say a word. She leaned in and kissed her daughter on the forehead. Anastasia's voice became almost child-like. "Mom?" she said as the tears began to flow down her face. "Is that really you? Mom?" She reached up and touched Nairi's face again.

Nairi went on to explain to her daughter why she'd given her up and why she hadn't been around. "I looked for you," said Nairi. I came back to America ten years ago to look for you, but I could not find you. One day, I went into a church; I think it was called The Master's Touch Ministries, and it was there that I got saved. I have gone to church every single day and prayed to God that He help me find my daughter — my only child. God finally answered my prayers!" Tears began to stream down Nairi's face as she stroked her daughter's hair. "I went back to Armenia two years ago. I was starting to think I'd never find you, but I came to realize that God took me back there so I could address some issues within my family — our family. I had a lot of healing to do. But while I was watching TV the other day, I saw the news and I was devastated to hear about that very wicked church and everything it has done to women. That's when I saw the most beautiful girl I'd ever seen. Before they said your name, I knew who you were. To hear that my baby ..." Nairi began to sob bitterly. "Everything I wanted to protect you from ... I stayed away for so long because I feared this thing would happen to you with my family. And now, some monster at a church ..." Nairi sat up and brushed her hair away from her face as she stared in the direction of the television set. "I want to be here for you," she said. "If you let me, I want to be a part of your life and I promise that I will never leave you again."

Anastasia was very accepting of her mother because Royce had always spoken well of her mother to her. He explained her mother's dilemma and he'd always told Anastasia that he believed that someday, Nairi would come looking for her. Nairi purchased the house right next to Royce after she discovered that it was empty. Having been her parents' only child, Nairi inherited close to a million dollars when they passed away. She'd used quite a bit of this money in her attempt to find Anastasia. She spent nearly every penny she had left buying her new home.

Three years later, the sound of construction workers filled

the air in Royce's home. "They said they ought to be finished in three weeks," said Royce to his new wife. Nairi smiled. "You still don't think the house will be too big?" she asked. "Anastasia's not having triplets, you know, plus, her husband is only one person." Royce wrapped his arms around Nairi. "It won't be big enough for the plans I have for you," he said as he leaned in to kiss his wife.

The Erickson's were joining their houses together. An architect had drawn up the perfect plans to connect the houses. He wanted to build a massive living space right between the two houses. He would burst out the walls that separated the buildings and and use the living room as a connector. Nevertheless, because of the distance between the two houses, he'd drawn a huge living room with a massive imperial staircase seated in the center of it. An imperial staircase is a double staircase with an equal amount of steps. Under the staircase was a single large door that led to a huge seating area. The staircases connected at the top of the stairs, revealing a wrap-around effect and several doors leading to several rooms, including two huge breezeways — one on the right and one on the left. The breezeways connected both homes on the second level, while the living room served as the central connector for the bottom level.

The couple had been married for two years and they'd

decided to connect their homes. They wanted Anastasia and her husband to sleep on the east wing of the house while they lived in the west wing. Anastasia and her husband were temporarily moving in with her parents to ready themselves for the birth of their twins, a girl and a boy. Excited to be a grandmother, Nairi had suggested that they connect the two homes and Royce loved the idea. She wanted to help out with her grandchildren as much as possible, especially considering the fact that Anastasia's husband traveled a lot with his job. The couple were planning to buy their first home as well, but they'd decided to move in with Anastasia's parents to save up the money they needed to get the house Anastasia so desperately wanted to have built.

The family thrived in their new home. Anastasia and her husband ended up staying with the Ericksons for two and a half years before their new home was move-in ready. This gave Nairi a lot of time to dote on her grandchildren.

Anastasia was like many believers today. She was so focused on what she did not have that she lost sight of what she did have. Some people are so curse-focused that they can't see their blessings. More than anything, Anastasia wanted to be married. In truth, she'd made an idol out of marriage and for this reason, she decided to leave her church to pursue what the Bible refers to as the doctrines of demons. Frustrated with God, Anastasia decided to test Him by going against her natural father. Her frustration with her natural father was a representation of her frustration with God. When she did not meet a man at the event her friend invited her to, she decided to lash out at Royce, her father. Nevertheless, after disconnecting from Royce and joining New Age Ministries, Anastasia found herself receiving the desires of her heart. Here's the problem. Her heart was wicked, therefore, her desires were wicked. This caused her results to be wicked.

Many believers don't understand the gift of prophecy. For example, if someone says that they will meet their God-appointed spouses at an event, they will accept every invite they receive. In this, they will be secretly wondering if the upcoming event will be the place they meet their idols. Needless to say, however, that some prophecies are not from God, while others are. However, when God tells us that we are going to receive something, He isn't telling us to position ourselves in the natural to receive what we're believing Him for. He is telling us to position ourselves in the spirit. How do we do this? It's simple. We repent of our sins, submit ourselves to God, resist the devil and seek the Kingdom of God, coupled with all His righteousness. We become like Christ, and when we do this, God will order our steps. But people who do not understand prophecy will follow many voices in an attempt to get what was spoken over their lives.

Even though Nairi, Anastasia's mother, wasn't initially in her life, Anastasia had the blessing of being raised by her father. Sure, our mothers are equally a blessing, but Anastasia needed her father. How so? Royce taught Anastasia how to survive difficult situations. As you'll notice in the story, Anastasia almost immediately calmed herself down, reminding herself of many of the survival lessons her father taught her. Had Anastasia been raised by her mother, she would not have survived the ordeal. Of course, some would argue that Nairi's history with sexual abuse would have made her more qualified to help Anastasia, but the truth is that Nairi wasn't saved or delivered enough to teach Anastasia what she needed to know. Instead, she would have taught her to be bitter and fearful. The point is, we were raised by the parent (mother, father, or both) who had the lessons that God wanted to deliver to us, regardless of how good or bad our teachers (parents) were. This is to say that we, as people of God, have to stop complaining about our childhoods so we can clearly understand what God wants us to take from our upbringings.

At the store, Anastasia had run into two leaders. The first

one was a leader whose credibility had been damaged by an adulterous affair. The other was Pastor Ron, a leader who had no history with Anastasia. The truth is, we tend to trust people who have no history more than we trust people whose credibility has been brought under question. This is why we must be moral and credible servants of God. At some point, we may have the words in our bellies to keep someone from falling into demonic traps and, in some cases, from falling into their graves prematurely. Nevertheless, if we allow temptation to lead us astray, we become voices crying out in the wilderness with no audience. Sure, we can repent and God will forgive us, but when a leader falls, it's hard for him or her to recover the trust of the people, especially if that leader does not repent. Now, had Anastasia been truly submitted to God, instead of bowing down at the altar of marriage, she could have easily discerned the voice of God and she would have not been led astray by Pastor Ron. She had a God-fearing father and enough Word in her to keep her, nonetheless, she chose to forsake what she had in attempt to get what she wanted. I've come across many believers who throw what can best be described as temper tantrums with God. They think that if they put their pain on display and highlight it with their rebellion, God will admit to being unfair and give them what they want. This is one of the reasons it is important for us to raise our children in the fear and admonition of the Lord; that way, they understand that tantrums don't move God ... at least, not in our favor. When people don't know God, they intentionally provoke Him to wrath in an attempt to provoke Him to bless them.

While in captivity, Anastasia finally decided to obey her father. Isn't this what many of us do as believers? We become obedient vessels of the Most High God when we find ourselves in need of Him. Thankfully, our God is just as forgiving as He is merciful. Prayer and determination helped Anastasia to free herself as well as Jeannette, Misty and their children.

Another lesson we can take from this is sometimes, our disobedience leads us into captivity, but God will still use us in those places to set the other captives free. First and foremost, we must free ourselves by repenting and then, we can effectively lead others to freedom. People who have been in captivity for a long time often give up on the idea of ever being free. For this reason, they settle in captivity and learn the language of their captor. Such was the case with Misty. She had never experienced true love, so she found herself being delivered from one prison to another one. Joshua didn't love her, but like many people who suffer from rejection, she chose to see love where there was no love. She told herself that Joshua loved her and then she continued to entertain the relationship in her head and not the one she was actually a part of. Joshua used her to manage the home and the other women, and to Misty, this meant that for the first time in her life, she was needed.

When Misty finally saw love on display, she was drawn to it. In that moment, the false love she'd experienced was overshadowed by true love. For the first time, she had something to compare what she believed to be love to, even though Royce and Anastasia's embrace was something she'd briefly witnessed. This is a picture of evangelism.

Matthew 6:33 reads, "But seek ye first the kingdom of God, and his righteousness; and all these things shall be added unto you." Just like most people, I read this scripture and understood it to mean that I should put God before all things. I have since come to understood the broadness and the depth of this scripture.

Merriam Webster's Online Dictionary defines the word "seek" this way:
1. to go in search of: look for
2. to ask for: request
3. to try to acquire or gain: aim at
4. to make an attempt

Seek: Jeremiah 29:13 (ESV) reads, "You will seek me and

find me, when you seek me with all your heart."

Ask For/ Request: Luke 11:9 (ESV) reads, "And I tell you, ask, and it will be given to you; seek, and you will find; knock, and it will be opened to you."

Try to Acquire or Gain: Philippians 3:14 (KJV) reads, "I press toward the mark for the prize of the high calling of God in Christ Jesus."

Make an Attempt: James 2:26 (ESV) reads, "For as the body apart from the spirit is dead, so also faith apart from works is dead."

What the Lord is instructing us to do in Matthew 6:33 is to pursue Him with our praise, worship, obedience, sacrifice, repentance, submission, and surrender. He wants us to want Him more than we want things and people. Going to church is not seeking God. Dancing around the church is not always seeking God. In some cases, it is, but in others, it's just a performance or an attempt to move the hand of God but not the heart of God. Going to conference after conference is not seeking God. Anastasia went to an event seeking a husband and not God. Please understand that whatever we seek, we will find, but if we seek something outside of God's will, we will find something or someone who is also not God's will for us. If you want a husband more than you want God, you will marry an ungodly man; that is, if you do not repent. Most of the women I've spoken to who are in abusive relationships made an idol out of marriage and this is how the enemy was able to pair them up with ungodly men. Don't let that end up being your testimony.

Lastly, the story has a good ending. Nairi, who was also a victim of a loveless home eventually found her way back to God. Notice that she wasn't found by Royce first. Instead, she sought and found God's heart first. Sure, in her youth, she'd had an encounter with Royce, but this wasn't an example of her being found; it was an example of her being discovered outside the will of God by a man who was also wandering around outside the will of God. Nevertheless, Nairi eventually gave her heart to God and when she did, God blessed her with the family she'd always wanted. She was able to reconcile with her daughter and marry the man who'd never truly gotten over her. She could have done like a lot of people and played the role of a victim for her entire life, but she decided to pick herself up and give life another try. Her diligence was eventually rewarded and she ended up having a massive home with a God-fearing husband, in addition to a newly restored relationship with her daughter. A son-in-law and two grandchildren was also added to her life. This is to say to you that regardless of how old you are, don't give up on happiness. Don't settle for false love, even if you've never experienced true love from a person. Galatians 6:9 (ESV) encourages us this way,

"And let us not grow weary of doing good, for in due season we will reap, if we do not give up."

Chapter 4

Warfare System, Welfare System

There's a story in the book of John that details one man's encounter with Jesus. The story reads, "Now there is in Jerusalem by the sheep gate a pool, which is called in Hebrew Bethesda, having five porticoes. In these lay a multitude of those who were sick, blind, lame, and withered, [waiting for the moving of the waters; for an angel of the Lord went down at certain seasons into the pool and stirred up the water; whoever then first, after the stirring up of the water, stepped in was made well from whatever disease with which he was afflicted.] A man was there who had been ill for thirty-eight years. When Jesus saw him lying there, and knew that he had already been a long time in that condition, He said to him, "Do you wish to get well?" The sick man answered Him, "Sir, I have no man to put me into the pool when the water is stirred up, but while I am coming, another steps down before me." Jesus said to him, "Get up, pick up your pallet and walk." Immediately the man became well, and picked up his pallet and began to walk" (John 5:2-9/ NASB).

What's interesting about this story is — Jesus didn't ask the man how long he'd been in his condition. He simply asked him if he wanted to be healed, nevertheless, the man did what we see many people do today: he started making excuses to explain his condition. Howbeit, Jesus didn't address the man's excuses or his condition; He addressed his mindset. He simply told the man to pick up his pallet (bed) and walk. In other words, Jesus gave him a set of instructions, and praises be to God, he followed those instructions. Nevertheless, many believers today are like the lame man who sat near the Pool of Bethesda, waiting on someone else to help them get what they clearly have access to if they would only use their heads.

———————

"Again, thank you so much! I don't call everybody a friend, but I feel confident in saying that you are not only my friend, but you are my best friend," said Raven as she exited Zuri's new Mercedes Benz. "We gotta do this again real soon. Next time, I'll get the tab." The women had just finished their lunch date and Zuri was in the process of dropping Raven back off at her house. "You're welcome," replied Zuri. "I'll call you later." Raven nodded her head as she unlocked the front door of her house.

"Ma!" Raven's eleven year old son, Drake, intercepted her at the door. "Collin ate some of your cookies!" Reality suddenly set in for Raven. Sure, she'd just enjoyed a wonderful kids-free day with her friend, Zuri, but she was now back at home with her three children: eleven year old Drake, nine year old Collin and six year old Elizabeth. Frustrated, Raven threw her hands in the air and continued walking toward her bedroom. "I don't have time for this mess today!" she shouted. "Drake, get in here and get your shoes off the floor! Collin, I'm gonna beat the silver lining out of you if any of my cookies are missing! And Elizabeth, why are you out of your room?! You are still on punishment! Like I told you yesterday, when you come home from school, go straight to your room and do not come out of it until I tell you to!"

Raven entered her bedroom and sat down on her bed. She let out a sigh of relief as she took her shoes off her feet. *Knock. Knock. Knock.* "What?!" screamed Raven. "Ma, we're hungry!" said Elizabeth as she gently pushed the door of her mother's bedroom open. "What happened to that spaghetti I left out for y'all?" Raven asked. With her big, brown eyes, Elizabeth looked at her mother and shrugged her shoulders. "I think Collin ate it up," she said. Raven sprung from her bed and made her way to the kitchen. Sure enough, all of the spaghetti was gone, but there was only one dish in the sink and it was obviously Collin's plate. Anytime Collin ate, he would always lick the plate clean. This is how Raven distinguished his plate from his siblings' plates. "Collin!" screamed Raven.

It was early the next morning and the school bus had just left with Raven's kids. Nevertheless, a frustrated Raven paced back and forth in her living room. "I'll hold," she said as she sat on her couch. Raven looked out the window and noticed Maybelle walking past her house, talking to herself again. Maybelle was a drug addict who frequented the neighborhood. Not only did it look like Maybelle was high, it was obvious that she was out looking for something to steal. Raven purposed in her heart to keep her eyes on Maybelle because two of her children's bicycles had been stolen in the last month. "Hello. Yes ma'am, I'm still here. Hi, my name Raven Stephens and I was just talking to — I think she said her name was Joy. Anyway, like I told Joy, I just checked my food-stamp card and noticed that it was short thirty dollars. I need to get that issue rectified today." Raven stood to her feet and began to pace again. She bit her lip and paced as Ms. Polk explained to her that she'd spent all the money on her card. "Ms. Stephens, as Joy explained to you, we sent you a notice three months ago, telling you that you'd be receiving $443 a month in foodstamps, instead of $473. You knew this and we even went over why there was a drop in your payments. For the last two months, you've received stamps and you accepted, without complaint, the money you received. If you want your case reviewed, you'll have to set up an appointment with your case manager, but we're not going to add thirty dollars to your card when this matter has already been resolved. And if you set up an interview with your case manager, we will hear your case, but more than likely, we won't change our minds. Just thought you should know that." Raven hated talking with Ms. Polk because Ms. Polk was what many referred to as the pit-bull down at the DHS office. They'd normally give her the phone whenever a foodstamp recipient became unruly. Raven suddenly disconnected the line. She looked at the calendar. It would be another two weeks before she got foodstamps again, nevertheless, her refrigerator was empty.

Ring. Ring. Raven continued to pace as she called Jamal. Jamal was Drake and Collin's father.

Raven: Hello, Jamal. I was calling you to see if you can help us out a little over here. They cut my stamps and our refrigerator is empty.

Jamal: Raven, like I told you last week and the week before that, they garnish my check for the boys. I don't have any extra money to give.

Raven: Jamal, your sons are growing up fast. Collin eats like a grown man. He's the reason we're out of food.

Jamal: Well, you need to control how much he eats! Put

your foot down. Anytime he's over here, I don't let him keep going back and forward to the refrigerator.

Raven: So, are you just gonna sit there and let your boys starve to death?

Jamal: What do you want me to say? Raven, I don't have any money.

Raven: Instead of telling me what you don't have, why don't you do like a real man and try to hustle some money up?

Jamal: So, I'm not a real man now? Just because I don't jump when Raven says jump?

Raven: No, you're not a real man cause you'll let your sons go hungry, instead of trying to find a way to feed them.

Jamal: Says the woman who works part-time at a gas station. You're about as ambitious as a brown recluse.

Click. Raven disconnected the line. "Pathetic waste of skin!" Raven shouted as she tossed her phone on the couch. She tried to think of another way she could find money, but the only other option she could think of was her mother. She couldn't call Elizabeth's father because he was in prison serving a fifteen-year sentence for possession of drugs with the intent to distribute. He'd been arrested just two months after Elizabeth was born.

Raven's mother had always been negative, religious, controlling, bitter and messy. For this reason, Raven had distanced herself from her mother several times, only to find herself reconciling with her when times got hard. Raven picked her phone up off the couch and stared at it. She hadn't spoken with her mother in four months. Calling her would mean listening to her go on and on about how disrespectful and unappreciative her kids were, and asking her for help would mean coming back under her control. Raven took a deep breath and started scrolling through her contacts list. Just as she was about to hit the call button, her phone rang. It was her friend, Sharon.

Sharon: What are you doing?

Raven: About to call Olivia Mae Stephens!

Sharon: Oh, Lord. What would possess you to do that?

Raven: Three hungry children and a sorry baby daddy.

Sharon: Did you call Jamal?

Raven: Yep and as always, he said he doesn't have any money.

Sharon: How much do you need?

Raven: At least a hundred.

Sharon: I just got my child support check today. I could loan you a hundred dollars.

Raven: Are you serious, Sharon? Girl, thank you so much! And I'll pay you back in two weeks when I get my paycheck.

Sharon: No problem. I just don't want to see you getting entangled with your mother again. The last time you did that, she had you arrested.

Raven: That's what I was thinking. Girl, it's safer to cuddle with an alligator than it is to try to get close to her.

Sharon: Right! Do you want me to bring the money to you?

Raven: Yeah. My car is still in the shop. If you can, will you take me to the store?

Sharon: Okay. Gotta make a couple of stops first. I'll be there in about an hour.

Raven: Okay, thanks. Love you.

Sharon: Love you too.

An hour later, Raven heard the sound of a car horn blowing. She grabbed her purse and keys and left. On the way to the store, the women talked about their children's fathers and their plans for the future. Raven's main plan was to take Jamal, her son's father, back to court for more child support. She also talked about changing the name of her blog to "Deadbeat Dungeon." She believed that if she appealed to the many mothers out there who felt like they were the victims of deadbeat baby daddies, she would become popular and make a lot of money. "After my blog kicks off, I want to write a book to encourage women who have to do it all by themselves," said Sharon. "I want to create t-shirts, coffee mugs and even have my own shoe line. Girl, I'm about to start a movement." Sharon, on the other hand, was planning to take her daughter's father off child support. After listening to her pastor give a sermon about the witchcraft of violating human will, Sharon realized that Nathan, her daughter's father, was paying child support against his will. He wanted nothing to do with his daughter, Katelyn, and Sharon was finally okay with that. Raven felt a little agitated with Sharon's decision to take Nathan off child support, especially given the fact that Nathan was a police officer. "Girl, I'd keep his behind on child support," Raven reasoned. "Police officers make some pretty good money, plus, they get a lot of benefits." Nevertheless, to Raven's dismay, Sharon was unmovable. She'd already made up her mind and was planning to start the paperwork that week to have Nathan taken off child support.

The women pulled up at the local supermarket and Raven got out of the car first. Clutching an over-sized hobo bag, Raven looked like a teenager holding her mother's purse. Standing at five foot, two inches tall, Raven was a beautiful petite woman with grayish brown eyes and flawless brown skin. Additionally, Raven was known for her bold approach to fashion. Her fiery red hair was the cross between a bob and a Mohawk. Wearing a bright yellow top and a pair of ripped jeans, Raven looked playfully adorable. Sharon, on the other hand, was a dark-skinned beauty, standing at five foot, four inches tall with long black hair and large, almond-shaped eyes. Even though her approach to fashion was more modest than Raven, Sharon almost seemed to garner more attention than Raven because her casually cute wardrobe seemed to perfectly match her meek, down-to-earth persona.

Raven: I was thinking. Instead of you giving me the hundred dollars, why don't I just get everything I need and you can pay for it that way? Because I may spend under a hundred.

Sharon: Are you sure? I think I'd rather just hand you the money.

Raven: No, I'm sure. This way, if I spend under a hundred dollars, I won't be tempted to keep the rest.

Sharon: Okay. That sounds fair.

The women walked into the supermarket and Raven grabbed a shopping cart.

Raven: And girl, like I was saying, I was thinking of the name Deadbeat Dungeon or maybe I can switch things up and just call it The Deadbeat Diaries. What do you think?

Sharon: Raven, you know what I think. I think you should just let that man be. Let him do what he's willing to do and move on.

Raven: That's easy for you to say because you have a good job.

Sharon: Okay, so why don't you go out and get yourself a good job too?

Raven: If I work full time, they'll cut my aid in half. If I can find a job where they pay me under the table, that would be perfect.

Sharon: Yeah, maybe you can start your own in-house salon. I'm thinking about starting a business on the side. I want to start painting again and sell my paintings online.

Raven: You remind me so much of my friend, Zuri. She owns a spa and she's talking about starting a gift basket business. She's one of them independent women like you.

Sharon: What's the name of her spa? I've probably been to it.

Raven: She named it after herself. It's called Zuri's. It's off Main Street, down there by that Chinese restaurant that you used to work at.

Sharon: I think I've been there before. My friend, Paige, took me there for my birthday last year. Very impressive.

Raven: Yeah, she's doing good. She just bought herself a brand new Mercedes Benz and she's about to close on a house.

Sharon: What a blessing. Is she Christian?

Raven: Yep. I told you, she reminds me of you. The only difference is, she doesn't have any kids and Zuri's nice, but she's more on the naïve side.

Sharon: How so?

Raven: Zuri is very smart when it comes to business type stuff, but with people, I sometimes feel like I have to protect her because she's a little too nice. For example, she told me about a woman who came into her spa and got a facial. The woman called her three days later, talking about the facial broke her skin out. Like I told Zuri, ain't no telling what that woman got into in those three days, but Zuri ended up giving the woman her money back. And even after that, the woman was still talking about suing Zuri. She wanted Zuri to give her a hundred thousand dollars and I believe Zuri was thinking about doing it until I put her in touch with the lawyer I used that time I slipped and fell at Jammy's Market. The lawyer called the woman and told her that they were gonna go after her for extortion and Zuri said she never heard from that woman again.

Sharon: People like that make my skin crawl.

While the women were talking, Sharon noticed that Raven was putting some expensive meats in the basket. She'd grabbed a t-bone steak and was now looking at a twenty dollar bag of lobster. Additionally, the cart was half full. Realizing that her friend was starting to pay more attention to what she was adding to the cart, Raven put the lobster back and said, "Girl, I have to get something for myself too. I'm always buying for the kids, so anytime I go shopping, I have to get myself at least one thing." Sharon didn't say a word. Instead, she started waving at a woman who was a few feet away from them. "That's my supervisor's daughter," said Sharon. "She has a beautiful spirit." Raven stopped and waved at the young lady as well. "I guess she would have to have a beautiful spirit with that face," Raven laughed. Sharon wasn't humored. "That's not nice, Raven," she said. "She's gorgeous, both inside and out." Raven started scratching her chin in contemplation. "You know what. I think I will get that lobster because I know when I get home, I'm gonna regret not getting it. I need to get three more things and then, I'll be ready." Sharon looked at Raven's shopping cart. She knew that there was no way that the total would be a hundred bucks or less. Feeling used and manipulated, Sharon tried to ensure that her frustration wasn't evident.

$147.54. The cashier grabbed a paper towel and started wiping off the conveyor belt on her register as she anticipated the payment. "Wait a minute," said Raven. "How in the world did this come out to be one hundred and fifty bucks? That cart did not have that much stuff in it. I believe some of this stuff is ringing up higher than what it's supposed to be." The cashier pushed a button and the receipt came out. Annoyed, the cashier seemed to be punishing her chewing gum as she read through the receipt. Sharon became annoyed too. She knew that Raven wasn't surprised by the price, after all, she'd gotten two t-bone steaks, a pack of lobsters, a big pack of shrimp and a whole lot of junk food. "That's okay," intercepted Sharon. "You'll just owe me $147. Let's not hold the line up

because even if she did a price check on everything, I'm confident that it'll come out to be the same thing." Not wanting to let go so easily, Raven asked the cashier for the receipt while Sharon proceeded to make the payment. "Why did the shrimp ring up to $19.99?" asked Raven. The cashier didn't mumble a word. She reached into one of the bags, pulled out the huge back of shrimp and pointed to the sticker on it. It read $19.99. Embarrassed, Raven said, "I don't know why it's twenty dollars in the first place. Darn near half of the bag is air."

The women were in traffic when the aroma of food started to enter the car. "Man! What I'd give to sink my teeth into a SuperSonic Double Bacon Cheeseburger right now," said Raven. Sharon didn't say a word. She knew that Raven was hinting for her to pull into Sonic's restaurant and buy her a meal. The light suddenly turned green, but Sharon didn't notice it at first. *Beep. Beep.* The car behind Sharon's car suddenly snapped her out of her daydream. "What's wrong with you?" asked Raven. Sharon put on her signal light so that she could get into the left lane. "Nothing," said Sharon. "I was just thinking about a homeless woman I met the other day when I was out evangelizing with my church. She told me that her mother was a drug addict before she died. She said the biggest regret she has is that she did not break the curse. Now, her daughter is on drugs. Her daughter started doing drugs the minute she got clean. Because of this, she doesn't feel like she should go to a shelter. She's punishing herself for not breaking the curse sooner. Sometimes, I just wonder what type of mother I am being to Katelyn." Raven looked out the window. She hated sentimental conversations. "Girl, you are a great mother to Katelyn. That girl has everything, including you. Do me a favor. Pull into Sonic's right quick. I want to see if my home-girl is at work. If she's there, I can get the food for free. Sharon let out a silent sigh. She knew that Raven was simply trying to manipulate her into buying her a meal. "Okay," said Sharon. "But remember, I'm pressed for time." Sharon got back in the right lane and quickly turned off into the restaurant. She pulled into one of the parking stations and put her car in park.

Raven pressed the call button at the station. "Is Ulanda in today?" she asked. A few seconds later, a voice came from the intercom. "Who?" The man's voice sounded rushed. "Ulanda Perkins" said Raven. The man waited an entire minute before responding. "We don't have anyone here by that name," he said. Raven looked confused. "Now, I know I ain't crazy. Ulanda told me that she worked at the Sonic on Lemon Street and this is Lemon Street. This is the only Sonic I know of on Lemon Street." Feeling annoyed, Sharon spoke up. "Just order your food and you can pay me back," she said. Raven looked at her friend. "No, you've done enough. I already went over at the store and I feel bad enough as it is." Sharon decided to call her friend's bluff. She put the car in reverse and waited for one of the bell-hops to move from behind her car. Realizing that they were about to leave, Raven spoke up again. "You're right. I'll just pay you back. I'm too hungry to cook right now. Since we're here, order me the SuperSonic Double Bacon Cheeseburger combo with extra bacon and onion rings. Make that large with a cherry limeade. I got a sweet tooth too so get me a hot fudge sundae with nuts and a lot of caramel."

Sharon's car pulled up in Raven's driveway. Raven had just finished eating her food and was now eating her ice cream sundae. The two women got out of the car and started grabbing some of the bags and taking them into the house. "Thank you again," said Raven. "I truly thank God for you and I'm being sincere when I say this ... you are not only a good friend to me, but you are my best friend." Sharon smiled. She didn't know how to respond, after all, she felt conflicted inside. On one hand, she believed that Raven was nice, but she was starting to see more of Raven's manipulative side. She suddenly realized that many of Raven's friends were successful women or women who were well on their way to becoming successful women. "Thanks and I love you too," said Sharon. "Wow! I love that painting!" Sharon shouted as she observed a large painting of what appeared to be the Garden of Eden on

Raven's wall. Raven grabbed a few bags and started making her way towards the kitchen. "My girl, Brandy, bought it for me. Isn't it nice?! She works with me at the gas station. I don't know why that girl is working. Her parents are filthy rich, but she's one of those women who want to do it on their own. She gave me another one. It's on my bedroom wall. Go check it out." Sharon made her way into Raven's bedroom and noticed a huge picture of Buddha on Raven's wall. "It's a creative photo, but Raven, you shouldn't have anything that represents another deity on your wall. That only opens demonic doors in your life." Raven made her way into the room. "No, that's not the painting Brandy gave me. She gave me that one," she said pointing to the wall to the right of the bed. That particular painting featured an image of a woman kneeling down to pray.

Raven: Anyway, I bought that picture of Buddha, or whatever his name is, at a carport sale. I don't believe in Buddha or nothing like that, but the colors matched my bedroom perfectly. Plus, I don't believe that God will punish me for a painting. He knows my heart.

Sharon: He's a jealous God, Raven. The punishment may not come from Him. It's the spirits that are attached to that image that will come after you.

Raven: Brandy told me the same thing when she brought the other paintings over, but like I told her, I don't believe in the whole demons philosophy.

Sharon: Do you believe that you shall reap what you sow?

Raven: Yeah, like if a man kills another man, I believe he'll be punished for it, but if a man steals to feed his family, for example, I don't think God would punish him for that.

Sharon: God's not punishing the guy. Reaping isn't designed to be a punishment; reaping is designed to help people to receive the blessings of God by thinking, reasoning and behaving like God. Nevertheless, there is another side of sowing and reaping too. If a man sows evil, he'll reap evil. The principle of sowing and reaping works at all times. There are no times when God shuts it off, no matter how noble we believe ourselves or our intentions to be. If a man steals to feed his family, he'll reap of that seed because he could have worked to feed his family.

Raven: I just don't believe that God is cruel like that. Anyway, let's change the subject cause I don't like to talk about that deep stuff.

Sharon: Quick question before we change the subject. Have you changed churches yet? Remember we talked about that.

Raven: No. I thought about it and like I told you last time, the women in my family have been going to Mt. Zion for three decades. I don't want to be the one who breaks that trend.

Sharon: You need to go where you can grow, Raven. The only thing that's happening down there at Mt. Zion is you keep getting into it with your mother.

Raven: My mama hasn't been to church in six months. She said that Reverend Albert tried to get fresh with her, so I don't bump into her at church anymore. And Mt. Zion isn't bad. There are no perfect churches.

Sharon: Okay. Well, I have got to head out, but love you and I'll call you tomorrow.

Raven: Love you too and thanks again, girl. I know that God's gonna bless you for having such a good heart.

Three weeks passed and Raven still hadn't paid Sharon back the money she'd borrowed from her. Instead, she'd bought Sharon a t-shirt, hoping that the kind gesture would be enough to make Sharon forgive her for the debt she owed. Nevertheless, Sharon was a firm business woman. She believed in creating and sticking to a monthly budget, so she finally called Raven to ask for the money back. Raven promised to give it to her within the next two to three weeks and Sharon explained to her that she was taking from next month's budget to cover the money Raven had borrowed. "Be sure to give it to me in two to three weeks so my budget won't be off," said Sharon. Raven was annoyed. She'd borrowed money from a couple of her friends and most of them had never asked for the money back. Sure, they may have expected it, but none of them had been bold enough to ask for it. Eventually, they moved on.

Later that evening, Raven clocked in at her job. Brandy was there waiting on Raven to relieve her. Noticing how angry Raven looked, Brandy asked her what was wrong.

Raven: Okay, so I have a friend named Sharon. Sharon is a Paralegal. She makes good money doing what she does. Anyhow, I borrowed $150 from her about three weeks ago and now, she's on my back about it. What pisses me off is that she knows my situation. She knows that I have three kids and not a lot of help from their fathers. She has one child. You would think that she would be more merciful towards me.

Brandy: Well, Raven, she may need the money. Sometimes, people appear to be doing well, but they aren't doing as good as you think they are.

Raven: That's true, but that's definitely not the case with Sharon. She just filed to have her daughter's father removed from paying her child support.

Brandy: That's weird, but it doesn't mean she's doing well. She may have another reason for doing that. Maybe the guy is crazy. Who knows?

Raven: No, she's doing it because her pastor said that forcing someone to do something they don't want to do is witchcraft.

Brandy: Wow, that's deep. I never thought of it that way.

Raven: And now, because she's not getting any money from him, she's decided to come after me.

Brandy: I don't think that's the case. Seriously, Raven.

Maybe she just needs the money and if she doesn't, she may have a budget that she tries to keep up with. I just started budgeting eight months ago and if I don't follow my budget, I could end up homeless.

Raven: Why are you defending her? You act like you know her.

Brandy: No, I've lost a couple of friends for similar reasons. People think that just because my parents are wealthy that I'm automatically wealthy, when I'm not. I don't ask my parents for anything, including money to help out with Carter. Well, I've had friends to borrow money from me and never give it back. They loved me when I gave them the money, but the minute I asked for it back, I became their archenemy. One of my friends told another friend of mine that I was cold-hearted because I knew her situation and still asked for the money back. I'm like, since when does her situation relieve her of her responsibilities? I tried to tell my situation to a bill collector and he did not change his tune. He kept threatening me and when I didn't pay on time, he took me to court, garnished my wages and I'm still paying that debt off to this day. Another former friend of mine started threatening to beat me up just because I asked for the five hundred dollars she'd borrowed. She told me that she didn't owe me anything because she didn't ask me to loan her the money — I volunteered. So, I'll say this: if she's a good friend to you, give her the money back and don't lose the friendship over it.

Raven: Honestly, I don't want the friendship anymore. Any person who could take food out of my children's mouths is not a friend of mine.

Two months passed and the children were out of school for summer break. Raven was at home, trying to figure out where she'd get some money from. Her refrigerator was empty again and Raven wasn't going to get her food stamps for another two weeks. "Ma, we're hungry," said Elizabeth as she peeped into her mother's room. "Collin ate up all the hot dogs and Drake said he's not feeling well." Raven stood to her feet. "Don't tell me that Collin sat there and ate six whole hot dogs by himself! Collin! Get in here!" A few seconds later, a slightly obese Collin made his way into his mother's bedroom. "Collin, did you eat up all the hot dogs?!" Collin froze in his steps. He stared at his mother, but did not utter a word. Instead, he took a few steps back. "Get out of my face!" screamed Raven as she picked her house shoe off the floor, threatening to throw it at her son. "I told you to stop being so greedy!" Collin ran out of the room and Raven sat back down on her bed. She called her sons' father, Jamal, but he did not answer his phone. As a matter of fact, he'd stopped calling and visiting his sons altogether because he grew weary of arguing with Raven. Raven then got off her bed and walked into the kitchen. Sure enough, there was only one plate in the sink and the refrigerator didn't have anything in it but an almost empty jar of mayonnaise and a small box of baking soda. That's when Raven suddenly thought of Drew.

Drew was a nice guy who had a crush on Raven. He lived just a few houses down from Raven and he was smitten with the feisty, petite beauty. Standing at five foot, two inches tall and weighing 135 pounds, Drew was not Raven's type. Additionally, his only source of income was a Social Security check. Raven called Drew's phone number for the first time since he'd given it to her. She'd had his number for several months.

Drew: Hello.

Raven: Hey Drew. This is Raven from up the street. How are you?

Drew: Hey pretty lady. I'm surprised to hear from you. How are you?

Raven: I'm good. I was just thinking about you and decided to give you a call. Are you busy?

Drew: Not anymore.

Raven: Okay. Come down to my house and keep me company if you will.

Drew: On my way!

Two minutes later, Drew knocked on Raven's door. He was out of breath and it was obvious that he'd sprayed a whole lot of cologne on his sweaty body. Additionally, he'd stepped in some dog poo on his way over. Drew took off his shoes and walked in. "Had to leave my shoes at the door," he said. "I stepped in some dog feces on my way over. Well, I hope it was dog feces. I remember seeing Maybelle taking a crap behind a house once." Raven laughed. "Have a seat," she said as she made her way towards a bottle of air freshener that she conveniently kept on one of her end tables. "So, Drew. Tell me more about you." Drew looked around as if he were surveying what was about to become his new house. He shook his head in approval before answering. "Well, I'm 36 years old and I like to fish. My favorite food is meatballs. I have never been married and I don't have any kids yet. I do not work because I want to gainfully employ myself." Raven held her laughter in. She knew that Drew was going out of his way to sound intelligent. "Oh, so you want to gainfully employ yourself?" she asked jokingly. "And what do you want to do?" Drew sat upright and clinched his fingers together. "I like to paint," said Drew. "My brother, George, works for a painting company and he takes me with him to help sometimes. I'm good at painting so I plan to start my own painting company. I want to call it Drew On the Wall. In every room I paint, I want to create a signature wall where I just make something creative — something that reflects how that room makes me feel." Raven was impressed. "That's creative," she said. "Drew On the Wall. I like that." With a look of smug satisfaction, Drew adjusted his shirt. He looked around the living room again, noticing the huge painting of the Garden of Eden. "I've been there," said Drew. Raven looked at the painting. "Been where?" she asked. By now, she looked concerned. "There," said Drew as he pointed to the picture on the wall. "I've been to the Garden of Eden. It looks a whole lot prettier than that in person. I couldn't go in though because there were a few angels guarding the place, but I stood outside of it. Can't wait to go back." Concerned, Raven called her son, Drake, into the room. Standing at five foot, three inches tall, Drake was taller than most eleven-year-old boys. Drake walked into the room, but did not utter a word. "Did you finish your homework?" asked Raven. Drake nodded in affirmation. Raven adjusted herself in her seat. "Okay, tell Elizabeth to come here." Drake walked away and a few seconds later, Elizabeth walked into the living room. "Did you do your homework?" Raven asked her daughter. Elizabeth looked sad. "No," she said. "I told you that we're hungry. I can't work when I'm hungry." Raven sighed. "We don't have any food here, Elizabeth! What do you want me to do?!" Elizabeth walked away pouting while her mother continued her manipulative rant. Drew felt horrible. He got out of the slouched position, reached into his pocket and pulled out a twenty dollar bill. "This is all I have," he said. "Take it and get the kids something to eat." Raven shook her head and threw up her hands. "No, I can't," she said. Drew stood to his feet and placed the twenty dollar bill on the table. "I insist," he said. "It bothers me to see a child hungry. Sometimes, when I watch those commercials that show starving children, I cry." Raven let the money remain on the table. "Thank you so much. You are really a good man."

An hour later, a happy Drew walked out of Raven's front door. He felt great because he'd given money to the woman he believed he'd someday marry. Raven then called one of her brothers and asked him to take her to the store. While in the car with her brother, Jeff, Raven found a five dollar bill on the floor. She didn't say a word about it. Instead, she covered it with her foot and picked it up after they arrived at the store.

While at the store, Jeff mentioned a guy named Terek to Raven. "He's a nice guy and I thought about introducing him to you, but I know how you are." Raven laughed. "How am I?" she asked. Jeff didn't mince words. "You take advantage of nice people and Terek is a nice guy."

Raven: I do not take advantage of nice people. How old is Terek?

Jeff: Twenty-seven.

Raven: Does he have a j-o-b?

Jeff: Of course, he does. He works at the plant with me.

Raven: What does he look like?

Jeff: Well, the ladies like him, but like I said, Terek is a nice guy. Raven, if you're going to take advantage of him, I'd rather you just pass it up.

Raven: You just think the worst of me! I'm not the girl you think I am. Give him my number and if I don't like him, I won't lead him on.

Jeff: Okay, but remember, he works with me. The only reason I'm telling you about him is because he saw a picture of you on my Facebook page and he hasn't shut up about you yet.

A week later, Terek pulled into Raven's driveway. A handsome but shy man, Terek stood at six feet tall. With a medium brown complexion, wide-set eyes and a neatly trimmed beard, Terek was reasonably handsome. Nevertheless, his athletic build had been slightly interrupted by a slightly enlarged belly. Raven looked out the window and saw Terek approaching her house. "He's okay, but he's not my type," she thought to herself. A few seconds later, Raven opened the door. "Come on in, handsome man," she said, noticing the wine colored Lexus parked out in her driveway. Terek handed Raven a single stem white rose. "First day, first rose," he said. "As time goes on, the color of the roses I give you will reflect where we stand. This white rose means newness. Hopefully, one day, I'll be able to give you a dozen red roses."

Everything was going well until there was a sudden loud knock on Raven's door. Drake ran past his mother and opened the door. Drew stepped into the living room. In his hand, he held a twenty dollar bill and two tickets. Nevertheless, Drew didn't look happy at all.

Drew: Who is this negro?

Raven: Drew, don't come over here and start insulting people. His name is Terek and he's pleased to meet you too.

Terek: It's okay. Is this your boyfriend?

Drew: Yes, I am.

Raven: No, you are not. I never said that you and I were in a relationship, Drew. We're just friends. At least, we were friends.

Drew: You didn't say that the other day when you kissed me.

Raven: It was a friendly kiss on the cheek! I've never kissed you on your lips! Drew, you need to leave!

Drew: I'm not leaving until you give me all of my money back!

Raven: What money?

Drew: I gave you money three times!

Raven: You gave me twenty dollars on three occasions, Drew! I owe you sixty dollars. I'll give it to you on the first.

Drew: That's okay. Keep it. Remember, God don't like ugly.

With that, Drew walked out of Raven's house and she

turned her attention to her son, Drake. "Boy, how many times do I have to tell you to ask who it is before you open the door? We don't live in Beverly Hills! This is Compton!" Drake shrugged his shoulders and walked back into his room. Terek continued to sit calmly on the couch and it was obvious that he was now thinking.

Raven: You be nice to some people and they think you're in a relationship with them.

Terek: Yeah, but as a mother, you have to be careful that you don't lead men on.

Raven: I didn't lead him on. I was just nice to him; that's all.

Terek: Taking a man's money is leading him on.

Raven: He offered and I took it. I didn't think he'd read into it.

Terek wondered if he should continue pursuing the beautiful Raven. He'd dated a woman who'd used him once and this made him very cautious. Nevertheless, he decided to take things slowly and see where they went. Raven, on the other hand, had experienced a change of heart. At first, she was going to tell Terek that they could only be friends, but after seeing his Lexus, she'd changed her mind.

Two months into their courtship, Terek decided to take Raven to church with him. He'd been telling his spiritual parents about Raven and they were anxious to meet her. Immediately after church service, Apostle Floyd walked up to Terek while Raven was talking with his wife. Apostle Floyd gave Terek a parable. He said, "A man once went to the pet store and looked at two snakes. One was venomous and the other was non-venomous. Because he had a toddler at home, he decided to go with the non-venomous snake. He brought the snake home and it grew and it grew. One night, it outgrew its enclosure and got out. The next day, the man found the snake wrapped around his lifeless daughter's neck. Do you believe it would have been safer for him to get the venomous snake or the non-venomous snake?" Terek wasted no time answering. "He shouldn't have gotten a snake at all. He should have dealt with whatever it was that made him attracted to snakes." Apostle Floyd smiled and placed his right hand on Terek's shoulder. "Bingo," he said as he walked away. Terek nodded his head and let out a sigh. He knew what he had to do. He needed to end his courtship with Raven, but he didn't know how. He worried that Jeff, Raven's brother, would be upset with him, so he prayed about the matter.

The next day, Terek received a call from Raven.

Raven: Can we talk?

Terek: Yeah; what's up?

Raven: Terek, you're a nice guy and all, but I don't think you're the one for me.

Terek: Okay, but what's wrong?

Raven: I'm just not feeling this. For example, I tried to kiss you, but you pulled back. One night my kids were gone to bed; they were sound asleep, but all you wanted to do was read the Bible. I think you're a good man and any woman will be lucky to have you, but you're just not the man for me.

Terek: *(Laughs)* What's his name?

Raven: What do you mean, what's his name?

Terek: The guy you're dumping me for. Is it Drew?

Raven: Heck naw! If you must know, I have met someone recently and his name is Malik.

Terek: No problem, Raven. I just wanted to prove a point to you, that's all.

Raven: What point is that?

Terek: That you can be straight-forward with people. You don't have to manipulate your way out of a relationship. You just have to be honest.

Raven: I wasn't dishonest with you! I just said it wasn't working and that's true! Who I am or am not dating is none of your business!

Terek: You're right. Blessings to you.

"911. What's your emergency?" The operator's voice was calm. "Hello!" shouted Raven. "Someone broke into my house while I was at work!" Raven gave the operator her

address and twenty minutes later, two cop cars pulled up. In one of the cars was Nathan, Sharon's ex-husband. After realizing that he was at Raven's house, Nathan walked over to the other officer's car. "I gotta let you handle this one," he said. "She's a friend of my ex-wife." Officer Sanchez nodded his head and got out of his car. He walked up to Raven with Nathan following him.

Officer Sanchez: Good evening ma'am. Tell us what happened.

Raven: Nathan? Is that you?

Officer Brunswick: In the flesh. No worries. He'll be taking the report. I'm just here to observe.

Raven: Okay. I don't care either way, but anyway, me and my kids walked over to a friend of mine's house and we stayed over there for about two hours. When I came home, I noticed that the front door was wide open. I told the kids to stay outside and I went in and that's when I noticed that two of my television sets were gone and my microwave is gone. When I went to the back of the house, I saw broken glass. I believe the thief got in through my bedroom window, but left out the front door because you need a key to open my back door, even from the inside.

Officer Sanchez: Okay. Stand out here and we're gonna check the house and the perimeter. We'll be right back.

While the officers were in the house, Drew walked by. He locked eyes with Raven, but he didn't utter a word.

Instead, he turned his head and kept on walking. Five minutes later, the officers returned and continued asking Raven a list of questions. "I think that guy right there did it! I was just trying to be nice to him one day and I invited him over to my house — you know —nothing romantic, just to talk. He's not my type. Anyhow, he read too much into it and when I was dating a guy named Terek, he showed up at my house and started acting crazy." Officer Brunswick looked up the street and saw Drew. "Drew Lancaster," he said. "No, Drew's a little slow, but he's not a thief. The worst thing he'll do to you is embarrass you with the truth." Raven was offended. She was confident that Drew had broken into her house. Why didn't Officer Brunswick believe her? She reasoned within her mind that Nathan had never liked her and for this reason, he was trying to help the bad guy get away. "I'm telling you, it was Drew!" shouted Raven. Officer Sanchez decided to speak up. "I'll ask him a few questions, but we cannot arrest him or take him in for questioning. I'm with Officer Brunswick — well, you know him as Nathan, but I'm with him. I've known Drew for years and he's harmless. He's not on any drugs, besides the medicine the doctors give him, and Drew's the kinda guy who, if he sees someone breaking into your house, he'll try to arrest the intruder."

Later that evening, Malik, Raven's new boyfriend, came over. A ruggedly handsome man, Malik stood five foot, eight inches tall and wore his pants halfway off his butt. His clothes reeked of marijuana and his eyes were bloodshot red. Raven immediately sent her children to bed and invited Malik into her bedroom. Malik kept cursing and talking about what he was gonna do with the thief if he found out who it was. The truth is, Malik needed somewhere to stay, so he started acting as if he'd be an asset to Raven's house, but the problem was, Raven was on Section Eight government assistance. Letting a man live with her could very well mean losing her benefits. Nevertheless, Raven decided to let Malik stay a few nights at her house. Those nights turned into weeks and those weeks turned into months. Three months later, Malik got his first item of mail at Raven's address and that's when she realized that Malik was no longer visiting her; he had moved in.

Knock. Knock. Knock. Malik answered the door. A shocked Zuri stood on the other side of the door and asked for Raven. "She's not here," said Malik. "But you can come in if you want — with your fine self!" Zuri declined. "Tell her that Zuri stopped by," she said as she walked off the steps. Malik continued to stare at Zuri as she rushed away. "Dang!" he shouted. "They don't make em' like that no more!" he said referring to Zuri's shape.

It was Raven's lunch hour and she saw that she had a text

message from Zuri. "Call me!" the text message read. Raven hadn't talked to Zuri in several months because she owed Zuri over five hundred dollars. Just like she'd done Sharon, she'd convinced Zuri to take her shopping one day, claiming to be out of food and supplies. Zuri took her to a Sam's Club and Raven bought four buggies of food and household items that day. Raven promised her that she'd pay her back in two weeks. Nevertheless, instead of paying her back, Raven tried to manipulate Zuri by inviting her out to eat. When Zuri asked for her money, Raven got offended and canceled the invitation, claiming that her daughter, Elizabeth, was suddenly complaining of a stomachache. After that, Raven stopped calling Zuri and she refused to answer her calls.

Raven reluctantly called Zuri back.

Raven: Hey. You called?

Zuri: Who is that man at your house? I stopped by and he wouldn't stop flirting! He was absolutely obnoxious — almost made me forget that I am saved!

Raven: That's Malik. He's harmless. Just a man being a man.

Zuri: And who is Malik, might I ask?

Raven: My boyfriend.

Zuri: Raven!

Raven: That's why I didn't tell you. I knew you'd judge me.

Zuri: Telling you the truth is not judging you. Raven, you have a daughter. You have to think about her. You can't just be letting men move in with you.

Raven: My lunch break is over. I gotta go.

Zuri: Wait. Did you stop calling me because of the money you owe me?

Raven: No, I've just been busy, that's all.

Zuri: Okay. I just called to tell you I forgive the debt. Keep it. I don't want it back anymore. God told me to release it.

Raven was stunned. She didn't realize that by Zuri releasing the debt, she was turning Raven over to the Debt-Collector Himself, Jesus. Not knowing what to say, Raven simply interjected, "Okay. I'll call you back." After that, she hung up the phone.

Six months passed and Raven was at the county fair with Malik. "Come on here, woman!" shouted Malik as he pulled Raven's arm. When the couple turned around, they almost bumped into two women who were walking together and laughing. They suddenly stopped and apologized. Nevertheless, when Raven looked up, she was surprised. "Sharon? Zuri? Hanging out together? How do you know each other?" Sharon answered. "Ironically enough, when you told me that Zuri owned the spa over there by that Chinese restaurant I used to work for, I made an appointment there for me and you. But I never heard back from you, so I went by myself." Zuri smiled and interjected.

"When they told me that a woman had an invitation for two, but the other party wasn't with her, I pulled up her order. When I saw your name, I went out to meet her. I tried to call you too, but you didn't answer my call. Well, Sharon and I got to talking and realized that we have a lot in common and we've been friends ever since." Raven was uncomfortable and it showed. "That's good," she said. "We gotta go." That's when Sharon pulled the sunglasses off Raven's face. "Why are you wearing sunglasses at night time?" she asked. Suddenly, Raven's black eye was on display for the world to see. "Raven!" Sharon shouted sympathetically. "Mind ya business!" shouted Malik as he pulled Raven away. Sharon wanted to take off after Raven, but Zuri grabbed her arm. "Let her go," she said. "I think we've both done enough for her. The only thing that we can do now is pray for her." Sharon reluctantly agreed.

"You know, I was thinking," said Raven to Malik. "I don't believe it was Drew who broke in my house. I think it was that crackhead, Maybelle." Malik tried to start his car, but it would not start. "Hold on," he said as he exited the car. He let the hood up and a few minutes later, he started beating something with his fist. He then let the hood down and got back in the car. The car started this time.

Malik: Why do you say that?

Raven: Why do I say what?

Malik: Woman, are you retarded? You said that you

believe that Maybelle was the one who broke into your house.

Raven: Oh. Yeah. Anyway, Drake and Collin's bicycles came up missing some time ago and a few people said they saw Maybelle riding around on a blue bike. Of course, she must have sold the bike. Nowadays, it seems like she passes by my house more than usual, plus, she's always looking at me.

Malik: Our house.

Raven: What?

Malik: You said "my house." I was just correcting you. It's our house now.

Raven: Okay. Our house.

Malik: That's the kinda stuff that ticks me off. You act like I haven't done anything.

Raven: How we go from talking about Maybelle breaking into my house — I mean our house — to you accusing me of saying something I haven't said?

Malik: That's alright though.

Raven: What does that mean?

Malik: It means that I'm gonna pack my stuff and move out of YOUR house!

Raven: Malik, stop reading into the stuff I say.

That night, Raven was in the house trying to calm Malik down when there was a loud knock on the door. Malik froze in his steps. "Who is it?" asked Raven. Malik rushed towards the bedroom. "Police! Open the door or we'll have to kick it in!" Confused, Raven answered the door and to her surprise, ten cops flooded into her living room. By this time, Malik had jumped out of Raven's bedroom window and straight into the arms of Officer Nathan Brunswick, Sharon's ex-husband. The officers found drug contraband in Raven's house, and even though she didn't know that Malik stored drugs in her house, Raven was still arrested. Six months later, she was sentenced to three years in prison. Jamal stepped up and took custody of his sons and Elizabeth had to go and live with her vindictive grandmother.

Two and a half years later, Raven was released early for good behavior. She was in the car with her mother, on their way to her mother's house, where Raven would be staying. As they drove down the highway, a sign caught Raven's attention. It read: Drew On the Wall. Raven turned around and stared at the sign as they passed by the store. Realizing that her daughter was looking at Drew On the Wall, Ms. Stephens said, "Do you know the guy who owns that store? He's a little slow, but he's a nice guy. Last year, a woman was being robbed and he saw the robbery taking place. They said he ran up to the robber and beat that guy within an inch of his life, but the robber had a gun. He shot Drew in the arm, but rumor has it that Drew kept on fighting. He beat that man until he was unconscious. The whole city hailed him a hero. Anyway, his mother started a GoFundMe account for him to get some help with his medical bills and people from all over the world started contributing. His bills were $65,000 but people donated well over $800,000 to him. He used some of the money to start his company and he moved his mother out of the ghetto. Of course, he lives with his mother and she helps him to run the business. From what I hear, his company is doing great. He hired a lot of guys who are like him — slow — and they've managed to put three local painting companies out of business. They said that man made over a million dollars last year. Isn't that something?" Something Zuri always said suddenly dawned on Raven. Zuri used to always say, "Good things come to good people eventually, if they don't let the bad things that happened to them make them forfeit their blessings."

Raven had no choice but to move back in with her mother. When she saw her daughter, Elizabeth, she wept bitterly because she realized that her daughter had been subjected to the same treatment her mother had subjected her to. Raven called Jamal and asked if she could see the boys and he agreed. When Jamal pulled up, he parked the car in Ms. Stephen's driveway and both of his car's back doors flung open. Out jumped a much taller Drake and a much skinnier and taller Collin. Raven hugged her sons, but she could not take her eyes off Collin. He looked like a new man. Knowing her thoughts, Jamal opened his car door and came outside the car. "Like I used to tell you ... if you just put some rules in place and enforce them, Collin wouldn't eat like he was losing his mind." Collin laughed. "Hey Mama," he said, revealing a much deeper voice than Raven remembered. Raven started crying. Prison life hadn't hardened her; it simply made her more compassionate. Raven hugged her sons and greeted the woman who was sitting on the passenger's side of Jamal's car. "Oh! My bad!" said Jamal. "Raven, I'd like you to meet Tamia — my wife."

Raven had to start back where she left off. She ended up living with her mother for a year and unfortunately her mother hadn't changed a bit. While living with her mother, Raven realized that she was just like her mother. She watched her mother use and abuse people. She watched her mother take advantage of people who genuinely tried to help her. Nevertheless, Raven wasn't ready to change just yet. She was still convinced that she was the victim. She felt abandoned by Zuri and Sharon. She felt victimized by her ex, Jamal, and she felt betrayed by her sons because they wanted to continue living with their father. She even felt rejected by God because it looked like everyone around her was succeeding — everyone, that is, but her.

One Sunday evening, Raven was on the computer at her

mother's house. Her brother, Jeff, had shared a picture of a well-groomed, fit and very handsome Terek, along with his new bride. Terek was carrying his new bride in his arms. The couple were laughing as white rose petals fell just above their heads. Terek's new wife was absolutely gorgeous. Her big white smile and long black hair made her look like she'd been ripped from the pages of a magazine. Raven saw the link leading back to Terek's page. It was as if her eyes were suddenly opened. Terek suddenly became the most handsome man she'd ever laid eyes on. Raven watched a video of Terek's wedding. He handed his new wife one hundred red roses. "Red symbolizes blood and that's why it's used to symbolize love. Whenever I met women, I would give them a single white rose to reflect the newness of our relationship. No one could ever get past that single white rose. No one ever got a pink rose or a red rose but you. Each of these roses represent the number of years I want to spend with you. Through the good times and the not-so-good times, I vow to love you, cover you, pray for you and lead you. I will never walk away from you, just as God has never walked away from me. I love you with every beat of my red heart and I say in the presence of every person in this room, every angel in this room and in the presence of the Lord, Jesus Christ, that you will be loved, provided for and protected as long as there is breath in my body." Raven was taken aback by how handsome and good of a man

Terek was. His enlarged belly was now a thing of the past. She was scrolling through Terek's photos when all of a sudden, she heard her mother's voice directly behind her. "I forgot Jeff tried to fix you up with him," said Ms. Stephens. "It wouldn't have worked between the two of you anyway. You're too stupid to hold on to a good man. All of your lovers belong at the animal shelter with a sign above their cages that read: Awaiting Euthanasia — or at least, sterilization." After those words were spoken, Raven and her mother got into an argument. That argument led to a fight and that led to Raven being incarcerated for three days. After that, Raven decided to start over again. She moved into a shelter and stayed there for a month. She started working full-time at a retail store and it was there that she discovered who'd broken into her house four years prior.

Raven met a woman named Heidi who'd bragged about once buying two new television sets and a microwave for a hundred bucks. When Heidi told Raven where she'd once lived, which was less than a block away from Raven's old house, plus, the year she'd bought the items, Raven froze in her steps. "Girl, I bought it all from a guy named Malik," said Heidi. "He was dating some girl who, he said, had more butt than she had sense." Heidi laughed hard; that was, until she realized that Raven wasn't laughing. She suddenly stopped laughing and looked at Raven. "Oh my goodness," she said. "You're her."

It took Raven eight more years before she started surrendering her life to Christ. Raven was sitting in her living room praying one day when a very pregnant Elizabeth walked in. "Ma. Can you keep Myron for me? I have a date tonight." Raven took her two-year-old grandson by the hand and placed him on her lap. "Liz, you're already pregnant! You could at least wait til the baby's born before you start dating new dudes!" Elizabeth rolled her eyes and walked away. She then mumbled, "When you preach to me something you've practiced, then I'll listen."

I grew up in a family and in communities where welfare was the norm. As a matter of fact, anyone who was not on welfare was said to "have money," meaning, they were well off. I don't think most of us realized that we were poor. You see, when you are surrounded by people like yourself, the concept of rich and poor does not exist. Every person is measured by his or her individual personality and choices. Nevertheless, the more I advanced in school, the more I became aware of money, status and social rank. I also got a chance to see the clashes between the classes — economic classes, that is. In public schools, there are kids from all walks of life and even though I've inwardly vowed to never send my children to public school, I must admit that the public school system is much like the system of the real world. For this reason, I cannot and will not bash public schools.

Who was Raven? Raven was:

- An Ahab
- A Jezebel in Training
- A User
- A Liar
- A Manipulator and Con Artist
- A Horrible Mother
- An Unrepentant Sinner

Raven, the Ahab: if you're not familiar with demonology, this term will go directly over your head. Ahab was the husband of Jezebel, of course. Jezebel controlled her husband and manipulated all of Israel. Ahab was king of Israel, nevertheless, Jezebel managed to bring him under submission. By usurping Ahab's authority, Jezebel became the king's king. Nowadays, when we speak of the Jezebel spirit, we are talking about a real demonic spirit that specializes in perversion. For example, the Bible says that a man is the head of his wife. This is the system that God has established. Nevertheless, when Jezebel steps into the picture, the wife will usurp the authority of her husband, thus, violating God's system. This demonic practice is called perversion and the behaviors of a perverted wife are referred to as witchcraft because she (the wife) is operating in the wrong role and therefore, working against the system that God has established. Raven's mother had the infamous Jezebel spirit and for this reason, she sought to control her daughter. Men and women whose mothers have the Jezebel spirit are oftentimes either fully under her control, trying to get from under her control or on the run from her. Nevertheless, Jezebel always manages to re-ensnare Ahab. Why is this? It's simple: Ahab is married to Jezebel and until a person infected with the Ahab spirit is delivered from that wicked spirit, that person will keep finding himself or herself back in Jezebel's web, attempting to justify being there.

Raven, the Jezebel in Training: Raven didn't realize this at first, but she was blossoming from an Ahab into a soul-snatching Jezebel. She was becoming her mother one scheme, one thought and one choice at a time. One of the things I taught about in my book, *Jezebellion*, is that most Ahabs are nothing but Jezebels in training bras. If they are not delivered, they will eventually become the parent they once complained about.

Raven, the User: Like her mother, Raven took advantage

of everyone who dared to call her "friend." Like her ex, Jamal, told her, she really did have the ambitions of a brown recluse spider. Brown recluses wait in their web for their meals. They don't move; they just build a web and wait for some wandering insect to get caught in it. Raven didn't want to get out and work full time because she didn't want to lose her public assistance. She decided to stay put mentally, spiritually and financially because she believed that her mindset was benefiting her. Nevertheless, people like Raven do successfully use some people, but their ways are only tolerated for short periods of time. Eventually, they find themselves surrounded by people who are like themselves: cold-hearted con artists who mistake kindness for weakness.

Raven, the Liar: Users are always liars. They have to be if they want to become better at using people. Raven lied when she said that she had a friend who worked at Sonic. She did this because she wanted a SuperSonic Double Bacon Cheeseburger combo. She didn't care about Sharon. She was more focused on getting what she could get out of Sharon versus being her friend.

Raven, the Manipulator and Con Artist: Raven wasn't your traditional con artist. She posed as a friend, a potential lover and a damsel in distress to get her wants and needs met. Some people would argue that she did what she had to do for her kids, but this is not true. If Raven truly loved her kids and wanted to provide for them, she would have gotten a full-time job, gone back to school and looked for ways to earn the money herself. Please understand that there is a difference between motherly instinct versus motherly love. Any animal can feed its children because instinct dictates that it does so, but love will make you sacrifice your wants, needs and desires for your kids. Raven wasn't willing to sacrifice herself; instead, she chose to manipulate others into making sacrifices on her behalf. Even in the grocery store, she was more concerned about getting expensive foods for herself than she was with buying foods that would carry her children over for two weeks. She invited Drew into her house because she wanted to manipulate him into giving her some money. People like Raven see other people as tools to accomplish their own agendas.

Raven, the Horrible Mother: Again, Raven was led by instincts to feed her children and not by love. She exposed her children to different men, she chased Drake and Collin's father away, and she did not correct Collin's behavior. Women like Raven raise their children, but they do not cultivate them. It's a fact that fruit trees can go without the help of humans. Nevertheless, like most of nature, many wild fruit trees will die because of lack of exposure or overexposure to necessities like the sun or water. Nevertheless, when a man cultivates a garden, he intentionally ensures the health and well-being of every fruit in that garden; that is, if he's a good farmer. A lazy farmer can go out and water his plants without doing much of anything else for them. Because he has a garden, he is known as a farmer, but this does not make him a good farmer. The same is true for a parent. Any parent can give his or her children the things they need to survive, but a good parent will take his or her time to teach, train, correct and nurture his or her children. Unfortunately, in this day and age, we see a lot of parents, but there seems to be a scarcity of good parents.

Raven, the Unrepentant Sinner: Sure, we are all sinners saved by grace. Rebellious souls love to point this truth out, but we must all realize that there is a difference between being a repentant sinner versus an unrepentant sinner. An unrepentant sinner is a rebellious soul who willfully serves Satan. A repentant sinner is one who has turned away from his/her evil ways to follow God. Raven had no desire to follow God. She wanted to extract everything she could from sin. She loved using people, pointing out the flaws of others and bringing attention to herself. Terek would not sleep with her, so she realized that she didn't have the kind of hold on him that she wanted to have. Nevertheless, Malik was as sinful and unrepentant as she was, and for this reason, she felt safer with Malik.

Reading this story, you're likely no fan of Raven's, but here's the thing: there are many men and women out there who are just like Raven. These people come from different backgrounds, races, economic statuses, etc. They are oftentimes overly friendly and down-to-earth. Additionally, they don't always attach themselves to people who are financially stable. They are also known to connect with people who have little to give and they'll take the little that those people have left. They are con artists with hard hearts and smooth tongues.

How did Raven come to have so many successful friends in the first place? The truth is, there are many men and women out there like Raven who are really skilled at making friends from all walks of life. The reason for this is they have an anointing on their lives for wealth and greatness, however, that anointing has been perverted or contaminated by the enemy. We tend to be drawn to people who are presently equal to or greater than us or who have the potential to be equal to or greater than us in our God-assigned roles. For example, a man anointed by God to cast out high-ranking demons will not be drawn to a man who is anointed to cast out low-ranking demons, however, the man who casts out low-ranking demons will be drawn to the man who casts out high-ranking demons.

This isn't God's way of establishing a who's who of deliverance ministry; this is God's way of establishing rank. The guy who needs to grow in the deliverance arena should be following or mentored by the guy who has grown and matured in his assignment. In other words, Raven's friends were drawn to who she had the potential to become, but they were eventually repelled by who she presently was.

In the beginning of the story, we witness Raven flattering Zuri as she gets out of her car. Zuri had just taken Raven out to eat and Raven decided to pay her back with flattery. People who specialize in using others love to use flattery as their means of currency. They believe that their words of affirmation should compensate for what they've taken from others. One of the reasons for this is, we often allow users in our lives when we have God-sized voids that need to be filled. Users see these voids and attempt to fill them, because they understand how we, as humans, are wired. Most (decent) people feel obligated to help anyone who they feel has been beneficial to helping them grow or heal. Users take advantage of people who feel broken or stuck or they'll present themselves as broken and stuck to pull on the heartstrings of others. Nevertheless, even when they attract people by presenting themselves as damsels in distress, they'll still look for areas in those people lives where they can make themselves a necessity. For example,

Raven believed that Zuri needed her because, according to Raven, Zuri was too nice. Nevertheless, it was Raven who needed Zuri.

As the story continues, we witness Raven borrowing money that she has no intentions of paying back. This is because Raven has a mindset that you will find in most opportunists — she believes that the friend who has the most is required to do the most. But get this: Raven doesn't have friends who have less than she has! This means that, according to Raven's rules, everyone in her life is obligated to do things for her, but she is not obligated to do anything for them. I've met people like this in life and they are parasites who are skilled at attaching themselves to kindhearted (successful) people. They will always use flattery or pity to get what they want, but anytime they borrow something or need something, they always say things like, "She knows my situation and that's why I'm mad." People like this will have you taking them back and forth to work, and the minute you ask them for gas money, they'll go and talk about you to anyone who'll listen. People like this will invite you out to eat with them, order more food than they can eat, and then wait for you to pay the tab. If you tell the waitress to bring out two tickets, you'll notice that their facial expressions and attitudes will begin to change for the worse. Even though they'll still smile, it's easy to tell that their smiles are forced and their words are laced with insults. They will fumble through their purses, acting like they can't find their wallets or their debit cards. They will act overwhelmed, frustrated and confused while frantically searching through their purses. They may even act as if they've suddenly remembered that they have a bill due. For example, they may grab their heads and say something to the effect of, "Darn it! I forgot I told that man I'd pay him today! Now, I'm over here spending his money! What was I thinking?!" They do this so you'll volunteer to pay for the meal. If you are not moved by their performances, they will pay for their meals and leave without giving you a proper goodbye. I've learned to sit still and let them carry the burden of their own bills. Some people may say that this isn't the Christian thing to do, but this is not true. If I invite someone out to eat, I'll pick up the tab, but if someone invites me out to eat, I'll pick up my tab and let them pay their own; that is, unless that person is pouring wisdom into me! I let opportunists pay their own tabs because I want to send a clear message to them or drive them away from me. I want them to understand that a relationship with me has to be equally beneficial to the both of us. If they do not want this, I do not want them in my life, unless it's ministry related. I can't tell you how many times I've listened to parasitic people talk about the folks who made them carry their own weight. Of course, I attempted to correct them each time, but parasites don't have ears to hear. They'll distance themselves from anyone who tells them the truth and surround themselves with people who tell them what they want to believe about themselves. I've literally seen cases where people opened up their homes to opportunists and told them they could live with them rent free! All they had to do was help out around the house. Nevertheless, somehow, the opportunists managed to convince themselves that they were being taken advantage of. They convinced themselves that they shouldn't have to help out, even though they were not paying rent. This is the deception that opportunists subject themselves and others to.

A parasite can only teach its young to be parasites. Ms. Stephens taught her daughter to be a calmer and more seductive version of herself. This is why it is absolutely necessary for us, not only to be born again, but we must also be raised in the Word of God. We have to shed the generational strongholds that we've inherited or picked up from our parents and then learn to clothe ourselves with the Word of God. We must forsake familiar paths and walk by faith on the paths that God has set before us.

In the end, Raven learned a valuable lesson: you can underestimate the potential of people, but whenever you underestimate God, He will prove you wrong. Raven underestimated Drew, but she didn't realize that God does not favor "normal" people over people we consider to be slow. As a matter of fact, some people who we've written off are actually more in touch with God than we'll ever learn to be in this life. This is especially true for people who have the innocence of children. Jesus said in Matthews 18:3 (ESV), "Truly, I say to you, unless you turn and become like children, you will never enter the kingdom of heaven."

Eventually, Raven found herself in a relationship with a man who did to her what she'd done to others: he took advantage of her, stole from her and abused her. Now, if you ever come across a character like Raven, she will cast herself as the victim, and to an extent, she'd be telling the truth. Nevertheless, she will not acknowledge the fact that she is also predatory. Instead, she may try to justify her ways by saying something like, "It's not personal. I'm a mother." This is her way of saying that she's a good mother being driven by instinct and love, but the truth is, she's nothing but a parasite who happens to have children. If she truly loved her children, she'd try to build a future for them in a classroom, instead of trying to secure a future for herself in her bedroom.

Understanding the Welfare System

It goes without saying that welfare is considered a demonstration of love and kindness, and this may be true in some cases. Nevertheless, welfare can be binding in itself. Let me explain.

I grew up on public assistance. What I remember the most was the period when I was around 12 or 13 years old. I'd gone to my mother and asked her to stop getting food stamps. Of course, this was a strange request, but my reasoning was that first and foremost, I was embarrassed. Almost every time we went to the store, I would run into one of my classmates and I didn't want my mother to whip out a fat book of food stamps in front of them. The second reason was, I didn't want to associate my identity with food stamps. I was at an age where I was struggling to find myself and I didn't want to be defined by the stigma associated with being on public assistance. Honestly, this was the way I reasoned back them. For whatever reason, my mom stopped getting stamps at one point and our refrigerator suffered because of it. My mother said that I'd come back to her one day and begged her to get back on stamps temporarily.

As I grew older, I tried more and more to distance myself from the images I'd learned to associate with public assistance. Don't get me wrong — I didn't think I was better than anyone, after all, my family was on public assistance and most of my friends' families were on it as well. Nevertheless, I had a different view of myself and my friends than the images portrayed by the media. I don't regret having this line of thinking because when I became a young woman and moved out on my own, it was that reasoning that kept me from falling into the generational snares I'd seen my family members settle down in.

I'd gotten married for the first time and my ex and I had just gotten laid off from our jobs. He came to me and said that we needed to go down to the DHS office and apply for food stamps. "No way!" I exclaimed. I explained to him that I wanted us to get so hungry that we had no choice but to get jobs. I reasoned within myself that my ex's family and my family were public assistance junkies, therefore, we had that gene in our blood. I knew that if we got on public assistance, we'd get too comfortable and settle down in our struggle. We went back and forth about the idea for a few days and we finally agreed to not apply for public assistance and this worked! Because our bills were mounting and our fridge was empty, we went job hunting everyday and it wasn't long before we were both employed.

Understand this: public assistance was designed to help families transition. For example, if a father lost his job and could not provide for his family, receiving public assistance is a good way to help him and his family while he searches for another job. He should not get comfortable in receiving public aid to the point where he refuses to work or he refuses to work full-time. When public assistance becomes a crutch, it becomes an idol, and when it becomes an idol, it sets the stage for the generational strongman of lack to establish itself in a bloodline. Most of us have seen this strongman in action. Understand that the Earth and everything in it is set up under a system. A system is an order of things that work together to accomplish a common goal. Our government, for example, is a system. Democracy is a system. Liberalism is a system. Capitalism is a system. Every family has a system and every church has a system. For this reason, Satan is systematic. What does this mean? It means that he is methodical or better yet, he uses the structure of systems. This means that he uses a system to attack a system. God's system is a man gets saved, sanctified and filled with the Holy Spirit. That man works and is able to provide for himself. As he works, he starts earning enough to provide for a family. In due season, that man finds his wife and marries her before they have sex. Children then enter the picture and the husband continues to provide for them and his wife. The wife can work if this is the culture of that household. The couple stays together in Christ Jesus all the days of their lives, putting God first in all things. Nevertheless, because Satan is systematic, he wants to pervert this order, so he encourages fornication, slothfulness and perversion. In Satan's system, the woman goes out and fornicates, hoping some man will marry her. The same goes for the man. He fornicates with several women and then leaves them all. This creates a trail of hurt, ungodly soul ties and distrust. Hurt, distrusting people fight systems. That man who has uncovered many women then meets the woman who has been hurt by many men. Neither are truly submitted to Christ, but they are determined to have one of the fruits that we find in God's system: marriage. The couple gets married, but because they have not submitted to God's system, their home begins to divide. One of the branches of division is divorce. A house divided cannot stand, therefore, their home is split until they get divorced.

Welfare is a system. It is a government within itself. When a person starts getting welfare, that person is not necessarily under the system of welfare. Instead, that person is like a foreigner visiting another country. The foreigner's goal is to visit the country and then return to his own country. Nevertheless, many foreigners have come to the United States and decided that they prefer to live under our governmental system. When this happens, they then apply for citizenship. This means they are attempting to leave one system and become a part of another one. The same is true when a person becomes too comfortable in the welfare system. Let's revisit the man who lost his job. It is possible for him to get too comfortable in the welfare system if he doesn't get out of it quick enough. We are creatures of habit and we adapt easily. It generally takes 17 to 21 days to establish a habit, therefore, if that man does not break out of the welfare system in that window of time, he is in danger of becoming a part of that system. Why is this bad?

Just like every system, the welfare system has laws, established authority figures and boundaries. One of the laws of the welfare system is a person getting welfare must report all of their income to the proper authorities (DHS Office for example). One of the boundaries established is a person is only allowed to make a certain amount of money to remain under the welfare system. If that person makes even a dollar over that amount, he or she will be disqualified from being a part of that system. A person who wants to remain a part of a system, but does not honor that system will start to manipulate it. In governmental terms, that person will become an illegal alien. There are many illegal aliens in the welfare system. They work for jobs where they are paid under the table and they do not report that income. Determined to remain a part of the welfare system, they become methodical like Satan. They start developing systems to manipulate the system that they don't want to be ejected from. Any person who violates the laws of a system is called a criminal. One thing you'll come to learn about criminals is they have to embrace a lot of ungodly patterns of thinking to get away with their crimes. Additionally, their appetites for sin continues to increase. This is why under every system where lawlessness abounds, you will find a lot of disorder and chaos. This includes the welfare system, which we all know needs to be reformed.

People who submit to the welfare system become a part of that government. Again, I'm not talking about everyone who receives welfare because you can visit a system without becoming a part of it. I lived in Germany for six months, and I had to honor the German laws, nevertheless, I remained a citizen of the United States. This means that I visited a system, but I did not become a part of it. People who become a part of the welfare system have to submit themselves to the laws and authorities of the welfare system. Their case workers are their law enforcement officers and they must submit to the requirements that their officers give them. They restrict their earnings to a certain amount of money each month. They are also confined to certain neighborhoods. Sure, someone may argue that they can live in Beverly Hills and still get public assistance, but while this is true, it is not feasible. The reason is if you're making enough money to live in Beverly Hills, you are automatically disqualified from receiving welfare. So, while the laws do not specifically restrict you from living wheresoever you please, the income restrictions limit you to certain areas. These limitations are harsh and for this reason, most people who get welfare are illegal aliens of the welfare system. The reason is, the welfare system doesn't have enough manpower to enforce or re-enforce the laws. This encourages lawless systems to be established under the welfare system. For example, a mother of three may not report that her boyfriend is living with her. This is because she does not want to be deported from the system she has submitted to.

Whether a criminal is caught or is roaming freely, that criminal is bound. Let's take a fugitive for example. A fugitive has to move to a region where the people are not familiar with her. That criminal may have to change her identity, refrain from having too many personal relationships and distance herself from her family. This means that the woman in question is bound! She is living in a prison of rules designed to keep her from getting caught, nevertheless, a prison is still a prison, even if it has no bars! This is why many criminals have come out of hiding and turned themselves in to the authorities. They got tired of living in one prison while trying to avoid another one. They eventually reasoned within themselves that it would be better for them to start serving their time so that they can finish their sentences and move on with their lives. They got tired of living in fear which, again, is a prison in and of itself. A criminal of the welfare system is bound as well. People who have become citizens of welfare and have violated the laws of the welfare system work tirelessly to ensure that they are not caught. This is bondage! For example, a woman getting a Social Security check on behalf of one of her children may receive random visits from her child's caseworker. If she is in violation of any of the rules, she has to coach her child and make sure her home is in order so that when the Social Worker arrives, she appears to be a law-abiding citizen of the system she is benefiting from. A woman on Section 8 may have an illegal live-in boyfriend who is a violation of the guidelines that qualify her to receive Section 8 assistance. For this reason, she has to stay on high alert because if she gets a sudden visit from her caseworker and her boyfriend is found in her house, she will lose her benefits. This means that such a woman is a part of several demonic systems that the enemy is using to bind her. Again, these are examples of bondage.

In every system, there is a language or a dialect. Sure, in the United States, most of us speak English, however, there are many dialects in the United States. Google defines "dialect" as: "a particular form of a language that is peculiar to a specific region or social group." This means there are many derivations of English. I was born and raised in Mississippi, therefore, I have a thick Southern accent. Additionally, in the South, we have a dialect that is slightly different from Northern dialect. In the welfare system, there are dialects that are customary to that system. How do I know? Again, I was brought up under that system. When I spoke against that system as a child, I was speaking a different dialect from my peers. This brought me unfavorable attention from the people I'd spoken it to. This wasn't because they were bad people; it was because I was speaking a dialect that they did not understand. When people don't understand you, they say things like, "You think you're better than us." While the accusation is unfounded and untrue, the person speaking is attempting to enforce the laws of the system he or she is submitted to. If there is no law to enforce, people start saying how they think you're thinking versus actually accusing you. For example, a police officer who is determined to arrest a person, but does not have legal standing to do so may falsely accuse the person. He may say, "You think you're smarter than me." While this is not true, he believes the words that he has just spoken, and for this reason, he may trump up charges against that person. This is why we have a court system. That person can take the matter to court and place it before a judge. A lawyer is someone who specializes in a particular system (law, civil matters, immigration). The lawyer of the accused would examine the case, come to court and use the very same law that the officer is using to condemn the defendant to exonerate him.

The point is, it's okay to pass through the welfare system, utilizing it only when you need to, but it is demonic to make that system your system because the principles of the welfare system go against the system of Heaven. John 10:10 reads, "The thief comes only to steal and kill and destroy. I came that they may have life and have it abundantly." Living beneath God's best for you is a violation of His system. It goes without saying that most of us are living beneath God's system, but everyone who lives under the system of Heaven is not a criminal. Let me explain.

A child is not subject to most of the laws in the United States until that child gets to an age where he or she can understand those laws. For example, a two-year-old will not be arrested for stealing a bag of chips. Instead, the parents of the two-year-old may be required to pay for the chips. This is because the toddler is too young to understand what he or she has done. For this reason, the child in question is not a criminal. The same applies in the Kingdom. Even though we are adults physically, it does not mean that we are adults spiritually. For example, a new believer does not understand a lot of what God requires him to do because he is a babe in Christ. As such, he cannot be a criminal. Now, once he's mature enough to understand the things of God, he is responsible for what he knows and what he does not know. Not reading the Bible or going to church will not exempt him from the standards that God has placed on him at that stage in his development.

Just as there is a welfare system, there is a warfare system. This means that warfare is not a random, disorganized attack; it is a well-thought-out, systematic attack against a believer. The system of warfare is a system designed to stop a system. For example, we can engage in warfare against the enemy, meaning, we are working towards destroying his works, or better yet, his systems. To do this, however, we must be strategic. We can't pray sloppy, emotional prayers against a system and expect it to come down. We understand that his ultimate goal in the believer's life is to kill, steal, and destroy. If we become emotional in an attack, we'll focus on what he's trying to steal, rather than how he's trying to steal it and whatever legal access he has to it. Satan specializes in legalities. He's the king of legalism. He understands that he can legally dwell in darkness or, better yet, sin. For this reason, he designs strategies to get darkness into the hearts of believers. This is why God instructs us in Ephesians 4:27 to give no place to the enemy. This means that we are able to provide a place for the enemy. Other translations (paraphrased) say don't give the devil a foothold or don't give the devil an opportunity. In other words, giving place to the devil is extending an opportunity for him to operate or set up systems in your life. Please understand that when the enemy is allowed to work in a believer's life, he will start attacking every godly system in operation in that believer's life. For example, if the believer is a faithful tither and does not have an ungodly relationship with his or her money, that believer is open to receive the blessings of God. Nevertheless, the believer needs to know how to access God's blessings and because many believers lack knowledge in this arena, they continue to live beneath God's standard for them. This is because many believers are faithful givers who still live under and give into an ungodly system. Systems aren't broken by money; they are broken in the heart. You can throw money at the right system, but still live under the wrong system. This means that you can give out of your abundance into the system of Heaven, but still pay monthly dues to live in the system of darkness. This is why Jesus said the woman who'd given out of her poverty had given more than those who'd given out of their abundance. Mark 12:41-44 (ESV) reads, "And he sat down opposite the treasury and watched the people putting money into the offering box. Many rich people put in large sums. And a poor widow came and put in two small copper coins, which make a penny. And he called his disciples to him and said to them, 'Truly, I say to you, this poor widow has put in more than all those who are contributing to the offering box. For they all contributed out of their abundance, but she out of her poverty has put in everything she had, all she had to live on.'" What Jesus was saying was that she bankrupted her system and gave everything that she had into the Kingdom of God. This is also why Elijah had the widow to sow into him first. He was bringing her under a different system because the system that she was under had been cursed. The story is found in 1 Kings 7:8-16 and it reads, "Then the word of the Lord came to him, "'Arise, go to Zarephath, which belongs to Sidon, and dwell there. Behold, I have commanded a widow there to feed you.' So he arose and went to Zarephath. And when he came to the gate of the city, behold, a widow was there gathering sticks. And he called to her and said, 'Bring me a little water in a vessel, that I may drink.' And as she was going to bring it, he called to her and said, 'Bring me a morsel of bread in your hand.' And she said, 'As the Lord your God lives, I have nothing baked, only a handful of flour in a jar and a little oil in a jug. And now I am gathering a couple of sticks that I may go in and prepare it for myself and my son, that we may eat it and die.' And Elijah said to her, 'Do not fear; go and do as you have said. But first make me a little cake of it and bring it to me, and afterward make something for yourself and your son. For thus says the Lord, the God of Israel, 'The jar of flour shall not be spent, and the jug of oil shall not be empty, until the day that the Lord sends rain upon the earth.' And she went and did as Elijah said. And she and he and her household ate for many days. The jar of flour was not spent, neither did the jug of oil become empty, according to the word of the Lord that he spoke by Elijah."

What happened in this story? Elijah had her to stop sowing into a failed system. He had her to apply the principles of first-fruits and sow into a Kingdom system. When she did this, her cup started running over.

The warfare system is a system of war. Google defines "war" as: *a state of armed conflict between different nations or states or different groups within a nation or state.* Google defines "fare" as: *perform in a specified way in a particular situation or over a particular period of time.* This means that warfare is a specific or strategic plan designed to assist a state, group or nation during a time of conflict. This plan is not enforced one, but is enforced or engaged over a particular period of time (season). We must understand the reason warfare has to be practiced for specific amounts of time and the reason is, some systems we live under have been in place for hundreds of years. Our ancestors lived under those systems, our grandparents lived under those systems, and our parents lived under those systems. Therefore, those systems have become our default actions; they are what we consider to be normal. To break those systems, we must implore a different system consistently for a certain period of time. Remember, it generally takes 17-21 days to break a habit, but it can take years to break a system that's been in place for centuries.

The welfare system is Satan's warfare system. It is an act of terrorism against the body of Christ. Let me reiterate this again: I'm not talking about a person being on public aid; I'm talking about a person being submitted to that system, meaning, that person has no plans to ever stop receiving public aid. When a person goes under the government of the welfare system, that person will learn to value that system, meaning, he or she will make an idol out of that system. For this reason, if you ever speak against the welfare system to someone who does not want to come out from under it, that person will not only get offended, but he or she will place a label on you. That label represents a file. We all place labels on people, and these labels help us to identify how we want to respond and deal with each person. For example, there are some people you may be quiet around because of a system that's in place in their lives. You understand that if you speak around them, they will hear your dialect and realize that you are not a part of their systems. This means that you have placed a label on them and this is not necessarily bad. It can be wisdom in a lot of cases. Then again, there are some people who you are not quiet around, but you're not necessarily your goofy self around. You may be professional around them because of a system you've seen in place in their lives. This doesn't mean you're being pretentious; it means that you can speak several dialects. Lastly, there are some people you are yourself around. This is because those people are familiar with or submitted to the same system that you are submitted to.

The welfare system is a system of lack, slothfulness and dependency. It is settling down under a demonic system that Satan has designed to keep believers from ascending into their wealthy places. Sure, we can say that it's the world's system and that's true, however, the enemy never designs a weapon to bind people who are already bound. He understands that whatever systems he develops and binds the world with, the believers who have not sanctified themselves or, better yet, separated themselves from the world will fall subject to those systems. They will then bring them into the church and began to bring people out of the church and into the world. This is the opposite of evangelism; it is called conformation. Romans 12:2 reads, "Do not be conformed to this world, but be transformed by the renewal of your mind, that by testing you may discern what is the will of God, what is good and acceptable and perfect" (ESV).

Raven grew up under the welfare system and she'd become a criminal of that system. For this reason, she developed, mastered, and exercised the cunning and manipulative ways of a criminal. Those ways bled over into her relationships. Remember the adage: *there's no honor amongst thieves.* This means that even a thief's children are not exempt from his or her dishonor. Amazingly enough, dishonor is a system as well. It is a demonic system designed to work against the system of honor. Raven made herself a part of that system and she paid greatly for it.

Remember to only submit yourself to godly systems. Do not engage in the systems of this world, otherwise, you'll receive the results of this world. Raven called herself a believer, but who would believe her after examining the fruit in her life? She submitted to the wrong system and she used that system against her friends, who happen to be godly women submitted to an entirely different system. God's system is the governing system; it is like the federal government of the spirit realm. This means that the enemy's system cannot override God's system, but must instead, submit to it when confronted. What Raven did to her friends rendered her a criminal in the system that her friends were submitted to. Eventually, God's system sprung into action and Raven ended up reaping what she had sown.

Chapter 5

Apple Sauce

Satan likes to mimic God; most of us are aware of this. For everything that God has created, Satan has unleashed a counterfeit. It goes without saying that the purpose of the counterfeit is to deceive the people of God and to ensnare them in one of Satan's many traps. Whatever it is that we desire, Satan uses that thing to bait us into his will. If we could see in the realm of the spirit, we'd see so many enslaved believers — people who appear to be moving, but are really limited in their movements by their lack of knowledge, iniquities, associations and beliefs. We'd see believers who appeared to be caught in mousetraps, locked in small cages and roaming around deserted islands, going in circles. Amazingly enough, every bound person can feel the frustration of their limitations, even though they don't necessarily see them. And when humans feel frustrated, they look for ways to free themselves.

The pressure was starting to mount and Edith was beginning to feel it. Nevertheless, she'd made up her mind that she would take her lover's secret with her to her grave, even though the three angry Russian soldiers standing in front of her were overly determined to extract it from her. Edith tried to adjust herself in her chair, but the arm and leg restraints made it very difficult for her to move. "Tell us where Vadim Petrov is!" shouted one soldier. The soldier proudly and angrily marched around Edith's chair with his hands gripped firmly behind his back. "If you do not tell us where he is, we will have to kill you! That's not what you want; is it? You're too pretty to die so young." Edith ignored the soldier's rant. She lowered her head all the more, allowing her dreadlocks to cover her face. She loved Vadim and if she had to die to prove her love for him, she was willing to do just that.

Without warning, Edith felt a pain in the right side of her neck. She knew this pain. One of the soldiers had injected her, once again, with some clear liquid he kept in a small needle. Seconds later, Edith could feel what she believed to be truth serum, starting to take effect.

How did Edith get caught up with the Russian government and who was Vadim? The story started two years ago when Edith was working at a bank. A well-respected loan officer, Edith had it all — good looks, a budding career, a new house and two young children from her first marriage. A recent divorcee, Edith was determined to get back in the dating game. Even though she had two children, Edith's ex-husband, Omar, had gotten custody of their sons: seven-year-old Omar, Jr. and four year old, Oscar. Nevertheless, Edith was confident she'd get them back, after all, she was a prayerful woman. She'd told any and everyone who'd listen that the judge who'd granted custody of her children to her ex was the woman she believed to be responsible for Omar's sudden decision to divorce her. According to Edith, she'd woken up late one night and discovered that Omar wasn't lying next to her. When she went looking for him, she found the patio door slightly open in the kitchen. She made her way to the sliding doors and before she could touch them, she heard Omar's voice. He was on his cell phone speaking with a woman he kept referring to as Marissa. Edith could hear the woman's voice, but she couldn't necessarily hear what she was saying, nevertheless, it was obvious that Omar was having an affair. After all, it was three o'clock in the morning. Not long after this, Omar left Edith and filed for divorce. The judge who oversaw their divorce, ironically enough, was named Marissa and Edith was more than sure she as the same Marissa who Omar had been up late speaking with that night.

"Excuse me, Ms. Doyle. There's a Vadim Petrov outside to

see you," said Julia, Edith's assistant. "Send him in," said Edith as she started to sort through the files on her desk. "Ah, here you are," said Edith. "Have a seat," she said, pointing to the chair on the opposite side of her desk. "Just one second." Edith spun around in her chair and started going through one of the file cabinets behind her. Suddenly, she pulled out a single piece of paper before gracefully spinning her chair back around, but this time, she made eye contact with Vadim. Vadim was a tall, handsome Russian man with a medium build and very little pigment in his skin. His green eyes seemed to perfectly highlight his honey blonde hair and his full pink lips. "Wow," said Edith. She'd never dated outside her race before and she'd never been interested in dating anyone outside her race, but there was something about Vadim that made her want to throw all caution to the wind. "I'm sorry. What did you say?" asked Vadim as he leaned forward in his seat. His eyes were mesmerizing and his accent made him even more appealing. "I'm sorry. Here's the paperwork you requested," said Edith, handing the document to Vadim. "What paperwork?" asked Vadim. "I didn't ask for any paperwork. I came in to apply for a loan. I want to open a school for pilots. I was a teacher at an aviation school in Russia for five years, and I've worked as a private pilot here in the United States for the last eight years. Now, I want to open my own school in the U.S. and that's why I'm here." Edith was embarrassed. Normally, she had her paperwork ready, but it was obvious she'd gotten him confused with someone else. "That wasn't you who called earlier? Wait. Of course, that wasn't you," said Edith, remembering that the caller didn't have an accent. "My apologies. What can I do for you?"

Mr. Petrov proceeded to tell his story again. He couldn't help but notice how engaged Edith seemed to be. She hadn't lost eye contact with him and it was obvious, at times, that she was daydreaming. "Forgive my English. I hope you don't mind me to say this, but you are beautiful — black woman! You are beautiful black woman. I never dated black woman before." Edith was caught off guard. Normally, a statement like that would have offended her, but Vadim's gorgeous smile made him easy to forgive. "No, you're okay. Thank you," said Edith as she lowered her head in an attempt to hide her smile. Vadim started staring at Edith all the more. "Eh! I know who you are! You are that beautiful woman from Cosby movie — right? The movie that you know ... it came on everyday when I was a boy! You are ... you are ..." Edith stared at Vadim as he attempted to remember the name of the Cosby Show character he was referring to. She already knew, however, what he wanted to say. "Lisa Bonet? The woman who played Denise Huxtable on the Cosby Show," responded Edith. Vadim's face lit up and it looked as if all of the blood in his body had suddenly rushed to his face. "Yes!" he screamed. "That is you? Yes! That is you! You are Denise!" Edith smiled and grabbed a tissue to wipe her face. In his excitement, Vadim had sprayed her with his saliva when he'd screamed. "Passionate man I see," said Edith. "No, Mr. Petrov. I'm not Denise. My name is Edith." Nevertheless, Vadim was unrelenting. "No, no, no. You lie to me. I am very good at remembering faces. You are beautiful black Cosby woman. Don't worry. I will keep your secret. It is our secret now." Edith chuckled. "Seriously, that's not me, but I do have another meeting in 15 minutes, so I'd better collect some information from you so we can get the ball rolling on that loan of yours."

After the meeting, Edith was more than determined to ensure that Vadim got the loan he was applying for, even though he wasn't necessarily qualified for it. Vadim called Edith's office over the next few weeks to check on the status of his application and Edith insisted that the secretary put all his calls through to her. Eight weeks after he'd filed the application, Edith called to tell him he'd been approved. Excited, Vadim rushed to the office to sign the rest of the paperwork. Before leaving, he asked Edith out on a date and even though this went against the bank's rules and her moral code as a Christian, Edith happily accepted his offer. "Friday at seven," she said, repeating Vadim's words. "See you there."

It was Friday night and Edith was waiting near the front entrance of Vitaly's, a popular Russian restaurant in uptown New York. Vadim was running a little late and Edith was beginning to feel anxious. Additionally, it didn't take her long to realize that she was overdressed, wearing a long, fitted evening gown with a matching scarf draped around her neck. Everyone else heading in the restaurant seemed to be clothed in semi-casual attire, plus, the music in the restaurant was loud; it was really loud. One man bumped Edith as he tried to make his way through the restaurant's front door. "Excuse you!" shouted Edith, noticing that the man hadn't apologized. The rude stranger turned to look at Edith, but before he could say a word, Vadim appeared. "Is there a problem?" Seeing Vadim, the strange man made his way on through the doors. "No, everything's fine," said Edith. "Some people are just rude." Vadim took Edith by the hand and gently spun her around. "No, you are not Denise Huxtable," he said. "I don't remember Denise having such a wonderful butt." Edith giggled. "Enough of that," she said. "What is this place?" Vadim appeared to be surprised by her question. "What is this place?! What? You don't know Vitaly's? You have not lived until you've eaten Russian food! Come! I show you!" Vadim took Edith by the hand and led her into the restaurant.

It was very obvious to Edith that the restaurant doubled

as a nightclub. Nevertheless, it did have a little more class than a traditional nightclub, plus, the restaurant part was separate from the area where the people went to dance. All the better, Vadim requested that the waitress seat them in an outdoor seating area.

The waitress led Vadim and Edith outside into a nice private area. The night air seemed to have a hint of a breeze and the sounds of the music had gotten faint. Vadim and Edith had their own private patio and Edith was starting to feel as if she wasn't overdressed. "Are you cold?" asked Vadim. "If you are cold, I can go to my car to get my jacket." Vadim's accent wasn't too thick. It was obvious that he'd been in the United States for a long time. "No," said Edith. "The weather is perfect. Tonight is perfect."

For the rest of the night, Vadim and Edith discussed a lot of things, including their childhoods. According to Vadim, he'd grown up in Saint Petersburg, Russia in a small farming community. He'd grown up very poor so he'd joined the Russian Air Force three days after his eighteenth birthday. Nevertheless, Vadim didn't want to discuss too much about his former military career or his family. It was obvious to Edith that Vadim had experienced something traumatic while in the Air Force because every time she brought up his former military career, he would look around before answering her. He would then lean forward and say in his lowest tone, "I do not wish to discuss that, okay? Please." This happened three times before Edith decided to leave the matter alone.

Edith told Vadim that she was divorced, but she did not tell him about her sons. She wasn't sure how he'd react, plus, they were a new couple, so in Edith's mind, there was no need to tell him everything about her past as well. Edith ate Russian food for the first time and loved it. After they finished eating, Vadim insisted that the couple go into the nightclub area and dance a little bit. Edith hadn't danced in years, but she reluctantly agreed.

Vadim surprised Edith on the dance floor. He didn't dance as awful as she'd expected him to dance. "Not bad for Russian man — eh? You like how I dance?" Edith smiled. "Not bad," she said. "Not bad at all." When a jazz-like song came on, Vadim pulled Edith close to him and the two began to slow dance. In Vadim's arms, Edith felt safe; she felt wanted, and she felt beautiful. "Sexy woman," Vadim said as he lowered his hands, placing them on Edith's derriere. Edith reached around and grabbed Vadim's hands and pulled them up to the small of her back. Nevertheless, she didn't utter a word. Vadim lowered his hands three more times and each time Edith responded by redirecting his hands to the small of her back.

It was Sunday morning and Edith was unusually chipper at church. She seemed to have a glow to her and most people noticed. Edith was a door-greeter at her church and she always appeared to be militant, unfriendly and focused. Her greetings never sounded friendly; they'd always sounded scripted and forced. Nevertheless, on this sunny Sunday morning, Edith was friendly. "Good morning!" she said as the members of Greater Mountainside Baptist Church poured through the doors. She'd even hugged a few people.

During service time, Edith listened as Pastor Winston Mabry taught about the dangers of unforgiveness. "Hmph," Edith grunted a few times. "You weren't the one married to Omar," she whispered under her breath. The other door greeter, Mrs. Hampton, heard Edith, but she did not utter a word. She didn't want to offend her, nor did she want Edith to go back to behaving the way she'd behaved in the past. For this reason, she chuckled and said, "I know what you mean. It ain't always easy." Edith agreed and went back to her duties.

Three months had passed since Edith met Vadim and she was happier than she'd ever been, even though Vadim was a very private man who had not taken her out much over the course of their relationship. Edith excused this by reminding herself that Vadim was in the process of building his own flight school, plus, he was obviously protecting her from some dark facet of his past. Howbeit, it was a Saturday night and Vadim seemed to be in a different kind of mood. He wanted to go back to Vitaly's with Edith and he asked if she'd wear the same dress she'd worn the first time they'd gone out. "No," said Edith. "I'll wear something even nicer."

Just like the first time, Vadim was late. When he did arrive, the couple went inside and the waitress took them back to the same spot they'd dined in the first time they'd gone out. This time, Vadim seemed more interested in Edith than he'd ever seemed. He complimented her red, fitted gown and her beautiful smile. He even complimented her long locks. The entire date felt perfect to Edith, and for this reason, she felt comfortable enough to ask him about his future plans.

Edith: So, do you plan to get married someday?

Vadim: Pardon me?

Edith: Do you plan to get married?

Vadim: Are you proposing marriage to me? I am flattered, but in my country, the man asks.

Edith: No, I'm not proposing. I was asking do you ever plan to get married?

Vadim: Oh. I never thought about it. Why you ask such complicated questions?

Edith: It's not complicated; it's just a question.

Vadim: Well, maybe. My parents have been married for 42 years, so I like marriage. Marriage is good.

Edith: What about children? Do you want children?

Vadim: No. Children are too complicated. My parents have ten children. I have many nieces and nephews. They are like my children to me. Why do you ask this question?

Edith: I'm just curious. Look. Vadim, there's something I haven't told you. I have two small children by my ex, Omar, but they live with their father.

Vadim: I know.

Edith: You know? How?

Vadim: You have Facebook page. I went to your Facebook page and looked at your pictures. You have strong sons. Very nice-looking.

Edith: Thank yo, but why didn't you say anything?

Vadim: Because you didn't say anything. It is none of my business unless you make it my business. I have secrets too, you know?

Edith: Like what?

Vadim: If I told you, they wouldn't be secrets — eh?

Edith lowered her head and smiled. "Touche," she said.

Over the next few weeks, Edith noticed that Vadim's calls had slowed down and when the couple did talk, he always seemed rushed. She blamed herself for this sudden shift in their relationship. She'd kept her sons a secret and now it was obvious that Vadim didn't trust her. Howbeit, Edith was in love with Vadim; she was in love with the idea of being his wife, having babies with him and maybe even moving to Russia someday. During this time, she'd stopped harassing Omar and she'd even stopped calling her sons. She wanted to focus all of her attention on her relationship with Vadim.

One night, Edith called Vadim and just like he'd done every night for the last month or so, Vadim said he needed to call her back. "Okay," said Edith. "I wanted to see if you would like to come over to my house and spend some time with me." Suddenly, Vadim's voice changed; he didn't sound sleepy anymore. "Your house? I can come to your house?" Vadim's questions sounded almost child-like. "Yes," said Edith. "I'll text you my address."

When Vadim arrived, he appeared to be wearing a military-style outfit. It was obvious that he'd just gotten a haircut. He looked even more handsome than Edith could remember. "Have a seat," said Edith, observing how impressed Vadim was with her house. Edith thought to herself that Vadim likely thought she lived in the ghetto, but instead, Edith had a nice, cozy and somewhat elegant home situated in the suburbs of Manhattan. Vadim didn't sit down. Instead, he started giving himself a tour. "This is your house?" he asked, walking into the kitchen. Edith followed him, smiling at his reaction. "Yes. This is my house." Vadim was noticeably impressed. "Wow. This is nice house. Now, I believe that you are Denise Huxtable again." Edith laughed. "No, my name is Edith Doyle; I've told you this like a thousand times. Follow me, please." Edith led Vadim back into the living room, but it was obvious that he wanted to see the entire house, so she decided to give him a tour.

Edith had a three bedroom, single-story home with an amazing open floor plan. She led Vadim into each room, describing what it was. Finally, the two entered Edith's bedroom. The bedroom was very elegant and spacious. Edith's beautifully decorated king-sized bed sat in the center of her large bedroom. It was covered by a wine-colored silk-like comforter and several gold and wine pillows to match it. "I like this room," said Vadim as he walked closer to the bed. Vadim ran his fingers across the comforter. "This is nice," he said as he slowly turned around to face Edith. "And you are very beautiful to me," he whispered. That's when the couple started to kiss.

What felt like a surge of electricity began to flood Edith's body. She'd never felt anything like that before. Vadim kissed her like he loved her. He kissed her as if they were kissing at the altar after their vows had been exchanged. Edith imagined that they were newly married and kissing for the first time as Mr. and Mrs. Petrov. The kissing carried on and the couple found themselves lying on the bed, kissing passionately. That night, Edith allowed Vadim to experience her; that night, the couple had sex for the first time.

It was a month later and Edith was more than "in love" with Vadim; she was obsessed with him. Even though Vadim still didn't call her a lot, he did make it a point to visit her every other day. Of course, the relationship had become a hot and heavy sexual relationship, but to Edith, the two were married — just not on paper. She would often refer to Vadim as her husband anytime she spoke of him, and this confused many of her family members and co-workers. Nevertheless, most people reasoned within themselves that she'd likely married Vadim in a private ceremony, after all, she was a very private person. One thing that did bother Edith was the fact that she didn't know where Vadim lived. He was even more private than she was, so one day, Edith decided to follow Vadim home after he'd left her house. She had another car parked in her garage that Vadim had never seen. It was a small, white Sedan; there was nothing fancy about it.

Edith followed Vadim to an apartment and immediately, noticed a few men standing outside who appeared to be wearing military clothing. Vadim seemed to get noticeably uncomfortable when he spotted the men, nevertheless, he was able to avoid them altogether and make his way into the apartment's entrance. As he closed the door, Edith noticed that one of the guys threw his cigarette to the ground, stepped on it, and then, made his way inside the building. The other two guys appeared to be looking out for something. Without warning, Edith heard a knocking sound coming from her left. She turned to see some guy wearing a Russian style hat knocking on her window. Afraid, Edith suddenly motioned for the guy to move out of her way, and then, she suddenly pulled off.

Edith found herself worrying about Vadim. As she drove home, she allowed her imagination to run rampant. Was Vadim a spy, or even worse, were the guys outside his apartment spies? Who exactly was Vadim Petrov and what did he want with her? "I sure hope he's okay," Edith said as she pulled into her driveway. After she was settled into her house, Edith decided to call Vadim, but he did not answer his phone. She waited another five minutes and called him again. Still no answer. Edith began to panic. What if those guys had done something to Vadim? What if the Russian government was after him? Everything started making sense to Edith. Vadim had been a private man since she'd known him, plus, he didn't like talking about his military career. He didn't like talking about his family either. Lastly, the two times they'd been to Vitaly's, Edith had noticed how alert Vadim appeared to be. He kept looking around and scanning the faces of anyone who passed them by.

Ten minutes had gone by since Edith called Vadim. Worried, she decided to call him again.

Vadim: Hello. What can I do for you?

Edith: Are you okay? Is everything okay?

Vadim: Yes. Why do you ask me this question?

Edith: I was just worried about you.

Vadim: Why do you worry? Do you know something I should know?

Edith: No, of course not. I was just worried. I wanted to make sure you'd made it home safely.

Vadim: Yes. I am preparing to return to Russia.

Edith: Russia? Why?

Vadim: My mother is not well. I need to go and care for her, so I will not speak with you again.

Edith was shocked. She loved Vadim and she'd already made so many plans for a life with him.

Edith: Why? Are you breaking up with me?

Vadim: Breaking up? Noooo ... We are not a couple, Edith. We just have fun, you know?

Edith: Fun? What are you talking about Vadim? I thought you said you loved me.

Vadim: You were naked. What do you want me to say?

Edith: Vadim, what's going on?

Vadim: Do you think I could marry you? Do you think I could marry a black girl? Ha! You are funny! That's why I like you.

Edith: Talk to me, Vadim. This is not you. What is really going on?

Vadim: I need to care for my mother. Please go and marry someone else. I cannot marry you.

With that, Vadim suddenly hung up the phone. Edith was heartbroken, however, she was sure that there was another reason behind Vadim's sudden change of tone. She called Vadim back several times, but he would not answer his phone. Worried, Edith drove back over to Vadim's apartment. This time, there were no men outside and Edith was in her own car. Suddenly, her phone rang. It was Vadim.

Vadim: Is that you outside my apartment? I see your car. Is that you?

Edith: I drove here to make sure you are okay. I was worried.

Vadim: Edith, do not come to my house — ever! How do you know where I live? I never showed you!

Edith: It's okay, Vadim. I only want to help. You can tell me anything.

Vadim: I told you to leave me alone. I do not want to

marry a black girl! I do not want to marry you, Edith! Never come to my house again ... please!

Vadim's voice sounded desperate. Edith was sure that he was under some type of duress. She was sure that Vadim didn't mean anything he'd said.

That night, Edith went to sleep and found herself having a dream. In the dream, she was holding a beautiful bi-racial newborn baby girl. The baby appeared to be no more than a month old. Suddenly, there was a knock on the door. Holding her baby firmly, Edith answered the door and in came three Russian spies. "Who are you and why are you walking in my house?!" screamed Edith as the men began to walk through her house as if they were looking for something or someone. Suddenly, one of the men went into Edith's room. A second later, he screamed, "He's in here!" The other two men rushed to the room and they all arrested Vadim. Edith screamed and kicked at the men as they escorted Vadim down the hall and out the living room door. Before the car pulled away, Vadim somehow lowered the window and said to Edith, "I will always love you. Take care of our daughter and do not try to rescue me. This is my fight; it is not your fight. I must do this alone. If I don't go, you won't be safe; our daughter won't be safe. So, I must go." With that, Edith suddenly woke up. It was all making sense to her now. Vadim broke up with her to protect her. He was obviously very much still a part of the Russian military or something had happened when he was in the military that had gotten him into a lot of trouble.

Edith was determined to fight for Vadim. Obviously, he didn't realize her strength; he didn't know what she'd gone through and Edith wanted him to know that she was willing to fight for him. Nevertheless, Vadim's phone was now disconnected.

Over the next few weeks, Edith's job performance grew from bad to worse. Dark bags began to form under her eyes and she became even crankier than she'd been before she met Vadim. It was clear to everyone who saw her that she was in a downward spiral, but no one dared to approach her, after all, Edith was known to be ruthless, dramatic, and overly emotional. She waited day after day, hoping to receive a call from Vadim, but it didn't happen.

One day, Edith decided to pull Vadim's application. She wrote down the address of the site he was using to build his new aviation school. She hoped that someone would be at the site and that person would be able to fill her in about Vadim. She was sure he was in Russia, but she was even more sure that he had not abandoned his project.

When Edith arrived at Vadim's worksite, she was

surprised to see several men and women working on a nearly completed building. There was a very impressive runway on the property, and there were three small freshly painted planes parked at the end of the runway. The sound of machinery and running motors made the site very noisy. As if the site wasn't noisy enough, there was a large field that some kids were using to play soccer. Edith hated noise, but she was determined to find out whatever came of Vadim. "Can I help you?" Edith turned around and noticed a rather large male. Judging by the man's accent, it was clear to Edith that he was Russian. Not wanting to draw any attention to herself, Edith looked at the folder she was carrying. She wanted to appear to be at the site for professional reasons. "I am looking for Vadim Petrov," she said, looking back at the large man. "Who are you?" asked the man. Edith told him that she was the loan officer from the bank that Vadim had received his loan from. "He should be ..." The man stopped to look at his watch. "He should be landing in about five minutes." Edith was surprised. "Here?" she asked. The man nodded his head in affirmation. "On that runway right there," he said pointing to the longest of all the runways. "Wait, I think I see him coming now." Edith's heart began to race. She wasn't expecting to see Vadim; she'd come to the site to find out where he was and how she could contact him. Howbeit, there she was ... watching Vadim make his ascension in a rather large plane. Five minutes later, the plane was landed and Vadim emerged from the it. The large guy walked over to Vadim and started talking to him while pointing at Edith. Vadim looked annoyed. He shook his head in affirmation and Edith could hear him saying, "I'll take care of it."

Vadim was wearing a uniform that made him look even more handsome than Edith could remember. The sun seemed to make his beautiful green eyes glisten all the more. He looked like a model on the runway as he made his way towards Edith.

Vadim: What are you doing here?! Are you crazy?! I told you to leave me alone. Why you come to my school?!
Edith: I wanted to check on you. Listen, before you say another word — I know.
Vadim: You know what? What do you know? That you're crazy? I wish you would have told me.
Edith: Stop Vadim. I know about the Russian spies that are after you. I know about your government's plans to assassinate you. I know, baby, and it's okay. I'm here for you. Let me be here for you.
Vadim: What?! You really are crazy woman!

With that, Vadim gestured to the large man who, by now, was already heading in their direction. "Please remove this crazy woman off my property!" Vadim screamed to the man as Edith attempted to follow him. Suddenly, Edith could feel her legs dangling from the ground. The large man had lifted her from her feet and was now carrying her towards her car. Edith continued to yell at Vadim, "Let me be here for you, baby! You do not have to protect me! I can help you!" Nevertheless, Vadim got onto one of the smaller planes and it was clear to Edith that he was about to take off again.

On the way home, Edith found herself trying to figure out how she could help Vadim. Suddenly, she remembered that Vadim had another confirmed flight to Saint Petersburg, Russia coming up. He'd bought the ticket a couple of months ago from her computer and he claimed that he was going back to Russia on June 11th to celebrate Russia Day with his parents. There were only four days left before the 11th and Edith knew she needed to move quickly, after all, she worried that Vadim would not be able to return to the United States.

Three days later, Edith found herself standing in her bathroom. Anxious and frustrated, Edith took a deep breath and pulled the small white plastic stick from a cup. It was now around nine o'clock that evening and she could not get the events from earlier out of her mind. Why didn't Vadim trust her? She laid the pregnancy test next to three other pregnancy tests that were neatly lined up on her counter. She didn't want to look at the results of the last test just yet, so she went into the hallway and took a deep breath. All of the other tests were saying the same thing and Edith did not want to believe what they were saying. Nevertheless, there was one test left and this one was the most popular brand of them all. It was supposed to be the most accurate one of them all as well. Edith made her way back into the bathroom and stood in front of the tests. She lifted up the last test she'd taken. Unlike the other tests, this particular test didn't show one or two lines; its screen would read "pregnant" or "not pregnant." The other three tests had to be wrong, Edith reasoned within her heart. She looked down at the test she was holding and read the screen. "Not Pregnant." The news was horrifying to Edith. She wanted to be pregnant by Vadim so badly. Angered, Edith threw the test against the wall, shattering it, before collapsing to the floor. She wept angrily for several minutes before heading to her computer. Vadim had listed his parents' Russian phone number in his application for a loan and Edith was determined to do a reverse search on the number to get their address. Ten minutes later, she had the Petrov's address and she was online looking for flights to Russia. She was sure that if she followed Vadim to Russia, he would see how much she loved him. "This is crazy," said Edith. "Am I losing my mind?"

Edith made her way to her bed. She needed to think things

over, after all, this was going to be a major step. Fifteen minutes later, Edith drifted off to sleep. After she was sound asleep, she started having a dream. In the dream, Edith found herself in a Russian cottage holding the baby girl she'd dreamed about previously. "Mom!" A voice broke the silence. "Oscar hit me!" It was her son, Omar. A few seconds later, Oscar came running into the living room, holding a water gun. The two boys started playing and running around the house. They appeared to be very happy. Edith looked at her daughter and said, "I'm gonna call you Emilia." The baby girl smiled at her and then, Edith heard Vadim's voice, but she did not see his face. "Thank you for coming with me," he said. "Now, I know you love me." That's when she woke up. It was now after twelve o'clock midnight.

Edith was sure that the dream was prophetic. Her church didn't necessarily believe in modern-day prophecies, but Edith had just experienced a change of heart. She rushed over to her computer and purchased flight tickets for herself and her sons. She then emailed her boss, saying that she was now resigning and would not be coming in the following day. Finally, she grabbed a small tote bag and packed a few clothes for herself in the bag. She then left the house and headed to a nearby Walmart. There, she purchased a few outfits and coats for her sons, along with two more suitcases.

Edith arrived home a little after three in the morning. She was starting to feel tired again, but the excitement of moving to a new country made it near impossible for her to sleep. How would she learn Russian at such a fast pace? She'd already started learning, but she only knew a few words; she needed to learn the language and fast! What would Vadim's parents think of her? How would she and the kids adjust to Russia's cold climates? Suddenly, her phone started vibrating. It was still in the bathroom on the counter next to the sink. Edith's heart leaped. Maybe it was Vadim. Her mind raced as she rushed towards the phone, accidentally hitting her pinky toe against one of the wooden posts on her bed. "Ouch, ouch, ouch!" Edith screamed as she reached for her phone. Looking at the caller identification, Edith found herself feeling enraged.

Edith: What do you want, Omar? And why are you calling me at three in the morning?

Omar: I'm sorry to call you so late — or so early — depending on how you look at it, but I just got a call from your witch friend, talking about she'd seen an ominous vision of you.

Edith: Who? Ms. Javelin?

Omar: I don't know what her name is. I just know she's a witch and I don't appreciate her calling my phone.

Edith: What did she say?

Omar: She just said she woke up from a bad dream about you; she said it was ominous and she needed me to call you and tell you to call her. Why didn't she call you herself?

Edith: She doesn't have this number, Omar. And how many times do I have to tell you, she's not a witch; she's a therapist.

Omar: Therapists give you medicine for yourself, not somebody else. She's a witch. Anyway, get a pen so you can jot down her number.

Edith: Don't bother. I don't consult with her anymore.

Omar: That's good news, but may I ask why?

Edith: You and I are divorced, Omar. I did everything she told me to do and it didn't work. We're divorced.

Omar: Witchcraft only works on witches, the people who seek them and people who are not submitted to God.

Edith: This wasn't witchcraft. Not the first time anyway. The first time, I was trying to fix our marriage. The second time, I was just angry at you because you filed for divorce.

Omar: Like I said — witchcraft. Anyhow, I have to get up early in the morning. I'll pretend that you asked about your sons and I'll tell the boys that you said hi.

Edith: Wait!

Omar: Yes, Edith.

Edith: Can I pick up the kids this Friday?

Omar: Edith, you already know the answer to this. I'm sorry but no! You're not complying with the terms; remember? And why are you suddenly interested in them? You haven't shown much interest in the past.

Edith: I just miss them; that's all. Honestly, I was thinking about doing a little traveling, but I want to see them before I go.

Omar: Where are you going?

Edith: That's not important. Can I see my sons or not?

Omar: No, Edith. You know what you need to do to see the boys. Anyhow, I just called you to tell you about your witch friend. I'll text you her number in a few. Bye Edith.

Omar suddenly disconnected and Edith placed the phone back on the bathroom counter. "Yeah, I know what I need to do," she said, looking at her reflection in the mirror.

Omar felt a little uneasy about Edith's tone. Even though she wasn't super kind, she was a lot nicer than she normally was whenever he spoke with her. He tried to go back to sleep, but he couldn't shake the feeling that something was wrong. "Am I believing a witch?" he asked himself. "How could I believe what a witch says?" Omar laid back down and cut off the lights in his bedroom. Ten minutes later, he sat up again and turned the lights back on. "No, I don't believe that witch, but I do know that something is wrong."

Omar rushed over to his computer and tried to pull up Edith's Facebook page, but could not. "You still have me blocked, I see," he whispered as he logged out of his page.

Omar felt anxious. He was tempted to do something he knew was illegal, but he knew Edith and he needed answers. She was about to do something crazy and he sensed it. Omar took a deep breath. He entered Edith's email and password into Facebook. He remembered it because it was the derivation of both of their sons' names, along with Edith's birth year. She hadn't changed her password because she had never realized that Omar had her password.

Omar typed the last letter of Edith's password and took a deep breath. His finger hovered over the "Enter" button and he knew there was no going back from there. Suddenly, he hit "Enter" and Edith's account opened. Omar went directly to her inbox and that's when he saw that she'd been messaging a guy named Vadim Petrov, but it was obvious that Vadim had blocked her on Facebook, because Omar could not click his picture. Nevertheless, Omar started reading some of the messages. The last message had been sent over a month ago, and in that message, Edith proclaimed her undying love for Petrov and her willingness to go anywhere in the world with him. "I've never experienced anything like this," wrote Edith. There were only two occasions where Vadim had responded to Edith. One of those responses was four months old and it read, "What are you wearing? I want to see you tonight." The next message was a month old and it read, "Leave me alone! I changed my phone number so you could leave me alone! You are crazy!" Omar giggled. "Yeah, that she is," he said, logging out of Edith's account. He then logged into his own account and did a search for Vadim Petrov. There were a lot of listings for the name Vadim Petrov, but it didn't take Omar long to find the one Edith had been writing, after all, she'd uploaded a few of his pictures to her Facebook page. In each picture, it was obvious that Vadim was at Edith's house and he was unaware of the fact that he'd been photographed.

Scrolling through Vadim's posts, Omar could clearly see that he wasn't the type of guy who'd consider marrying any woman outside his race. His entire friends' list consisted of nothing but Caucasians. His posts were laced with racism. As a matter of fact, he had even uploaded a picture of a pinata of then President Barack Obama. There was a rope tied around his neck and a bunch of blindfolded children swinging at him. To his surprise, Edith had even commented on that photo. She'd written, "Ha! Clever!" Omar shook his head in disgust. Nevertheless, he had to redirect his thoughts so he could figure out what was going on with Edith.

According to Vadim's profile, he was from Saint Petersburg, Russia, but he was currently living in New York, New York. He listed his occupation as "Pilot" and he'd recently uploaded pictures of a very impressive building with Petrov's Aviation School on the front. He tagged the photo, "Almost finished!" Omar logged out of his account. "So, let me guess what happened," he mumbled. "You probably went into her office, looking to get a loan. You messed around with her, trying to ensure that you got that loan, and now, she won't leave you alone. Ha! That's catchy. She gave you a loan, now she won't leave you alone," Omar joked. Omar's dry humor helped to relax him a bit. He reasoned with himself that he'd investigate a little further once he woke up, but he needed to get some sleep.

The sound of the alarm pierced the silence and scared Edith. She'd packed her bags and now, it was time for her to put her plan into action. She loaded her car and went back to lock up her house. It was still somewhat dark outside, but the morning light was beginning to shine through. Edith searched her purse and found her passport. She then began to search frantically for her sons' passports. Omar had obviously forgotten to get them from her once they divorced. Edith let out a sigh of relief once she found the boys' passports. Now, all she had to do was to go to the boys' school and wait for them to get off the school bus.

Edith parked near the fenced-in bus lot. She knew that the

man who drove the bus her sons rode on was always frustrated and distracted. For this reason, he would let all of the kids get off the bus, and then, he'd get off the bus five minutes later, after he'd checked the bus to ensure that none of the children were hiding out on it. The kids would rush towards their classes while the driver was still on the bus. There would be no teacher on the lot to guide them.

Edith stood outside her truck and waited for Omar and Oscar to exit the bus. "Omar! Oscar!" she screamed when she saw their faces. The children's faces lit up. "Mommy!" screamed Oscar as he made his way around the fence and towards his mother. Oscar followed behind his big brother. Edith held her index finger close to her mouth. "Shhhh," she said, gesturing for the boys to whisper. "Do you want to come with me? I'm gonna get on an airplane today." The boys both nodded their heads in excitement. "Okay, get in," Edith said as she opened the passenger's side door of her SUV. The boys got into the car. Edith closed the door and rushed back to her side of the vehicle, looking around to see if anyone saw her. One little boy had seen her. He stood near the fence staring at Edith as she placed her index finger over her mouth again, gesturing for him to keep silent. After that, they were on their way to the airport and to their new lives. Three hours later, Edith and the boys were seated on an airplane scheduled to take off in less than fifteen minutes.

Omar owned his own company, so he'd decided to take the day off. He'd gone into the office for a very important meeting earlier, but now, he was back at home, attempting to log into Edith's Facebook account again. Nevertheless, this time, it had been deleted. "Do you want to reactivate your account?" the pop-up read. Suddenly, Omar's phone rung. The call was coming from Edith's job; he recognized the number right away.

Omar: What do you want, Edith?

Amy: Hello, Mr. Doyle?

Omar: Yes, this is Mr. Doyle?

Amy: Hi, you probably don't remember me. I spoke with you a few years ago about your wife, Edith? I'm her co-worker. Remember, I asked you to call me Marissa just in case Edith overheard you talking with me?

Omar: Yeah, I remember you. We spoke late that night, I think it was, because I was asleep when you'd called earlier. I still feel weird about that.

Amy: It's okay. Better safe than sorry, right? After all, my husband understood.

Omar: Awesome. What's going on?

Amy: Well, I know that you and Edith are divorced, but I didn't know who else to call because your number is still the only number she has listed under emergency contacts. Anyhow, Ms. Doyle sent an email to the boss last night saying that she was quitting.

Omar: What?!

Amy: Yeah, and that's not the worst of it. We also received a notification from another bank stating that she'd closed both of her accounts. Mr. Doyle, she's lost a significant amount of weight in a matter of weeks, plus, Mr. Parkinson was going to fire her anyway because we got a complaint from a customer who said he'd been involved with her — you know — sexually, and now, she is harassing him. The guy was threatening to sue the bank.

Omar: Wait! Was his name Petrov? Vadim Petrov?

Amy: Yes, I think so! How did you know?

"I have to go! Thanks! I have to go!" Omar screamed as he grabbed his keys. It was all starting to come together. Edith quitting her job, wanting to get the boys, claiming she was about to do some traveling — it was all coming together! Omar called the boys' school but got no answer. He then jumped inside his car and sped towards the boys' school, weaving through traffic, all the while, attempting to call Edith. Her phone was now disconnected. Omar's heart raced as he drove through red lights and ran stop signs, nearly causing a few accidents. "Come on! Come on!" he said, listening to the school's voicemail. A few minutes later, Omar parked his truck and jumped out of it. He ran into the school, past the office and towards Omar's classroom. The secretary chased behind him, after seeing him run past her office.

The door swung opened to Omar Jr.'s classroom and this startled a few of the children, along with the teacher. "I'm sorry, I'm so sorry. Please tell me that Omar came to class! Where's Omar?!" Omar shouted, looking at Omar Jr.'s empty seat. "I'm sorry, Mr. Doyle," responded Mrs. Whitaker. "He didn't come to class today." The secretary was just starting to catch up with Omar when he took off running again, this time, towards Oscar's class. A minute later, the door to Oscar's classroom swung open and started the children. "I'm sorry!" shouted Omar. "Where's Oscar?! Where's Oscar?!" he said, looking at Oscar's empty seat. "He didn't come to class today, Mr. Doyle," responded Mrs. Juniper. Omar began to panic. He ran again, just as the secretary was catching up to him. "Call the police!" he shouted to the secretary. "My ex-wife kidnapped my boys! Tell them to meet me at the airport!"

Omar got back in his truck and sped towards the airport. With tears in his eyes, he began to pray. "Lord, don't let her take my boys from me! Please don't let her take them!" Twenty-five minutes later, Omar pulled into a parking space at the airport. He ran into the building, but to his surprise, the police were already there waiting for him. Recognizing him immediately, Officer Petrowski rushed over to Omar. He and Omar were dear friends and he knew the situation regarding Edith and Omar. "Calm down, man. We'll get them back. I promise. They are contacting the authorities in Saint Petersburg right now, and I'm confident that they'll nab her as soon as she gets off the plane. We'll get your boys back to you. I promise." Those words were too heavy for Omar. Edith had successfully kidnapped their boys and was on her way to Russia with them. Omar sat on the floor, weeping bitterly and covering his head with his hands. "Please, just get my boys back," he said. "Man, I'm counting on you to get them back. I'm counting on you." Officer Petrowski sat next to Omar on the floor. "I promise you, we will get them back if I have to get on an airplane and go get them myself."

Edith's plane landed without incident, but she noticed a lot of Russian officers heading towards the plane the minute it landed. She told herself that the soldiers were either there for someone else or Vadim had been monitoring her and knew she was landing. She'd often imagined that Vadim had her phone line tapped. After she got off the plane, the officers took her and her sons into custody.

The Russian authorities were getting more and more desperate. After injecting Edith with truth serum into her neck, one of the officers grabbed a spoon and dipped it into a small bowl. Edith was sure that it was poison and she was willing to take it. She wanted to die before the truth serum kicked in. As the spoon got closer to her mouth, Edith lifted her head. She wasn't going to resist death. "Just don't hurt my boys," she said to the officer before she opened her mouth to receive the contents of the spoon. Suddenly, the taste of apple sauce awoke her senses. Edith gagged, spitting the apple sauce out. Suddenly, the officers' uniforms seemed to vanish and Edith realized that she was surrounded by nurses. "She still won't eat," said one of the nurses to the doctor standing nearby. "She keeps telling me not to hurt her boys." The doctor walked towards Edith, leaning into her face. He then pointed a scope at her left eye and said, "This is one of the worst cases of schizophrenia I've ever seen." The nurse agreed. "She'll eat anything, but I don't understand why she is so terrified of apple sauce."

Edith knew why. When she had been married to Omar, she had been a very contentious and jealous wife. She was always afraid that Omar would cheat on her, so she would repeatedly check his phone, follow him around, and call him repeatedly whenever he was at work. Omar took her to church, to counseling and to any place he could think of, trying to get her the help she so desperately needed, but nothing seemed to work. Edith was convinced that she was a victim; she was convinced that Omar was a professional liar who prided himself on making her look crazy.

While married to Omar, Edith became so desperate to control him that she contacted a therapist who also referred to herself as a herbalist. Ms. Javelin promised Edith that she could make Omar a better man and force him to stop cheating. She also told her that she had a special formula that would cause any woman who kissed Omar, outside of Edith, to become gravely ill. She asked Edith what Omar's favorite food was, and to that, Edith responded, "Omar loves apple sauce." The witch then gave Edith a small container. "Put this in his apple sauce," she said. Edith complied, and a few days later, she'd found Omar outside at three in the morning, talking to another woman whom he referred to as Marissa. A few days after that, Omar left Edith and filed for divorce. She later learned that Omar hadn't eaten the apple sauce and the kids swore they hadn't eaten it either. It had simply disappeared from the refrigerator and Edith never knew what came of it. For this reason, she was afraid of apple sauce.

Edith remained institutionalized for more than seven years. When she was finally released, she met and married another guy who was completely unaware of her past. A year later, Roman, Edith's new husband, filed for divorce after she would not stop talking about having been kidnapped by the Russian government. She claimed that the government had taken her sons and turned them against her. She also claimed that she was pregnant when they'd taken her. According to Edith, she'd given birth to a healthy baby girl named Emilia, who the Russian authorities had taken away from her. She believed that a popular bi-racial Russian model named Natalya was actually her daughter. For this reason, she would obsessively watch Natalya's website, shows, interviews and the like. She'd even attempted to contact Natalya, but she had never gotten a response.

Of course, Edith never had a daughter. She'd never even been kidnapped by the Russian authorities. Omar hadn't cheated on Edith and Vadim was simply a man who was sexually curious. He'd never had sex with a Black woman before he met Edith, plus, Edith looked a lot like Denise Huxtable to him. Edith read more into their relationship than what was there.

What exactly happened to Edith? What made her so delusional? Edith had become a witch by association. How is this? She consulted with Ms. Javelin, who undoubtedly was a witch. Edith did what so many Christian women do: she tried to call witchcraft by a different name, hoping that she could deceive God when, in truth, she only ended up deceiving herself. By attempting to perform witchcraft on her husband, Omar, she gave demons the right to attack her. Because Omar was covered by the blood of Jesus, the demons assigned to attack him had no choice but to return to her. Demons don't favor one person over another. They want blood and if they can't get it from the person they are sent to attack, they'll take it from the person who sent them.

By worldly terms, Edith was schizophrenic, but by godly terms, Edith was demonized. Her desire to control her husband was the stronghold that led her into witchcraft. And it's obvious that Edith's issues didn't stem from her marriage to Omar. They likely stemmed from some trauma in her past ... maybe it was parental rejection or rejection she'd suffered while in a previous relationship. Whenever we experience trauma, it is only natural for us to look for ways to protect ourselves from experiencing that trauma again. However, it is necessary for us to forgive the people who've hurt us. Forgiveness gives us access to healing and healing gives us access to knowledge. This means that God will give us the information we need to move forward. After we receive knowledge, we then need understanding. Without understanding, knowledge is just information. Understanding helps us to retain the information we've received; it takes us deeper than mere words spoken or black and white letters on a page. It gives us the answers to the questions that keep us from moving on. Understanding then gives us access to wisdom. Understand this: wisdom has to be intentionally sought; it won't just fall on our laps and start comforting us. God will give us a personal invitation to receive wisdom, but if we do not accept it, the enemy will start to challenge our understanding. From there, he'll get us to receive a different report and once we reject understanding, we officially start progressing towards rebellion which 1 Samuel 15:33 tells us is the same as the sin of witchcraft.

Edith received a painful reminder of what she'd done. The taste of apple sauce was a reminder to her of what she'd attempted to do to her husband. Demons especially love to attack people who identify themselves as Christians because Satan wants to give Christianity a bad name. When we help him do this, we unintentionally ally ourselves with him.

Proverbs 14:1 (ESV): The wisest of women builds her house, but folly with her own hands tears it down.

What then should Edith have done? First and foremost, before she ever considered marriage or being in a relationship with anyone, she should have worked on her relationship with God. She needed healing; she needed deliverance, and it's obvious that she had not sought these things. Instead, she got married and from there, she allowed her past to attack her present. Her present then attacked her future. Please understand that everything we do is a progression into something, whether it be the will of God or the will of Satan. Like most hurting people, she wanted to protect herself from being hurt again, so she tried to control her husband. This opened her up for the Jezebel spirit which, of course, is a spirit closely associated with witchcraft.

Edith's progression into witchcraft was as systematic as our progression into wisdom. It was a step by step process that led her to the foothills of insanity. Her desire to control others ended up costing her her marriage, her children, her freedom, her career, and most of all, her relationship with God. After all, we cannot serve two gods. Again, she should have sought the living God first.

Next, Edith should have intentionally forgiven everyone who has ever hurt her. This would have given her legal access to healing. You cannot receive healing if you do not first forgive the people who've hurt you. Forgiveness is an open invitation to knowledge and understanding; it's like saying to the two that they are welcome into your heart. Remember this: you must invite knowledge and understanding into your heart, but you have to accept wisdom's invitation to receive it. Peter asked Jesus how often we should forgive one another and the Lord gave him a parable.

Matthew 18:23-35 (ESV): "Therefore the kingdom of Heaven may be compared to a king who wished to settle accounts with his servants. When he began to settle, one was brought to him who owed him ten thousand talents. And since he could not pay, his master ordered him to be sold, with his wife and children and all that he had, and payment to be made. So the servant fell on his knees, imploring him, 'Have patience with me, and I will pay you everything.' And out of pity for him, the master of that servant released him and forgave him the debt. But when that same servant went out, he found one of his fellow servants who owed him a hundred denarii, and seizing him, he began to choke him, saying, 'Pay what you owe.' So his fellow servant fell down and pleaded with him, 'Have patience with me, and I will pay you.' He refused and went and put him in prison until he should pay the debt. When his fellow servants saw what had taken place, they were greatly distressed, and they went and reported to their master all that had taken place. Then his master summoned him and said to him, 'You wicked servant! I forgave you all that debt because you pleaded with me. And should not you have had mercy on your fellow servant, as I had mercy on you?' And in anger his master delivered him to the jailers, until he should pay all his debt. So also my Heavenly Father will do to every one of you, if you do not forgive your brother from your heart."

The King James version says that the unforgiving servant was turned over to the tormentors. Who are the tormentors? Demons! Whenever a person chooses not to forgive another person for hurting him or her, that person forfeits his/her right to God's forgiveness. This means that they are guilty of every sin they've ever committed. They forfeit the benefits of Jesus's blood! Why is this? Because by not forgiving others, we totally disregard the whole purpose of Jesus's death and resurrection. In a sense, we inwardly make ourselves greater than God, thus, implying that we are entitled to God's forgiveness, but the people who hurt us are deserving of eternal damnation. This is the evidence of a very wicked heart and a severe case of selective amnesia, whereas, we choose to forget the sins we've committed against God, all the while, choosing to remember the offenses others have committed against us.

Vadim wasn't interested in Edith; he wasn't even saved. Edith allowed her eyes and her rejection to deceive her. Vadim simply saw a woman who he considered attractive, even though he was somewhat racist. Perverted people tend to be very curious and will sleep with anything that ignites their lusts. A good example is — some perverted guy heads out to the mall and comes across a seductive midget, for lack of a better term. Now, don't get me wrong;

there's nothing wrong with being short and I'm not using the term midget to be offensive; this is just an illustration. The man has never slept with an unusually short woman before so he starts flirting with her. If he is allowed the opportunity to explore the woman the way he wants to explore her, his curiosity will be filled. He will have no other need for her. The same is true with a short man who becomes sexually fascinated with an unusually tall woman. His interest in her is simple perversion; it's sexual curiosity at most. With that being said, Vadim didn't deceive Edith; she deceived herself. She created an alternate fantasy for herself and she started to live in it, rather than face her own reality. This is similar to what alcoholics do. Alcohol gives them the ability to create another universe for themselves — one where they can escape the pressures of life.

Lastly, she should have corrected herself. At some point, she should have said, "Maybe I need help. Why am I so insecure? Why do I feel the need to control Omar? What's going on in my heart of hearts? What part of my past is attacking my present?" From there, she should have started praying about her heart, sought Christian counseling and did whatever she needed to do to make herself a candidate for the ministry of deliverance. Howbeit, she chose to progress in wickedness, all the while, serving at her church, meaning, she chose to be double-minded.

James 1:8 (ESV): A double minded man is unstable in all his ways.

Again, every choice we make is a step forward, either in the right direction or the wrong direction. It is a progression towards a harvest. What we find growing for ourselves is a representation of the seeds we've planted and the paths we've chosen for ourselves. Edith planted evil seeds and therefore, she reaped an evil harvest. This is common for people who choose self over God, sin over righteousness, hatred over forgiveness, and war over peace.

What are you progressing toward? What seeds do you have in the ground? What's progressing toward you? Sure, we can be religious and speak what we want to come to pass, but the seeds we've sown are going to eventually grow up for us; that is, if we have not repented and uprooted them. Regardless of what you experience in life and how bad those experiences hurt, you have to predetermine within yourself that you will stay in God's will. You have to war for your love and your peace because the enemy is trying to steal them both! Sadly enough, a lot of believers have allowed the enemy to bind them by allowing him to steal their love and burden them with chaotic lives. Instead of repenting and getting back on the paths that God, through His Son, Jesus Christ, has blazed for them, many believers choose to continue their progression into sin, hoping that someday, they will reap a blessing. Not surprising, this just doesn't happen. Instead, many believers grow old and realize that all they have to their names is a religious title, a bunch of church hats or shoes and a few scriptures to toss against the wall.

Don't be like Edith. If you need healing, get healing; if you need deliverance, seek deliverance. Don't rush off into a marriage, hoping that your husband can fix you or vice versa. If you choose marriage before you are completely submitted to God, you may find yourself standing in front of a witch with tears in your eyes, thinking that she (or he) is the answer to your prayers.

Chapter 6

Battered Reflections

A wife is the reflection of her husband; a husband is the reflection of his wife. But what happens when one spouse doesn't like his or her own reflection? They try to break the mirror. In other words, rather than attempting to fix themselves, they try to break their spouses. Of course, this only leads to more problems.

Not too long ago, I stood in front of my bathroom mirror and noticed that I had discoloration under my right eye. I'm not in a relationship (yet) and no one has been hitting me, so it goes without saying that I was baffled. I didn't know why there was a dark spot under my right eye, so I did some research. I discovered that I'd simply rubbed my eye too hard, after all, it was allergy season and my eyes had been itching a lot. The point is, when I looked in the mirror, I did not like my reflection. Wiping the mirror off would not change the picture it was casting back at me; it would only make it clearer. Breaking the mirror wouldn't change the fact that I had a black eye. It

would only cause me to hurt myself even more, plus, I'd have to clean up the broken shards of glass and then, replace the mirror. Additionally, it would only cause me to go into denial. To get the results I wanted, I had to allow my eye to heal and refrain from rubbing it with so much force.

Realizing that her feet were no longer touching the ground, Farrah began to claw at Kane's eyes. Kane closed his eyes and tightened his grip around his wife's neck. He could feel the pain of the skin breaking on his face, nevertheless, a sudden rush of adrenaline made that pain bearable. Farrah, on the other hand, was starting to feel weaker. Realizing that she could not breathe, Farrah stopped clawing her husband. That's when Kane threw her body to the floor and kicked her.

After kicking his wife, Kane picked up one of Farrah's concrete candle holders and threw it through the living room window, shattering the glass. Enraged, he then rushed over to Farrah, grabbed her by her hair and started dragging her to their bedroom. "This is what you wanted!" he shouted angrily. "I'm giving you what you wanted! I told you to leave me alone, but you wouldn't! Now, look at you! You're about to learn a lesson on this day!" Farrah grabbed her hair in an attempt to keep it from being pulled out by the roots. She cried out in pain as her husband dragged her to the bedroom.

Once in the bedroom, Kane grabbed a pillow and put it over his wife's face. He pressed down on the pillow for ten seconds before tossing it across the room. He then looked down at his wife and stood to his feet. Almost out of breath, Kane grabbed his car keys and left. Farrah curled her body up in the fetal position and began to weep bitterly. She wasn't weeping because her husband had physically assaulted her. She wasn't even weeping because of the pain she was in. As a matter of fact, she wasn't aware of the pain because the adrenaline in her body was high at that moment. Farrah wept for her marriage. She wanted her husband more than anything, but she couldn't think of anything to do or say to save her marriage. Was Kane gone for good this time? What time would he be home? If he comes home, how long will he punish her for offending him? Farrah had many questions, but the answers were nowhere in sight.

Farrah and Kane had been married for two years and they were coming up on their three-year anniversary. Fights in the Anderson household had become more commonplace and even more violent, nevertheless, the makeup sex had become more passionate and more intense.

Farrah opened her eyes and looked at the clock. It was now two in the morning and Kane still hadn't come home. Sore from the attack, Farrah lifted her weary body and went to the bathroom. "Ouch, ouch, ouch!" Farrah hissed in pain as she lifted her shirt. She placed her hand just above her stomach and began to press into the swollen, red bruise that had formed. She turned toward the mirror so she could get a better look at her bruise. It was huge! It was obvious to Farrah that Kane had really put some force behind his kick. She leaned closer to the mirror to observe the dark circle that was now forming under her left eye. "I can't go to work like this," she said to herself. The sound of the front door opening caught Farrah's attention. Kane was finally home. Determined not to upset him, Farrah went back into their bedroom. She knew that Kane would likely sleep on the living room couch, so Farrah laid face down on her bed and began to cry as quietly as she could. Thoughts of suicide began to race through Farrah's mind. She imagined her own funeral. In her imagination, a brokenhearted Kane stood near her coffin, weeping bitterly, so much so that several men had to get up and hold him back. "I'm sorry! Baby, please wake up! I'm sorry!" screamed Kane repeatedly, but it was too little too late. The imagination faded away as Farrah dozed off to sleep.

"I'm sorry, baby." The sound of Kane's voice woke Farrah

up from her sleep. It was now five in the morning and still dark outside. Farrah couldn't see much of Kane's face, but she could smell his cologne and his breath. It was obvious that he'd just brushed his teeth and was now lying next to her, with his face just above her face. "Farrah, I promise you that I love you. I am scared to death of losing you. I wish we didn't fight so much. Baby, I just wish you'd realize sometimes that I'm under a lot of pressure at work. When I come home, I just want to relax. When you start arguing and accusing me of stuff I haven't done, I get angry. Baby, I love you and I want our marriage to work, but you've got to change your ways. I'm serious. You have got to change. I know I was wrong too, and I'm gonna change. I'm sorry for hitting you. I shouldn't have done that, but I need you to stop provoking me, baby. I mean, look at my face. How am I going to go to work like this?" Seeing her opportunity to finally speak with her husband, Farrah spoke up. "I love you too," she said. "But Kane, when I see you hugging another woman, I'm gonna ask questions. I don't know any wife who would keep quiet. I feel like I'm being punished for loving you. And look at me. I can't go to work like this either. I got a black eye, a busted lip, and if this bruise on my stomach doesn't go down, I may have to go to the hospital." Kane leaned across the bed, turned on the light, and lifted Farrah's shirt. After seeing the big red bruise just above her stomach, his countenance changed. He looked sad, sorrowful and repentant. He leaned forward and kissed his wife's bruise before gently laying his head on it. "I'm so sorry," he whispered. A few seconds later, Farrah felt Kane's body jerking. She could hear him sniffing and before long, she felt warm tears bleeding down her belly. She lifted her right hand and moved it down towards his head. She then placed her hand on his head and began to run her fingers gently through his hair. "I'm sorry too," she said. "I didn't mean to hurt you, baby."

"Hey, Mrs. Culpepper. This is Farrah Anderson. I think I'm coming down with the flu, so I won't be coming in today." Farrah tried to sound as sick as she possibly could. While Mrs. Culpepper spoke, Farrah coughed repeatedly. "Yes, ma'am," said Farrah. "Well, I wasn't planning to go to the doctor unless it gets worse. Do I have any more personal days left?" Farrah waited for Mrs. Culpepper's answer. "Yes, I'll hold," she said, looking at Kane. A few minutes later, Mrs. Culpepper came back on the line and told Farrah she'd used all of her personal and sick days. "Okay," said Farrah. "Can I use two days of my vacation? I'm off Sunday, Monday and Tuesday anyway. If I take today and tomorrow off, I should be okay." Mrs. Culpepper put Farrah back on hold. Farrah looked over at Kane and shrugged her shoulders. Kane laughed. Farrah giggled and placed her finger over her mouth, gesturing for Kane to be quiet. "Yes, ma'am," she said. "I'm still here. Okay. Yeah. I heard you. I will. Okay. Thanks." With that, Farrah got off the phone.

Kane: Did she let you take off?

Farrah: Yeah, but you know she had to give me a lecture first.

Kane: I'm so glad I don't have to go through all that. All I have to say is, "Mr. Dudley, I can't come in today," with no questions asked.

Farrah: Yeah, that's because you are a man. You know the workplace treats men better than they treat women, plus, I think Mrs. Culpepper's miserable. I don't think her husband spends that much time with her. Ashley said that Mr. Culpepper is always going out of town.

Kane: Can you blame him? Look at her. She looks like a science project. I wouldn't want to come home either. I'd be like, "Baby, I just got an email from NASA and they said they are looking for volunteers to go to the moon. I hope you don't mind, but I kinda volunteered."

Farrah: *(Laughs)* So, you'd do me like that?

Kane: Heck yeah! If you looked like Mrs. Culpepper, I wouldn't have much of a choice. It would be either leave and give my eyes extended vacations or climb out of our bedroom window and howl at the moon every night. I'd be looking forward to those nights when there was a full moon.

Farrah: *(Laughs)* She's not that bad.

Kane: Who?! Are we talking about the same person? I'm

surprised somebody even married that woman. If he gets off work at five, I bet he starts feeling suicidal at 4:30. Anyway, so are you packed?

Farrah: Yeah, I just have to put my shoes on and I'm ready.

Fifteen minutes later, the couple started loading their car and preparing for the seven-hour trip from Raleigh, North Carolina to Jacksonville, Florida. They'd decided to take a miniature vacation to work on their damaged marriage.

During the drive, Kane looked over at his wife. Now asleep, she looked very angelic. He reached over and gently held her hand. "I love you, baby," Kane whispered. Half asleep, Farrah heard Kane's words. She wanted to open her eyes and tell him that she loved him too, but she didn't want to ruin the moment. Suddenly, Kane pulled into a gas station. Noticing that the car was coming to a stop, Farrah opened her eyes. Confused, she looked around and then over at Kane. "Baby, didn't we just fill up? Is it time to fill up again?" Kane locked his fingers with her fingers. "I just pulled over to tell you that I love you." Kane then leaned in to hug his wife. The two kissed briefly before Kane pulled back onto the highway.

The couple finally arrived in Jacksonville and checked into one of the hotels on the beach. Seeing how beautiful Jacksonville was and how nice their hotel was, Farrah became overly excited. After check-in, Farrah and Kane rushed to their beautiful suite. Farrah's eyes lit up as she saw how elaborate their room was. "Wow," said Farrah as she lifted her phone to take pictures of their room. Kane smiled. "Let's go to the beach," he said. "We have all night to enjoy the room." Farrah excitedly agreed. Like a kid in a candy store, Farrah ran through the hotel, pointing at every beautiful feature that she noticed. Outside the hotel, the couple rushed over to the beach. Still reeling with excitement, Farrah ran ahead of Kane towards the ocean. Kane lifted his phone and took a picture of his wife. He loved seeing Farrah dancing with excitement. The couple held hands, played in the ocean, and took a long moonlit stroll. Farrah let out a sigh of relief. "This is what an answered prayer looks like," she whispered to herself as Kane wrote their names in the sand. **Kane and Farrah Anderson ~Forever.** Infused in the sand, those words looked immortal. Even though a sudden wave rushed ashore and washed the words away, Farrah told herself that the sea was simply immortalizing their love.

It was dark outside and the couple decided to stop and grab a bite to eat before returning to the hotel. In the car, Kane turned on one of Farrah's favorite songs. The lyrics pierced Farrah's heart and mind. She leaned her head back on the seat, closed her eyes and basked in the ambiance of the moment. "I love you," Kane said as he reached for his wife's hand. "I love you too," said Farrah as she placed her hand in his. She then leaned forward to kiss Kane's bruised hand.

The evening was perfect; the restaurant was perfect, and the couple was now back in their hotel room. "I ran a bubble bath for you," said Kane. "Go and get in." Farrah stood to her feet and reached for her husband's hand. "Come with me," she said flirtatiously. Kane stepped back a few paces. With a grin on his face, he said, "No, I have plans for you. I showered when you were napping. Now, I want you to go and take your bath so I can get the room ready." Farrah agreed. She went into her suitcase and grabbed a few things before heading to the bathroom. When she emerged from the bathroom after a thirty-minute soaking, Farrah was awestruck. The dim light that emitted from the candles gave the atmosphere a romantic ambiance. Sweet, slow sounds of R&B filled the room. Kane stood to his feet and took in the beauty that was his wife. Wearing a sheer pink baby-doll gown, Farrah looked breathtakingly beautiful. Taking his wife's hand in his, Kane pulled her body close to his and the couple began to sway to the music. Farrah let herself get lost in the moment. She laid her head on Kane's chest as they continued to dance. In that moment, she felt loved. In that moment, she felt safe and protected. This was the moment she'd been praying for. "God, don't let this moment end," she prayed in her heart. Kane kissed his wife and then leaned back a little to look into her eyes. "Baby, I want it to be like this with us forever," he said. "I'm madly in love with you." The couple got lost in one another's eyes and then, they began to kiss again. Farrah tried to move towards the bed, but Kane stopped her. "No," he said, pulling her body back close to his. "We've got all night for that. I just want to hold you right now. Please let me hold you."

It was early the next morning when Farrah woke up. Kane was still sleeping, but Farrah had a hard time going back to sleep after her trip to the bathroom. As she lay next to her husband, Farrah replayed the events of the previous night. "I want you to have my baby." Those words kept replaying in Farrah's mind. They were so enchanting that hearing them sent chills down Farrah's spine. When Kane and Farrah met, they were both in college, even though they went to different universities. For the first year and a half of their marriage, Farrah was still a student, even though she did most of her studies online. For this reason, she'd always refused Kane's many requests to start a family. Nevertheless, she'd recently graduated from college and Kane had dropped out of college after he'd started working as a painter for a small company.

"Hey, you." Kane's voice brought Farrah out of her daze.

"How are you feeling?" Farrah leaned forward and kissed her husband. "Still in awe," she said. "I know we've talked about children, but just knowing that we are officially trying to get pregnant is mind-blowing."

Kane: Yeah, for a while there, I was beginning to think that you didn't want children or that you didn't want them with me.

Farrah: I do. I just didn't want to go that far in college and then have to quit.

Kane: What do you want to do today?

Farrah: I want a replay of yesterday.

Kane: *(Laughs)* No, we gotta switch things up a little.

Farrah: Okay. We can do something different today, but tonight, I want to relive last night. You're laughing but I'm serious. My head is still spinning.

The next couple of days were surreal. Kane and Farrah shopped, frequented the beach and spent a lot of quality time together as a couple. When they checked out of the hotel, Farrah felt a wave of sadness hit her. It was time to go back home, back to reality and away from all of the enchantment of Florida.

"Did you get everything?" Kane asked as he closed the hotel room door. Farrah looked at her bag and replied. "Yeah, I double-checked." With that, the couple checked out of the hotel and started their journey back to North

Carolina.

A few days later, Farrah came home from work and laid her body on the couch. She began to weep as she waited for her husband to come home. She called and requested prayer from one of her aunts who happened to be an evangelist. "I'll call you back," said Farrah as Kane's car pulled up in the driveway. Her heart raced as she anticipated Kane's reaction to the news. Kane walked into the house and closed the door. That's when he saw Farrah standing to her feet. She was holding a piece of paper in one of her hands and she did not look happy.

Kane: What's wrong?

Farrah: They fired me today.

Kane: Farrah? Please tell me you're joking. Baby, please tell me that you're joking.

Farrah: I wish I was.

Kane: Why? What did you do?

Farrah: I forgot to change the settings on my Facebook page. I uploaded the pictures of us in Florida and somebody showed Mrs. Culpepper.

Kane: Wait. Didn't you use two of your vacation days? They can't fire you when you're using vacation time.

Farrah: That's what I said, but Mrs. Culpepper kept saying that I called in sick when I wasn't sick.

Kane: I told you not to upload those pictures to Facebook! I knew this would happen. You wouldn't listen to me. You never do. Now, what are we gonna do?

Farrah: I'm gonna call Mr. Savage on Monday and explain the situation to him.

Kane: You're gonna have to do something cause I used the rent money for that vacation we took.

Farrah: I thought you said you paid the rent.

Kane: How, Farrah? Did you think I magically found a thousand bucks? No! That was the rent money. If I had known you'd be stupid enough to post the pictures to social media, I would have just paid the rent instead.

Farrah: Kane, I told you, I forgot to change my settings.

Kane: Yeah, right.

Farrah: What's that supposed to mean?

Kane: It means I don't believe you. Is that chimp-looking dude still on your page?

Farrah: Who?

Kane: You know who I'm talking about.

Farrah: Melvin?

Kane: Like I said, you know who I'm talking about.

Farrah: How does Melvin fit into this?

Kane: I don't want to talk about it, Farrah. You were too busy trying to make him jealous that you forgot you'd called in sick.

Farrah: How was I trying to make him jealous? I told you that Melvin and I dated when I was in high school. I don't even think about Melvin anymore. You think about him more than I do. Like I said, I'll try to sort it all out on

Monday. Let's not fight about it.

Kane: Why do you have to wait until Monday to call Mr. Savage?

Farrah: Because he only comes to our office on Mondays. Baby, please calm down. I'll sort it all out.

With that, Farrah went into the bedroom and closed the door. The atmosphere in the Anderson home was very tense. Farrah's heart raced as she flipped through the television set, inwardly praying that Kane would just drop the matter, but she knew that he wouldn't. A few minutes later, she heard the front door slamming. Panicked, Farrah ran from the room and tried to catch Kane before he pulled off, but it was too late. She watched in agony as his car pulled out the driveway.

"Hi, you've reached the voicemail of Kane Anderson. I'm sorry, but I'm not available to take your call. Please leave me a message and I'll be sure to call you back at my earliest convenience." *Beep.* Kane's voicemail was beginning to sound irritating. "Kane, please call me back," said Farrah. Nevertheless, hours went by and still no call from Kane. Farrah couldn't sleep at all that night. She repeatedly called Kane's phone, but she kept getting his voicemail.

It was now seven o'clock in the morning and the sound of birds singing was beginning to annoy Farrah. Kane hadn't come by the house to pick up any work clothes and Farrah wondered if he'd even go to work that day. An hour and a half later, Farrah called Kane's job. "I'm sorry, Mrs. Anderson, but Mr. Anderson called in this morning," said the secretary. "I think he said he was taking the rest of the week off." Farrah's heart raced with fear. Why would Kane take an entire week off after she'd lost her job? She waited all day to hear from Kane, but he did not call, come home or return her calls.

It was now nine o'clock that evening and Farrah was starting to become desperate. Kane had never stayed out that long before. What if he'd been in a car accident? What if he was lying on the side of the road dead? Terrifying thoughts raced through Farrah's mind as her agony intensified. She called Kane's phone again, but this time, the call didn't immediately go to voicemail. Instead, it rang until it finally went to voicemail on its own. Farrah let out a sigh of relief. Obviously Kane was okay. Nevertheless, the panic seemed to reignite itself as Farrah considered the possibilities. What if someone stole his phone? What if Kane was out with his ex, Kendra, because he was convinced that Farrah wasn't over Melvin? Farrah waited a few minutes and then downloaded a free phone call app to her phone. The app would allow her to have a second number that she could call and receive calls from. *Ring. Ring. Ring.* "Hello." Kane finally answered his phone.

"Kane, why haven't you been answering my calls?" Farrah's voice was firm. *Click.* Kane disconnected the call and Farrah started calling him repeatedly once again, but he would not answer. Instead, he turned his phone back off and she continued to go to voicemail for the remainder of the night.

It was early the next morning and the sound of the garbage truck broke the silence. Farrah still hadn't slept much, only dozing off once that night, but waking up less than an hour later. She was tormented; she was becoming more and more desperate. "Call me back." This was the thirtieth voicemail Farrah had left for her husband. Farrah laid her phone down on the coffee table in her living room. She then stood to her feet and made her way to the kitchen. Suddenly, her phone started ringing. *Finally!* Farrah raced back to the living room, determined not to miss Kane's call. She didn't take the time to even look at the caller I.D. because she was sure that it was Kane calling her back. "Hello ... hello." The desperation could be heard in Farrah's voice. "Hey baby. This is Pastor Gloria. How are you doing?" Farrah's heart dropped, her body tensed up and the disappointment in her voice was unmistakable. "I'm okay, Pastor. How are you?"

Pastor Gloria: Blessed and highly favored of the Lord. I was worried about you. You kept falling on my spirit last night and we haven't seen you at church for a while, so I decided to give you a call before you left for work to make sure that everything was okay.

Farrah: Well, I got fired the other day, so I don't have a job to go to.

Pastor Gloria: Oh, Lord! I'm sorry to hear that. How's Kane? Is he still working?

Farrah: Kane is fine, I guess. Yes, he's still working.

Pastor Gloria: What do you mean you guess?

Farrah: He left home day before yesterday and I haven't seen him since.

Pastor Gloria: That ain't nothing but the devil! How are you doing? Are you okay? Would you like me to stop by?

Farrah: No, I'm fine. I'll be okay. I'm probably gonna go out job hunting today. Kane is just having a temper tantrum. He'll come home when he's ready.

Pastor Gloria: Yes, and you must remember that he is an unbeliever. They have their own language, their own world and their own way of reasoning. If you try to communicate with him from a Kingdom standpoint, it'll only end in an argument. You have to speak to him on his level, but pray on your level. This doesn't mean you argue with him. It simply means you refrain from being too deep with someone who has yet to start digging.

Farrah: I will. Keep me lifted, Pastor.

Pastor Gloria: Well, you call me if you need anything and please know that Pastor Harry and I will be praying for you over this way.

Farrah: Okay, thanks, Pastor.

Pastor Gloria: You're welcome, sweetie. Oh and Farrah?

Farrah: Yes, ma'am?

Pastor Gloria: To chase the devil away, you must get closer to God. The further away you get from God, the more access the devil will have to you and your marriage.

Farrah: I'm starting to see that. Gonna spend some time in prayer today.

After Farrah got off the phone with Pastor Gloria, she called her friend, Tina. When Tina answered the phone, Farrah asked, "What are you doing today? I need you to do my hair." At first, Tina seemed disinterested. "Girl, I have to drop these kids off at school and then, I have to go pay the bills and stop by the laundromat. Can it wait till tomorrow?" Farrah let out a sigh before she started crying. "Yes, I guess. I just wanted to get out this house. I got fired the other day and now Kane is mad at me. He left two days ago and I haven't seen him since."

Tina: Hold on, girl. Marvell, Re-Re and Junior! Put your shoes on right now and let's go! I'm not playing with y'all on today! I'm sorry, girl. I'm back. Why didn't you call me? Are you okay?

Farrah: I guess I've been trying to deal with it on my own.

Tina: Do you want me to come to your house or do you want to come to mine?

Farrah: Come over here because the landlord is supposed

to be coming by today to look at the broken window.

Tina: Who broke your window?

Farrah: Long story. What time are you coming?

Tina: Give me about three hours. I'm gonna drop these kids off at school and then, run some errands. Do you want me to bring you something?

Farrah: No. If you have some hair dye, bring it. Maybe a reddish color.

Tina: I think I have one. Hold on. Re-Re, look under that cabinet in the bathroom and bring me that box of hair dye! You'll see a picture of a woman with red hair on the box! Hold on, Farrah. She's getting it now. Okay, give Mommy a kiss and go put on your shoes. Farrah? I'm back. I think the box says it's honey blonde. Did you want to go that light? I think it would look cute on you.

Farrah: Honey blonde is perfect.

Tina: Okay, and after I finish, we can go out to eat — my treat.

Farrah: Thanks girl. I need to get out of this house before I lose my mind.

It was two o'clock that afternoon when Tina finally arrived. "I'm sorry, girl," she said. "I had to go up to Marvell's school again. His teacher called me and said he hasn't turned in any homework for the last week. Anyway, that woman held me up, talking about Marvell. He done traumatized her — I can tell. I told her that she needed to go see the school counselor to get a load off. I also called Craig and asked him if he'd pick the kids up from school and drop them off at Bridgette's house. He said yes, so it looks like it's gonna be ladies' day and night for us. " Farrah opened the door wide so Tina could come in. "Girl, you're the only person I know who calls her mother by her first name." Tina set her bag on the floor next to the couch. "She hasn't been much of a mother to me. She didn't raise me, so she better be happy that I call her period."

It was two hours later and an excited Farrah looked in the hand mirror that Tina had just given her. "Yes!" she shouted. "Look at all that bounce! I love it! Thanks Tina!" Tina collected the rest of her hair tools and placed them in her bag. "You know you're always welcome," she said. "Wait til Kane sees you. He's gonna start stuttering. Ba- ba- ba, where you go- go- going?!" Farrah laughed. "Girl, I'm not studying Kane anymore. Let me go get ready, cause I'm starving."

The women went to a restaurant called The Front Porch. There they ate and talked more about men. Tina held up her phone and took a snapshot of Farrah. "You are looking too cute!" she exclaimed. I'm about to send the photo to your phone. Post it up to your Facebook page and I bet you Kane will come home tonight." *Ding.* Farrah's phone chimed, indicating that she'd just received a text message.

She looked at the photo attachment and smiled. "Done," she said with a big grin on her face. "Girl, you are a jack of all trades. Beautiful hair — check. Perfect makeup — check. Jealous husband — pending."

Tina: Thanks sis. What worries me though is that he's hitting on you. Farrah, he's a man. He shouldn't be putting his hands on you. He could hit you too hard and end up killing you.

Farrah: I know but I have to stop provoking him. Sometimes, I lose my temper and start talking crazy. I have to remind myself sometimes that Kane wasn't brought up by a loving mother. He's not a bad person, but when he gets mad, he loses control. When he's calm, he's the sweetest man you can ever know.

Tina: That's not an excuse for him to be putting his hands on you. It couldn't be me. Girl, Marvell's dad hit me one time and that was it. You've seen that big scar on the side of his face. Yeah, that's my handiwork. That man flinches to this day every time he sees me. Crazy recognizes crazy.

Farrah: Oh, you know I don't just be laying there getting my butt kicked. I fight, bite, scratch and do whatever I can to get my point across. Right now, Kane is somewhere with no less than six scabs on his face.

Suddenly, Farrah's phone rang. She fumbled through her purse, hoping that the call was coming from Kane. Frustrated, Farrah shouted, "I can never find this phone until it hangs up!" Right before the caller went to voicemail, Farrah found her phone and hit the answer key. "Hello ... hello," she said. "Hey stranger. How have you been? I just called to check in with you." Farrah's heart dropped. "Hey Aisha," she said. "I'm good. How are you?" Farrah looked up and noticed that Tina was trying to get her attention. "I'll be right back. I need to make a call too," she whispered. Farrah nodded her head.

Aisha: No complaints this way. I had a dream about you last night that had me worried.

Farrah: What did you dream?

Aisha: I dreamed that you were holding a blanket with something wrapped up in it. It was one of those blankets that people wrap their babies up in. I could tell that you were breastfeeding. I rushed over to see the baby and when you opened the blanket, there was no baby. You were breastfeeding a colorful baby snake.

Farrah: What? What does that mean?

Aisha: I'm not sure, but that dream felt too real to ignore. I remember feeling scared and I kept telling you that it was a snake, but you looked at me and said, "This is my baby." I told you to stop feeding it because you were making it grow. I told you to chop its head off. You got mad at me and started throwing dirt at me.

Farrah: Wow, that's crazy.

Aisha: Yep and I had almost forgotten to call you until I saw that you'd updated your profile picture on Facebook.

Farrah, what made you dye that pretty black hair of yours?

Farrah: I just wanted to go with something different.

Aisha: Okay. Just wanted to make sure that everything was okay. We've been missing you at church. I told Pastor Gloria that one of these Sundays, I'm gonna come by your house and drag you to church.

Farrah: *(Laughs)* She called me today. I told her I've just been going through a lot; that's all.

Aisha: What's wrong, Farrah? You haven't called and told me anything.

Farrah: I got fired Wednesday.

Aisha: Are you serious? What happened?

Farrah: I did the dumbest thing. I called in sick last Friday because I knew I had the weekend off, plus, I had Monday and Tuesday off. I told Mrs. Culpepper I was coming down with something and asked her if I could use two of my vacation days for Friday and Saturday. Kane and I wanted to drive down to Jacksonville and take a mini-vacation. We went down there and everything was beautiful. Of course, you know me. I took out my camera and started snapping pictures.

Aisha: Don't tell me you uploaded them to Facebook.

Farrah: Guilty. And somebody saw the pictures and showed them to Mrs. Culpepper. She didn't even let me clock in. She intercepted me at the clock and told me to follow her to her office. I knew then that she was about to fire me.

Aisha: Well, the blessing is that Kane's working, so that should hold you guys over until you get another job.

Farrah: Kane's job is on a call-by-call basis. He doesn't make that much money, plus, when I told him that I'd got fired, he got mad and left. I haven't seen him since Wednesday.

Aisha: Farrah, today is Friday.

Farrah: I know. I've been calling and calling him, but he won't answer his phone.

Aisha: Let me ask you this. Don't be mad at me, but is he still hitting on you?

Farrah: Not really. Okay. Well, yeah. We got in a fight last Wednesday. That's why I asked to take Thursday and Friday off.

Aisha: Farrah, this may be a blessing from God. I don't advocate divorce, but that man needs some serious help.

Farrah: I know. I've been looking for marriage counselors for months now, but just about everyone I pick out, he finds some reason not to like them. He's a good man. His mother just messed him up.

Aisha: Farrah! I just realized what my dream meant. The baby snake was Kane! You keep trying to nurture Kane back to a stable mind, but the only thing you're doing is helping what's on the inside of him to grow!

Farrah: No, I don't think that's what that dream meant. Anyhow, I gotta go. I'm out with Tina right now.

Aisha: Not a good idea, Farrah. Tina was not the right

person to call. I'm telling you this because I love you. Don't tell her your business and don't take any of her advice. Spit it all out and pray.

Farrah: I hear you, girl. Gotta go. I'll call you later tonight or tomorrow.

A few minutes later, Tina made her way back to the table.

Tina: I had to call Bridgette to check on my kids. She said that Marvell is scared to come home. He knows I'm gonna get in that butt when I see him.

Farrah: I don't blame him. You're heavy-handed. That was Aisha who just called me.

Tina: *(rolls eyes)* Little Ms. Perfect, herself. How many times did she say Jesus this time?

Farrah: None, I don't think. She said that she had a dream that I was breastfeeding a baby snake.

Tina: Kane! That's who the snake is!

Farrah: That's what she said. Anyway, no marriage is perfect. I remember that time when her and Kwan got into an argument over a piece of chicken.

Tina: Did he hit her?

Farrah: No, I just thought it was petty to be arguing over who ate the last piece of chicken. Anyway, are you ready?

Tina: Yeah, let's go. I'm not tipping the waitress. She sucked.

Farrah: What's annoying is Aisha's supposed to be Christian, but she keeps trying to get me to leave Kane.

What happened to forgiveness and mercy?

Tina: Right! I'm no fan of Kane's, but if you want to be with him, I won't try to pressure you to leave. Isn't there a story in the Bible where some crazy dude was walking around a cemetery or something and Jesus cast a whole lot of demons out of him?

Farrah: Exactly. That's why I keep trying to get Kane to come to one of our deliverance conferences. He just needs deliverance, that's all. She's always putting her nose where it doesn't belong. That's why I stopped calling her in the first place.

Tina: I bet her husband be cheating on her with everything that walks by. He's gotta get tired of hearing Jesus-this and Jesus-that.

Farrah: No, I think Kwan is a good guy, but I agree. I'm sure he gets tired of her holier than thou attitude. She used to be married to a guy named Danny and I remember he used to kick her butt all over North Carolina. One time, we were at the supermarket together and he walked in looking for her. Girl, he walked right up to her and slapped her so hard that she slid past three registers.

Tina: For real? And now, she's got the nerve to tell you how to run your marriage. You gotta tell me more. Give me the dirt!

Hearing the word "dirt," suddenly got Farrah's attention. Aisha had just told her that in the dream, she'd warned

Farrah that she was breastfeeding a snake; she'd told Farrah to cut its head off. When this happened, Farrah had started chasing her and throwing dirt at her. In that moment, she realized that she was throwing dirt at her best friend. "Let's go," said Farrah. "I think the waitress is starting to realize that we didn't leave her a tip."

Farrah wanted to go directly home, but Tina had a few stops to make. Irritated, Farrah considered calling herself a cab, but just when she was ready to find another ride home, Tina came running out of her mother's house. "Here I come!" she shouted. A few minutes later, Tina got in the car and explained her dilemma. "Girl, Bridgette was trying to convince me to take the kids home with me tonight, but like I told her, duty calls. My girl needs me. She finally agreed to keep them after I promised her that I'd come out tomorrow and do her hair." Tina started her car and pulled off. A few minutes later, they turned on Farrah's street. In the distance, they noticed two cars parked in Farrah's driveway. One of them was Farrah's car. "Girl, is that Kane?" Tina laughed. Farrah's heart started racing. "Yep, that's his car." Tina pulled into the driveway and put her car in park. "I told you," she said. "That picture you posted to Facebook made him nervous." Farrah nervously grabbed the door handle. "Rain-check?" she said, looking over at Tina. "Okay," said Tina. "But call me if he starts acting crazy. You know I carry a blade on me at all times."

When Farrah entered the house, the unusual calm in the house made her jittery. At first, she didn't see Kane. The only sound that could be heard was the sound Farrah's six-inch blue high heels made as she made her way towards the bedroom. As she passed by the kitchen, she noticed Kane sitting at the bar, eating a sandwich. At first, Kane didn't say anything, so Farrah continued towards their bedroom. "Where have you been?" asked Kane calmly. Farrah became annoyed. "I should be asking you the same thing!" she countered. "I haven't seen you since Wednesday." Kane finished off his sandwich and then grabbed a paper towel. Wiping his hands, he stood to his feet and threw the paper towel in the trash.

Kane: So, was he better than me?

Farrah: What? Was who better than you? What are you talking about now?

Kane: Melvin. A little birdie told me that you spent the night with Melvin last night.

Farrah: Well, that little birdie lied to you! And how are you gonna come home after being gone for two days and start questioning me about my whereabouts?! If you were here, you would've known that I was at home trying to call you!

Kane: So, Melvin screwed you in our bed ...

Farrah: Kane, nobody's been here but Tina!

Kane: That's why you went and changed your hair; right? So, you could look good for Melvin.

Farrah: Tina just did my hair today! I know what you're doing! You're trying to redirect the blame away from yourself. Who have you been with these last two days?

Kane: It wasn't you.

Farrah: Well, I guess we both can say the same thing.

With that, Kane pinned his wife up against the wall in the hallway. He stared at her for a couple of seconds before leaning in as if he wanted to kiss her. Farrah turned her head. Farrah screamed out in agony as the pain intensified. Kane was biting her cheek with so much force that Farrah knew he'd left a bruise. He then grabbed a handful of Farrah's hair and started pulling her towards their bedroom. "Stop!" screamed Farrah as Kane lifted her above his head and threw her on the bed. He then mounted Farrah and started choking her. As he was choking her, he made eye contact with her. Something about his eyes was different and Farrah could see it. They seemed darker and more dilated than usual. Farrah clawed away at Kane's face, all the while, gasping for air. "You made love to another man in our bed," said Kane with an unusual calmness. Farrah managed to lift her right leg and slightly throw Kane's body off her body. Kane suddenly sat up and began to strike Farrah across her face repeatedly. He then returned to choking her and he did this until she finally passed out.

Farrah woke up three hours later in a puddle of her own urine. Kane had obviously moved her body to the floor and threw a blanket over her as if he was trying to keep her warm. The sound of the blender and the smell of food was overwhelming. Farrah lifted her sore body from the floor and noticed that she had another bruise forming on her stomach. Kane had obviously kicked her while she was unconscious. *Should I call the police?* Farrah's mind started racing with thoughts. Calling the police would ensure her safety, but it would also end her marriage to Kane, after all, the last time Kane had been arrested for domestic violence, he'd swore to Farrah that if she'd ever had him arrested again, he would leave and not look back. Scared, Farrah limped her way into the bathroom to observe her face. There were no obvious new bruises on her face, but her body had many bruises on it and they were all very sore.

Farrah walked into the kitchen, right past her husband and grabbed a mop. She made her way into the bedroom and started mopping up the urine that now covered a large part of the floor. After mopping the floor, Farrah went into the bathroom and took a shower. The house remained quiet for the next couple of hours. Farrah laid in her bed and stared at the wall. The sound of her phone ringing startled her.

Farrah: Hello *(coughs)*.

Aisha: Farrah, this is Aisha. I'm worried about you. Are you okay?

Farrah: Not really. I'll call you back.

Aisha: Is he there? Do you want me to call the police?

Farrah: He's here, but no. I'll be okay. He's not speaking to me, that's all.

Aisha: Okay. You call me if you need me. I'm gonna keep my ringer on.

Farrah: Okay, thanks.

Looking at her phone, Farrah realized that she had a few missed calls from Tina. She decided to call her back.

Tina: Farrah, girl, I was just about to come by your house. Is everything okay?

Farrah: Not really.

Tina: Should I call the cops?

Farrah: No, I'll be okay.

Tina: He didn't put his hands on you, did he?

Farrah: Yep.

Tina: He did?!

Farrah: Yep.

Tina: Farrah, let me make a phone call. One call, that's all. Please.

Farrah: No, I'm okay. He's in the living room now and I'm in the bedroom.

Tina: You need to leave his sorry behind! I bet he wouldn't lift his hands to fight a man.

Farrah: You're right and I will.

Tina: You will what?

Farrah: Leave.

Tina: When?

Farrah: Soon.

Tina: Okay. Well, call me if you need me. I'm serious, Farrah.

Farrah: I will.

Farrah was surprised that her husband still hadn't come to the room to check on her. He'd seen her briefly when she'd gone to the kitchen to get the mop and that was it. She could hear the sound of a spoon scraping up against a plate. It was obvious that Kane was just finishing up on his meal. Realizing that he would come into the bedroom soon, Farrah pulled the covers up to her neck and closed her eyes. Just as she'd predicted, Kane made his way into the bedroom. He took off his clothes, turned on the television set and let out a loud burp. Farrah laid next to Kane with her eyes closed, wishing that the show he was watching would hurry up and go off. She wanted so badly to talk to Kane, but she also wanted him to initiate the conversation.

Forty minutes later, the show went off and Kane turned off the television, leaving the room in utter darkness. He then turned his back away from his wife and waited for her to speak.

Farrah: Kane?

Kane: What?

Farrah: This isn't working.

Kane: I know. I think we should call it quits now before it gets worse.

Farrah: *(Sobs)* What bothers me is I do everything to make our marriage work and somehow, it all backfires.

Kane: Farrah, do you know what I did today? I almost cheated on you. I have never cheated on you, but today, I almost did. That let me know that this marriage is over.

Farrah: Almost cheated with who?

Kane: That's not important. The point is, I don't trust you, you don't trust me and now, I don't trust myself.

Farrah: I don't understand what I've done that was so bad to make you hate me the way you do.

Kane: I don't hate you, Farrah. We just don't get along. I tell you one thing and you hear another. If I tell you to go left, you'll intentionally go right. Everything you do is about you. You're selfish.

Farrah: Me? Selfish? Everything I do is for you. That's why it hurts so bad. I even took that time off so we could work on our marriage. Yeah, it was stupid for me to upload the photos to Facebook, but I guess I just wanted to share my joy with the world.

Kane: Did you go to Facebook to share with the world that you're now unemployed?

Farrah: I have a degree, Kane. I won't be unemployed long.

Kane: Tell that to the bill collectors when they start cutting *your* utilities off.

Farrah: The way I see it, it's a blessing from God because that job was paying me way less than entry-level pay anyway.

Kane: There you go! I was wondering when you'd try to drag God into this. Did He tell you to upload those pictures to Facebook?

Farrah: No, Kane. He did not.

Kane: Anyhow, I agree. This is not working. My feelings toward you are changing. I love you, but I'm falling out of love with you.

Farrah: You abuse me with your hands and kill me with your words.

It was two days later and Farrah's body was so sore that she could barely move around. For this reason, she opted to stay in the bed. Kane came into the room carrying a feeding tray. "Here you go, madam," he said as he lowered the tray. "Kane's famous chicken noodle soup and a few croutons to tease your palate." Farrah loved being nursed by Kane. Moments like those made her feel loved and wanted and moments like those made Kane feel respected and needed. Suddenly, Kane's phone rang. It was his mother.

Farrah hated when Kane's mother called because she would always say something to upset him. He'd then take out his anger on Farrah. Kane walked out of the room as he answered the phone. A few minutes later, Farrah could hear Kane talking loudly to his mother. "How many times do I have to tell you to keep my name out of your mouth?!" Kane screamed. "That wasn't any of her business! What?! No, I'm wondering why you would tell my ex-girlfriend that my wife was unemployed. That is none of her business!" With that, Kane hung up the line and Farrah sat up on the bed. "What was that about?" asked Farrah. "Nothing," said Kane. "Mom ole messy butt told my ex-girlfriend, Kendra, that you were unemployed."

Farrah: Why did she do that?

Kane: She said that Kendra asked about me and she told her that I was married now. When Kendra asked her what I did for a living, she told her that I was a painter. Then, Kendra asked what you did for a living and Mom told her that you were unemployed.

Farrah: That was none of her business.

Kane: That's what I said. And she wonders why she can't keep a man. Always in somebody's business. She could have said that you have a degree in Social Work or she could have said that you were in between jobs, but she's messy. Always has been.

Farrah: It's okay.

Kane: No, it's not okay. You're my wife and she needs to respect that.

Farrah: Amen to that.

Kane leaned over and kissed his wife. A few seconds later, the doorbell rang. "I'll get it," he said smiling. A minute later, Kane came back into the room holding a large bouquet of flowers, three balloons that read, "I love you," a rather large teddy bear and a box of chocolates. Farrah smiled and took a deep breath. Kane sat on the bed, leaned forward to kiss his wife and then proceeded with his speech. He said, "Farrah, I know that we've had a lot of problems in our marriage and we've even talked about getting a divorce, but I want you to know that I love you. I didn't marry you to divorce you. I know I have got to get some help; we both do. But Farrah Monique Anderson, I cannot and will never leave you. No one may understand our marriage. Sometimes, I don't even understand our marriage, but what I do know is this: you complete me. I love you; I'm in love with you, and baby, I need you more than you know." Farrah leaned forward to kiss her husband again.

It was three weeks later and Farrah was excited about an interview. She combed through her hair one last time, making sure that every curl was in its proper place. "Don't be late," said Kane as he handed Farrah her purse and keys. "We need the money." Farrah kissed her husband and rushed out the door. Work, for Kane, had slowed down tremendously and their rent payment was almost due. Farrah knew that if this job didn't come through, Kane would get stressed out and they'd end up fighting again.

Two hours later, Farrah returned home. She had a big grin on her face. "I think I may have the job," she announced excitedly. Kane gestured for her to sit next to him. "Tell me what happened," he said. Farrah told him about the interview and how the interviewer had said that she was the most qualified candidate for the job. She'd told Farrah to look for a callback within the next three to five days. "Let's celebrate," said Kane. "Let's go to the park and have a picnic." Farrah was excited. She relished those spontaneous dates that she and Kane had anytime something good happened.

At the park, the couple walked, held hands and talked about Farrah's new job. They started making plans as to what they'd do with the money. After walking for about thirty minutes, Farrah went back to their car and pulled out a blanket and a picnic basket. They walked to a large field area and set up their picnic. As they lay on the blanket, they laughed and talked about a few of the people at the park. Farrah basked in this moment. It was everything she'd prayed for.

Kane: I need to tell you something, but I don't want you to get mad. Promise you won't get mad.

Farrah: I won't get mad.

Kane: Promise?

Farrah: I promise.

Kane: My mom called me the other day with Kendra on the phone.

Farrah: When?

Kane: I think it was Tuesday. I talked with her for a few minutes just to be nice, but I told her that I am married.

Farrah: What did she say?

Kane: She asked me if I was happy.

Farrah: And what did you say?

Kane: I said yes. I think my mom thinks I should have married Kendra because Kendra and I never fought. The only reason we broke up was because she joined the military and went overseas for a few years.

Farrah: So, are you still in love with her?

Kane: I'm not gonna lie. I felt something when I was talking to her, but I didn't entertain it because I love you. I could tell that she wants us to get back together, but I'm not gonna throw our marriage away to entertain what's probably nothing but curiosity on both of our parts.

Farrah wasn't sure how she should feel. This was one of those moments when she felt like she should be happy and grateful, but instead, she felt disrespected. Nevertheless, she didn't want to ruin what could possibly be a great day over something she wasn't sure about. The couple went out to eat, and after that, they went home. "I want you to have my baby. I want us to have a family," said Kane as he pulled his wife's body close to his. With that, the lights went off and the Andersons enjoyed another night of marital bliss.

Two weeks later, Farrah stood in front of the mirror putting on her earrings. She'd finally gotten the job and was excited about starting her first day at work. Kane sat in the bathtub and watched his wife beautify herself. Conflicted within himself, Kane was happy that Farrah had gotten the job, but on the other hand, he worried that the job would inflate Farrah's ego. Jealousy crept in as Kane watched his wife put on her lipstick. *Splash.* "What was that for?" shouted Farrah. Kane had splashed a little water on her clothes. Kane didn't respond. He simply stared at his wife in a threatening manner. Farrah's excitement turned to worry. She rushed out of the bathroom, grabbed her blow dryer and started using it to dry the wet area on her shirt.

Over the next few days, Kane's jealousy continued to intensify. He watched his wife leave the house looking professionally adorable. He hated the sudden surge in her confidence and he despised the fact that the company had given her another cell phone. Determined to humble her,

Kane decided to start an argument about Melvin again. It was Friday evening and Kane knew that Farrah would be off for the weekend.

Farrah: I don't know why you keep bringing Melvin's name up! I've deleted the man off my Facebook page, even though you still have three of your exes, including Kendra, on your page!

Kane: Like I said, a little birdie told me that you've been going to visit Melvin when you get off work. That's why you keep coming home late.

Farrah: I wish you'd tell me who that little birdie is so I could prove to you that it ain't a bird, it's a bat!

Kane: I'm not gonna worry about it. It's not like I don't have options too.

Farrah: What options? Kendra? Oh, please. I checked her Facebook profile and she's in a relationship.

Kane: Okay. If that's what you want to believe.

Farrah: What's that supposed to mean?

Kane: It means you can believe what you want. Besides, Kendra isn't the only woman who wants me. Remember that.

With that, Kane grabbed his keys and left. In his mind, it was time to punish and humble Farrah again and he knew just how to do it. He came home the next morning and he didn't speak to Farrah until Sunday night. For the next few weeks, Farrah came home early. She rushed through her assignments at work, determined to be home no later than 5:30. On some days, Kane would treat her like a precious jewel, but on other days, he would emotionally torture her. This was the norm in their marriage.

"I'm pregnant." Kane turned around and saw his gleaming wife holding a pregnancy test. Kane froze as he stared at the positive pregnancy test. Excited, he wrapped his arms around her and started to kiss her neck. "I love you so much, baby," he said. "This is definitely an answered prayer." Hearing Kane use the word "prayer" in a sentence, gave Farrah hope. Maybe God had been dealing with his heart after all.

Over the next few weeks, the couple's emotional highs and lows continued. Kane slapped his wife one day after he said she was wearing too much makeup for work. On another day, he'd punched her and when she fell down, he kicked in the direction of her stomach, barely missing her. Farrah started realizing that Kane was now using their unborn baby as a tool to get what he wanted. Scared that he'd kick or hit her stomach, Farrah went out of her way to refrain from angering Kane.

Ding dong. Farrah stood to her feet. Who on Earth could it be at the door? Kane had just left to go to the store and he had his own set of keys, so it was obviously not him. "Who is it?" No one answered. Farrah made her way towards the door. By now, she was five months pregnant. "Fairy Canary!" screamed Tyler as he opened his arms to embrace his sister. "Tyler!" Farrah was excited. Standing in her doorway was her oldest brother. A handsome specimen of a man, Tyler was tall and athletic. A brown-skinned masterpiece, Tyler had a square face, strong jawline and very intense eyes. Farrah wrapped her arms around her brother and hugged him for more than a minute before inviting him in. Still dressed in his army uniform, Tyler looked like the epitome of an army guy. "That Uber driver had me laughing," said Tyler. "She flirted with me the whole way here. If someone comes by here in a silver Murano, just say that I went back to Afghanistan." Farrah laughed. "Could you blame her?" she said. "Look at you. My brother grew up to be a ladies' man." The siblings sat down and talked for a few minutes before Tyler asked Farrah about a box of old photos that Farrah had taken from their mother's house. "It's in the attic," said Farrah. "I'll have Kane to get it as soon as he gets home." Tyler laughed. "Nonsense," he said. "I think I'm in better shape than Kane anyway."

The only entrance to the attic was in the hallway. The stairs to the attic were broken and Kane had removed them altogether, so getting up into the attic meant jumping and climbing. Nevertheless, the job proved to be a simple task for the agile Tyler. A few minutes later, Kane walked into the house and was already starting an argument. Not realizing that his brother-in-law was in the attic, Kane repeatedly accused his wife of cheating on him, even claiming that he believed that the baby was not his baby. Frustrated, Farrah shouted, "Shut up!" That's when Kane attacked her. He started choking and punching her as if she were a man. Hearing the commotion, Tyler leaped down out of the attic and rushed to his sister's aid. He elbowed Kane on the back of his head and pinned him up against the wall. He then began to mercilessly beat his brother-in-law while Farrah stood nearby begging him to stop. Kane's soul begged for mercy. When was the beating going to end and why did it hurt so bad? It seemed as if adrenaline had forsaken Kane once and for all. Tyler picked Kane up over his head and threw him as far as he could. He then mounted his brother-in-law and gave him a grown-man's spanking he'd never forget.

Thirty minutes later, the police were at the Anderson's house, taking Kane's report. "And then, he picked me up and threw me onto the coffee table," said Kane as he held a wet towel over his left eye. His right eye was swollen and it was obvious that Kane was developing two black eyes. A few seconds later, one of the officers walked up to Kane and told him to stand to his feet. Assuming that the officer was about to take him outside so he could identify his assailant, Kane stood up, but to his surprise, the officer told him to place his hands behind his back. "Yes, officer," said Farrah. "My brother was just defending me." The officer shook his head. "That's all we need ma'am," he said. Looking at Tyler, the officer saluted and said, "Thank you for your service, sir. Take care of your sister. We'll take care of this scumbag."

"Battered Wives' Syndrome." Dr. Smallwood was certain that Farrah was suffering from Battered Wives' Syndrome. "What is that?" asked Farrah as she held her belly. Tyler spoke up before Dr. Smallwood could say a thing. "It's pretty much Post Traumatic Stress Syndrome for spouses," he said. "Dr. Smallwood helped me to move past PTSD and that's why I knew she'd be perfect for you. Plus, y'all kinda look alike." Dr. Smallwood smiled. "Thanks for the compliment," she said posing. "Your sister's absolutely beautiful — but wait ... " Ms. Smallwood's demeanor seemed to suddenly change. "If I look like your sister, that means I don't have a chance in Hell with you," she said. Tyler smiled and winked at the Psychiatrist. "There's always Heaven," he said.

Three months later, Farrah could still feel the effects of the soul tie she had with her husband. A big part of her wanted to reconcile with him so that she could experience every plan they'd made together. Nevertheless, after getting her restraining order extended, Farrah walked into her lawyer's office with her best friend, Aisha, by her side. "I'm here to file for divorce," she said. The lump that began to form in Farrah's throat started to subside as Aisha rubbed her back. "It's gonna be okay. I survived Danny and God blessed me with Kwan. Kwan and I have been married for ten years and he has never lifted a finger to hurt me. Like Pastor Gloria said, you have us. We are here for you. You don't have to do this alone." Knowing that she would be giving birth to baby Karrah soon without her husband made Farrah even sadder. Nevertheless, she knew that her church family, her brother Tyler and her best friend would be there. She thought of something Pastor Gloria said to her. She'd said, "Sometimes, we imagine the major events that we want to occur in our lives like our weddings, our marriages, childbirth and so on. During our immaturity, we've mentally created pictures of these events and placed the wrong people on these pictures. We then hung them up in our hearts. Then, the truth hits us like a tsunami and God washes those people out of our lives, even though the pictures are still up. It's up to us to take the pictures off the wall and realize that God is not saying no to us someday experiencing the desires of our hearts. Instead, He simply has us to take the pictures down so He can change the faces on them."

Five years later, Farrah finally experienced what Pastor

Gloria had spoken to her. She was in the process of giving birth to her second child, a little boy she'd already named Stanley, after his father. Her husband, Stanley Sr., stood next to her and held her hand as she pushed out their first child together. Farrah got to experience the desires of her heart, but with a different man. During her single season, she'd finally came to terms with the fact that she'd made an idol out of Kane and she'd made an idol out of herself. She repented of these sins and asked the Lord to retake His place in her heart. She committed herself to a life of purity and three years after her divorce was finalized, she met Stanley. The couple started courting and they maintained their purity throughout the courtship.

Three years after they were married, Farrah stood in front of an audience of women and shared her testimony. She said, "When I was married to my first husband, I would give anything to experience a romantic moment with him. I loved those spontaneous moments when he'd be in a good mood and take me out to a beach, a park or out to eat. Those moments fueled my belief that everything would work out in the end. But that's all they were: fleeting moments that were few and far between. As crazy as it sounds, even after he'd beat me, I would try to think of ways to recreate those romantic moments that seemed to draw us closer together. He seemed so genuine, so authentic. I thought that no one would understand our love. I believed that I was the only woman who understood him. His mother had abandoned him when he was small and then, when she came back, she mistreated him. I believed I was the woman who God wanted to use to heal the damage she'd done, to change his views of women. I did everything in my power to make him happy, but he always seemed to find some fault in me. He separated me from my family by highlighting the fact that just about every one of my family members was dysfunctional. He could not separate me from my brother Tyler, though. Tyler and I have always been close. There was no way I would have let him separate me from Tyler. While going through a divorce, he threatened to take our daughter, Karrah, from me. He threatened to kill me; he threatened to ruin my reputation, and he threatened to kill himself. I kept calling his bluff. I was finally tired; I was finally fed up. Listen up, you will never think to yourself, 'I'm ready to leave him for good now.' That just doesn't happen. Instead, one day, you'll tell yourself, 'I need to leave him for good and I have to do it now!' It takes a made-up and settled mind to leave an abuser. But if you've made up your mind to come to this conference, that means that you've already taken the first step towards freedom. My goal is to help you to take the next one and the next one until you learn to walk away on your own. Leaving an abuser is like being a baby all over again. You take one step and then you fall. You take another step and then you fall. Eventually, you'll get so tired of falling that you'll learn to stand. Once you learn to stand without the help of others, you'll learn to walk away. Take a look at this handsome gentleman to my right. This is my husband, Stanley. With my ex, I used to beg and search for romantic moments, but amazingly enough, my entire marriage to Stanley has been non-stop love and romance. Do we argue? Yes, but it's rare and we apologize within ten minutes. We truly love each other. I don't have to beg for moments anymore. I'm living the life I always wanted, but I had to put God first. If you put a man before God, the Lord will show you how terrible of a god a man would be. Guess where my ex-husband is at now? He's locked up in Raleigh's Central Prison, serving a life sentence for strangling his pregnant girlfriend to death. That could have been me, y'all. That would have been me. I had to stop waiting for the strength to walk away and just walk away in my weakness, trusting that God would hold me up. That girl lost her life and her baby, and for what? Because my ex-hated not being in control. When she refused to talk to him, he got up and attacked her. Like me, she probably thought it was just another fight. She didn't know she was gonna die that day. I often wonder if she'd known that Kane Anderson would take her life, would she have stayed with him? I have no doubt that the answer to this question is no. Just like many of you would not stay in the abusive relationships you are in or were in if you knew the end of them. I know we hate starting over, but starting over means a new start at life. Some women will stick around with their abusive husbands, only to realize one day that you can't change somebody who doesn't want to be changed. I thank God for saving my life and my mind. He wants to do the same for you. If you're ready for a new start, stand to your feet, so we can pray for you."

As a former victim of domestic violence, I wrote this story to shed some light into what happens behind the scenes in an abusive marriage. Most people think that an abused woman is mishandled and mistreated twenty-four hours a day, seven days a week and this is not true. Perpetrators of domestic violence tend to be very charming and very good at convincing their lovers that they themselves are the victims. One of the feats abusers manage to accomplish is to convince their victims that they are not being abused. This is usually done through comparison. An abuser will befriend men who are more violent than himself. He will then contrast what his friends are doing to their lovers with what he's doing to his lover. For example, Kane would say to Farrah, "I had to go over to Jake's house today to stop him from killing Michelle. Do you know he broke a chair over her back? I had to punch the dude to get his attention. I told him, 'Look man, that's a woman. I understand that people fight, but you're taking it too far.'" In this, Kane would be casting himself as a hero, saving a damsel in distress from an abusive monster. Kane's friendship with Jake would only serve to justify his beliefs that he has the right to abuse his wife.

In this story, I shared one or two scenes I've heard from domestic violence victims, including the part where Kane choked Farrah until she passed out. She eventually woke up in a puddle of her own urine. I remember a co-worker sharing a similar testimony with me maybe twenty years ago. She'd been separated from her abusive husband for more than two years and the couple had recently reconciled. At first, it looked like everything was going great. He would send her flowers to work all the time and she would brag about the expensive dinner dates and gifts that he lavished upon her. But one day, she came to work late and told us about the horrific night she'd had. According to her, her ex-husband had come over to her house and they'd argued. He became so angry that he started choking her. He did this until she was finally unconscious. She woke up the next morning in her own urine. This is the reality of domestic violence and if we keep trying to tell cute little non-gory stories, we'll help to conceal the true horrors that happen behind closed doors.

One of the first things I'd like to mention is this: most

people who are victims of domestic violence have made idols out of the people they are being abused by. I know this seems unfair because we want to embrace the victim, but one thing we must understand is if a heart condition is not dealt with, we can help to rescue the victim from the victimizer, but as long as their minds have not been changed, they'll only go out and attract the same devil in a different man. This is why victims of domestic abuse repeatedly find themselves in abusive relationships. When I was in an abusive marriage, I was guilty of idolizing the man I was married to. Of course, I didn't realize this at first. I thought my obsession with him was unfiltered love, but it wasn't. It was idolatry, and one of the things I learned from that experience is that the emotional pull of idolatry is far stronger than the pull of love. Let me explain.

Idolatry is a heart condition; it is a stronghold. In love, we learn to hold people close and let people go when necessary. We grow up and move out of our parents' houses, not because we don't love them, but because we have to build lives for ourselves outside of them. This doesn't mean that we don't appreciate all they've done for us. It simply means that we've grown up. Additionally, we learn to love some of our teachers, but once we're promoted to the next grade, we have to move on. We can't keep frequenting our former teachers' classrooms. This means that the love we have for them doesn't die; it simply transitions. In idolatry, there is no release or transition; there is only obsession, need, desperation, rejection, fear of rejection and fear of the unknown. I didn't realize that I'd made an idol out of the man I was married to until we started breaking up. Because I was brokenhearted, my prayer life got stronger. I drew closer to God and that's when I began to hear more from Him. One day, I heard Him clearly say to me that I'd made an idol out of my husband. I couldn't deny it. I thought back to all of the things I'd done and I confessed to God that He was speaking the truth. I repented in that moment and that repentance sealed the fate of that marriage because it was established on an altar and once I tore the altar down, the man walked away. After all, there was no place left for him. Since then, I've met and counseled many victims of abuse and I've noticed that they all have that one thing in common: their husbands (or wives) are their everything. They sinned to get them and they kept sinning to keep them.

Instead of pointing out the details of the story, I want to point out the ways of an abuser and the mindset/ways of an abuse victim. Of course, you'll notice that both Farrah and Kane were guilty of some of these pointers.

1. **Abusers convince their victims that everyone is against them.** They do this because they want to

create an "us against the world" syndrome in the victim. This is designed to make the victim feel safe, loved and wanted by the abuser and to establish distrust in the victim towards others.

2. **Abusers and abuse victims tend to magnify the problems in other people's relationships in an attempt to minimize the problems in their own.** Farrah pointed out that Aisha and her husband had argued over a piece of chicken. This was a minor disagreement, but Farrah used it to justify staying with Kane.

3. **Abusers are often very funny and likable people.** This helps them to appear to be sensitive and changeable. Abuse victims, like most people, have their hearts set on a target. Without hope, a victim would not remain a victim. Abusers have to instill hope in their victims and they do this through charm, flattery and gift-giving.

4. **Abusers have a system that utilizes both flattery and condemnation.** An abuser is always trying to master and manipulate the personality of the person he or she is abusing. To do this, they flatter their lovers when they think flattery will help them to accomplish their desired results, and they condemn their lovers when they think condemnation will help them to achieve their desired results.

5. **Murder and suicide are two spirits that haunt abuse victims.** Earlier on in the story, you'll notice that Farrah starts fantasizing about her funeral. In her fantasy, her husband is standing near her coffin, crying and screaming that he's sorry. Believe it or not, this is a common fantasy for an abuse victim. When I was a victim, I would always fantasize about dying. This was the spirit of suicide trying to attach itself to me, but praises be to God, my dad had scared all of us away from the idea of suicide when we were younger. He'd always told us that if we killed ourselves, we'd go to Hell. He reasoned this way: God told us that we are not to murder anyone. My dad told us that our last act on Earth would be us murdering ourselves and we would have no time to repent for that. Now, I do understand that we are no longer under the law of works, but standing before God as a murderer was not a part of my fantasy. The spirit of murder stepped in and tempted me many times, just like it does most abuse victims. I wasn't just tempted; I tried to act out what I'd envisioned in my head. One day, I grabbed a pair of scissors and planned to drive them in my ex's chest. Another day, I tried to run him over with my car. Again, if you come across an abuse victim, please know that two of the spirits that need to be cast out of them are murder and

suicide.

6. **Many abuse victims don't realize they're victims.** Identifying where we are makes us want to change, so Satan works tirelessly to ensure that anyone under his deception believes they are further along than they really are. For example, most abuse victims will talk about people who are being abused. They'll say things like, "That couldn't be me," or "I wish somebody would try that with me." This is because they refer to every abusive encounter this way: "We got into a fight." This helps to equally distribute the guilt to both parties, thus, allowing the victim to justify staying in the relationship.

7. **Abusers love the extremes.** They love to give their victims extremely great times, followed by extreme bad times. The purpose of the great times is to get their victims to believe that they are changing and to give them something to hold on to during the downtime.

8. **Abusers can go weeks or months without physically assaulting their lovers.** Most people, including victims of abuse, believe that true abusers harass and attack their lovers everyday. This is not true. The reality is, an abuser doesn't necessarily have to repeatedly use his hands to get what he wants. Most abusers use manipulation (silent

treatment, leaving for hours or days at a time, saying they're getting tired, saying they've checked out of the relationship, exes and whatever tools they can use) to get what they want. Most victims are manipulated on a daily basis. Physical assaults do tend to escalate over time. This is especially true if the victim is strong-willed.

9. **Abuse victims live more in their heads than they do in reality.** Understand this: we will always choose the channel where the signal is clearer. What does this mean? It's simple. It is human nature to fantasize; we all know this, but whenever our fantasies are better than our realities, we will spend more time fantasizing than we do living. Abuse victims are often married to two men: the man in their heads and the man they live with. Now, both of these men have the same face and many of the same traits, but their personalities are almost night and day. This means that the victim is oftentimes more in love with what they can see versus the actual person. Abuse victims often marry their fantasies, but divorce their realities. I've learned that the real fight in an abusive relationship is both parties trying to coach, coerce and drag their lovers from the personalities that they actually have to the ones they want them to have. Once an abuse victim accepts that his or her lover is not going to

change, the victim will stop being a victim and walk away.

10. **Most abusers and abuse victims are the products of dysfunctional upbringings.** Telling an abuse victim that her husband is not treating her right is like telling a colorblind woman to wear a red shirt to the company picnic. To her, red and green look the same. To an abuse victim, all relationships are dysfunctional. This is because they have never experienced a functional relationship. Oftentimes, they'll even believe that people who appear to be happy are simply putting on a performance. When God has me ministering to abuse victims, He rarely has me telling them to run away from their abusive lovers. Instead, He has me to hang out with them and let them see that His love for me and my love for myself are both functional. This is very effective because victims of abuse often believe that being single and starting over is far worse than the abuse they are suffering. They need to see a demonstration of love functioning the way it's supposed to function, even if the person who's demonstrating love to them is single. Oftentimes, this causes the victim to mentally create a side-by-side video of their lives and their mentor's lives. Slowly but surely, they start to realize that their abusive lovers do not truly love them, but are

instead self-centered, demonized people who are hell-bent on controlling them.

11. **Abusers love to use futuristic terms with their victims.** For example, an abusive husband may say to his wife, "When we get old, I'm gonna remind you that you said that." Phrases like these are designed to make the victim feel that there is a future and that the future will be better than the present. This is just the abuser's way of buying more time.

12. **Abuse victims often become as manipulative and as crafty as their abusive partners.** In the aforementioned story, you'll notice that Farrah changed the color of her hair to appear more attractive to her husband. She posted her picture online to entice him into coming back home. This is done to arouse his curiosity or his fear. Abuse victims will often play mind games with their lovers. This is because their lovers tend to be manipulative, so they learn to be manipulative as well.

13. **Abuse victims often use other people as pawns in their attempts to get what they want.** For example, you can have a friend who is the victim of abuse and her husband or lover may despise you wholeheartedly. He will request or suggest that his wife or partner stays away from you and she will do exactly what he's suggested when things are going

well between them. However, one day, he will hurt her and to get back at him, she will call you and ask you if you want to hang out. This is done to provoke her lover. They will use exes, friends, former friends, and family members to provoke their lovers. If you stay near the victim's house or someone the abuser tends the visit, you may get a surprise visit from the victim. You'll notice that she's overly dressed to be making house visits. She'll pretend that she's there to see you, but in truth, she wants her husband or lover to see her. For this reason, she may suddenly request to sit outside or ask if you'd like to go walking. This is why you must always be prayerful when dealing with a victim of abuse.

14. **Most abusers cast themselves as the victims.** It starts off with them accusing their parents of mishandling, mistreating or abandoning them. This is the abuser's attempt to justify his ways. This is his way of saying, "I'm not a bad person. I just had a really difficult life. That's why I am the way that I am. If you leave me, you are no better than my mother" (for example). As a matter of fact, during the good times (before the abuse starts), most abusers will tell their victims a lot of horrific things that they've experienced and then they'll say something like, "Everyone I love leaves me." This is

to get their lovers to vow to not leave them. If their victims start talking about leaving them, attempts to leave them or successfully leaves them, they will cry and say, "You are just like everyone else! You said you wouldn't leave me, but you lied! You are just like everyone else!" Most abusive men claim to be victims of immoral women. When provoked or hurt, they'll often generalize women, saying things like, "All you women are the same!" Knowing the abuser's history with women, the victim suddenly feels obligated to not be like every woman the abuser once complained about.

15. **Abuse victims tend to take mental snapshots of moments or words.** For example, when Kane used the term "answered prayer," Farrah got excited. It's moments like those that fuel the victim's belief that he or she is making progress.

16. **Abuse victims tend to believe that if they get their lovers in the right church, they'll go through deliverance and suddenly become great men.** This belief drives the victim and gives her hope. For this reason, a victim will spend a lot of time trying to convince her partner to come to church with her. When and if he does, she will have high expectations in regards to the person (minister) officiating the service. She will pray for deliverance to break out in hopes that the dark

personality that she's witnessed manifesting in her husband or lover will be cast out. Nevertheless, she will leave several deliverance services disappointed, not because deliverance didn't break out in the place, but because her lover didn't get any prayer. This is because God doesn't force His hands on anyone. The predator must want to be free and ask for freedom before God will touch him. This is why many abuse victims go from church to church in search of someone who can "discern" them in the spirit and help them with their abusive lovers.

17. **Most abusers will convince their victims to nurse them back to health.** Aisha dreamed that Farrah was breastfeeding a baby snake. This was symbolic of what Farrah was doing with Kane. She knew that he'd been through a lot with his mother, so she was attempting to nurse him back to sanity. Nevertheless, a snake is a snake. Feeding it is only helping it to grow big enough to swallow you whole.

18. **Abusers want to have babies with their victims to gain another method of control over them.** I've been in one abusive marriage, but I've been in two potentially abusive relationships before I entered that abusive marriage. In every one of those cases, the men spoke a lot about children. Of course, I ended the two relationships that could have been potentially abusive the moment I realized that the

guys had anger issues. From the start of one of those relationships, the guy I had been dating kept talking about us having a baby together. He was obsessed with the idea and I didn't know why at first, but it didn't take me long to find out. After he'd got drunk one day, we got into an argument. That's when he picked me up, threw me on his bed, and started threatening to punch me if I got up. Still enraged, he threw his glass against the wall, shattering it. He kept screaming at the top of his lungs and threatening to hit me. I didn't know what to do, so I started crying and pretending to see his point of view. Once he calmed down, I convinced him that all was well, but I needed to go home. When he felt safe enough to let me leave, I left. When he called me, I promptly ended the relationship, but he didn't want to hear it. He stalked me for a few months. He even tried to kidnap me. I learned young that a man who is in a rush to become a father is oftentimes an abuser looking to anchor himself in his intended victim's life.

19. **Abusers punish their victims for disappointing them.** In the aforementioned story, Kane would not only physically assault his wife whenever she upset him, he would also leave for a day or more. This is a very common method of control that's used by

abusers. The thought of losing them is designed to scare their victims into submission.

20. **Most male abusers objectify women.** This is the same thing that serial killers do. By objectifying women, an abuser can easily shut off his emotions when he's attacking or mistreating his victim. This is why trying to change an abuser is like falling into a lion's den and trying to talk a hungry lion out of doing what comes naturally to it: making a skin sandwich out of you!

21. **Victims often change their appearance in an attempt to reignite their lovers' interest.** Abuse victims will suddenly change the color of their hair, cut their hair, suddenly start wearing makeup, buy new clothes or try to lose weight in their attempts to rekindle their relationships with their lovers. This is why Farrah dyed her hair honey blonde.

22. **Abusers often request demeaning sexual favors.** This hasn't happened to me personally, but many of the women I've counseled testified about their husbands refusing to have sex with them. Instead, they'd request odd or demeaning sexual favors. This is an attempt to belittle the woman and make her feel cheap. This is also the abusers' way of punishing his victim.

23. **Victims of domestic violence often tell their abusive lovers when someone tells them to**

leave. This is the victim's way of making a sacrifice. Some victims believe that by informing their lovers about an attempt to break them up, their abusers will suddenly see how loyal they are to them. They believe that by making this sacrifice, their relationships will take a turn for the better. This is especially true when the person who told the victim to leave is very close to the victim. The greater the influence that person has on the victim, the greater the sacrifice. Abusers will often reward their victims for ratting out their friends and family members by sleeping with them, being overly kind to them or taking them out. This is to get the victim to share more information and to acclimate the victim to the "rewards system" the victimizer has in place.

24. **Abusers often convince their lovers that there is someone else out there who was better suited for them, but somehow, they'd managed to be separated from those people, but not through a contentious breakup.** They will then go on to say or imply that the person wants them back. This is to make the victim feel lucky to have them. It also serves as an indirect threat to the victim, basically letting the victim know that the only thing that's keeping them and the love of their lives from being together is the victim. They will oftentimes use the

words "us, ours, and we" when referencing their exes. This is a manipulation tactic designed to make the victim feel like a third wheel who's interrupting what could potentially be a great relationship. For example, the abuser will say something like, "<u>We</u> decided that breaking up was best for <u>us</u> because <u>we</u> were gonna live so far apart. <u>We</u> didn't want to hold each other's lives up and <u>we</u> knew that staying together would be selfish on both of <u>our</u> ends. When I spoke with her yesterday, <u>we</u> both joked about how <u>we've</u> ruined a lot of relationships trying to turn <u>our</u> lovers into each other." Such conversations are designed to make the victim feel "lucky" to have the abuser and to make the victim jealous of what the abuser is pretending to have with his ex. It is to make the victim feel that the ex knows what he wants and needs, whereas, the victim has yet to figure him out. This is the abuser's way of casting himself as the victim.

25. **Abuse victims tend to abandon the friends who tell them the truth and they often draw closer to the ones who tell them what they want to hear.** Even though Tina told Farrah that she needed to leave Kane, she didn't try to press the matter. Instead, she entertained Farrah's desire to make her husband jealous. She came to her house, styled her hair, hung out with her and then allowed her to

send her away the minute she realized that Kane was home. For this reason, Farrah preferred Tina as a friend over Aisha; that was, until she was ready to hear the uncompromising truth.

26. **Abusers often convince their victims that they are at fault for the treatment they are receiving.** Sadly enough, this mind control is so effective that the victims start blaming themselves without the help of their abusers. Here's the truth: we can look at almost every argument, disagreement or uncomfortable situation and find a way to blame ourselves. Nevertheless, the choice to strike another human being is entirely the fault of the striker. For example, I live in Georgia where people drive like they've lost their minds in a card game. Oftentimes, I have to slam on breaks because some overly proud and anxious driver decided to cut me off. Nevertheless, as frightening and offensive as their actions were, I exercised my ability to choose how I handled the offense. Yes, I could have chased them, rammed them with my car and threw rocks at their windows. I could have screamed obscenities at them or tried to run them off the road, but I don't behave like this because I am not a city without walls. In other words, evil thoughts are not entertained. I just have to keep on driving, even though I may be grumbling in my car or shouting

phrases like, "Are you serious?!" This means that even though I couldn't control their actions, I could control my reaction. In other words, there is absolutely no justifiable excuse for a human being to strike another human being unless that person is defending himself/herself.

There's much more that you can extract from Kane and Farrah's story, but the most important thing is:

1. You cannot control another human being.
2. People change when they want to change, not when you want them to change.
3. An abuser is abusive because he or she chooses to be that way. It's a choice, not a default!
4. Any person who outranks God in your life will eventually show you what God doesn't look like.
5. There is no excuse for a person to prey on another human being! Having a bad mother or father is not a justifiable excuse; it's the predator's way of saying that he (or she) does not want to change! When people want to change, they stop making excuses and start seeking help.

Note: It is absolutely foolish and dangerous to tell a victim to fight back. Most people who've never endured domestic violence say silly things like, "It couldn't have been me," or "If he did that to me, I'd snap." The person may be speaking what he or she truly believes, but those words have not been tested. Additionally, not all abusers are the same. One abuser may learn his lesson if his wife suddenly becomes crazier than he is, but another abuser may take her life. I often tell a story of when I was pinned up against the wall, feet dangling in the air and fighting my ex back. I heard a voice say, "Stop fighting. Be still." I knew God at that time and I was saved, even though I wasn't completely submitted to Him. I don't know if I realized that I was hearing from God, but I somehow knew to adhere to instructions I'd just received. I stopped fighting and just stared at my ex until he dropped me. I didn't see love or humanity in his eyes; I saw utter darkness. I now know that if I had listened to the people who'd told me to snap, I wouldn't be here to share my testimony today. The best thing for an abuse victim to do is to stop being a victim and leave. Why does it have to happen in this order? Because a victim will be a victim wheresoever she goes, but when she decides to become a victor, her mind will change and she will not submit to a victimizer anymore. Remember this key: victimizers rule over victims, but they cannot rule over victors because victors are more than conquerors through Christ Jesus.

Chapter 7

Rejected Legacy

Names are very important to God. As a matter of fact, as we search the scriptures, we learn that God changed the names of several people. He changed Abram's name to Abraham. He changed Sarai's name to Sarah. He changed Simon's name to Cephas (Peter) and He changed Saul's name to Paul.

The Bible speaks about the Book of Life, where our names are written. It also talks about names being blotted out from the Book of Life. Lastly, God talks about making a man's name great; this meant that God was going to bless that man and his lineage. So, as we can see, our names are more important than we realize. Additionally, our surnames are just as important.

———————

Amanda let a few tears fall from her eyes as she signed her name to the divorce papers that had been just handed to her. "There," she said to her lawyer, handing the papers back to him. "It's done. Can I leave now?" The lawyer nodded his head. "Take care of yourself Mrs. Mallory," he said as Amanda left his office.

The cold breeze met Amanda at the door. The day felt dead and dry; it was almost as if the weather was grieving as much as Amanda was. Suddenly, Amanda remembered a question that she'd forgotten to ask her lawyer. She reached into her purse and grabbed her cell phone. "Hello," she said. "Can I have Mr. Kyle's office? This is Amanda Mallory calling." The operator placed Amanda on hold and a few seconds later, Amanda's lawyer picked up the line. "Kyle speaking," he said. Amanda rushed into a nearby store to ensure that Mr. Kyle would be able to hear her. "Mr. Kyle, this is Amanda Mallory. I forgot to ask you ... do I have to change my last name? I mean, do I have to stop using his last name once the divorce is final?" Mr. Kyle's answer was quick and somewhat rushed. "No," he said. "That's completely up to you. The courts will never force you to change your last name. Okay?" Amanda thanked the attorney and hung up the line. "Stupid boy," Amanda whispered to herself as she made her way out of the store and towards her car. "I gave you two children and this is how you repay me."

Seven months later, Amanda's divorce was finalized and her growing belly ousted her secret. Amanda was five months pregnant by a man she'd met at church. His name was Luke and both he and Amanda were excited to know that she was finally going to have a boy. She had two daughters by her ex-husband, Anthony, and now, she was due to deliver what the doctors said was a healthy baby boy that following September.

Luke was a very handsome man. Standing at six foot, three inches tall and weighing 225 pounds, Luke was athletic and charming. He looked like an upgrade from Anthony — Amanda's ex-husband. Anthony was a mere five foot, six inches tall and weighed 274 pounds, meaning Anthony was slightly overweight.

Amanda loved showing off her handsome, well-mannered boyfriend. Even though Luke didn't have a great job (he worked as a barber at a local shop), he did seem to have a promising future. After all, Luke had aspirations of someday opening his own barber shop. Amanda loved taking him to church with her for two reasons. The first reason was — she wanted to show him off, especially since her ex's mother was a member of her church. The second reason was that she secretly hoped that by doing so, the pastor would say something indirectly or directly to Luke that would make him want to surrender his life to God. Nevertheless, Amanda's manipulative ways were not unnoticed or appreciated by Luke. He didn't like the fact that she was trying to save him, plus, he reasoned within himself that she was a hypocrite. After all, she'd slept with him, knowing that she was not married to him. As a matter of fact, their sexual relationship started long before Amanda's divorce was final.

Fed up with Amanda's ways, Luke decided to end the relationship with her. "I'll help out with Luke, Jr." he said as he entered his car. He'd spent a few nights with Amanda, reasoning within himself that he wanted to have sex with her a few more times before ending the relationship. After he'd had his fill of her, Luke started an argument on Saturday night after Amanda asked him if he had brought something with him to wear to church. He used that opportunity to break up with Amanda. "Who said I'm going to name *my* son Luke, Jr.?!" Amanda snarled as she hit the driver's side window with the palm of her right hand. "You're a punk! You're not a real man! What kind of man breaks up with a pregnant woman?!" Amanda screamed as Luke pulled away. Once again, Amanda was heartbroken and now, she would have to raise three children by herself.

Two months later, Amanda gave birth to a baby boy who she named Alvion. She did this to spite Luke. Additionally, she didn't give Alvion his father's surname. Angry that Amanda hadn't named his first and only son after him,

Luke decided to disown the boy altogether. After all, he was now in what he believed to be a promising relationship with a woman who owned her own hair salon.

On the other side of the world, Anthony, Amanda's ex-husband, had just received the news that his girlfriend, Nova, had given birth to their twin daughters. Anthony was in the United States Army and was stationed in Kuwait. The news of his daughters' births was exciting news for him, but at the same time, it was somewhat scary. After all, before Anthony met Amanda, he already had three daughters. He then had two with Amanda, and now, his new girlfriend had just given birth to twins, bringing the number of children he'd be responsible for to seven. He'd already been complaining about the amount of child support that he was being forced to pay and now he'd have to pay more. Additionally, Anthony desperately wanted to have a son, but at the rate he was going, he was starting to believe that he could only produce girls. And lastly, Anthony was beginning to experience a change of heart towards Nova. Sure, she was a nice, quiet and decent woman, but she was a little too quiet for Anthony. She rarely responded to anything Anthony said. Instead, she'd smile and respond using body language; for example, if Anthony asked her a question, she'd shrug her shoulders if she didn't know the answer. She'd nod if the answer was "yes," but when the answer was "no," she was sure to verbalize it. On top of that, she had a very odd relationship with her father. She seemed to be more vocal, playful and open with him, but with Anthony, she was somewhat quiet, reserved and secretive. For this reason, Anthony knew that he was going to be stuck paying child support for his daughters with Nova as well.

Anthony was no longer in touch with his daughters by Amanda because every time he called to speak with them, Amanda would antagonize him and ask for more money. She would then threaten to take him back to court for more child support. Anthony finally grew weary of Amanda's bitterness towards him, so he disassociated himself from his daughters altogether. Nevertheless, he'd been engaged in some heavy combat for the last few days, so he reasoned within himself that he needed to reach out to Amber and Antoinette: his daughters with Amanda.

Amber was seven years old and Antoinette was four. Amber was slowly beginning to harbor feelings of anger and unforgiveness towards her father, but to Antoinette, her dad could do no wrong.

Amanda: Hello?

Anthony: Hey. This is Anthony. How are the kids?

Amanda: What kids?

Anthony: Don't start, Amanda. How are Amber and

Antoinette?

Amanda: I didn't think you realized you had kids over here. We haven't heard from you in what ... four or five months?

Anthony: I'm in Kuwait, Amanda. I'm in the middle of a war. I can't call like I want to call. Can I please speak with Amber?

Amanda: Plus, I heard that congratulations are in order. So, you're now the father of two twin girls, right? When were you going to tell me this?

Anthony: When it became your business. Amanda, please let me talk to Amber. I didn't call to fight.

Amanda: As far as I'm concerned, you don't have any kids over here. Call that Nova girl and ask to speak with her kids ... if they are even yours!

Anthony: See, this is why I don't call. Don't you have a son now? Why is it that it's okay for you to move on, but it's a sin if I do the same? Don't take out your frustrations on me, Amanda. I just want to talk with my children.

Amanda: What children?

With that, Amanda hung up the phone. She was angry with Anthony for moving on; she was angry with Anthony for not calling his daughters, and she was angry with Anthony for divorcing her. Additionally, she inwardly blamed Anthony for her breakup with Luke, after all, the only reason she'd pressured Luke to go to church was because of what she'd gone through with Anthony. She didn't want a repeat of her marriage with Anthony, so she would often ask Luke to do the things that Anthony once refused to do.

A few days later, Amanda received notice that Anthony had been killed in combat. Not sure how to feel, Amanda decided to keep the news from his daughters for a few days. She knew that she wouldn't be able to get around taking the kids to his funeral, but at the same time, she worried mostly about Amber's reaction. Even though Amber was angry with her father, most of her anger had been the result of what she'd heard her mother say.

The day of Anthony's funeral finally arrived and just as Amanda predicted, Amber was not only heartbroken, she was furious with her mother. She walked up to her father's casket and placed a single stem red rose on his chest. "I'm sorry, Daddy," she said as the tears began to pour from her eyes. "If you can hear me, please know that I'm sorry!" Amber continued to scream apologies to her father and her voice grew louder and louder, so much so that Amanda's mother rushed over to grab her. Antoinette, on the other hand, didn't understand death. To her, Anthony was simply sleeping. Nevertheless, when she saw her sister crying, she began to cry. Amanda picked up her ailing daughter and both her and her mother led the children out of the sanctuary.

Outside the sanctuary was Anthony's stepfather. He was sitting one of the steps, holding onto the purple heart the military had given him for Anthony. "You know, he was my only son," said Mr. Mallory. "He wasn't my blood, but he was my son. I met his mother when she was pregnant with him; I even asked her to give him my name. And now, look. I've lost my only son," said Mr. Mallory as the tears began to pour down his face. "This pain is a pain I've never felt before. My baby boy is dead! And most folks don't even know I'm grieving cause they figure he ain't my blood, but I loved him like he was my own!" Amanda didn't know what to say. The entire family knew how contentious her relationship had been with Anthony, plus, they knew that she'd went out of her way to keep him away from his daughters. "I'm sure he's in a better place," said Amanda. "Be strong, Mr. Mallory. He wouldn't want to see you hurting."

Suddenly, a loud voice cried out from behind Amanda. "How would you know what he wants, you self-righteous witch?! You kept him away from the one thing he loved the most: his children!" It was Anthony's older sister and she was clearly ready to fight. Amanda placed her arms around her daughters in an attempt to shield herself as Laila rushed over in her direction, spewing obscenities at her. That's when a few of Anthony's relatives rushed over and grabbed her. "It's stupid women like you who make men scared to settle down! Anthony broke up with you, not his daughters! He told me that you turned Amber against him! Stupid! Did you tell her that her father called for her three days before he was killed?! Did you tell her?!" Amanda was stunned. She looked at Amber who was starting to back away from her. "Yeah!" screamed Laila. "Your dad called you three days before he died, but your stupid mother wouldn't let him speak to you because she was still mad that he didn't want her! So, I blame her for his death! If he had talked with his children, things probably would have been different!"

By this time, a group of Anthony's family members had gathered around Laila. They were hugging her and trying to carry her back into the sanctuary. Mr. Mallory didn't say a word to Amanda. He simply got up and made his way over to his daughter. "Let's go inside," he said. Laila looked at her father and began to weep. "I'm sorry, Daddy," she said. "I'm so sorry." With that, she laid her head on her father's shoulder and walked back into the church with him.

Amber's little fists were now clinched. "My daddy called me and you didn't let him talk to me?!" she asked. "Tell me it's not true, Mom! Tell me it's not true!" Amanda looked at her daughter. She wanted to lie to her, but there were still a few of Anthony's family members standing around watching her. "Let's go," said Amanda. "No!" screamed Amber. "You want to get me in the car so you can lie to me! Tell me the truth right here! Did my daddy call and ask to speak to me before he died?!" Amanda looked at her daughter and then looked up at a few of Anthony's family members. "Yes," she said. "I was just mad at him. I'm sorry." With that, Amber kicked her mother's right leg with all of her might before running back into the church. "I do not want to live with you anymore! Leave me alone!" A week later, Amanda gave in to her daughter's demand and let her go and live with Anthony's mother.

A year later, Amanda found herself in the hospital again; this time, giving birth to another baby girl. The father of this child was named Blaine and he looked like a promising prospect for a husband.

Amanda met Blaine outside of her lawyer's office and the two of them seemed to complete each other — that is, at least in Amanda's eyes. Blaine was unemployed, but he made a little money doing odd jobs like painting, lawncare and furniture assembly. Occasionally, he would even work the door at a few local nightclubs, acting as a bouncer.

Blaine had two children, a boy and a girl, from a previous relationship and he was very active in his children's lives. Seeing how good of a father he was to his children made

Amanda want to secure her relationship with him. For this reason, she told him that she was taking birth control pills when she was not. She wanted to have Blaine's child because Blaine represented everything she hadn't gotten from Anthony or Luke. Additionally, Anthony didn't know that Amanda had three children; he believed she only had two children by her deceased ex-husband, Anthony. Since Amber was no longer living with Amanda, Blaine was led to believe that Antoinette and Alvion were both Anthony's children. Amanda also led him to believe that her and Anthony were still married when he'd died. He'd met Amanda a month after Anthony's death. Amanda was leaving her lawyer's office after signing some paperwork. The military was paying out a total of $100,000 to Anthony's children, which of course, would be divided up equally. Since Amanda had two children with Anthony, she was supposed to receive a payout of $28,571.43. Nevertheless, Anthony's mother hired an attorney and demanded a paternity test. She was starting to believe that Antoinette was not Anthony's daughter because her skin was much darker than Anthony and Amanda's skin. Additionally, her nose was wider.

Frustrated after hearing the news that she wasn't going to receive her payout that day, Amanda left the building in tears. That's when she met Blaine. Blaine was heading into the lawyer's office to sign his final paperwork, giving him the right to see his children outside of their mother's supervision. Like Amanda, Blaine's ex was bitter and overly determined to keep him away from his children, even though she insisted that he pay more than half of his wages in child support. Of course, child support was just her way of getting revenge and attempting to control him. Natalie and Blaine had broken up seven months prior to him meeting Amanda. They'd ended their relationship after Blaine discovered that Natalie had unwittingly given her phone number to one of his cousins. Tyree, Blaine's cousin, had flown into Texas from Delaware to attend the family's reunion. When he'd seen Natalie at a local gas station, he didn't know that she was Blaine's fiance. Being the suave, handsome man that he was, he'd approached her and struck up a conversation. Natalie told him that she was in a dead-end relationship and was about to break it off with her boyfriend. She'd given Tyree her phone number and a day later, Tyree realized that Natalie was Blaine's fiance. This happened after Natalie said Blaine's name and he'd figured the rest out. Blaine had always talked about his wife-to-be, Natalie. Of course, Natalie didn't know that Tyree was Blaine's cousin. Tyree wanted to honor the man-code so he told his cousin, Blaine, who, in turn, ended his relationship with Natalie.

While leaving the lawyer's office, Blaine noticed a distraught Amanda heading down the steps. Sure, she was beautiful, but Blaine wasn't romantically interested in her initially because she was obviously hurting. Being the gentlemen that he was, Blaine made his way over to Amanda and asked her if everything was okay. The only words Amanda could seem to get out, however, were, "He died and now ... " From there, she'd started crying uncontrollably, but her tears were not for Anthony; they were centered around the fact that Anthony's family was fighting to keep her from receiving the amount of money she believed she deserved. To comfort her, Blaine shared his story about Natalie with her. Realizing how similar she was to Natalie, Amanda decided to lie about her and Anthony's relationship. Two months later, Amanda was pregnant and Blaine was sure he'd found the woman of his dreams — despite Amanda's tendencies to become easily enraged.

Amanda gave birth to a healthy baby girl who she named Briana and Blaine was ecstatic. Nevertheless, Amanda's lies would meet her head-on while she was in the hospital recovering after Briana's birth. That's because Laila (Anthony's sister) and Nova (the mother of Anthony's twins) both worked as nurses at that hospital.

Laila found out that Amanda was in the hospital twelve minutes after Amanda arrived. This is because she was initially scheduled to help with the delivery, but once she saw Amanda's name and peeped into her room, she immediately went to her supervisors and made them aware of her connection to Amanda. The supervisors placed Laila on another floor, but they were unaware of Nova's knowledge of Amanda. Nova didn't personally know Amanda, but she knew of her. Nova worked the main desk on the third floor so she wouldn't be visiting anyone's room, but she was able to see who went in and who came out. That's how she'd met Blaine.

Blaine was rushing to Amanda's room with an arm full of roses. The doting father beamed with pride as he made his way towards the desk where Nova was sitting. "I think they told me that Amanda Mallory, my fiance, was in room 404," he said. "Do I just go in?" Nova smiled and nodded her head. "Go right ahead, sir," she said.

Blaine walked into Amanda's room and kissed her on the forehead. "I got you these. Beautiful flowers for a beautiful woman," he said. Amanda smiled as she smelled the flowers. "Thank you," she said as she attempted to place the flowers on the table next to her bed. It was obvious that she'd just had a baby. Her skin looked pale and her hair was disheveled. The intravenous needle in her right arm made it difficult for her to reach for anything. "Can you sit these on the table for me and pass me that remote?" Amanda asked, pointing at the controller just below her knees. Blaine happily obliged, grabbing the remote and handing it to the mother of his child. He then grabbed the flowers from her hand and placed them on the table next to her. "How are you feeling?" he asked, caressing Amanda's feet with his hands. "Tired," said Amanda as she crunched on the ice cubes that one of the nurses had given her. "This was the hardest and most draining childbirth I've ever gone through. Amber was easy, but Antoinette had to be suctioned out." Blaine was surprised. "Wait. Who's Amber?" he asked. Realizing that she'd just exposed the fact that she had another daughter, Amanda suddenly stopped talking and started staring at Blaine. "Who's Amber, Amanda? I've heard that name before. I remember Antoinette asking about her, but I thought she was your niece. Amanda? Who's Amber?"

Suddenly, a nurse walked into the room. "How are you feeling, Ms. Mallory? We've just checked on little Briana and she's doing well. We'll be bringing her into the room in an hour or less. Is this handsome guy the father?" Amanda was still in shock. "Yes," she said. "He's the father." In that moment, Blaine felt a wave of emotions hit him. He suddenly realized that he did not know Amanda the way he thought he knew her. But before he could get a word out, the door swung open again, but this time, it was Mrs. Mallory — Anthony's mother. Laila called and told her that Amanda was in the hospital, having given birth to another child, so Mrs. Mallory decided to come to the hospital to let Amber meet her little sister and to ask about the blood test. The test had been delayed because Amanda had used every excuse she could think of to keep from taking it, including the fact that she was pregnant. This kept the money from being released to the rest of Anthony's children.

Amanda's eyes seemed to double in size when she saw Mrs. Mallory walking through the door with Amber. "What's going on? What are you doing here?" asked Amanda. Mrs. Mallory stopped and placed her hands on her hips. "What does it look like? Amber wanted to come and meet her little sister." The nurse looked shocked. "I'll be back in to check on you in a few minutes," she said, giggling as she walked out of the room. Blaine looked directly at Amber. She looked just like her mother. It was obvious that she was Amanda's daughter. "Ma, why didn't you tell me you were having another baby?" asked Amber. "I know I live with Grandma, but at the end of the day, I'm still your daughter," scoffed Amber.

Blaine: Excuse me. My name is Blaine.
Mrs. Mallory: So, you're the baby's father, right?
Blaine: Yes, ma'am. It looks that way.
Amanda: What do you mean it looks that way?
Blaine: I was just answering the question.

Amanda: Blaine, please leave and call me later. I'll explain everything then.

Mrs. Mallory: Leave for what? I'm not here to cause any trouble. I'm just here to bring your daughter by. Young man, you don't have to leave on my account.

Amanda: Mrs. Mallory, now is not the time ...

Mrs. Mallory: Time for what? Oh, you think I want to talk about the paternity test? No. We'll deal with that later. I'm here because Amber wanted to come.

Blaine: Paternity test? Wait. Are you Anthony's mother?

Mrs. Mallory: Yes, I am.

Blaine: Ma'am, I'm so sorry. I didn't realize ...

Mrs. Mallory: It's okay. Amanda, does Luke know you've had another baby?

Amanda: Mrs. Mallory, please ...

Blaine: Wait. Who's Luke?

Mrs. Mallory: He seriously doesn't know who Luke is? Luke is Alvion's father.

Blaine: Wait. Hold up; hold up. I thought Anthony was Alvion's father.

Mrs. Mallory: Anthony? My Anthony?

Amanda: Mrs. Mallory. Let it go ... Please!

Mrs. Mallory: Let what go? No, sir. Anthony and Amanda were going through a divorce when she conceived Alvion. His daddy is named Luke.

With that, Amanda pressed the nurse call button. "I'm

sorry, Mrs. Mallory. You need to leave," she said as the nurses entered the room. "Please escort her out of here." Mrs. Mallory was enraged. "Wait! What did I do wrong?! Tell the truth?! It's obvious that you haven't told this man the truth about who you are! Why are you getting mad at me when all I did was bring your daughter here to visit her new sister? Don't touch me. I'll leave on my own, but remember this, Amanda. You won't be able to avoid taking the blood test for long. And what was your name again? Blaine? Be sure to get a blood test done. That ain't no Proverbs 31 woman!"

After Mrs. Mallory left, there was a deafening silence in the room. Blaine stared at the floor for a few minutes before rising to his feet. "Blaine," said Amanda as Blaine walked out of the door. "Blaine!"

Blaine made his way towards the elevator, but he was intercepted by Nova. "Is everything okay?" she asked. Blaine couldn't seem to focus on Nova or anything. "Yeah," he said. "I'll be alright." Nevertheless, Nova wouldn't let up. "No, you seem distraught. I don't think you need to drive until you clear your head. Come in here," she said, as she grabbed Blaine's left arm and started pulling him towards the break room. "I was about to go on break anyway." Blaine didn't resist; he was too hurt to resist. "Wait. Won't you get in trouble for having me in here?" he asked, but Nova assured him that the room was for staff and patients alike, even though it was rarely used.

Ten minutes later, Blaine found himself sitting across from Nova at a long but empty table.

Nova: So, tell me what's going on?

Blaine: I don't want to burden you with my problems.

Nova: No burden at all, but first, let me introduce myself. My name is Nova, and so you won't think I'm being messy, I know your wife, Amanda.

Blaine: She's not my wife. Wait. How do you know Amanda and why would I think you were being messy? What is going on around here?

Nova: I don't personally know her, but she and I both have children by Anthony Mallory. She used to be married to Anthony, but they were divorced by the time I met him.

Blaine: What?! Wow! So, your children are younger than hers? Anthony had more children after he and Amanda broke up? Is Amanda aware of this?

Nova: Yep. Twins. I have twin daughters by Anthony and yes, she knew.

Blaine: You know, all this time I thought Amanda and Anthony were married when he ...

Nova: ... when he died? No. Anthony was in Kuwait and he really wanted a relationship with his daughters but Amanda wouldn't let him talk with them. That's why ...

Blaine: I get it now. That's why his family hates her. And here it was, I thought they just hated her for no reason other than she'd left Anthony ...

Nova: I could lose my job for having this conversation with you. This was probably not a good idea.

Blaine: No, you're fine. This conversation won't go out of this room. I just need the truth. I mean ... get this ... I just had a baby with a liar who hid a whole daughter from me.

Nova: What?

Blaine: I didn't know about Amber. She let me think that Antoinette and Alvion were Anthony's children. I thought they were her only two children. I didn't know she had another daughter.

Nova: Oh no. I'm sorry to hear that. Amber and Antoinette are Anthony's children. What happened was Anthony called Amanda three days before he was killed. He asked to speak with Amber but Amanda wouldn't let him. He said she kept going off on him about everything, including the fact that she'd heard that Anthony and I had just had our twin daughters. She hung up in his face and three days later, he was dead. Laila, Anthony's sister, confronted her at the funeral and that's when Amber heard what her mother had done. After that, Amber refused to live with her mother which is how she came to stay with Mrs. Mallory.

Blaine: It's all starting to make sense to me now. But why does Anthony's family want a blood test on Antoinette?

Nova: They want a blood test on both children because

Anthony and Amanda were broken up around the time that Amanda got pregnant with Amber. Rumor has it that she was seeing some married man. Anyhow, Anthony told me that she came to his apartment one day begging to reconcile with him. They weren't married at that time, but they'd briefly lived together. According to Anthony, Amanda started seducing him and one thing led to another. A month or two later, she told him she was pregnant. Anthony's a stand-up guy, so he decided to marry her. Around the time she'd gotten pregnant with Antoinette, they were talking about separating. As a matter of fact, Anthony said he'd started moving his stuff out, but before he could move completely out, Amanda told him the news. She was four months pregnant. I mean ... who hides a pregnancy for four months? He said she didn't take a pregnancy test or go to the doctor. She just announced it and she'd even told him how far along she was. Of course, Anthony didn't believe her so he went to the store and bought a pregnancy test. Sure enough, she was pregnant, so he moved his stuff back in and tried to work on his marriage.

Blaine: Wow. I'm literally speechless. I was supposed to be coming here to meet my daughter for the first time, but as it turns out, I'm meeting Amanda, the mother of my child, for the first time. This is a lot to take in.

Nova: I understand.

Blaine: This girl had a whole daughter that she didn't tell me about. Then, Alvion's dad is some guy named Luke. Today was the first time I'd ever heard the name Luke. Talk about some Jerry Springer type ...

Nova: Ironically enough, I know Luke. We went to high school together. He's a really cool guy. He told me that he broke up with Amanda because she kept trying to change him, plus, she lied a lot. He said that she would lie for no apparent reason. He works over on Second Street at a barbershop called I'll Cut Ya! *(giggles)* And yes, that's the actual name of the shop.

Blaine: I can now agree with him about the lying. I remember her telling me that some famous radio personality was her father, but one day, we went to visit her mother's house. I asked about her dad and Amanda got angry. I don't think I'd ever seen her so angry. Nevertheless, the question was out there so her mother answered.

Nova: What did she say?

Blaine: She said that she didn't know who Amanda's father was. According to her, around the time she conceived Amanda, she was on drugs and she would do anything to get high. Amanda's father was likely one of the guys who traded drugs for sex.

Nova: Well, you know that makes sense with her feeling the need to tell so many lies. I don't think she's a bad person; I just think she's lost. That's all.

Blaine: Yeah and I can sympathize with her, but I can't be with a woman if I gotta question or second guess everything that comes out of her mouth. I just don't trust her anymore.

Nova: Talk it out first. I remember not long before Anthony passed away, he opened up to me. He told me that he had been thinking about ending things with me because, as he put it, I was an odd child. I didn't talk much back then. I was just intimidated by him. I didn't know what to say whenever I was around him, so I would just nod my head or gesture with my hands. Anthony saw my relationship with my father as odd because I would talk and play with him, but whenever I was alone with Anthony, I was quiet. After he told me this, I apologized and started talking more *(laughs).* I remember one day, Anthony told me that he wished he'd never had that conversation with me because, according to him, I talked far too much. But anyhow. Talk it out first. You may be able to help her out.

Blaine: I have to make her face all of her lies. I can't lie to you. The relationship is over; there's no way I can continue seeing her after this, but I will work towards having a solid friendship with her — if that's at all possible.

Nova: Yeah, that's probably not gonna happen. She hated Anthony after they broke up and Luke said she came to his job the day after they broke up and broke two of his car windows out. She ended up spending two nights in jail because of that incident.

Blaine: Amanda? Jail? Whoa!

Nova: Yeah, so the friend thing — not gonna happen, I'm sure.

Blaine and Nova continued to talk for another twenty minutes before Nova's break was over. After that, Blaine left the hospital and didn't return until the next day.

Amanda heard a knock on her room's door. "Come in," she said, hoping that it was Blaine. She'd been calling him nonstop ever since he'd left the day prior, but Blaine hadn't answered any of her calls. A few seconds later, in walked Blaine, but to Amanda's surprise, he was holding the door for someone. That someone turned out to be Luke. Amanda's heart began to race as she felt the coldness of fear gripping her entire body. "You need to leave!" she shouted, looking at Luke. Amanda pushed the nurse call button again, but it had somehow jammed. "Leave! You need to leave!" shouted Amanda as she tried to find a way to fix the button. Nevertheless, Luke was unmoved by Amanda's anger. He'd seen it before. "Why won't you let me see my son?" he asked. "Is Alvion even mine?" Amanda grew even angrier. "Leave! Nurse! Nurse!" she screamed as loud as she could. With that, Luke turned to leave and Blaine followed behind him. "Blaine!" shouted Amanda. "We need to talk." Blaine didn't look back; he continued to walk until he heard Amanda say something that shocked him entirely. "If you're breaking up with me, you need to take your daughter," she said. "I can't afford to raise her alone." Blaine turned around. The angered look he'd once sported was now replaced with the look of sheer shock and horror. "What?" he said. Amanda sat up on her bed. "If it's over, you need to take your daughter. I'll sign the papers. I can't afford to raise her by myself." Blaine didn't know what to say. On one hand, the idea of raising his daughter outside of Amanda's influence was great, but on the other hand, he was shocked to see a mother willing to give up her child without a fight. Obviously, Amanda hadn't bonded with Briana or any of her children, for that matter. "I'll talk to you later," said Blaine as he made his way out of the room.

A few months later, the paperwork was complete. Amanda signed over custody of Briana to Blaine. She knew that she couldn't get much child support out of Blaine because he was an unemployed handyman. She also went ahead and agreed to the paternity test. Just as everyone had suspected, Amber was Anthony's daughter, but Antoinette was not. When questioned about the paternity of Antoinette, Amber finally admitted that she'd had an affair with a married guy named Ivan. Ivan had been the same married guy that Amanda had been seeing when she and Anthony had broken up the first time. This meant that

Amanda's relationship with Ivan had long started before she'd married Anthony and obviously, it had continued.

Ivan wanted nothing to do with Antoinette. His wife learned of his infidelities when he was served with documents requesting a paternity test, but she did not leave him. Amber went on to have two more children by two more guys. Sadly enough, her daughters grew up and started walking in her footsteps. Because of what he'd gone through with Natalie and Amanda, Blaine stopped trusting women altogether. For this reason, he ended up in a lot of casual relationships until he got saved four years later. During his season of promiscuity, Blaine went on to father two more children. After salvation, Blaine went on to marry a woman he'd met in his church.

One thing you'll notice about this story is there's not too much movement. What I mean by this is — the story talks more about conversations and babies being born than people moving around. It's not an action story or some mind-blowing mystery that has you on the edge of your seat. It's the story of a broken woman named Amanda who went from bed to bed and pillow to pillow in search of love. Sadly enough, her search wasn't just reserved for the streets; Amanda used the church as a dating site as well.

She was the product of rejection. She didn't know who her father was, so she felt rejected.

Amanda's children were nothing but a representation of her own attempt to fix her life. Like many women do, Amanda had babies, hoping to live vicariously through them, meaning, she wanted to live out a father-daughter relationship by watching her children with their fathers. Nevertheless, every time she was rejected by a man she would, in turn, reject her own children. Antoinette and Alvion won't be raised by a loving mother. Instead, they'll just be raised. Women like Amanda think their only jobs as mothers is to feed, clothe and provide homes for their children. They think their only responsibility is to send them off to school and make sure that they don't rub their teachers the wrong way. Women like Amanda often don't discipline their children; they abuse them with words. This is largely due to the frustration they feel in raising those kids. You see, Amanda cannot live vicariously through Antoinette because Antoinette's father is not in her life. So, Antoinette, by default, becomes nothing but a burden for her mother. Feeling rejected, Antoinette will likely follow in her mother's footsteps in search of love and acceptance. This is how rejection works. When a person is not healed or delivered from the spirit of rejection, they will repeatedly involve themselves in relationships that are doomed to fail. This causes them to feel rejected over and over again, all the while, the spirit of rejection in them grows stronger. As that spirit grows, the person bound by it becomes more and more desperate to get and receive love. Before long, they begin to reject themselves and the evidence of this self-rejection can often be seen:

1. **In their friendships:** People who suffer from rejection often surround themselves with gossips, liars and profane people. They do this because gossips, liars and profane people are often very accepting of others. This helps the rejected soul to feel wanted and safe.

2. **In their self-adornment:** Rejected souls usually reject their own appearances as the spirit of rejection grows stronger. They do this by drastically changing their appearances; for example, a dark complexioned African American woman may suddenly start wearing blonde wigs, blue contact lenses, false eyelashes and a lot of makeup. With a Caucasian American woman, the evidence may show through excessive tanning, Botox injections, breast implants, hair extensions and so on. Even though many bound by this spirit would disagree, this honestly is a manifestation of self-rejection. This is their attempt to find an identity they believe would be more accepted, celebrated and loved by others.

3. **In their conversations:** Rejected people complain a lot and often cast themselves as victims. Additionally, they tend to be very prideful and self-absorbed. They can rarely go five minutes without talking about themselves, what they've been through and what they've accomplished. They often start talking about sex early in their relationships because sex, to them, is currency. It's their way of paying people for being interested in them and it's also their way to hold on to their relationships.

4. **In their finances:** Rejected people spend a lot of money trying to impress others. There are many different cultures and classes of people, so rejection often manifests the same way, but on different levels.

5. **In their choices:** Rejection often leads people to make poor choices in their attempts to "fit in" or be accepted by others, especially the people who once rejected them. A good example of this is — I lived in bad areas up until I was around 13 years old. Additionally, I loved to hang out in seedy neighborhoods when I was younger and one of the manifestations of rejection is men pouring every dime they have into their cars. It is not uncommon to see a man driving an older car with flashy rims, a flashy paint job and custom seats. This flamboyant cry for attention is rejection on full display.

We see what happened in Amanda's life, but what we often do not see is what has happened or is happening behind the scenes. Amanda was not wearing her father's surname because she didn't know him. For this reason, she likely wore her maternal grandfather's last name or her maternal great-grandfather's surname. Amber, Amanda's daughter, was wearing Anthony's surname, but Anthony was not carrying on the legacy of his natural father because he was named after his step-father. Antoinette was carrying Anthony's surname, even though time revealed that Anthony was not her biological father. Her real father was a married man who had absolutely no interest in sharing his name with her. Because of Amanda's bitterness towards Luke, Alvion cannot be traced back to his father through his surname. Instead, he would only be able to trace his surname back to his maternal great-grandfather or great-great grandfather. Let's say, for example's sake, that Blaine shared his surname with Briana. If Blaine is carrying his father's surname, Briana could trace herself to him, but understand this: children can only trace themselves back to to the first paternal rejection. What this means is that rejection isn't just a bad experience that we have; it's a spirit that enters into a bloodline through sin and rebellion. This means that rejection was embedded in the DNA of the sperm of some of our fathers, grandfathers, great-grandfathers and so on. Rejection can almost always be traced back to rebellion. For example, let's say that the Smith bloodline has been faithful to God. The men have abstained from fornication, all having married their high-school sweethearts for the last seven generations. What you'll notice is that in this bloodline, there are a lot of happy and successful people. Nevertheless, one of the Smith boys ventures off and has a child with a girl he met in high school. The two didn't wait until marriage to have sex and for this reason, they had a baby out of wedlock.

Because the Smith boys tend to marry their high school sweethearts, George wants to follow suit, but his girlfriend, Susan, doesn't feel genuinely loved by George. She feels as if George's relationship with her lacks passion, spontaneity and it's too monotonous. Susan believes that George does not love her, but he's only asking to marry her so that he can please his parents. For this reason, Susan breaks up with George and starts dating a guy named Maximus. Two years later, Susan gives birth to her first child with Maximus. What you've just witnessed is rejection entering the Smith's bloodline. From there, it will work to cloud the men and the women's judgment, end every relationship that the Smiths enter into and destroy the Smith legacy altogether.

How far can you trace back a paternal father figure in your bloodline? Understand this: the fathers were the ones who invoked the blessings upon their children in the biblical days. Let's look at some examples of fathers blessing their sons.

God blesses Abraham: God, Himself, changed Abram's name to Abraham. He also called him the father of many nations. This was the blessing from the Father to Abraham.

Abraham blesses Isaac: "Abraham gave all he had to Isaac. But to the sons of his concubines Abraham gave gifts, and while he was still living he sent them away from his son Isaac, eastward to the east country" Genesis 25:5-6 (ESV).

Isaac blesses Jacob: "Then his father Isaac said to him, "Come near and kiss me, my son." So he came near and kissed him. And Isaac smelled the smell of his garments and blessed him and said, 'See, the smell of my son is as the smell of a field that the Lord has blessed! May God give you of the dew of Heaven and of the fatness of the earth and plenty of grain and wine. Let peoples serve you, and nations bow down to you. Be lord over your brothers, and may your mother's sons bow down to you. Cursed be everyone who curses you, and blessed be everyone who blesses you!"

Over the years, especially throughout the Old Testament, fathers would speak blessings over their sons. They would also instruct and train them. During that time, fathers would protect their daughters. A man (or his father) would have to ask a father for his daughter's hand in marriage. The father of the potential bride would ensure that the man came from a godly bloodline, he could provide for the woman and that he was a man of integrity. He would also make the groom pay a bridewealth (bride price). Now, this sounds like the father "sold" his daughter to the highest bidder, but this is not true. Unlike sons, daughters would not carry on their fathers' last names or legacies, but like sons, they worked very hard around the house. People in those days often made their money through farming and agriculture, so the daughters and sons worked a lot in the fields. When a man gained a wife, he gained a helper; he gained someone who could help him with whatever it was that he did. So, the bride price had three objectives:

1. To give the father back what he would have made if he'd kept his daughter.
2. To scare away any man who could not afford to provide for the woman whose hand he was asking for.
3. To serve as a contractual agreement between the bride's father and the groom or the groom's family.

In other words, the bride price was a father's way of maintaining honor and protecting his daughter.

These days, there are no bride prices (in Western countries) and this isn't a bad thing, but the issue nowadays is that potential brides are choosing their husbands without the direction of a father. This means that the dishonorable guys who the father once protected his daughters from are now able to seduce many young women. This also means that young men who have not received the direction of a father are often led astray by lustful, ungodly women. So, what we see is the spirit of rejection is able to keep reproducing itself. Until this stops, we'll see a surge of teenage pregnancies, failed marriages and the like. Nowadays, there are a lot of children who cannot trace themselves back to a father-figure. This is because the spirit of rejection has lorded itself over their bloodlines, and when it is not bound and cast out, it will continue to strengthen and reproduce itself.

Women like Amanda are often hard, but not impossible, to reach. The reason for this is — she has a plan for her life. Even though her plan is not working, she's sold out to it. What has to happen is, her plans will continue to fail her until she realizes that they are not working for her. Amanda would have to come to realize that everything she needs (healing, love, deliverance, provision) is in Christ Jesus. Until she reaches this reality, it will be hard to reach her. Nevertheless, if you have a friend like Amanda, keep praying for her. She has to be delivered from idolatry, pride, rebellion, rejection and a whole host of spirits. Even though things may look bleak, God is able to set her free.

Lastly, in the biblical days, the men of God would do anything to have sons because they understood the value of a legacy. Nowadays, the enemy has deceived many men into believing that children are burdens. Children are blessings and any man who provides for his children will experience the blessings of a father because he is behaving like a father. Any man who rejects his own legacy has decided to wipe his own name out from the face of the Earth. This is why it's important for you, as a woman, to wait for God to send you the husband who knows the value of a wife and the value of a legacy. One of the best gifts you can give a child isn't given after the child is conceived; it is given the moment you choose who that child's father will be. If you let God choose the father of your children, you have allowed God to use you as a garden to plant seeds that He Himself will water. If not, you'll continue to reproduce the spirit of rejection in your children, while strengthening it in yourself. Amazingly enough, it is not uncommon these days to see mothers yelling at their daughters as they watch them follow the trail of rejection that they once blazed. Remember, a wise man leaves an inheritance for his children and his children's children. On the other side of the token, a foolish man or woman takes from their children (fathers, legacies, love) before they're even born.

Chapter 8

A Marked Woman

It is human nature to mark special moments. We like to write our names on things or have names, words or images drawn on us as a representation of what we've experienced. Tattoos don't just serve as markers for special moments; they also serve as markers for certain mindsets and cultures. In reality, when a person gets a tattoo, that person is freezing a moment of time and engraving it into his or her skin. The reality is — we also do this with our hearts.

Aphrica was here. Aphrica stood still and looked at the new carving she'd just made on a tree. It was a tree that stood not too far from her dad's grave. Little did she know, her signature there had just created a permanent marker in her life — one that she would someday have to revisit.

James Sibley, Aphrica's father, had passed away three years ago. He'd been killed by a drunk driver. His daughter decided to visit his grave often, especially on the anniversary of his death. She believed that by doing so, she was honoring her father and showing him once and for all that her love superseded the grave.

"Nice handiwork." The voice came from behind Aphrica. When she turned around, she saw a very handsome young man standing a few feet away from her. "Hello, my name is Roderick, but everyone calls me Rod." Aphrica's heart began to race. She wasn't sure if it was because she was alone in a deserted Georgian graveyard with a complete stranger or if it was because the stranger happened to be the most handsome man she'd ever laid eyes on. "I'm Aphrica," she responded. "Wow, beautiful name. Nice to meet you." Roderick was a medium built young man with copper brown skin, big brown eyes, short wavy hair and relatively thick eyebrows. Aphrica, on the other hand, was a petite woman with smooth, peanut butter-like skin and honey brown eyes. Her hair was shoulder length, thick and full of tightly twisted curls.

Roderick: Why'd you do that to your face?
Aphrica: What? This nose ring? I've had this for a year or so now. Why? You don't like it?
Roderick: I like nose rings, but I hate those kind of nose rings. Makes you like a boar.
Aphrica: A boar as in a pig?
Roderick: Yeah. Looks like something they'd put in a pig's

snout.

Aphrica: Wow. I tell you my name and you immediately start insulting me. I don't recall asking for your opinion.

Roderick: My apologies. I'm honestly not trying to offend you. Let's start over. My name is Roderick. What's yours?

Aphrica: Ms. Piggy.

Roderick: *(Laughs)* Okay, Ms. Piggy. What are you doing here ... in the graveyard? Aren't you scared to be out here by yourself?

Aphrica: I'm visiting my dad's grave and no, I'm not scared. The worst thing that's ever happened to me out here was I got called a wild boar. Other than that, everyone else tends to keep to themselves.

Roderick: Funny woman I see. Well, I guess I should have asked for your phone number before insulting you. I've got to learn to stop putting my foot in my mouth.

Aphrica: You're probably right because now there's no way I'd give you my digits ... not even two of them.

Roderick: That's fair. Well, it was nice to meet you, Ms. Aphrica. I hope to see you again someday, and maybe next time, you will have forgotten this encounter and we can start over.

Aphrica: I doubt it, but it was nice meeting you.

Roderick: Wait. I am curious though. Don't take this question the wrong way, but what would make a woman as beautiful as you get a bull's ring in her nose?

Aphrica: Oh, so first, I looked like a pig, and now I look like a bull?

Roderick: Don't take it that way. It's just a question.

Aphrica: Have a good day, Roger.

Roderick: That's Roderick.

Aphrica: Whatever.

Aphrica was what most people would call a "free spirit." She hated social conformity, organized religion and anything she felt was a violation of her rights. She was polytheistic, meaning, she believed in the existence of many gods. Aphrica believed in JEHOVAH to a certain degree, but she also believed in many gods. She hated injustice, pollution and the slaughtering of animals. For this reason, she was a raw vegan. Her normal everyday attire consisted of African-style clothing and jewelry. A perfectly placed mole rested on the left side of her face, just above her top lip. Another birthmark rested on the right side of her face, not far from her right ear. This particular birthmark was the size of a quarter and almost looked like the map of Africa.

Aphrica didn't work a traditional job. Instead, she made a living making and selling perfumed oils, candles and clothing. Since this didn't bring in a lot of money, Aphrica was on public assistance to help raise her six-year-old son, Aadil.

Aphrica had once been married to Aadil's father, Zidan. Zidan started off as a Christian. Eventually, he turned away from Christianity and joined a movement called the Black Hebrew Israelite movement. A few years later, he left that movement and became a Muslim. He'd met and married Aphrica while he still identified himself as a Christian, even though he wasn't an active believer. Two months after marrying Aphrica, Zidan crossed over into the Hebrew Israelite faith and two years later, he identified himself as a Muslim.

A large scar on Aphrica's back served as a reminder to her about Zidan's temper. He'd always been an abusive man towards her, but the worst attack occurred one summer night while Aphrica was asleep. Zidan was the type of man who hated working traditional jobs, so he would do odd jobs to make money. Needless to say, Zidan and Aphrica had some severe money issues, even though she worked part time at a bank. For this reason, he hated running the air conditioner during the summer or the heater during the winter. Being that the couple lived in Georgia, their house was always very uncomfortable. For the sake of keeping the peace, Aphrica had always abode by Zidan's rules, but being that it was mid-August and she was pregnant with Aadil, Aphrica decided to run the air conditioner for an hour and then, turn it off before Zidan returned home. The issue was ... the air relaxed Aphrica and she fell asleep face-down on their couch.

Two hours later, Aphrica woke up to the worst pain she'd ever experienced outside of childbirth. She screamed and rolled off the couch. When she looked up, she saw her infuriated husband holding a smoking iron. He'd plugged the iron in and used it to punish Aphrica for running the air conditioner by holding it to her bare back. This incident left a scar on Aphrica's back and on her soul. Of course, Aphrica ended up in the hospital and thankfully, little Aadil was okay. Aphrica had Zidan arrested and while he was in jail, she finally mustered up the courage to file for divorce.

After Zidan was released from jail on bond, he went looking for his estranged wife. Armed with a gun, Zidan walked into the bank that Aphrica was working for at that time and pointed the gun at her. He then pointed the gun at Aphrica's swollen belly and pulled the trigger. Thankfully, the gun jammed and a retired war veteran happened to be in the bank at that time. He'd tackled Zidan to the ground, knocking the gun out of his hand. The gun went off as Zidan was being tackled, but the bullet went into the wall just above Aphrica's head, barely missing her. The heroic veteran was able to restrain Zidan until the police arrived. Zidan was eventually sentenced to twenty years in prison behind that incident. That term was increased by another ten to fifteen years after Zidan offered to pay another fellow prisoner to kill Aphrica. The prisoner was set to be released in six months and because of the prisoner's violent past towards women, Zidan was sure he'd agree to do the hit. Instead, the prisoner became an informant and Zidan was booked, charged and convicted of conspiracy. Aphrica was relieved to hear about her ex-husband's new conviction. Twenty years had never felt like it would be enough time. She was confident that ten to fifteen more years of added on time would help her to securely build the empire she wanted to build and use her wealth to move to Africa.

Aadil had just celebrated his sixth birthday and he and his mom were now living in a small apartment in South Atlanta. Their home was decorated with all types of pagan artifacts, including several large pictures of African goddesses, deities that were commonly worshipped in some African countries and villages. The smell of burning incense was now embedded in the drapes, the sofa and anything that was made of cloth. A large Buddha statue sat a few feet away from Aphrica's large animal print sofa.

"Did you finish your homework?" Aphrica asked her son. Aadil was in his bedroom with a Hindu coloring book his mother had given him. Ignoring his mother's voice, Aadil continued to color the diagram with precision. "Mom, my head is hurting," said Aadil as he finished off the picture. "That's not what I asked you, Aadil. Did you finish your homework yet?" Still, Aadil didn't answer his mother. Instead, Aphrica heard a thumping sound. Frustrated, Aphrica made her way into his room and there, she found her son lying on the floor. His coloring book was lying next to him. Aphrica panicked. She tried to wake Aadil up, but to no avail. She immediately grabbed her phone and called 911. An ambulance came twenty minutes later and when they arrived, a panicked Aphrica was outside, holding her son.

It was now two hours later and the doctor had finally come up with a prognosis. "Ma'am, we believe your son had an aneurysm," said Dr. Floyd. "We're not confident yet, but we're still running tests. Has he been complaining about a headache or anything like that?" Aphrica was frantic. "Only today," she said. "Right before I found him, he said he had a headache." Dr. Floyd nodded his head and took notes. "Okay," he said. "We're going to run some more tests on him. You can stay with him in his room tonight or you can go home. It's entirely up to you."

How could this have happened? Why hadn't the gods protected her son? Aphrica was scared, angry and most of all, confused. She put her hand in Aadil's hand. He looked so lifeless; he looked dead and this scared Aphrica to her core. What would she do without him? The doctor said that things weren't looking good for him; they said they may have to operate and that an operation on the brain was risky. Scared, Aphrica began to pace back and forth. She didn't know what god to call on or who she could turn to. She sat back down next to her son, reminding herself that Aadil could feel her negative energy. "Remain positive," she said to herself before dozing off.

While asleep, Aphrica began to dream. In her dream, she and Aadil were in Egypt. They were walking into a beautiful palace that looked like it had been made from sand. Inside the palace, there were long hallways. On each wall, there were many drawings of various Egyptian deities and pharaohs. Aphrica held Aadil's hand in hers and walked into a large room where she saw a lot of statues. In the center of those statues was an empty throne. On the throne was a white piece of paper. Aphrica picked it up and read it. It read: *Place your god here.* Aphrica then looked up and saw Aadil heading towards the throne. "Don't sit there," she screamed, but it was too late. Aadil sat on the throne and all of a sudden, the throne was surrounded by snakes. One medium-sized snake made its way up the throne and wrapped itself around Aadil's head. Aadil then began to scream for his mother. Aphrica screamed for her son, but it seemed as if the floor between them began to get longer and longer, placing

Aphrica further and further away from her son. Suddenly, she found herself in another room and the door shut between her and Aadil. That's when Aphrica woke up.

When Aphrica opened her eyes, she realized that what was attacking her son was an evil spirit, but which evil spirit was it? Aphrica began to think about some of the things her spiritual mentor, a woman named Ebony, had taught her. Nevertheless, because her mind was clouded, she decided to give Ebony a call.

Ebony: Hello.

Aphrica: Hey there. This is Aphrica Sibley. How are you?

Ebony: Good, doll. How are you?

Aphrica: Not so good. Aadil's in the hospital. They think he had an aneurysm.

Ebony: Oh no! Is he okay?

Aphrica: I hope so. They are still running tests. Listen, I dreamed that Aadil and I were in Africa; we were in Egypt as a matter of fact. Anyhow, we walked into a castle and walked through some very long hallways until we came to this big, big room. In the room, there were a lot of statues and in the center of these statues, there was a throne. On the throne, I found a piece of paper that read, "Sit your god here," or something like that. When I looked up, Aadil was sitting on the throne. I screamed at him, but it was too late. All of a sudden, a black snake climbed up the throne and wrapped itself around Aadil's head. He started screaming my name and I couldn't do anything. It's like the floor was getting longer, putting more and more distance between Aadil and I. That's when a door suddenly appeared and it shut, separating me from Aadil. I don't know what any of this means. Can you explain it to me?

Ebony: Oh my. It seems as if you've upset the gods. You know they are jealous, Aphrica. Somehow, they must've felt like you were giving Aadil more attention than you gave them, so now, they are trying to move him out of the way.

Aphrica: What do you mean ... move him out of the way?

Ebony: *(Sighs)*. Aphrica, Aadil is gonna die. They've chosen him as a sacrifice to them because he's so important to you.

Aphrica: I will not sacrifice my son to them or no one for that matter! What kind of crazy mess is this, anyway?

Ebony: Don't speak while angry. You may say something that will upset the gods. Consider it an honor that they are considering Aadil. If he's taken, he will become one of them.

Aphrica hung up the phone. At that moment, she realized that Ebony was an evil woman and the spirits she'd been consulting were all evil. She felt an urgency in her spirit to pray, but who should she pray to? She hated organized religion and this was the reason she'd turned to worshipping various deities. Aphrica pulled her hair back into a ponytail and looked at her watch. It was now seven in the morning and she knew where she wanted to go.

Thirty minutes later, Aphrica pulled into the graveyard where her father was resting. After parking her car, she made her way over to his grave. There she knelt down and began to cry aloud. "Daddy! I know it's you trying to take Aadil from me! You've always been a jealous man! I forgave you for asking my mom to abort me! I forgave you for not being in my life for the first twelve years of my life! I forgave you for running my mom crazy. You're the reason she's in an institution to this day! I forgave you for telling me that you wish you'd never met my mother! I even forgave you for telling me to abort Aadil! And this is how you repay me?! By trying to take my son away from me? I know it's you! Leave my son alone! Leave me alone! Leave us alone!"

Suddenly, a voice came from behind Aphrica? "Are you okay?" The voice sounded somewhat familiar. Aphrica turned around and saw the guy she'd met a few days earlier. It was Roderick.

Aphrica: No, I'm not okay. My son's in the hospital.

Roderick: Oh wow, what's his name? I want to pray for him.

Aphrica: Who do you pray to?

Roderick: God, of course.

Aphrica: Yeah, but who is your god?

Roderick: JEHOVAH.

Aphrica: No thanks. My mom served Him and she went crazy. I'll figure something else out.

Aphrica rushed to her car, wiping the tears from her eyes. She couldn't help but to acknowledge that the sound of the name JEHOVAH had made something within her leap. She got in her car and tried to crank it up, but it wouldn't start. She tried several times to start her car, but it would not start. Aphrica then began to scream and beat her steering wheel hysterically. That's when she saw something moving out of the corner of her right eye. When she looked over, she noticed a small black snake on the passenger's side floor. Aphrica panicked and climbed out the window of her car, even though the door handle was working properly. Roderick saw and heard the commotion from a distance, so he came rushing over to her aid. He helped Aphrica off the ground and she began to yell hysterically. "There's a snake in my car! There's a snake in my car!" Roderick looked into the car and noticed a small black snake on the passenger's side floor. He rushed over to the passenger's side, carefully grabbed the snake, took it to a wooded area and threw it with all his might. Aphrica paced back and forth in fear.

Aphrica: What's happening?! What's happening to me?! I

think I'm losing it! Just like my mom! I think I'm losing it! The gods are mad at me because I would not give them my son! Now, they are after me!

Roderick: Gods? What gods? There is only one true God and that's JEHOVAH.

Aphrica: I need to get back to the hospital with my son, but that stupid car won't crank! They want to keep me away from my son so they can take him! They're trying to put distance between me and him — just like in my dream! I can't lose my son! I just can't!

Roderick: Calm down. What hospital is he in? I'll take you.

Aphrica: He's over at Grady Memorial.

Roderick: Follow me. My car's over here.

The drive to the hospital would take just a little over an hour. As they were riding, Roderick began to question Aphrica.

Roderick: So, can I ask you a question?

Aphrica: Yeah.

Roderick: What god or gods do you worship?

Aphrica: I don't have one specific god. I believe there are many gods in the universe and if you do well, they will reward you. I worship Hindu gods, African gods, and many more, but I'm not in any organized religion. For example, I am not Buddhist, even though I talk to Buddha.

Roderick: Why did you turn from JEHOVAH? I heard you say that He let your mother down.

Aphrica: My mom and dad dated; they were high school sweethearts. Well, my mom was a very devout Christian. She kept me and my brother at church. Anyhow, she loved my dad with every fiber of her being, but my aunt said that when my mother got pregnant with me, my dad panicked. He didn't want me. They were both just 19 years old and living with their parents. He went and got himself a job to pay for my mom to get an abortion, but she didn't know this. She thought he'd started working so he could help take care of me. My Aunt Chevelle said that when my dad got his first paycheck, he came straight over to my grandparents' house and asked my mother to come outside. Everybody there knew she was pregnant, so they all thought he was about to propose marriage to her, but he had a different proposal. He got down on his knees and handed her a bunch of cash. He then started begging her to get an abortion. My aunt said from that moment on, my mother seemed to have checked out on life. When she refused to abort me, my daddy left town. I didn't meet him until I was 12 years old and the only reason he reached out to me was because he needed a kidney transplant and they couldn't find a suitable donor. My Aunt Chevelle was raising me by that time because my mom was in and out of the hospital, so my aunt was completely against me giving my dad one of my kidneys. She would not agree to it, and since I wasn't of age to give legal consent, her word mattered. She was my legal guardian and I couldn't get past it. I hated her for that. I felt like — here it was, I was being given a chance to get to know my father and my aunt was ruining it for me. Anyhow, I prayed that God would give him a kidney and He did. That's why I believe in JEHOVAH, but at the same time, my mom was a devout Christian.

Roderick: Do you and your brother have the same father?

Aphrica: Oh no. My mom got pregnant while at fruitcake university.

Roderick: Fruitcake university?

Aphrica: She's in a mental institution.

Roderick: Oh.

Aphrica: We don't know who my brother's father is. We just know that she got released and a few months later, my brother was born. She didn't talk about it and we never pressured her for answers.

Roderick: Both of my parents are ministers. Let me ask you this. Would you be willing to give JEHOVAH another try?

Aphrica: *(Sighs).* Honestly, at this point, I'd be willing to give Wonder Woman a try.

Roderick: Okay. Once we get to the hospital, I'm gonna give my parents a call. What room is your son in?

Aphrica: He's in room 46B.

Roderick: Room 46B. Okay. If they won't let us come up, I'll call the room.

Aphrica: Okay.

They finally arrived at the hospital and Aphrica rushed back up towards her son's room. She was stopped by Dr. Floyd, Aadil's doctor, and he gave her some bad news. "It's not looking good," Ms. Sibly. "We've been doing everything we can do, but it seems as if he's only getting worse. Surgery is not even looking like a viable option right now. He's too weak and it's too risky. All we can do is wait and hope his condition improves. We put him back in Room 46B and we're monitoring him closely." Aphrica could feel her legs growing weaker. She looked at her phone, trying to figure out who she could call. She called her best friend, Jada, but she didn't answer her phone. She called her Aunt Chevelle, but then she remembered that Chevelle and her husband were vacationing in Barbados. She had no one left to call, so she called on the name of Jesus. "Jesus, I know I haven't spoken with you in a while. I don't even know how to talk to you anymore or what to say. My son is dying and I don't know what to do or who to call, so I've decided to give you another try. If you will save my son, I promise I will serve you and you alone. I really need you. Please don't let me down. Please!" Aphrica got off the floor and made her way into her son's room. He looked somewhat bloated. Seeing all the machines that he was hooked up to broke Aphrica's heart all the more. She sat down on the chair next to Aadil's bed and began to weep. In that moment, she knew that she was responsible for her son's condition. In that moment, something changed on the inside of her and she regretted worshipping all the deities she'd been worshipping. Tears fell from Aphrica's eyes as she held her dying son's hand. "I'm so sorry," she said. "I'm sorry, Aadil. Mommy's sorry." Aadil's vital signs seemed to be getting weaker. His hand felt cold. Remembering what her Aunt Chevelle had taught her, Aphrica looked up to the sky and said three words. She said, "Lord, I surrender."

All of a sudden, there was a knock on the door. "Come in," said Aphrica. An older woman who looked to be around 50 years old entered the room, followed by an older gentleman who was obviously her husband. Aphrica didn't recognize the couple, but a few seconds later, Roderick came into the room. "These are my parents. Mom, Dad, this is Aphrica — the girl I told you about. Aphrica, this is my Dad, Apostle Roderick Melborne, Sr. and this is my mother, Pastor Shirley Melborne."

After the formalities, Aphrica noticed that Pastor Shirley kept rubbing her shoulders. "My, my, my. I feel a lot of tension in my head and shoulders. You've been around a lot of witchcraft," she said. Aphrica dropped her head. "Yes, ma'am," she replied. Apostle Roderick was now standing next to Aadil and both he and his son, Roderick Jr., were praying. The Apostle stopped praying, looked over at Aphrica and said, "I saw a snake wrapped around his brain while I was praying for him." Aphrica began to weep. She told the couple about her dream, followed by her encounter with a snake in her car. "What's that tattoo about?" asked Apostle Rod, pointing to a tattoo on Aphrica's arm. It was the image of a large serpent wrapping itself around Aphrica's right arm. "It represents a Greek goddess named Pythia," said Aphrica. Apostle Roderick interrupted. "It's Python, he said. The Python spirit is known to coil itself around people. What's attacking your son is in you. We can't get to him until we cast out what's on the inside of you. If you don't mind, I want to pray for you right now and take you through what we call deliverance."

Aphrica: I'm familiar with the term deliverance. My Aunt Chevelle took me to church with her when I was young. I've never seen it, but I'm familiar with it.

Apostle Roderick: Okay. Good. Are you saved?

Aphrica: I was, but then, I turned away.

Apostle Roderick: That's okay. You're about to be restored today. Do you believe that Jesus is the Son of God? Do you believe that He died for your sins and He rose on the third day? Do you believe He now sits on the right hand of God.

Aphrica: Yes.

Apostle Roderick: Say it out your mouth. You have to confess it.

Aphrica: I believe that Jesus Christ is Lord. He is the Son of God. He was crucified and He died for my sins. He rose on the third day and He now sits on the right hand of God. Jesus Christ is Lord.

Apostle Roderick: Excellent! Now, Aphrica, what you're about to experience may be scary to you, but don't stop the process. I want you to renounce all those other gods you've been worshiping. Also, renounce ancestral worship. When you were talking to your dead father, you were engaging in ancestral worship. I'll explain this to you later.

Aphrica began to renounce the names of the deities she'd been worshiping, including ancestral worship. The more she renounced, the more she began to cough and the more the machines showed an improvement in her son's vital signs. When she was done, Apostle Roderick took over. "Spirit of Python, you heard her. She has renounced you! You come out of her now, you foul spirit!" At first, Aphrica didn't move. She couldn't move. She looked at the Apostle and thought to herself, "This isn't working." That's when her phone rang. It was Ebony calling her. At that moment, Aphrica felt tension in her body. Suddenly, the Apostle spoke again. His tone was authoritative. "Python! You heard me. Come out of her now in the name of Jesus Christ!" Suddenly, Aphrica felt like something was trying to come out of her mouth. "I can't breathe,"she gasped. Nevertheless, the Apostle did not acknowledge Aphrica's complaint. He kept speaking to the demon that was now manifesting. "Python, you will not strangle her. Come out of her now and cause her no pain! You will not rip nor tear her! Come out in the name of Jesus Christ!" All of a sudden, Aphrica found herself falling backwards, but thankfully, Roderick Jr. was standing behind her. He caught her and laid her on the floor gently. That's when the room door opened and in walked another guy. Aphrica couldn't see his face very well, but she heard his voice. "Apostle, I'm here. I got caught up in the five o'clock traffic." The man's voice was deep and very authoritative as well. "That's okay," said Apostle Roderick. "As you can see, we've already gotten started." With that, the Apostle continued to address the different spirits that were in Aphrica. Aphrica could hear the people around her speaking in tongues, but everyone's face was now blurry. All of a sudden, a loud scream came out of Aphrica's mouth and just like that, it was over. Whatever had just come out of her mouth seemed to leave behind a pungent odor. The odor seemed to clear as Aphrica's eyesight was restored.

The men were now placing Aphrica on the chair next to her son's bed. "No, everything's fine in here," said a nurse. As it turned out, one of the nurses happened to walk in with the man who'd come late. A devout Christian herself, Nurse Allison Stone was very familiar with the ministry of deliverance, after all, her dad had also been a very powerful deliverance minister before his death. She'd stayed in the room, guarding the door because she knew that no other nurse would understand what was taking place in that room. The good nurse rushed over and handed Apostle Roderick a small barf bag. He hurriedly placed it under Aphrica's mouth. He was right on time. Aphrica vomited out the residue and in that moment, she felt lighter, happier and more at peace. Apostle Roderick then laid his hands on her and began to pray for her to receive the infilling of the Holy Spirit. Aphrica fell forward, with her head resting on the bed, right next to her son. When she opened her eyes again, Apostle Roderick, his wife, Apostle Louis King (the man who'd come in mid-deliverance) and Roderick Jr. were all holding hands and praying around Aadil's bed. The nurse was still guarding the door and praying in tongues herself.

Aphrica looked at her son and to her amazement, he no longer looked bloated or dead. He looked healthy! Aphrica began to cry as she watched the complete strangers all gathering together in unity to pray for her son. It was the most beautiful sight she'd ever witnessed. Suddenly, Aphrica felt Aadil gripping her hand. "He's waking up!" she screamed. "My baby is waking up!" With that, the nurse peeped out the room and said, "The doctor's coming, y'all." Dr. Floyd walked into the room and saw Nurse Allison checking Aadil's vitals. He also saw the people gathered around and praying for Aadil. A devout Scientologist, Dr. Floyd didn't know how to respond, so he stood still and watched. Aadil's legs began to move and when the doctor saw this, he rushed in and began to check his vitals himself. "Sorry guys. I'm gonna need everyone to leave the room," he said. "We gotta make sure everything's okay." With that, everyone left the room.

In the waiting room, everyone kept praying while Aphrica paced back and forth. An hour had passed and still no word from the doctor. Suddenly, Dr. Floyd emerged and everyone stood to their feet. He looked dazed, amazed and surprised. He looked as if he'd seen a ghost. "It's a miracle," he said. Before he could finish, the sound of laughter and cheering erupted in the waiting room. "I knew it!" said Roderick, Jr. "Our God is an awesome God!" Dr. Floyd sat down. "In all my years as a doctor, I've never seen anything like this. And I do mean never! We can't find any trace of an aneurysm. There are no broken vessels, no blood on his brain — nothing! There was blood on his brain when he first came here. I can't explain it, but it's gone. He's sitting up in the room, talking now as if nothing happened." With that, Aphrica took off running towards her son's room, leaving the stunned doctor and the cheering leaders behind.

When she entered Room 46B, Aphrica briefly saw what

she later described as a large angel standing near her son's bed. After that, she couldn't see the angel anymore. Nevertheless, Aadil was sitting up on the bed watching television. He looked over at his mother and said, "Mom. When we get home, can you please throw away that coloring book. That thing gave me a headache." Aphrica laughed as she wrapped her arms around her son.

"Excuse me, sir. Can I speak with you for just a second?" Apostle Roderick turned around to see who was addressing him. It was Dr. Floyd. "Sure," said the Apostle. "How can I help you?" Dr. Floyd appeared baffled. "Look, my mother was a Christian and I left the faith after going to medical school. Anyhow, what I just saw in that room was nothing short of a miracle. How do I return to ...?" Dr. Floyd looked around to ensure no one else was listening in. "How do I return to Jesus? Is it too late for me?" Apostle Roderick smiled. "It's never too late unless you're dead," said the Apostle. "I'll tell you what. I'll give you my business card. Give me a call whenever you can. I'd love to help you out." Dr. Floyd smiled. "Yeah, I definitely will. I will call you tomorrow around two o'clock. My wife is gonna be excited to hear the news. She's a devout Christian. She's been praying for me to return to the faith for years. Well, it looks like her prayers have just been answered."

A few days later, Aadil was released from the hospital, leaving behind a bunch of confused doctors. Dr. Floyd kept his word and reached out to Apostle Roderick. Just as he said he'd do, he returned to the faith, got baptized and eventually went into ministry himself.

Aphrica refused to return to the apartment she'd been living in. It was filled with witchcraft and pagan items. She spoke with her Aunt Chevelle who'd just returned from Barbados and as expected, her aunt and uncle were happy to welcome her and Aadil back into their home. Aphrica hired a cleanup team to go into her old apartment. "Throw everything away except for the pictures of my son," said Aphrica. "I don't want nothing from that era in my life."

A month after Aphrica returned home, she called Roderick to express her feelings for him. "Look, I know that I'm no pastor's daughter and the church would probably not support a relationship between you and me. But, I do want you to know that I like you and more than that, I appreciate everything you and my new church family has done for me and Aadil." Roderick didn't know what to say. He liked Aphrica, but he knew that she had a long journey ahead of her. "Look, Aphrica," he said. "I really do like you. Really, but you're not ready for a relationship right now. I want you to focus on building your relationship with the Lord and if He says someday that you and I are for each other, we'll come together. If not, I trust that the man He's assigned you to will love you the way you deserve to be loved. God is processing you right now and I don't want to interrupt that process by being selfish." Aphrica understood and she loved Roderick all the more for putting God before he put himself or her.

Three months later, Aphrica went to the graveyard where her father was buried, but she wasn't there to speak to her father's corpse anymore. Instead, she came for an entirely different reason. She came because she'd dreamed about the tree that she'd signed her name to. With a blade in her hand, Aphrica looked at her signature once again. It read: Aphrica was here. A few seconds later, the word "was" had been crossed out and Aphrica replaced it with "is no longer," so that it now read, "Aphrica is no longer here." After that, she walked past her father's grave and got into her new car.

A year later Aphrica had healed nicely from the tattoo removal surgery she'd had. She turned sideways to look at her arm in the mirror. Her skin was still a little red, but it was no longer sore. "Are you ready?" Aunt Chevelle's voice was loud. It was obvious that she was downstairs, standing at the front door. "I'm coming," said Aphrica as she grabbed her purse and slipped on her shoes. They were all heading to church and Aphrica was more excited than she'd ever been. Her son was about to be baptized and she did not want to be late. Aadil was already at the church with his Uncle Nolan, Chevelle's husband.

When the duo arrived at the church, they were surprised to see the number of cars parked at the church. A medium-sized church, Mountain Movers Ministries normally seated around 250 members, but it was very clear to Aphrica that the house was packed. Thankfully, because she was the mother of one of the children being baptized, she, along with the people who came with her, would be able to sit at the front of the church.

When Aadil saw his mother, he relaxed. The thought of someone else dunking him underwater made him a little nervous. Normally, he'd go underwater in the bathtub, plus, he loved to swim in his Uncle and Aunt's pool, but baptism was different. Someone else would be in control and this made Aadil nervous. "Mom!" Aadil's voice was loud. "I thought you weren't coming. I told Uncle Nolan — I said watch Mama be late." Nolan laughed. Trying to catch his breath, he said, "Yeah. He asked your apostle if there was such a thing as a demon that makes people late for everything. He said to him, 'Apostle, if there is such a demon, can you please do altar call today? I want to bring my Mom to the altar so she can get set free.'" After that, Nolan started laughing hysterically again while Aphrica looked at her son in dismay. "Aadil," she said. Apostle Roderick's voice broke the silence. "Every person who's here for the baptism, please follow this woman right over here wearing the pink blouse to the back. Thank you." With that, the smile on Aadil's face went away. He was excited but scared. "It'll be okay," said Aphrica. "I got baptized when I was around your age too. Let's go. I'm coming with you." With that, Aphrica and Aadil followed behind Sister Beatrice and a few other people as they made their way through a single door just behind the pulpit. A few minutes later, Aadil watched two other people get baptized before him. It didn't look so scary anymore. When his turn came, Aadil climbed into the large tub and said to the pastor, "Today's my birthday, so take it easy on me." Everyone in the church laughed. "Happy birthday, young prophet," said Apostle Roderick. "How old are you today?" With childish excitement, Aadil happily answered. "I'm seven today. I'm almost a grown man." The church erupted in laughter again. "Yes, you are," said Apostle Roderick. "But don't be in a rush to grow up. Wow. Seven. That's the year of completion. I prophesy to you that everything that once tried to destroy you is now behind you. It is in the abyss. No weapon that is ever formed against you shall prosper. Today starts a new chapter in your life and everything the devil tried to take from you is restored to you right now! I baptize you in the name of the Father, the Son and the Holy Spirit." With that,

Apostle Roderick baptized Aadil and an excited Aadil bounced back out of the water. It wasn't nearly as bad as he thought it would be.

Two years later, Aphrica stood to her feet and slowly approached the mic. It was Resurrection Sunday and Aphrica was already feeling God's glory all over her. She leaned forward to speak into the mic. "I want to sing a beautiful song that I heard. It expresses my love and gratitude to the Lord for all He has done. Lord, what you did for me on the cross that day, I can never forget. You saved me, delivered me and loved me, even though I didn't deserve it. Lord, I love and adore you. Some of you may not know this but just over three years ago, I was a mess. I was a witch and I didn't know it. I worshiped several gods. I was miserable, hateful, prideful — just a mess of a soul. I'd gone to the graveyard to visit my dad one day. I felt like I needed answers so I would speak to him, not realizing that he couldn't hear me. Y'all, I didn't know I was praying to the dead. But God arranged it that on that day, a man with His heart would approach me. At first, he insulted me. Told me I looked like a wild pig because I had an earring right here — right in the center of my nose. It was one of those hoop earrings. I didn't think I'd ever see him again, but that divine encounter was orchestrated in Heaven and the next time I saw brother Roderick, I was broken. The doctors had given up on my son and I thought my dad's spirit was behind the attack my son was suffering. Brother Roderick happened to be at that graveyard again that day. Ironically enough, just like the first time, he'd come there to give the groundskeeper his paycheck. I didn't know this at the time, but the church that would become my future home owned the graveyard that my dad is buried in. Anyhow, the grounds-keeper's paycheck had bounced for the second time and get this — they still don't know why his check bounced. The money was there to pay him. Anyhow, Brother Roderick saw me there yelling at my dad's grave. I was broken and out of my mind. My son was dying and I was scared. I had never been that scared in my life. I had made up my mind that if my son died, I was gonna kill myself too. But God had another plan. In the nick of time, He sent His servant to encourage and deliver me. Y'all, Apostle Roderick, Pastor Shirley, Apostle Louis, Rod Jr. (my new husband), and a nurse on duty came into my son's room and prayed for him. They cast so many demons out of me that Apostle Rod got tired and started calling them out in groups *(laughs)*. But this is why I love the Lord so much. Even in the midst of my darkness, His light shined so brightly that it got my attention. He saved my baby boy. He saved me. Just last year, Apostle Roderick and some of the leaders here at Mountain Movers Ministries walked through the doors of Central State Hospital where my mother was staying. She'd been in the hospital most of her adult life.

Y'all, God set my mother free! The doctors couldn't believe it! They kept my mother another week to run some tests, but after that, they couldn't hold her. My Mom walked straight out of the mental hospital and she's here today in her right mind! And that's why I want to honor Him on today with one of my favorite songs, entitled *Lord, Do it Again.* For those of you who appreciate His love and kindness, stand to your feet as we give honor to the King of kings and the Lord of lords. First, I wanna read a poem to you and then we'll move directly into the song."

Another

Another idol. Another day.
Another teardrop. Another way.
Another lover. Another high.
Another chance to say goodbye.
Another smile. Another friend.
Another fight, but I did not win.
Another helper. I cannot lose.
Another closed door. Another bruise.
Another piece of my broken heart.
Another lie. Another dart.
Another day. I can't complain.
Another mercy. Another gain.
Another chance. Another song.
Let us praise Him all day long.

Lord, Do it Again (The Intercessor's Song)

Lord, do it again (Show your power)
Lord, do it again (Make us whole)
Lord, do it again (In this hour)
Lord, do it again (We say ohh)
Ohhh Ohh Ohhh (Lord, do it again)

Verse
Lord, do it again
Do for others what you did for me
Lord, heal the brokenhearted
And set the captives free

Lord, do it again
Nothing is too hard for you
Hide them underneath your wings
And heal them through and through

Lord, do it again
Rebuke the storms and calm the winds
Feed the hungry and clothe the poor
Lord, do it again; we need more

Chorus
Lord, do it again (Show your power)
Lord, do it again (Make us whole)
Lord, do it again (In this hour)
Lord, do it again (We say ohh)

Ohhh Ohh Ohhh (Lord, do it again)

Verse
Lord, heal the brokenhearted
Make the dry bones live
Take the brokenhearted
And teach them to forgive

Lord, do it again
Go to the woman at the well
And deliver the man in the tombs
Let them know you've torn the veil
And heaven has opened her womb

Lord, do it again
Rebuke the storms and calm the waters
Save your sons and heal your daughters
Lord, do it again; we need more of you
Hide us in your love and heal us through and through

Chorus
Lord, do it again (Show your power)
Lord, do it again (Make us whole)
Lord, do it again (In this hour)
Lord, do it again (We say ohh)
Ohhh Ohh Ohhh (Lord, do it again)

Lord, do it again (Show your power)
Lord, do it again (Make us whole)

Lord, do it again (In this hour)
Lord, do it again (We say ohh)
Ohhh Ohh Ohhh (Lord, do it again)

Lord, do it again
Lord, do it again
Lord, do it again
Please do it again

Most birthmarks are the result of the clustering of cells called pigment cells. Some are caused by abnormal blood vessels. Aphrica had a birthmark on the side of her face. No one has proved any spiritual significance behind birthmarks, but what we do know is that birthmarks can be used as identifying marks. For example, if you knew Aphrica and someone asked you to describe her, you'd point out the fact that she had a quarter-sized birthmark on the side of her face. What's interesting, however, is that if Aphrica was asked by someone to describe herself, she would not mention her birthmark. The reason for this is — the markings on our skin are not used by us to identify ourselves; they are used by others to identify us. The same is true for self-inflicted marks like tattoos. This means that we mark ourselves for others to see. The reason is when we are in a certain mindset, we tend to believe that marking ourselves increases our value and helps to shape others' perceptions or beliefs about us. People who mark themselves want to send a message to others and that message can vary from:

"I'm immortal."

"I'm abnormally strong."

"I'm crazy."

"I'm unique."

"I miss this person."

"I'm sexually adventurous."

"I'm different."

"I'm affiliated with _____ organization."

"I'm affiliated with _____ gang."

There are many reasons that we choose to communicate through body markings and some (not all) of those reasons include:

- We fear others' opinions of us, and therefore, want to shape their opinions.
- We believe that a tattoo can communicate in a matter of seconds something that could take us months, years or a lifetime to communicate.
- We only want to draw like-minded people to ourselves.
- We believe that tattoos make us stand out more.
- We believe that tattoos cast us as the characters that we want to be or we believe ourselves to be.

Again, there are many reasons that we tend to tattoo ourselves. Think about some of the men you see wearing leather jackets, riding on motorcycles and covered in tattoos. What message do you believe they're trying to send? It's obvious, right? They want to communicate to others that they are not to be messed with. Many want to appear to be immune to pain, immortal even. But do you believe that this is how they were created? Of course not! God created us, but we try to make revisions, not because who we are isn't good enough, but because somehow we've come to believe that who we are is not good enough!

I got a tattoo when I was 17 or 18 years old. I had my cousin to tattoo the word "Scandalous" on my arm. Honestly, I wanted praying hands, but my cousin said he needed a stencil to do this. I didn't have a stencil, but I was eager to get a tattoo. I chose the word "Scandalous" because I loved Tupac's song, "Scandalous." I felt like it represented who I was. In my young, twisted and misinformed mind, I believed that I was a cold-hearted woman who could discard a man at the drop of a hat. I was deceived. I wasn't cold; I was numb because I'd been hurt a lot and I secretly feared being hurt again. My tattoo served as a warning to any man I found myself in a relationship with that I could and would live without him if pushed. I had another female cousin with me that day and she had her name tattooed on her fist. Why is this? She was communicating that she was a fighter and that she was! She'd spent most of her life fighting, so her message was designed for the many women she'd fought and the ones she knew she'd fight someday. Again, tattoos send messages to others; despite what we believe or what we say, we do not tattoo ourselves for ourselves. Sure, we can say, "I like the way it looked," in reference to a piece of artwork, but we could always have that artwork printed on a canvas and hang it up in our living rooms. We put the art on ourselves because we want to use it as a means of communication.

Aphrica was a marked woman. Why is this? First off, we must understand generational strongholds. Generational strongholds are inherited or learned patterns of thinking and reasoning passed down from one generation to the next. Next, we must understand generational strongmen. A generational strongman, in this case, is a demonic spirit that is passed down from one generation to the next. It is usually the strongest demon in an army of demonic spirits, the one who gives the orders and the one who has the most power. I like to liken mindsets to leashes or chains. Demons don't mind allowing the people they've bound to roam around mentally, as long as they don't get so far away that they threaten to break the mental leashes they are on. In other words, people who are bound are allowed to call themselves Christians and be religious, but serving Christ truly and wholeheartedly is prohibited. If a bound person starts venturing off too much, whatever spirits are binding that person will work overtime to drive them further into captivity.

Our identities are what make us unique. We all identify one another by our faces. A Biologist could identify us by our blood or DNA, a Police Officer could identify us by our fingerprints, a Forensic Odontologist could identify us by our teeth, and our parents can sometimes identify us by our voices and our birthmarks. All of these are unique marks that distinguish us from others.

Aphrica was marked by the enemy for destruction from the time she was born. How so? She was the product of a mentally unstable mother and an absent father. Her father reentered her life, but his re-entry brought more hurt and confusion than it did healing.

Because of what Aphrica experienced with her mother, Aphrica turned away from the faith. She did like many African Americans and decided to embrace her roots. There's nothing wrong with wanting to be who you are uniquely designed to be, whether you are white, black, brown or red. However, it is not always a good idea to return to the mindsets or the gods that our ancestors once worshiped. After all, this is similar to returning to Egypt. We all know the story of Moses. The Jews were in Egypt for 430 years and God used Moses to deliver them from the bondage that Pharaoh had placed them in. God could have easily wiped out the Egyptians and allowed the Jews to remain in Egypt, but He chose to bring His people out of Egypt. This is because the systems of Egypt were demonic, plus, He had already prepared a place for the Jews. Nevertheless, the Jews did like many of us today. They wanted to be free from the oppression that Pharaoh had placed them under, but they did not want to be free from the systems and the mindset of the Egyptians. This is why what should have been an eleven-day journey (see Deuteronomy 1:1-2) ended up taking 40 years to complete! This is similar to what happened to Aphrica. She should have ventured forward, but instead, she decided to embrace what she did not understand. She decided to go back (spiritually and mentally) to a place (paganism, polytheism and ancestral worship) that God had delivered her ancestors from.

Many of our ancestors (African Americans) practiced ancestral worship and other pagan rituals. For this reason, we shouldn't look back and desire to return to their ways. Instead, we should be moving forward in Christ Jesus. This doesn't mean that we have to completely disregard our identities; it simply means that we need to turn away from any and everything that threatens to take us back to our Egyptian mindsets. Think about it — just because many of our ancestors were worshipping pagan gods when they were taken into slavery doesn't mean that they were worshipping the gods their ancestors had once worshipped. Our problem is that we often trace ourselves back to the place where we became the victims, instead of going further and tracing our roots back to the places where we were once victorious. This only enables and empowers the victim mindset and helps us to justify staying there. We can't be both victims and overcomers.

Aphrica's desire to be polytheistic or, in layman's terms, worship many gods, was brought on by the many traumas she'd experienced in her life. After having survived an abusive husband who was hellbent on destroying her, Aphrica made many changes to her life. Her desire to not work for anyone could be traced back to her one estranged husband, Zidan, walking into her place of employment and pointing a gun at her. This trauma scared Aphrica so much that she decided to work from the comfort and safety of her own home. Her desire to return to Africa was likely birthed in curiosity, but Zidan's determination to end her life was the motivation behind her wanting to save up enough money to move to Africa. Sometimes, we have desires, but they are nothing but desires brought on by curiosity or fear. Nothing more, nothing less. Additionally, sometimes we try to find ourselves by embracing who we were or who we want to be.

Every self-inflicted mark on Aphrica's skin represented a mindset, a belief and a stronghold. Google defines the word "stronghold" this way: *a place where a particular cause or belief is strongly defended or upheld.* We all visit certain mindsets in our life's journeys, but here's the thing: we're not supposed to stay there. Most of the time, we shouldn't have been "there" in the first place, but because of our families, our communities and our limited knowledge, venturing through some mindsets is almost inevitable. Nevertheless, we must continue to press forward until we are out of the wilderness and living in the promises of God. Aphrica's tattoos represented rebellion (her unwillingness to move forward) or her belief that she had already arrived in the right place both mentally and spiritually. Understand this: every time we mark our skin, we are, in a sense, immortalizing or memorializing a certain mindset. In other words, we are refusing to let that mindset die or we're placing a marker on ourselves to represent where we were because we don't plan to go much further.

The mark that Aphrica received from her husband, Zidan, was a burn mark from an iron. It represented his desire to drive her back into a mindset that she'd come out of or drive her into a mindset he believed was better suited for him (not her). Of course, he'd been controlling her and this is very dangerous. Here's why. We all understand that controlling another human being is a form of witchcraft because the controller overrides the will of that human being. God, Himself does not control us. Anytime you allow people to control you, you allow them to adjust to the belief that they own you, therefore, punishing you is, in their minds, an acceptable response to you disobeying them, after all, to them, you are their property. Control is a form of power and because God did not design us to be controlled by others, a person who taps into this power can easily become addicted to it. That's why you'll hear people saying things like, "She's drunk with power," or "He's power hungry." This is a representation of the fact that having and exercising power over another human being's will does stimulate something in the oppressor. This is why an abuser, for example, could beat his wife and then get turned on by every blow he dishes out. He will then rape his wife because he's in the midst of an adrenaline rush and he wants to experience what he believes will be a heightened sexual encounter, followed by a heightened, adrenaline-fueled orgasm. So, by allowing her husband to control her, Aphrica allowed control to become his drug of choice and we all know that addicts can do some cruel things when they want to get high.

Zidan burned his wife with the iron because he felt disrespected and dishonored due to the fact that his wife had cut on the air conditioner. Sounds silly, right? It is! However, whenever you're dealing with a twisted soul like Zidan, you'll find that they don't reason like normal human beings. Because he was drunk with power and bound himself, he thought he had the right to punish his wife for not obeying him.

There are many people who visit certain mindsets, get comfortable in then and refuse to move past them. This is why we experience the storms of life. Some storms are just God's way of forcing us to evacuate mindsets, cultures or beliefs that are offensive to Him. It's God's way of driving us out of our comfort zones of bondage. People who get comfortable in the wrong mindsets often learn to master those mindsets and they can sometimes make bondage look good. For example, can you imagine how appealing Aphrica's bold stance would have been to a younger woman who was insecure, hurting and didn't know who she was? Let's say that the young woman worked with the overly confident Aphrica and wondered how she'd survived an abusive ex-husband and a dysfunctional family. She'd likely marvel at what appeared to be Aphrica's strength and her unwillingness to conform to society's definition of beautiful. That young woman would attempt to befriend Aphrica so that she could study her ways and find out what makes her who she is. Nevertheless, as time went on, she would have discovered how unstable and unhappy Aphrica was.

Aphrica, like Jezebel, had many gods that she turned to because she did not trust the living God. Nevertheless, there came a time when every god she trusted in failed her. Some may say, "Well, she also trusted JEHOVAH as one of her gods," and my answer to this is ... well, so did Ahab and look what happened to him. God won't be "one" of your gods; He is and has to be the only true and living God in your life, otherwise, He will turn you over to the gods (demons) in which you trust.

Aphrica was so into witchcraft that she gave her son a Hindu coloring book. In other words, she handed her son over to the gods she trusted in. In her dream, she saw an empty throne; that throne represented the seat in which God was supposed to be seated on in her heart. Nevertheless, it was an empty throne and her son went to take God's place on that throne. Well, because she didn't serve YAHWEH, the gods in which she did serve became jealous and decided to remove their competition. The truth of the matter is — some people have lost children to the very demons they were serving. What did Jesus say in John 10:10? He said, "The thief comes only to steal and kill and destroy. I came that they may have life and have it abundantly" (John 10:10 ESV). Sure, we'd like to believe that Satan can't touch us or our children, but if we become rebellious, religious and unrepentant, we will unintentionally and unknowingly hand our children over to him. This is why we cannot afford to be double-minded or lukewarm. If we're going to serve God, we'd better serve Him wholeheartedly. This doesn't mean that we'll be perfect; what it means is that we have to be intentional about doing what is right in the eyes of God. It means that if we mess up, we need to repent immediately and turn our hearts completely back to God.

When the most important relationship in her life almost ended, Aphrica had to reevaluate all of her relationships. She also had to re-position her son in her heart so that he would not be number one. Aphrica had to give God His seat back in her heart; that way, He could now put everything that was rising up against Aphrica under His feet. Thankfully, Aphrica made a choice to renounce her idolatrous ways, witchcraft, bitterness, fear and everything that kept her separated from God. When she did this, she watched God work a miracle right before her eyes.

God has to be our only God, plus, He has to be seated on the thrones of our hearts if we want His will to be done in our lives. We cannot and should never serve any other gods but the living God, Himself: JEHOVAH (YAHWEH).